Shaken and Stirred

Crystal Black Davis

Hudson Row Publishing

First edition June 2009
Second edition June 2013

SHAKEN AND STIRRED

A Hudson Row Publishing Novel

ISBN-13: 978-0615816029 (Hudson Row Publishing)
ISBN-10: 0615816029

Copyright © 2009 by Crystal Black Davis
Poem entitled *Queen* written by Crystal Black Davis

All rights reserved, including the right to reproduce
this book or portions thereof in any form whatsoever
without written permission.
For permission please contact
Hudson Row Publishing c/o Savvy Events & Marketing
1375 Broadway, #1100
New York, New York, 10018

This is a work of fiction. All characters in this book have
no existence outside the imagination of the author and
have no relation whatsoever to anyone bearing the same
name or names. Any resemblance to actual events or locales
or persons, living or dead, is entirely coincidental.

Lolita Smith, Editor
Cover Photograph, Diane Diederich
Cover Design, Savvy Events and Marketing

shakenandstirredbook.com
hudsonrowpublishing.com

DEDICATION

To my family and friends, on earth and in heaven,
I love you and appreciate your support

THE START OF A NEW BEGINNING

Change is like noticing your baby sister grow up. Though you know it's inevitable, you won't pick up on it if you look too hard or too often. It's when you're not paying attention and life preoccupies your time with stress and responsibility that you then notice, her chubby round cheeks are gone, her legs are long and lanky and before your eyes she's become a young woman—that's when you think to yourself, where did all the time go? Better yet, where was I when it happened?

So, in the spirit of reclamation and to finally notice life's subtle changes, I went out and bought this journal. Too many major events have happened in my life that are just blurs, so I figure, now's the time to start documenting them. After I fill this book with words and come back to it years later, I'm very curious to see if I'm really the person I think I am.

When I asked for guidance on how to effectively record my life on a day-to-day basis, the woman who sold me the journal recommended a few main points. One, that I be honest. She suggested that I not leave out the good things that my enemies do at times, nor should I leave out the bad things I may be embarrassed to acknowledge about myself. The second point was for me to record the experiences of each day at night, right before bed. She said that the mind is obviously more at peace, but also that the mind is more fair and partial just before rest. Another point she recommended is that I always write descriptively as if I were telling a story. The reason is simple. Years from now when I go back and read my life's events, I'll still be able to taste the tastes, smell the smells and see the colors just as vividly as I do today. Along with being descriptive, she also recommended that I describe myself just as I am today, as well as describing my closest friends at the beginning of each new journal.

"You'll be amazed with your progression and the lessons you've learned when you revisit this journal years from now," the woman said, unaware that she was not only a sales clerk but also a life maven.

Now, armed with the capability and desire to remember my life just as it is in the present, I'm ready to dot the first I and cross the first T. Hello world, this is my story. The trials and tribulations, life and times, and thoughts and vibes of Christian Maureen Cullen.

MY LIFE

Okay, I'm a control freak. Not in a possessive or diabolical kind of way, it's just that I prefer to be the agent of change in my life. I don't know if it's a flaw or just a normal human reaction, but if I'm not in control of my career, my love life or my future, I feel powerless and defeated. With that in mind, on a scale of one to ten my current happiness ranks at a high eight. Even though there are a few areas in my life that I'd definitely like to have more control over, mainly my love life, overall I'm a happy girl. I'm thirty-two years old, I have great friends, one heck of a family, I sit on the boards of three major art organizations and I run my own successful events and marketing firm, Image Brokers.

I'm extremely passionate about the little things in life that make me happy: music, food, art, travel, and of course fashion. I would consider myself a purist when it comes to all of my interests. With music, I'm strictly neo-soul, real hip-hop and classic jazz. I'm not trying to wobble, twerk or drop anything like it's hot, I prefer soul vocalists to sound more human and less machine and if I hear another saxophone rendition of a Janet or Luther tune I'm going to lose my mind. Give me Common, Jill Scott and John Coltrane any day of the week. With food, make it healthy and ethnic. I have a gluttonous obsession for Ethiopian, Indian and Mediterranean foods—and oh yes, soul, but it has to be healthy soul. My love of art is a little more complex. I appreciate the color and fluidity of Matisse, dimension of Bearden, abstractness of Picasso and rawness of Basquiat as well as the emotion of real life captured through the eyes of Van Der Zee and

7

Parks. My favorite travel destinations tend to be more urban and less remote. Though I'd like to explore more tropical locales, I can't seem to stay away from London, Paris, Toronto and NYC. It all ties in and makes perfect sense. All of my favorite places allow me to be stimulated by the very best of all of my interests, especially fashion. I've heard the phrase "death by chocolate," but I prefer fashion over chocolate any day. With a few exceptions, this season's television seems to lack shows with highly fashionable characters, à la *Sex and The City* and *Girlfriends*, so my must-see TV consists of predicting fashion's next "it" designer on *Project Runway* and watching the live streaming video coverage from Fashion Week. Diane Von Furstenberg, Tory Burch and Tracy Reese are my favorite designers, however a bit hard on the budget. So when I'm in between clients and my bank account is looking a little thin, all I can say is thank goodness for Simply Vera Wang for Kohl's and Missoni for Target.

On the romance front, I'm currently in the tail end of a pseudo-relationship with Mekhi Singleton, a telecom executive by day and party promoter by night. Honestly, I'm not that into him anymore, I'm just dealing with him until I find something better. On that note, it's time for something better. Finding Mr. Right has proven to be an exhausting task to undertake, requiring time, energy and patience that I haven't been able to devote. One thing's for certain, I can't waste anymore time dealing with Mekhi. Nipping him in the bud will at least open my world to better possibilities. Whether I find Mr. Right after a diligent search or if he falls in my lap, I'm ready to experience a new range of emotions with a new man.

The people who are the closest to me consist of my three best friends: Carra, Reese and Celeste.

Carra Smith-Knotts is a married, thirty-three year old veterinarian who wants to have a baby because she thinks it will save her marriage—even a wild animal can see the flaw in that theory. Carra can best be described as "sweet-spoiled." She's the nicest person you could ever meet. She sings to the birds, talks to her plants and lets her dog sleep in her bed. Extremely Mary Poppin'ish. On the other hand when things don't go her way, watch out for a flying bottom lip because she will pout and throw a fit until she's satisfied with the outcome.

Reese Cambridge is divorced, thirty-two years old and is the assistant marketing director for UniLink World Media. Since the divorce, Reese has not been interested in new love with commitment. She simply believes in living for the moment and loving every minute of it. At times, Reese can be an amazing and hilarious creature to watch in action. She can best be described as "bourgeois-street smart." Growing up, she's was extended all of the privileges in life, a prep school education, equestrian lessons, cotillions and frequent international travel, yet there was one thing that set her apart from all of her other classmates. She lived on the Southside of Chicago as a product of a well-to-do family that never left the "hood" and didn't believe in moving to the suburbs. So as good as she's had it she's still a product of her environment—one part executive, one part snob and one hundred percent sistergirl.

Celeste Venditore is thirty-three years old, a pharmaceutical sales rep and is stressed out over the long distance relationship with her boyfriend of five years, John, a stockbroker who lives in Cleveland. Celeste has been patiently waiting for John to propose over the past three years. She wasn't in any hurry to get hitched but at the beginning of that three-year mark John began putting the bug in her ear. He started bringing up marriage and hinting around about rings and honeymoon locations, then abruptly stopped about a year ago leaving her confused and a bit perturbed. Celeste can best be described as an "out of sight, out of mind workaholic." She consumes herself with her career therefore she doesn't have time to think about what's going on, or shall I say not going on between her and John.

My fair-weather best friend is my own sister, Angela. I hate this, but somewhere down the line our relationship has taken on the title of the John Jake novel, *Love and War.* Angela is twenty-eight years old and freelances as a graphic artist for a small advertising agency and on occasion works for me. Angela is the type of person who backpacks in Europe for six weeks without confirmed accommodations, will hang out all day in a coffee shop strumming her guitar belting out Kate Bush tunes and is somehow okay with not having a steady gig. Sometimes when we're together we could be having the time of our lives, but all it takes is one small factor, one itty-bitty disagreement between us and I won't see or hear from her for weeks. My best description of Angela would be "windy-worldly," a free-spirited and worldly person who can sometimes be as unpredictable as the direction of the very oxygen we breathe.

I was born and raised in Indianapolis to two loving parents who completely went above and beyond the normal parental call of duty to make sure their children were the happiest kids alive. We were the average black upper-middle class family with two extremely hard working parents. Dad, now retired, was an R&D supervisor for a large pharmaceutical company and my mother is a middle school guidance counselor. I have three siblings and despite the vast age difference we're very close-knit. I'm the oldest, Angela is the textbook "middle child" and the babies of the family are my sixteen year-old twin sister and brother, Eva and Everett.

I'm a graduate of Central Indiana University and I often think back to my college years missing the fun, freedom and frivolity I once had. I'm a third generation legacy of the prestigious Gamma Kappa Gamma Sorority, which I pledged my freshman year and was president by my junior year. I served as secretary for the student chapter of the American Marketing Society, was committee chairperson for the Minority Business Association, an active member of the Union Council and Black Student Union, played intramural tennis, was a driver for Woman's Wheels and volunteered as a new student ambassador. Obviously my college years served as the catalyst for my I-can-do-it-all attitude.

I met Carra, Reese and Celeste in college. Carra was a bookworm who rarely left the library. On the weeks I had research projects and would actually have to go to beyond the main lobby of the library into the stacks, I would always see her in a study carrel with her head buried in a book. She would never hang out downstairs in the main lobby, otherwise known as "party central", with everyone else because unlike some of us she was actually in the library to study. It was a surprise to everyone that she submitted her application to be a member of our sorority the same year I did. I didn't really get to know

11

her until our first pledge night when we were introduced to our new line sisters. I remember looking to my left and seeing Carra looking nervous with anxiety in her eyes and Reese to the right looking smug with a sly grin. Reese was the typical light-skinned, long hair, big boobed sister that all the brothers seemed to love. I met Reese during our freshman orientation weekend and instantly hated her. At the new student sessions she did everything in her power to get all the guys to notice her. Black, White, Asian or Hispanic, it didn't matter. All that mattered was that *she* was the center of attention. From the sneezing spells to the constant question asking, even my mother periodically flashed a *would-she-please-shut-up* glare every time Reese raised her hand.

"Is it true that freshman can't have cars on campus?" or "When is it recommended that we declare our major?" she would ask while batting her eyes and swinging her long brown hair. Every question she asked had been covered religiously in our new student manuals.

"I bet she's going to end up being your roommate," I remembered my mother whispering.

I recall the feeling of relief when we pulled in front of my new residence hall and I saw Reese getting out of her parents Range Rover at a dorm across the street. It wasn't until we pledged together that Carra and Reese became my best friends. It's funny how you can see people in passing for years and never know that they may be someone you'll love and cherish for the rest of your life.

Celeste and I eventually became best friends after being college roommates for two years. If things had gone my way we may not have ever met. I remember it as clear as day. On my student housing form, I requested that my roommate was to be a non-smoking, African-

12

American woman from Indianapolis. Instead I got Celeste, a chain smoking Greek-Italian from East Rutherford, New Jersey.

THE HERE AND NOW
THURSDAY, 8/24

"Christian, I hate to be the bearer of obvious news, but you need to kick Mekhi to the curb. Last night he was at happy hour getting way too happy with a little Jada Pinkett-Smith looking waitress. If you get this message before you go to bed do me one big favor, call Nathan's sexy ass and have some fun in Hotlanta! It's going to take hooking up with an ex to create a new one. I don't want to hear your mouth, just do it! By the way, don't forget we have dinner reservations Saturday night at nine-thirty. I'm forewarning you, we expect to hear some juicy stories about your trip so don't come back boring us to death talking about work."

I chuckled as I erased Reese's voicemail message. She had nothing to worry about because I was one step ahead of her. I called Nathan as soon as my plane landed yesterday. Words could not explain the sense of empowerment that came over me as I made plans to rendezvous with him. I'm moving on and it's liberating, even if it is with an ex-flame.

I hadn't seen Nathan since his job transferred him to Atlanta two years ago. We broke up on good terms because I figured it was best to part ways rather than endure the stress of maintaining a long distance relationship. Not to say it was easy to do. No man has ever made me melt the way Nathan did. Although his looks are incredible, something he is well aware of, he never exploited it by being arrogant. No, his appeal spans way beyond the physical. It's his gentle mix of confidence, assurance and humility that had me hooked from the start. He has a presence that is indescribable, a warm-spirit men rarely possess. Because of that, I had to go through a weaning process after our break-up. With every week that passed, I called him one less time until finally we just caught up with each other every now and then.

I checked him out as I walked towards the cozy corner window spot where he was seated. Nathan looked better than ever. Cuff links sparkling, hair cut superb, skin radiating, facial hair groomed to perfection and that smile. Oh, he had a smile to die for. He stood when he noticed me approaching and opened his arms. I was butter during the duration of our embrace taking in the cologne, warmth and strength that was once so familiar. How did I let this go?

"It's so good to see you," he said smiling. "My soul mate."

"It's good seeing you too," I said, trying to tone down my giddiness. Why did he have to remind me of our soul mate status? He definitely wasn't going to make this easy for me.

"I took the liberty of ordering one of your favorites, Bailey's shaken but served straight."

"Good memory."

"You're memorable, what can I say."

An hour and two drinks later marked the end of small talk and the official start of "what's up" talk.

"So what's up with you now? Are you seeing anyone?" he asked, taking a long sip of port.

"Not seriously," I said then thought back to Reese's message. "Actually, no."

"Did you just decide that?" he asked laughing as he lounged back into his chair.

"As a matter of fact, I did."

"Well alright. I hate to see how you're going to break it to him. You have a track record of lovin' them and leaving them," he joked while staring me square in the eyes.

"I'm going to let that slide. How about you? Are you seeing anyone?"

"I guess you can say that. It's in the early stages though."

"Oh," I said in the most neutral tone I could find, although deep down inside my inner Florida Evans was screaming *"Damn, damn, damn!"*

"I don't know if it's going to turn into anything serious. It's hard for anyone to replace you."

"Stop it."

"Seriously, I mean it."

There was nothing I could do to mask my blushing. This is leading exactly where I hoped it would.

"Well then, let's toast to my irreplaceability," I said as I lifted my glass.

"Even though irreplaceability isn't a word, *you* my dear are the definition," he said, tapping his glass against mine.

"What are your plans for the rest of the night?" he asked, motioning for the waitress to bring the check.

"I have some work to finish when I get back to the hotel," was the best I could come up with knowing I had every intention of spending the rest of the evening with him.

"Work? Nah, don't think so," he said as he walked behind my chair and ran his fingers down the side of my neck. "Work can wait. I want you to come by and check out the new crib. We can have dinner, chill out on the lake and continue this wonderful conversation."

"I don't know if I should," I managed to say, trying to keep a straight face.

"I can give you a backrub."

"Well..."

"And a foot massage."

"Oh my..."

"And a bubblebath in my Jacuzzi."

"Okay, okay since you've twisted my arm," I joked while my heart raced out of my chest at the excitement that awaited me.

To say that Nathan's home was something out of a magazine would be putting it mildly. No expense was spared in the architecture and interior of his immaculately designed home.

"Nathan...wow."

"Ya like it?"

"I love it. You stepped your game up about fifty notches."

"Well, you know how it is. Brother gets a JD/MBA, then a promotion..."

"The car and crib come next...I know," I laughed. "I'm proud of you."

"It's a lot different from my place back home."

"To say the least! Gone are the days of black lacquer Nathan, you've come up to this," I said as I rubbed my hand across the back of his modern leather sofa.

"It's from the Andre Marselle line," he mentioned in a jokingly smug tone.

"Andre Marselle!"

"I see you've heard of him."

"Heard of him? He hosts *the* most popular show on the design network! He's in virtually every interior design book known to man. Damn Nathan!"

"His firm basically did the whole house."

"Wait until I tell the girls."

"Speaking of your girls, how are they?"

"They're doing good. Reese moved up to assistant marketing director at the beginning of the year."

"Is she still a hot mess?"

"Hot to trot! Carra is still Carra, serial wife and lover of all things four-legged."

"Yeah, I used to call her Snow Black," he said, cracking up remembering how that name used to irritate her.

"And Celeste is still a work-a-holic. We're trying to get her to take a vacation but she refuses."

"Sounds like someone I know."

"Who?"

"*Who?* You know who. This is coming from the same person who was trying to go back to work tonight."

"Oh but the difference is that I run my own company."

"Touché."

"Thank you."

"You still need to make more time for yourself though."

"What do you think I'm doing now?"

"What are you doing now?" he asked as his hand lightly grazed my inner wrist.

"I'm making time for myself," I said then paused, "and falling for you again although I told myself not to."

"Why?"

"You know why."

"I think we can reassess this whole distance relationship thing."

"*You're* not in the position to do that. Remember, you're involved with someone right now."

"Chris, just say the word and I'm all yours."

"So it's that easy?"

"It's done," he said as he pulled me close and slowly kissed my neck, forehead then passionately on my lips.

"I'm going to start the tub, why don't you make yourself comfortable," he said as he made his way upstairs. "Make sure you go out on the patio and check out the view."

To get to Nathan's patio you have to go through a long dramatic foyer, a gourmet kitchen rivaled only by the studio kitchens on the *Food Network* and a sunken family room with custom built cabinetry to house Nathan's entire home entertainment system.

"Did you see the painting?" Nathan yelled from upstairs.

"I've seen many paintings! All of them equally fabulous I might add."

"Then you haven't seen *the* painting. Take a look in my office."

I couldn't believe my eyes as I walked into Nathan's mahogany-clad office. He had an original Basquiat hanging on the wall above his credenza.

"It's real!" he yelled.

"How in the hell..."

"I've got connections."

"Obviously! Whose gallery did you rob to snag this?"

"Someone's got jokes! Did you check out the desk? It's from Andre Marselle's Basquiat inspired line."

"It's beautiful," I yelled back, inspecting the craftsmanship of the design while noticing a bouquet of flowers on his desk. "You know, pillows are the only thing I can afford from Andre's line!" I said purely to get a response to make sure he was still busy upstairs.

"I've seen your client list. You can afford way more than that!" he yelled back as I took the heart-shaped card out of the bouquet. I should've been ashamed of myself for being so nosey but I had to scope out the competition.

"Nathan, they say the eyes are the windows into the soul, well your eyes reveal the world to me. I'm enjoying this journey and I hope it never ends. We have an intrinsic connection that I've never felt with anyone before. Your love is truly unbelievable..."

"What did you think of the patio?" Nathan called out as he hopped down the stairs.

I tossed the card back on his desk and dashed to meet him in the foyer. Nathan greeted me with a bare, lightly oiled chest, white linen pants and his trademark bedroom eyes.

"It's nice."

"Nice? I just dropped over a half a million dollars for the view alone and you only think it's nice?"

"It's spectacular," I said, knowing good and well that I never saw it.

"That's more like it," he said as he walked behind me and lifted my hair. "Is this still your spot?"

Although my knees nearly gave in as Nathan nibbled on the nape of my neck, I was preoccupied with the fact that he was obviously still involved with someone.

"What about your woman?" I whispered as I tried to pull away.

"You're the only person worthy of that title," he said as his lips grazed the side of my neck with every word. He smelled delicious, looked amazing and felt wonderful.

I tried hard to resist, okay maybe not that hard as we walked hand in hand up his grandeur staircase. The closer we got to the top of the stairs, the more I heard R. Kelly singing, "*My mind is telling me no…but my body, my body's telling me yes!*"

Nathan's master bathroom was magnificent! I've been to spas that didn't even scratch the surface. As I stood there watching him check the bath water, something inside me clicked. I don't know if it was the scent of the nag champa incense, calming zen décor, the flicker of the candlelight glistening against his copper chest or my sheer desire to be with him, but at that very moment I lost all inhibition and made

22

the next move. I hadn't kissed anyone that passionately since, well since Nathan and I were last together. If it weren't for the love that Nathan and I shared when we were a couple I would've dismissed his claims to drop everything to be with me. Men will typically say anything if they think they have a good chance at getting some. This felt different. I know Nathan and I know his heart. I initiated the break-up. Yes, I broke up with him although he tried to convince me that the long distance thing would work. Second chances don't come often and at that moment I decided to reclaim Nathan as my man.

"Feel free to take a look around up here while I go down to the wine cellar. Oh, yeah, a brother's got a wine cellar."

"Look at you!"

"Well what can I say?" he said, walking out the door before peeking back in. "I need to pick out a good Moscato. As I recall, that's someone's other favorite."

"Again, you remembered."

"And you know it," he winked.

Of course the one and only room I was truly interested in checking out was his bedroom. By that point, I was well aware that Nathan's place was gorgeous and I fully anticipated that the rest of his upstairs was as well. What I was concerned with was trying to find a picture of the other woman. I don't know why, I just felt that I needed to know what she looked like. I immediately went over to the nightstand on the right side of his bed only to find some loose change, his keys and some random mail. The drawer on the left nightstand was a different story. Jackpot! There she was. A petite, light skinned woman with long flowing weave, wearing fire-engine red lipstick. In the picture they appeared to be at a barbecue and although they were hugging each other, he looked like he was just going through the motions. I know Nathan's happy look and that wasn't it. Yeah, he's mine again, no question about it. She's cute but she's not me, that's one thing I'm confident about.

Lounging in Nathan's tub allowed me to ease into a deeper state of relaxation. I became one with the sounds of Terence Blanchard as I imagined a future with Nathan back in my life. I thought back on how he used to serve me peppermint tea every night before bed, how I would lay in between his legs engrossed in a novel while he lovingly massaged my scalp and how he would pause to smile and gaze into my eyes when we made love. With those thoughts, I melted into the steady jets of his tub and closed my eyes.

I was startled back to consciousness by the sound of voices downstairs. I figured I'd been asleep for about forty-five minutes or so because the water had gone from can-barely-stand-it hot to one notch under lukewarm. Since Nathan obviously had company, I figured that our Jacuzzi rendezvous wasn't likely to happen. As I was getting dressed, I overheard Nathan say, "Let's go talk about this out back." After that, dead silence. I wonder if Ms. Red Lipstick decided to drop by, I thought as curiosity got the best of me.

I tiptoed through the foyer into his kitchen, trying to plot the best route to get within earshot of the patio. As I slid through the butler's pantry to make a mad dash to the family room I crashed into Nathan and was startled speechless.

"Who the hell is this? Hello Nathan, I'm talking to you. Who is she?" The words directed at Nathan pierced through my ears as Andre Marselle shouted through the family room.

"You need to stop yelling in my house," Nathan replied, trying to remain calm.

"Nathan, what's going on here?"

"Nothing," Nathan replied.

Andre squinted and began walking towards me, looking me up and down, "So this is my competition. A video hoochie look-alike who only wants you for your money."

I felt a hot wave flush over my body as I looked my longtime design idol directly in the eyes and said in the most controlled manner I could project, "You not only need to change your tone, you need to get out of my face," then turned to face Nathan, "You mean to tell me you and Andre..." I asked as I watched him cringe before I said the word.

"Christian, no..." he said as Andre interrupted him.

"Like hell. Oh, I'm sorry I forgot, you call it experimenting. Isn't that right? Too embarrassed to admit that you're bi and in complete denial that you're with me!" Andre yelled then directed his attention back to me. "So you're Christian. Damn, I guess I was wrong. You're not the slut I took you for, no you're Christian Cullen, the one person Nathan would drop everything for. Well you know what, you can have him back," Andre said, standing right in front of my face. "I admit, I was forewarned about you. Nathan always said that if he had another chance with you that he'd take it. Here she is

Nathan, your beloved Christian! Live your life, be happy and from this day on you better hope that I don't ever see you in public. Trust me, I can't be responsible for my actions if I cause a scene!" Andre said as he snatched his jacket off the sofa and walked out, nearly slamming the front door off the hinges.

"Damnit!" Nathan yelled as he turned away from me.

"Nathan, take me back to my hotel."

"Christian, let me exp…"

"Please, just take me back to the hotel."

"Christian, it's not what you think."

"Nathan! Take me back to my hotel!"

"Christian, please hear me out."

"There's nothing for you to explain, it's all black and white," I said as Nathan collapsed on his sofa and held his head in his hands, rocking back and forth.

I stormed into the foyer and gathered my belongings out of the coat closet.

"I'm calling a cab, what's your address?"

"Christian, it's after midnight. No cab is going to come way out here until the morning. Just stay here. You can take one of the guest bedrooms."

"I'll take my chances. Where's your phone book?"

After eight failed attempts at getting a cab to come out to the suburbs in the late hour, I marched upstairs to get Nathan.

"Nathan, I'm going to ask you one last time, take me to my hotel," I said as I tried turning the handle of his bedroom doorknob. "Nathan, unlock the door."

"Christian, I can't right now. I can't...," he slurred from inside the bedroom. "I can't."

"Oh, so now you're drunk. It figures," I said as I stomped into one of the guest rooms and slammed the door.

Why me? Why did my day have to end up like this? I went from the high of feeling love to the rock bottom feeling of being totally blindsided all in a matter of a few hours. I was so distraught that I couldn't cry nor could I calm down to rest, so I just laid there staring at the ceiling.

FRIDAY, 8/25

Morning came with a blur. It felt like last night had been a figment of my imagination, but if that were the case I would be waking up in Nathan's arms. My flight back home wasn't until five o'clock but the sense of urgency to leave was dire, not only because I needed to get back to the hotel and check out, I simply needed to emotionally sever ties with Nathan once and for all.

As I applied Nathan's expensive face wash on my cheeks, I felt like I was washing away a chapter of my life. The more I splashed the cold sobering water on my face, the more I came to grips with the situation at hand. After showering, I headed down the hall noticing Nathan's open bedroom door. When I went downstairs, he was in the kitchen on the phone talking to his mother.

"No ma, I'm doing alright...I'll be home to see you soon, I promise...Yes, I know that Christian's out here..." he said as he noticed me walk in the room. "As a matter of fact she's right here," he said handing me the phone.

"You must be crazy," I whispered as I pushed the phone away.

"Please," he whispered back, holding his hand over the receiver.

"No, Nathan."

"Sorry ma, she just went to the bathroom...Yeah, she stayed with me for a few days...We had a wonderful time together...No mom, no wedding bells just yet, don't jump to conclusions...Well, we're about to eat breakfast, I'll call you later on today...Love ya."

"Why in the world would you tell your mother that?"

"Christian, what was I supposed to say?"

"How about the truth?"

You could cut the tension with a knife during the silent forty minute drive to the hotel. When we arrived, Nathan pulled into the parking lot and turned off the ignition instead of pulling up to the door.

"Christian, I know you don't understand what's going on and I don't expect you to, I just need for you to hear me out. I do and will always love you. You can hate me, curse me, whatever—no matter what, I'm going to continue to love you more than anything in this world. I know that probably won't change things but I just wanted you to know that."

"Okay, you said what you had to say, pop the trunk."

"There's one more thing. I'm *begging* you, please don't tell anyone about what happened. I'm going to work this situation out on my own, I just can't risk my family finding out," he said as he closed his eyes and leaned his head back into the headrest. "I know you and your grandmother are close but she and my mom are best friends. Please Christian, don't say anything to her."

"Fine Nathan," I said as I opened the car door.

Nathan grabbed my arm and pulled me back in, "Christian, I'm begging you."

"Look, I won't say anything."

"Thank you," he said, still holding on to my arm with tears in his eyes. "I love you. Always have and I always will."

On my way to the airport, I came to the realization that I was a free woman literally and figuratively. I was about to call it quits with Mekhi and my mind was no longer preoccupied with getting back with Nathan. It is time to focus on Christian and not on Christian's potential companion. If Mr. Right comes along, that's great, but I'm not going to sweat it. When that perfect relationship happens it needs to happen organically. I'm not going to force it, seek it out or question it—I'm just going to let it be.

SATURDAY, 8/26

I slept until ten-thirty today. I guess the emotional stress of letting go of Nathan and the anticipation of breaking it off with Mekhi completely took its toll on me. Thankfully I had yoga class at three. I needed to breathe, stretch and relax my way into a higher state of mind. To further enhance my *me time* I booked a four-thirty pedicure to accentuate the new snakeskin peep toe pumps I plan on wearing to dinner tonight.

On my way out, I checked my home voicemail which I'd neglected for over a week. The one and only message was from Mekhi's best friend Darius:

"Hey Christian, it's Friday night around ten and I'm calling to see if you've heard from Mekhi. He was supposed to drop through 'cause some of our boys from school are in town this weekend. If you see him tonight tell him to call me, okay? Oh, don't forget to hook me up with one of your girls. Later."

Just as I saved the message my phone beeped.

"Hey girlie!"

"Hey Celeste! What are you up to?"

"Suffering in the hot sun at this golf outing. I can't take it any longer," she mumbled. "Enough about me, did you see Nathan while you were in Atlanta?"

"Yes."

"Uh, oh, anything juicy?"

"Oh, it's juicy alright."

"I can't wait to hear all about it tonight," she said as she was interrupted by someone. "Hey, I'll see you later. I have to get back to my nine iron. Take care!"

After hanging up with Celeste, I returned Darius's call.

"I'm going to kill that knucklehead man of yours."

"So it's safe to assume you never heard from Mekhi."

"No. Christian, I don't know what the hell is wrong with him. We've had this weekend planned since May and leave it up to Mekhi to forget. Our boy Mark is in town from D.C. and his old roommate Kevin is in from Miami. Have you talked to him?"

"No, I just got back from Atlanta last night. I haven't talked to him in over a week."

"When you do talk to him, tell him that he better get his ass over here tonight because the crew leaves first thing tomorrow morning."

"I'll try calling him later on this afternoon," I said, noticing the time. "Darius, I don't mean to hurry off the phone but I'm running late for an appointment. I'll talk to you soon."

On my way to Yoga, I decided to take a chance and call Mekhi to relay Darius's message.

"Hello?" Mekhi answered in a groggy voice.

"Hey Mekhi, it's me. Are you still asleep?"

"Yeah, what time is it?"

"It's two forty-five."

"Shit. I should have been up. What time did your flight get in last night?"

"A little after nine."

"I was planning on calling you but I got caught up."

"What did you end up doing?"

"I went out to Linebackers Sports Lounge with Darius and the boys."

"Oh, *really?*" I replied as I listened to him to lie about where he was. "So you were with Darius last night?"

"Yeah, we hung out, watched the game then went and got something to eat."

"Is that so?"

"Yeah, I can't even remember what time we got in…"

"Mekhi, I'm pulling in the parking lot of my yoga class," I said, cutting him off. "Let's continue this conversation when I get done."

"Before you hang up, I think I left my green polo over your house. Will you be home later on?"

"I'll be home around six."

"Cool, I'll be over there about a quarter after."

Mekhi is such a lying punk! My instinct was to bust him out right there over the phone but I realized that catching him in a lie in person would be more fun.

"Center and stabilize all toxins and negative energies with a deep breath in, then force all of those impurities out with a slow, steady exhale," the yoga instructor said, practically whispering from the back of the dark room. "The next pose we're moving into is downward facing dog."

Downward facing Mekhi would be a more accurate description, I thought to myself as a hot waved rushed through my body. This was Mekhi's last and final day in my life.

"That fool put me in his lie?"

"He said he was with you all night."

"Christian, I've known you for over five years so I feel I can be honest. I hate that I was the one who hooked you two up and as hypocritical as this may sound, you need to drop him."

"Trust me Darius, in a few minutes Mekhi will officially be black history."

"I'm glad to hear that because even though he's my boy, you deserve better. Much better."

"I concur."

I made it a point to not only toss Mekhi's green shirt into a trash bag, but all of his other belongings as well. There will be no getting comfortable tonight buddy, you're going to grab your things and go—for good.

"You know you need to go ahead and give me a key," Mekhi said as he stood in my doorway before I let him in.

"Trust me, there's no need for that."

"What's that supposed to mean?"

"It means I think we need to take a breather."

"A breather?"

"Actually, a breather implies that there will be some sort of reconnection. Let me rephrase that, I think we need to let it go."

"What?"

"You know as well as I do that this isn't working."

"What is this about?" he said, trying to move in close as I held out my arm to stop him in his tracks. "Baby, is this about last night? I promise I would have called you if it hadn't been so late, plus I forgot my cell phone at home."

"This has nothing to do with you not calling, but everything to do with last night. Even more than that, let's be honest with each other. You want to see other people and so do I. We're wasting each other's time."

"Baby, you got me. I'm not feeling anybody else. Last night I was just telling Darius about how lucky I am."

"Mekhi, you weren't with Darius last night."

"Huh? Quit trippin', I picked Darius up from his house and we went to Champps."

"I thought you said you went to the Linebackers."

"We did, but...uh...we went to Champps afterwards to get something to eat. I can call Darius right now and he can tell you," he said as he picked up the phone on my desk and pushed the speakerphone button.

"Hello?"

"What up D!" Mekhi barked like he was on campus yelling across the yard. "I'm over Christian's house trying to convince her that we hung out last night. Would you please tell her..."

"Dog, she already knows."

"Man what are you talkin' about?"

"Mekhi, give it up. It would have been nice to have gone out last night since Mark, Juan and Kev are in town. If you had checked the many messages I left on your phone, you would've known that I called Christian's house trying to hunt your ass down last night. Bruh, you need to tighten it up."

After Mekhi hung up the phone, he stood there and looked at me like he'd just seen a ghost. I pointed to his bag of stuff by the door and he quickly got the picture.

"That was easy," I thought to myself as I slammed the door behind him. It felt like a huge weight had been lifted off of my shoulders. Although hindsight is twenty-twenty, if I'd used my gut instincts we would've never hooked up in the first place. It was New Year's Eve and Carra, Reese, Celeste and I decided to go to The Hang Suite at the last minute. From the moment we arrived, Mekhi stared at me all night. Everywhere I went his eyes followed. When I walked to the restroom, he was watching. When I was out on the dance floor, he was sitting at the closest table watching me. The moment I ended up at the bar, he was standing right there.

"I'm Mekhi Jeffries," he said as if I was supposed to be impressed. "Can I buy you a drink?"

"I've got it, I'm good," I said, not really in the mood to go through the whole "meeting a dude in the club" drill.

"I insist."

"Really, I'm okay. I've got it."

"Would you please let a man be a man," he joked.

"Oh, goodness gracious," I said under my breath. "Fine, since you're offering I'll have a socialitini."

"Okay, you're going to have to help me out, what is a socialitini?"

"It's a drink my girl Reese invented. It's basically a cosmopolitan with ginger ale and lime juice.

"A socialitini it is," Mekhi said as he leaned in to yell to the bartender. "Hey Ron, get me a cosmo mixed with Canada Dry and a twist of lime, and a rum and coke for me."

The bartender dropped everything he was doing at the busy bar to cater to Mekhi's request.

"Is this your first time here?"

"No, but it's been a while."

"I guess that explains why I've never seen you before," Mekhi said as the bartender walked over to deliver our drinks. "I would have remembered you."

"So you spend all of your time here at the club?"

"Not all, just most."

"That's interesting," I said, noticing my girls motioning for me to come back to the table. "I guess I'd better be going. Thanks for the drink."

"So soon? I was hoping that I could get to know you better."

"I need to get back to my girls—you know, keep them out of trouble."

"Well I hope you and your friends enjoy yourselves this evening," he said looking a little disappointed. "This is my event so if there's anything that you ladies need tonight, it's on me. Oh, before I forget, I'm having another set at the Velvet Room next Friday. I hope you can make it."

"I'll check my calendar."

"Hey, you never told me your name."

"Christian."

"Do you have a last name?"

"Cullen."

"So *you're* Christian Cullen. You're the force behind Image Brokers right?"

"That's me."

"I've heard some good things about you."

"Is that so?"

"Yeah but I'd like to learn more first hand."

"Maybe someday," I said as I walked away.

"Who was that?" Reese said, turning her nose up at my admirer.

"Why'd you ask like that? I think he's kind of cute," Carra replied.

"His name is Mekhi. He's the promoter for this party."

"Well in that case he's fine as wine," Reese said changing her tune as she squinted to get a better look at him.

"He's a nice looking guy," Celeste added.

"Not my type," I said trying to change the subject.

"Just a minute ago you were over there batting your eyes and accepting drinks now you're trying to act all uninterested. What happened?" Reese asked jokingly.

"I was not batting my eyes. Anyway, like I said, he's not my type so can we please talk about something else," I said as they pursed their lips together and playfully rolled their eyes at me. "Thank you."

A few hours later, Darius rushed over with a sense of urgency, "Hey Christian! I have a friend upstairs whose been wanting to meet you all night."

"Darius, I'm typically not that fond of meeting people in clubs. Who is it?"

"Come with me and I'll introduce you two."

"I'm trusting you on this one."

"He's good people. I wouldn't steer you wrong."

I followed Darius upstairs to the V.I.P. section and as security let us through, I immediately saw Mekhi. As luck would have it, Darius led me directly to him.

"Christian, this is Mekhi," Darius said smiling at me. "And Mekhi, this is Christian."

"We've already met," I said, a bit annoyed.

"Man, you told me that you wanted me to introduce you two," Darius said to Mekhi then lightly tagged him on the arm.

"That was before I saw her downstairs at the bar."

"Well since you two know each other already, I guess my job here is done," Darius said as he squeezed my shoulders and headed back downstairs. "I'll be right back. I've got to grab the rest of the crew before the countdown."

"Well get Reese and the girls while you're at it."

"Will do," Darius said then made a "handle your business" face at Mekhi.

"So Christian, are you originally from Indianapolis?"

"Yeah, how about yourself?"

"I'm originally from Philly but I moved here with my parents when I was about 10 years old..."

After getting to know him a little better I began to let my guard down and even embraced the notion of going out with him. And though I'm usually cautious about letting someone move too fast with me, I surprised myself by not getting mad after he completely caught me off guard and kissed me following the countdown. Yes, he was a little cocky but interestingly enough I found it sexy. By the time I left the club, I seemed ready to begin the New Year on a new leaf with a new man, or so I thought.

About a half hour after Mekhi left I was starving. I tried to tie myself over with a handful of grapes but who was I kidding. Even though I had dinner reservations with the girls in a few of hours, I went across the street to Taj Mahal Indian To Go and ordered two pieces of tandori chicken, a side of dal makhani and two pieces of naan. I swear living next door to City Market will be the reason I gain fifty pounds before the end of the year. That may not be such a huge exaggeration because I've only lived here since March and have already gained seven. From Indian to Jamaican or pizza to cheesecake, it is way too convenient for me to walk a few yards and pig out at a moment's notice.

Just as I was putting the fork to my mouth, the phone rang.

"Hey Christian, it's Darius again."

"Hey."

"I'm sorry about what happened earlier."

"No reason to be. Actually the timing couldn't have been better," I said with a mouth full of food.

"My boy Kev and I were just talking about how Mekhi hasn't changed a bit since college."

"It's a shame that someone so smart can be so immature."

"Tell me about it. He'll come to his senses one day."

"One can only hope," I managed to say in between bites of naan.

"I can tell that you're eating so I'll let you go."

"We'll talk soon."

"Maybe we can catch up for lunch or something next week."

"Sounds like a plan. Just email me some dates and we'll make it happen."

With at least an hour and a half before meeting up with the girls I washed my face and wrapped my hair to take a much needed cat nap. About an hour in, I was abruptly awakened by yet another phone call. My goodness, I have never spent so much time on the phone in one day, I thought as I answered.

"You need to wake your lazy ass up and get ready."

"Reese, what time is it?"

"Nine o'clock."

"Fine, I'm up. I'll be there in about forty five minutes or so. You guys can go ahead and be seated."

"Just hurry up. Oh, before I forget, I need you to bring your black Gucci clutch. I have a date tomorrow night and it will go perfectly with my outfit. Don't forget," Reese said then abruptly hung up the phone.

There once was a time when I would think Reese and I were accidentally disconnected or worse, worried that something had happened to her whenever the phone would cut off like that. Time has taught me otherwise. That's just one of Reese's many signature traits. I don't think that I've ever once told Reese goodbye before ending a phone call with her. As for my clutch, she needed to return my silver belt before I hand over anything else.

After a deep yawn, I was jolted with a sudden burst of energy. I felt like running a marathon, climbing a tree and marching in the Circle City Classic Parade. As I walked across the living room and hit the power button on my surround sound, I was overcome by the exhilarating feeling of freedom.

"You must not know 'bout me, you must not know 'bout me..."

"Sing Bey!" I said aloud as I grooved into my bedroom closet.

Usually Meridian Lounge is a low key, chill out spot but tonight it was wall to wall. I spent almost a half hour searching for a parking space and once inside, it was so crowded that it was a struggle to make it back to the booth where the girls usually sit. Never once did it cross my mind that today was the last Saturday of the month or that Mekhi's promotions company could very well be hosting this party. It was confirmed once I saw Mekhi in his infamous green shirt wheelin' and dealin' with the club manager behind the bar. Oh well, I thought to myself. No point in feeling awkward because I was on a mission to have a good time with my girls and I planned to accomplish just that.

"Hey girlie!" Celeste, Carra and Reese squealed when I walked over to the booth.

I leaned in to hug all of my girls, "What's up, what's up!"

"So did you and Nathan break the headboard?" Reese asked before I could even sit down.

"Reese!" Carra scolded, elbowing her in the arm.

"What?" Reese replied smiling, eager to hear some juicy details.

"No Reese. Nothing happened."

"Give me my money," Celeste said to Reese as she held out her hand. "I told you she wasn't going to do anything."

Reese opened her purse and pulled out a crisp ten dollar bill.

"So my love life is worth a measly ten dollars," I laughed.

"It's been worth more in the past, but lately…" Celeste said as she threw her arm around me.

"I can't believe you guys."

"You guys? Don't rope me in with those two," Carra joked. "Trust me, I haven't participated in any of their tacky bets."

"Well Celeste, buy something real nice with your huge winnings and if you have more riding on Nathan and me, my suggestion would be to collect now."

"Uh oh, what happened?" Celeste asked.

"Nathan is seeing someone else."

"Is *that* all?" Reese said looking at me like I was completely out of my mind. "That's what's holding you back? I thought you had a little more go-getter in you. You went all the way to Atlanta to reclaim your man and you're gonna let some other chick stand in your way?"

"Reese, I'm over him. We're just two different people."

"He must have a baby on the way because I can't think of anything that would prevent you from rekindling a relationship with such a fine ass brother," Reese stated matter-of-factly.

"Either that or he's engaged," Celeste chimed in.

"That's never stopped *me* before," Reese joked.

"He's not dabbling in illegal substances is he?" Carra asked with a concerned look on her face.

"No, no and no."

"I got it! Maybe he went to Atlanta and decided to get down with the down low!" Reese said.

I attempted to shield any reaction on my face as the girls giggled at Reese's claim. I tried laughing with them but I know it came off fake.

"Hold on ladies, something ain't right. Christian, why are you looking like that?" Reese said, staring me square in the eyes.

"What?"

"Christian." Reese said as if to say, *this is us you're talking to.*

Without thinking, I shook my head in surrender.

"What! I did not see that coming!" Carra said wide-eyed.

"How did you find out?" Celeste asked with her hand over her mouth.

"By accident. Look guys, even though Nathan and I don't have a future together, I still care about his feelings. Don't mention this to anyone, please," I said, directing the majority of my attention and words to Reese who sat there smiling with her mouth wide open as she took in the juicy conversation. "Okay Reese?"

"Girl, I'm not going to say anything I'm just in shock. My gaydar didn't pick up on this at all. I'm usually dead on!"

"So am I, but obviously I'm not as perceptive as I once thought," I said wanting to desperately change the subject. "Enough about me, what's going on with you guys?"

"So be specific, how did you find out?" Celeste asked with eyes as big as saucers.

"Celeste, let's please change the subject."

"Fine then, let's change the subject," Reese interjected as she cut her eyes over to the bar. "I'm sure you noticed mister popularity over there."

"I saw him when I came in. I cut him off earlier today."

"No more Nathan, no more Mekhi. Wow, you're not playing are you?" Reese said.

"Honestly, enough about me. Don't you all have anything to fill me in on?"

Carra clapped her hands in excitement, "Yes, yes yes! Okay I'll start! I got an ovulation test yesterday. I have a good feeling about this," Carra said, smiling from ear to ear.

"I'll be praying for you," I said hugging her.

"That's my little news, although I'm positive it's not nearly as big as Celeste's," Carra smirked.

"What news does Celeste have?" I asked noticing Celeste's flushed cheeks.

"Well," she said smirking. "I have an announcement to make."

Just then Celeste opened her purse and pulled out a small black velvet box. She opened it to reveal one of the most stunning rings I'd ever seen.

"Isn't it beautiful! It's two sizes too big so I have to get it resized before I can wear it."

"Wow! Congrats Celeste! When did John propose?" I asked as we all took turns inspecting the gorgeous piece of jewelry.

"Who cares about that, I want to know how many karats is this boulder?" Reese said trying to determine the weight as she let the gravity of the box weigh her hand down.

"Alright, you better not drop my ring."

"I was there when he proposed, but I'll let her tell the story," Carra squealed.

"Okay first of all, you guys know that I had no clue John was still even thinking about marriage so needless to say I was completely shocked!"

"So was it the traditional down on one knee or did he do something completely out of the box?" I asked.

"It was the old school down on one knee, but also out of the box."

"When?" Resse chimed in.

"Thursday night, right before I took him to the airport. I'll be quite honest, I almost broke up with him that same day."

"Uh huh," Carra mumbled as she looked at Reese and I like she was privy to the juicy details.

"Why, what happened?" I asked.

"I didn't feel like I was a priority in his life anymore," Celeste said, taking a sip of wine. "You know how he flaked out on me at the last minute and cancelled our weekend get-away to Chicago, right? Well, that was two weeks ago. Then he promised to at least come and visit me last week, which technically he did—but he didn't."

"What do you mean?" Reese asked.

"Well he was here physically, but his mind wasn't. The whole time he was too preoccupied to focus on me."

"Was his mind still at work? I hear the stock market is volatile these days," I said as Resse looked at me like I was talking crazy.

"What the hell do you know about a volatile market?" she laughed. "A sister reads the Wall Street Journal once, three years ago, and now she's an expert."

"Shut up girl," I said, chuckling at her slight yet accurate observation. "I'm just trying to relate. Anyway Celeste, you were saying."

"Between work, hanging out with his brother and catching up with friends, he basically put me on the back burner. After a few days, I decided to enjoy the peace and quiet of my time off and pretended he wasn't even in town."

"Okay, so what happened in between the time of him ignoring you and all of a sudden proposing?" Reese asked while scanning the menu.

"I'll get to that later, but first let me tell you how the rest of the week turned out. I went from having a ton of things planned for us to do together to ultimately spending every night reading or shopping by myself. After two days of this, I told him to stay at his brother's place since that's where he was spending the majority of his time. By Thursday, I had my mind made up about ending the relationship and I left a voice message informing him that it was over."

"That's where I come in!" Carra proclaimed. "I had a hunch that something was wrong because when I stopped by on Thursday, Celeste was outside gardening like a mad women, yanking weeds, soil flying all over the place. I suggested we go to the spa for some de-stressification and after a mud wrap and massage she was starting to feel better."

"Now what day was this again?" Reese interrupted.

"Thursday. Why?"

"Because you could've called somebody to let them know that you were going. I'm past due for a massage!"

"Would you please let her finish the story?" I said, squeezing Reese's arm.

"Anyway, when we got back to her house, we pulled out her Taste of the Mediterranean cookbook and by eight o'clock we were enjoying delicious sun-dried tomato and seared skirt steak with bowtie pasta, Romano garlic toast and a bottle of 1997 Sunset Valley Pinot Grigio. Everything was going fine until the doorbell rang."

"You gotta let me take over from here," Celeste said, her voice oozing with climax as she poured mineral water into her glass. "There stood John, dressed in his navy blue Brooks Brothers suit with tears in his eyes. Here's how the whole scenario played out..."

"John, what are you doing here?"

"Celeste you know I love you and I can't live without you."

"John, actions speak louder than words, it's over."

"There's something I need to say to you before you take me to the airport."

"What makes you think I'm taking you to the airport? You need to call your brother, I'm sure he'll take you because I'm not."

"Celeste forget the airport, I need to talk to you," he said, leaning in to hug me.

"As I backed away, tears began rolling down his face. He took a few steps back then fell to his knees. As I watched his dramatic performance I didn't know what to think. He was actually starting to scare me because he looked borderline suicidal."

He said, "Celeste, I've been going through some things lately and I can't go on…" as he reached inside his coat pocket pulling out the ring. "Without you."

"And just when I thought Celeste was going to cuss him out, she stood there frozen for a moment then ran over to him screaming yes!" Carra said, looking at us still in disbelief.

"Okay, that was interesting. I didn't know how this story was going to unfold and I still don't quite get it but nonetheless, I wish you all the best. Congratulations," I said as I lifted my glass to propose a toast.

"Uh, uh," Reese said with a raised eyebrow. "I don't mean to sound rude but that shit was just flat out weird."

"Reese!" Carra replied.

"I'm for real," Reese said.

"I know it's a little unorthodox, but we have a history and we need each other. I love him and that's all I can say."

"If you say so. So when do I pick up my bridesmaid dress?" Reese asked sounding unconvinced.

"In October."

"October?" Reese and I said in unison.

"You do mean *next* October, right?" I asked.

"She better mean next October because it's already the end of August," Reese said looking directly at Celeste.

"I mean this October," Celeste said. "We decided there was no reason to prolong the engagement. John accepted a job offer here in Indy and he's moving next month."

Reese still had a look of skepticism on her face, "Not to keep beating a dead horse but this is bothering me. What was his excuse for ignoring you?"

"Nerves. When he wasn't spending time finalizing his new job situation, he was hanging out with his brother in an attempt to calm down. John always said that when he proposed, he would do anything in his power to make it as unpredictable as possible."

"Well he is definitely a man of his word," I replied.

"The official date for our wedding is October 1st, on a Sunday. It's tradition in our family to marry on a Sunday afternoon in autumn. Lucky for me everything is pretty easy to come by since October is not a popular month for weddings."

"Well I'm excited for you," Carra said getting misty eyed. "It seems like just yesterday when Aaron and I exchanged those sacred vows. I still get emotional when I think about it. I remember…"

"Okay, okay!" Reese snapped jokingly at Carra.

"Hater," Carra said, tossing a balled up cocktail napkin at Reese.

While we all sat laughing together, my attention veered inadvertently towards the bar where Mekhi was cuddled up with another chick. The fact that he's already gone public with his other woman just hours after leaving my house was starting to piss me off. Even more, all the time I wasted with Mekhi I probably missed out on my perfect mate. But not Mekhi, *nooo*. He kept his options open and played the field. Why had I been so slow in breaking it off with him? I knew all along that Mekhi and I would never materialize.

"What church service are you going to tomorrow?" Carra asked, startling me out of my self-pity thoughts.

"Three-thirty service."

"Three-thirty service? What three-thirty service?" she replied.

"At bedside Baptist on channel eleven."

"You are going to burn eternally!" Carra said, smiling as she shook her head.

"At least she's making an effort to get the Word somehow. It may be a bootleg way of going about it, but she's getting it," Reese replied, looking at me out of the corner of her green eyes.

SUNDAY, 8/27

This morning I made two day altering mistakes. One, I set my alarm to the wrong time yesterday night and two, I fell into bed last night without closing the blinds in my bedroom. So not only was I being disturbed out of some much needed sleep by the buzzing of an annoying alarm clock, I couldn't go back to sleep because I'd already seen the light of day. After lying in bed for a couple of hours unable to fall back asleep, I got out of bed and looked around my apartment in disbelief at the mess that had accumulated for two weeks. After declaring my apartment a national disaster, I mopped, dusted, vacuumed and scrubbed until it literally sparkled. As my reward I went downstairs to El Torrito for a well deserved carry-out order of Nacho Extreme so I could eat it just in time for church service on TV. Who needs to get up early and deal with the pomp and circumstance when you can just get straight to the point and watch the sermon from the comforts of your own home.

Today's sermon about cherishing and honoring our elders reminded me to call my grandmother. She is my last living grandparent and I love talking to her as much as I love chatting it up with my girlfriends.

"Hi Nanna, how are you?"

"Hey baby, I'm fine. I was just wrapping up the food from dinner."

"What did you cook?"

"Oh, honey. I fixed a big pot of Gumbo with brown rice and your favorite sweet cornbread. I can keep the food out if you want to come by."

"No, you can go ahead and wrap it up, I've already eaten."

"Oh, I bet that cute mocha man took you out to dinner today."

"No, I went across the street to the Mexican place and got a big nacho plate."

"Nachos on a Sunday? Girl what's wrong with you? You should've come over after church with your boyfriend. It could've been you two, Mr. Otis and me."

"Mr. Otis? Why's he over there?"

"Since when did I ever have to answer to you? He's my friend, a really good friend. Just like your what's his name."

"You're thinking about Mekhi."

"Oh, yes Mekhi. I can never remember that young man's name. He just doesn't look like his name should be Mekhi."

"Nan, it doesn't matter what his name is, we're not seeing each other anymore."

"How old are you again?"

"You know that I'm thirty-two."

"That's exactly my point. Isn't your clock beginning to wind down?"

"No, my clock is not winding down and obviously yours isn't either," I joked.

"*Ooh wee*, aren't we testy today. What did he do? Did he cheat on you baby?"

"Nan, we just decided to move on with our lives and explore other options."

"Well he's crazy if he let you go without a fight. He just lost out on the prettiest, thirty-two year old woman in this entire city. Mark my word, he'll come crawling back."

"I don't even want him back."

"Then don't worry, you'll find somebody. I feel it in my bones," she said laughing.

"That's just your rheumatism," I giggled.

"Hey watch it little whipper snapper," she replied laughing with Mr. Otis joining in the background.

"Well Nan, I guess I'll get off the phone. I'll talk to you later on this week. Take care."

"You too. Love you."

"I love you too."

Half the day had passed and although I went out for a split second to grab dinner, I felt like I needed to go out and get some fresh air. A quick jog would do me some good. Lord knows after eating those nachos I could stand to burn a few calories. As I stretched in front of the main door to my building, I saw Reese pulling into the parking lot.

"Where are you going in those booty shorts?" she asked referring to my old high school cross-country shorts.

"**They**'re not that short."

"If you say so."

"Just jealous," I joked as I playfully sashayed down the stairs. "I'm about to go for a quick jog."

"How long are you going to be gone?"

"About a half hour or so. Do you want to wait for me here?"

"Yeah. I know you don't have anything to eat up there."

"Nothing at all. You better go to El Torrito because they're about to close."

"Uh, uh that place is rat infested. Give me your keys, I'll find something."

When I returned home from my jog, there was a large El Torrito bag lying in the middle of my living room floor.

"So how was the rat burrito?" I yelled out to Reese, kicking off my running shoes.

"Shut up," she yelled laughing from my bedroom.

"What are you doing back there? I thought you were in the bathroom," I said as I walked in my room to find Reese checking herself out in one of my new dresses.

"This is cute on me."

"No it isn't. The waist is way too tight," I said jokingly.

"This is what is known as hourglass," she said smiling with a phony attitude as she ran her hands alongside her curvy physique.

"Reese, take off my dress."

"Fine. Did they have this in a size ten?"

"Nothing above an eight," I said as Reese looked at me like I was lying.

"Imma go check tomorrow," she said as she looked at the tag before tossing the dress on the bed.

"Oh, no no. Let's try that once again," I said like a mother to a spoiled child. "You are going to delicately put my dress back on the hanger, slide the garment-bag back over it and hang it up just like you found it."

"Yes mother."

"Did you come over just because you wanted to borrow some clothes?"

"No, sweetie I wouldn't do that," she said sarcastically. "I just wanted to come by and help you celebrate your first sucker free Sunday."

"First of all, you're crazy. Second of all, I know you all too well. You didn't come over here to be consoling miss nosey pants. You just want the juicy details that I refused tell you yesterday."

"You know me better than that," she said then paused. "So what happened?"

"You pretty much know," I said plopping down on the bed beside her. "Mekhi's a player which I don't have time for, and Nathan, well Nathan's just plain confused."

"To hell with the both of them."

"What was I thinking all this time, walking around ignoring the warning signs with Mekhi. And Nathan, just think if I had agreed to the long distance thing while he was living on the D.L."

"I know but look at it this way, you're in total control now. Get out there and enjoy the dating scene again. If you happen to meet the one, it'll be on your terms. You'll find Mr. Right. Someone who will be perfect for you with no surprises or extra-curricular activities. You deserve to be in love, but you also need to be with someone who deserves you."

"I'm surprised to hear you say that, miss anti-relationship."

"Don't get it twisted, I said when *you* find the one, not me."

"Just when I thought you were reformed."

"I love men too much to settle down with just one."

"Well I guess I shouldn't ask you about Martin."

"Girl, Martin is just my old faithful when I'm in a dry spell."

"That's cold. Martin's a nice guy."

"Which is why he's the perfect fall back."

"Damn, I guess when it's all said and done I was Mekhi's fallback. Never again."

MONDAY, 8/28

I woke up quite cheerful this morning. Maybe it had something to do with the fact that it's Monday—the day that I get paid, in a sense. Mondays are my invoicing days and every week after I send out bills to my clients, I calculate what portion of my lifestyle each particular invoice will cover. From the invoices sent out today, I should be able to completely take care of all necessities such as rent, car, insurance, food and entertainment for the next three months.

My largest client to date is a denim company based in Chicago, Jean Co. Jeans, owned by a young Russian woman by the name of, you guessed it, Jean. I landed the account this past May which entails managing the promotional campaign for their new collection comprising of field marketing, coordinating a few meetings and producing their launch party and fashion show in the next couple of weeks. Although Jean Co. is a really great account that has taken care of me for a couple of months, there is one piece of business that I've been trying to lock down since February and if it goes through I'll be set on all of my necessities for almost a year. Illum, a new cosmetics company based in Manhattan, is the hippest thing to hit the fashion world this year. I met one of the owners and the creative director last September while hanging out at Lincoln Center during Fashion Week. At the time, Illum wasn't quite known by the mainstream, but within a matter of months they were deemed the next "it" make-up brand. Meeting them was purely by chance, totally the perfect place at the perfect time. I was hanging out in front of the main entrance trying to sweet talk a couple of security guards into giving me a pass. All the while I noticed two stylish guys in the massive crowd smiling at me while shaking their heads. The way they were watching me led me to believe a few of things. One, they could probably figure out what I was trying to do from a mile away. Two, they've probably already tried it themselves and didn't succeed. And three, although they were both attractive, they weren't in the least bit interested in me for a couple of obvious reasons. As I stood on the stairs trying to make idle conversation with the guards, one of them mentioned to the other that he was going on break and he'd be back in a half hour. Once that guard left and I made my last attempt and plea with the other, the two men from the curb casually walked up the stairs behind me and went through the door without a pass. One of the guards from the sidewalk spotted them and ran up the stairs behind them. Just as the guard confronted the pair, they each pulled out passes from their jacket pockets and after a moment of conversation they were granted access. Just as I was on the verge of giving up, the two men motioned for me to join them.

"Unless they have a pass for you don't think about trying anything funny," the guard said to me as I walked to the top of the stairs.

Once I met up with them, one of the men pulled out a chained pass and placed it around my neck. When the guard saw that, he just shook his head then turned around to face the crowd.

"Hey, I'm Faire."

"And I'm Guy," both men said while shaking my hand.

"Christian Cullen," I said trying not to be star struck as I absorbed the glitz and glamour of my surroundings. "Thank you."

"This must be your first fashion week," Faire stated.

"Yeah it is."

"Well if you come back in February there are a couple of things you need to remember," Guy said, trying to school me. "Never, I mean never, look obvious. Everyone at the curb knew exactly what you were trying to do. And never chum up with a guard, they *will* remember your face. Remember that."

"He's right. We knew that we couldn't get anywhere near the door unless the main guard you were talking to left the scene."

"I don't get it, you have passes," I said.

"You're right! Digitally re-mastered by the wonderful people in our art department," Faire laughed.

"The guard who left turned us away last night. He was the only one who realized these were fake," Guy said, trying to look like the most important person at the event. "We better find a seat because Carolina Herrera's about to start."

I hung out with the Illum guys for the rest of the evening and was so impressed to learn about the overnight success they were experiencing. They were as equally impressed with me when I met with them at the beginning of the year with a sharp proposal detailing my vision for the product launch events for their new perfume line. They're supposed to make a decision soon so I'm keeping my fingers crossed.

Although I don't have the Illum account, yet, I'm satisfied with the progress of my company. I'll be the first to admit, when I started I didn't know if I would make it or not. I gambled a large chunk of my savings on my marketing and development budget to purchase print materials, a website, registration for industry conferences and the purchase of a mailing list of twenty-five hundred start-up companies in the Midwest. From then on I've had my ups and downs but for the most part it's been smooth sailing, especially after securing an investor. My new stream of capital has prepared me to move from my cramped home office into a hip converted warehouse space in a few days.

As I stuck the last stamp on my final invoice, I received a call on my company phone line.

"Hey Chris."

"Hey mom, how are you?"

"I'm fine. Haven't heard from you in a while."

"I'm sorry," I said, feeling guilty. "I promise that I'll get over to see you guys by the end of the week."

"So what's been up with you? How was your weekend?"

"It was okay. Ran some errands, cleaned house and got some rest."

"Did you go to church yesterday?"

"Not physically."

"Chris, you have to take a little time out of your life and give it back to God."

"Mom, I watched service on TV. I get just as much out of it that way as I do sitting up in a hot sanctuary."

"It's not the same," my mother scolded. "Actually getting up and putting forth the effort to go is symbolic to your commitment to God."

"How many times do we have to go through this? You know what happened to me the last time I went to church."

"Let me just say this one thing and I'll leave it alone. You cannot let people interfere with your walk with God. People are going to be people whether they're church going or not. You just have to overlook the few who try to bring you down and keep moving on with your life."

"Alright. I'll give it another chance."

"That's all I wanted to hear," she said, ending that chapter of our conversation. "You know, Eva's been asking about you."

"Really, how's she been?"

"She and Ev have been bopping around the house, happy to finally be upperclassmen. They've been begging us for a car for the past couple of weeks."

"Tell them that they'll just have to borrow yours like Angela and I did."

"I don't know. We're actually considering it."

"That's not fair!" I joked, sounding like a six year old.

"Your dad told me you would say that," mom said laughing on the other end.

"Not only did Angela and I have to borrow your cars, we'd have to turn back flips for the chance."

"You know that's not true," she said, laughing even harder.

"Remember when you guys finally broke down to help me get a car. That raggedy old grey Chevette with the one leather seat. All of the other seats were made of that weird carpet texture," I said cracking up, reminiscing on my old hooptie that lacked air conditioning and FM radio. "It barely got me from point A to point F. So what are they getting, new or used?"

"New."

"New? What kind?"

"We haven't decided yet, probably a Mini Cooper."

"Those two are so spoiled!"

"Oh, stop it. You know that you and Angela had your fair share of goodies when you were younger."

"I know, I'm just joking. Tell Eva I'll come by to help her with her cotillion speech."

"I need you to do something else. When you get a chance, sit her down so you guys can talk?"

"About what?"

"You know. Growing up, becoming a woman."

"Haven't you two already had *that* talk?"

"Yes, but you're younger and cooler. She idolizes you. When I talk to her about those things, she starts squirming all over the place, making faces like she doesn't want to hear me talk about it."

"I'll talk to her, don't worry."

"Thanks. Well, I'll let you get back to work."

"Talk to you later."

"Alright," she said then paused. "Oh, and don't forget what I said about church."

Every week my mom gives me the church lecture and every week I give her the same response. I know a lot of people are probably ready to call me a brazen heathen, but so what. I love the Lord and

I'm a believer, I've just had some bad experiences at church. The last two times I went were enough for me to stop going. The first instance I was called a whore as I stood in line waiting to be seated in the sanctuary. That day I'd decided to wear a sundress to church, nothing revealing or sultry just a classy, black, ankle-length sundress. While I waited in the lobby for the usher to come back and guide me to my seat, an elderly woman behind me began mumbling something under her breath. As the choir started to come to the end of their hymn and the deacon began the responsive reading, I heard the lady loud and clear.

"Hussy."

Who is this woman talking about, I thought to myself.

"Just whorish."

I turned around to find the old lady sneering at me. After a moment of complete and utter disbelief, I decided to politely respond to her un-Christian like behavior but couldn't because the usher opened the door and motioned me in. The second incident was similar to the first. My morning had already begun on a bad note because I woke up late after a power outage screwed up my alarm clock. To top it off, I had a crook in my neck and my hair was sweated out because I was too lazy to put on a scarf the night before. Like always, anytime I'm having a bad hair day my ritual is to pull my hair back in a high ponytail. So once again at church, minding my own business and waiting to be seated, three women behind me started snickering and singing "*Yaketty yak, don't talk back.*" I didn't think anything of it until I noticed them gawking and pointing at my ponytail through the reflection of the sanctuary window. They were convinced I was wearing a ponytail extension. I have nothing against women wearing weaves, it's just the fact that I wasn't wearing one. To top it all off, the ring leader, who had a head full of micro braids that hung down to the middle of her back, decided to get really bold and said, "There are gonna be some cold horses at the Derby this year." Instances like those show how hypocritical church folk can be. So if anyone's ever wondering about where I am on Sunday, they can find me in front of the TV with a big plate of nachos getting the word. That's just how it has to be.

While going through my emails before wrapping up for the day, I received a chain-message from Carra about signing a petition to stop the U.S. Postal Service from discontinuing the African American stamps series, one from Celeste asking for help with the wedding and one from Guy of Illum.

"Christian, I'm sorry that I haven't been able to keep in contact with you but I've been up to my neck in work, you know how it is. Unfortunately, I regret having to tell you that we chose a local firm to handle the perfume campaign. I want to mention that it was a very hard decision to make because your proposal absolutely blew our minds, but we just feel that a Manhattan based company would better suit our needs. Don't hesitate to keep in touch. Ciao!"

TUESDAY, 8/29

Boy did I pound the pavement today. I hit up nearly thirty businesses looking for new clients and everyone said the same thing, not right now. The joys of entrepreneurship are also the pains of it. The freedom and control to call the shots but also the responsibility of keeping your head above water. I try not to get discouraged after days like today. Although I have enough business to get me by for now, what worries me is that most of my contracts end in the spring. I should have gotten that Illum account. It pisses me off that I didn't get it just because of where I live.

"Hey girl, are you still going to the event at the Walker Theatre tonight?" Reese yelled, trying to speak over the sounds of cheering in the background.

"Yeah. Where are you?"

"I'm at a back-to-school rally hosted by the Colts."

"Are you going tonight?"

"No, but I wanted to give you a heads up that Mekhi's going to be there. Who are you going with?"

"I'm going by myself."

"Serious mistake."

"And why is that?"

"Because word is he's taking one of the Colts cheerleaders."

"Reese, I really don't care. Plus it's too last minute to ask anyone."

"No it's not. Just say the word and I can hook you up while I'm here."

"Thank you but no thank you."

"Alright, I tried. I just know that I don't want to hear you talking about how awkward it was being at a gala without a date while your ex was out with his rebound."

"Trust me I'll be fine."

After I parked my car, I took one last look in the rearview mirror, smoothed the flyaway hairs back in place and reapplied my lipstick. As I blotted my lips, a thud on my driver's side window nearly scared me half to death.

"You look fine," Darius said, staring at me through the glass.

"Boy, you scared the crap out of me! You can't do that kind of stuff at night!"

"I'm sorry, Chris," he said laughing as he opened the door for me. "I tried calling you Sunday."

"I was probably out getting something for dinner."

"No, this was earlier in the day."

"You probably caught me while I was in the shower."

When I said that, Darius paused, let out an "um, um, um" then made a shivering gesture.

"I'm sorry," he said, embarrassed by actions. "You kind of took my mind somewhere else."

I didn't know how to react to that. Darius had never once made a pass at me or ever given me any indication that he was attracted to me, so needless to say I was a little caught off guard.

"Are you meeting someone tonight?"

"No, originally Mekhi was supposed to have been my date."

"Well even if you guys were still kicking it he wouldn't have been able to make it. He just found out that he has to be in Denver for a meeting first thing tomorrow morning. He flew out about an hour ago."

"Poor Ms. Colts cheerleader."

"Oh you knew about Sherri?"

"You know how word gets around in this city," I said as I handed my ticket to the host. "Are you meeting someone tonight?"

"Nah. I figured I'd just fly solo. Maybe I'll meet a nice girl or maybe I'll swoop one up from a relationship gone sour," he said, smiling at me.

I must admit, I had a good time hanging with Darius tonight. I saw people looking at us and I'm sure they're going to start talking, but so what. I've been knowing him for years and there's nothing wrong with friends hanging out. I deserve to have fun so who cares.

"Christian, call me as soon as you get in. I don't care how late it is, just call me. 212-555-5555."

"Can you come to New York this week?" Guy asked in a panic.

"This week? Why?"

"I need you present your proposal again."

"What happened to the other firm?"

"Conflict of interest. We just found out they signed a non-compete agreement with another cosmetics company."

"How soon do you need me there?"

"Thursday afternoon. Just email me your itinerary with the airfare and hotel costs and we'll have a check waiting for you when you get here."

I could barely get the phone back on the base before my scream came out. Words could not describe my happiness to hear that I was back in the running.

WEDNESDAY, 8/30

This morning, my first appointment was thirty-five minutes late. Robert Hemmingway is the human resources director for an old paper manufacturing company that I'm doing marketing for. I met him a couple of months ago after we exchanged business cards at a gallery opening I coordinated. I was a little leery about him when we first met because he came off kind of used car salesman tacky, but my gallery client assured me that he was a good contact. Unfortunately, he was mistaken. Robert was supposed to be meeting me at his office at nine so we could discuss the details of his annual report and client appreciation party. He even called me twice this week to confirm. After twenty minutes passed, I got up and asked his secretary if she expected him in any time soon.

"Oh, honey he's on his way. I just spoke to him and he's leaving the dog groomer's now."

He's late because he's at the friggin' dog groomers? I thought as I convinced myself to sit back down and wait for him a little while longer. Once he finally arrived, he acted as if it were no big deal that he was late. He even had the nerve to ask if he could make a few phone calls before we got started. By the time our meeting was over, I realized that Robert was definitely as tacky as I first suspected. Throughout the meeting it was rare that he would look me in the eye since he was having such a great conversation with my chest. On top of that, he slashed three-fourths of his budget and is demanding that we move their client appreciation party, once scheduled at a ritzy golf course club house, to their dusty old supply warehouse. All I can say is Lord please let me get the Illum account.

After my morning appointments, I rushed back home to finalize all the logistics for my big fashion fundraiser, make my travel arrangements to New York, write a chairman's report for my museum board meeting and follow up on email. I had to do all of this before heading out to three more meetings. By the time I got home for the evening I barely had enough energy to walk from my car to the building and turn the keys in the locks. I kicked my shoes off across the living room then dragged myself to the kitchen and opened my refrigerator, only to be gravely disappointed. There were four bottles of Cakebread Cellars Chardonnay left over from a gallery opening, a half jug of water, two carry-out boxes that I was too afraid to open and a bunch of grapes that were converting into raisindom. As I was about to commit the most severe act of laziness known to man, calling the Thai restaurant downstairs to have them deliver my food to me, Reese called.

"What are your plans for dinner tonight?"

"I was just about to order Thai from downstairs."

"Not anymore because I'm grilling. I've got shrimp kabobs, chicken, swordfish..."

As Reese continued to rattle off her menu my stomach growled like a bear, "What time should I be there?"

"It's practically ready now."

"Just give me about a half hour to get some energy back and I'll be on my way."

I took a well deserved twenty-minute power nap, then after freshening up I grabbed a bottle of wine from the fridge and headed out. When I arrived at Reese's, there was a black Range Rover in her driveway that I didn't recognize. I was surprised to be greeted by a bald, muscular, six-foot something man when I rang her bell. He stood there smiling as Reese danced behind him, threw her arms around his waist and peaked out from around his left side.

"Christian this is Tee."

"Nice to meet you," I said extending my hand.

While attempting to shake my hand but instead crushing my fingers, Tee replied with a thick southern drawl, "Nice meeting you too."

"Tee's a new running back for the Colts," Reese purred. "He and I go way back."

Way back? I've been knowing Reese for over ten years and this is the first time I've ever heard about Tee.

"You need me to take that?" Tee pointed to the bag of wine in my hand.

"Yeah, thanks."

"I'm 'bout to go out back baby," Tee said, pinching Reese on the cheek.

"Umm, umm, umm!" Reese said, pretending to fall out as he walked away. "100% pure dark chocolate, bittersweet and scrumptious!"

"When did you meet him?"

"Girl, earlier this year at a client's Super Bowl party."

"Ah, right—way back."

"Shut up silly."

"So how come you didn't tell me about him when you two first met?"

"Because he wasn't a starter."

"Shameful," I said, smiling yet shaking my head in disbelief. "So where's Martin these days?"

"Who cares. I'm taking a sabbatical from him for a while."

"Why don't you just leave that poor man alone?"

"Naw, can't do that. He's taking me back to Negril in October."

"You know that's not right," I said.

"What? You're looking at me like I'm leading the brother on. He knows what he's gotten himself into."

"I guess," I replied following Reese into her kitchen. "Do you need help with anything?"

"No. Everything's already out on the patio. I'm about to change real quick so go on outside and relax."

As I approached the sliding glass doors that led to Reese's patio, I saw Tee outside laughing with a light skinned guy about the same build and height. Before I could turn around, Tee noticed me then ran up to open the door.

"Romeo, this is the chick Reese told you about," Tee said then looked at me. "Kristin right?"

"Actually, it's Christian," I said as Romeo smiled exposing a row of platinum teeth across the front of his grill, bobbing his head up and down and rubbing his hands together. It was like little red riding hood's first encounter with the big bad wolf.

"How you doin' Miss Lady?" he said, as I caught another glimpse of those god-awful teeth.

I am going to murder Reese, I thought as I tried to come up with a good escape. I politely excused myself by telling them that I needed to go help Reese with the rest of the food. As I slid the patio door shut, I saw Tee and Romeo give each other dap and laughing as if Romeo was about to get lucky.

"Oh, hell no!" I snarled at Reese as I entered the kitchen.

"Just stop it. Romeo is single and paid."

"Is that all it takes to qualify in your book? Romeo may be paid, but there is an obvious reason why he's still single and it's sitting smack dab in the front of his mouth. And is Romeo even his real name?"

"Quit being picky and try to have some fun for once."

"Reese I'm not going back out there."

"I thought you wanted to start dating again."

"You know good and well he's not my type."

"Okay, what do you want?"

"I don't know, but it ain't that."

Dinner with the guys was just as bad as I expected. Played out jokes, unnecessary references about how much money they make and even worse, the two of them reminiscing about some women they met last week at a D.C. strip club. At the end of the night, Romeo went through the typical, watered down ritual of trying to see if he could get to know me better. I had to tell him straight up that now isn't a good time and that it was a pleasure meeting him.

On my way home, I stopped at Target to pick up a pair of tights, the latest *Essence* and *Dwell* magazines, some trail mix and a pack of gum for my trip tomorrow. While I was in the check-out line, Darius called to invite me to the Sonny Rollins concert on Saturday night. After I hung up with him I had to wonder if it was just my imagination or was Darius starting to catch feelings? Ever since the Mekhi fiasco Darius has seriously been trying to step up to the plate.

As I was in the middle of preparing my presentation for tomorrow's meeting I felt a sharp tightness in my abdomen. All I could do to brace the pain was to cling onto the bottom of my desk and breathe in deep and long. First warning, I thought as the piercing jolt began to subside. Every month, a couple of days before I start my period, I'm always inconvenienced with a sudden burst of unexpected pain. Good thing that it didn't happen earlier or big man Romeo may've gotten those teeth knocked out. Once I recovered, I remembered that I forgot to take my birth control pill today. This was the second time this week that I'd forgotten to take my pill. Why I'm even taking them right now is beyond me. I hadn't had sex in over two months plus I was tired of feeling bloated and hungry all of the time. Taking a rest from the pill would be a healthy choice, plus it would force me to be more disciplined in the one thing that I'd been contemplating on and off for a while now, celibacy.

THURSDAY, 8/31

"Hey sugar! How was your trip?" Guy welcomed me with an embrace immediately after I entered the doors of the ultra chic headquarters of Illum.

"Just fine. How have you been?"

"I've been good—really good," he said with sly look, nodding his head. "I'll tell you all about it later."

"Are you one of the models?" a handsome man, who seemed to come out of nowhere, asked as I followed Guy down a long corridor.

"I'm flattered but no," I responded.

"Well you should be," he said smiling then extended his hand and made a face like he just remembered something. "I'm so rude. I forgot to introduce myself. My name's Toussaint. And you are?"

"Christian Cullen."

"Christian. Well it's good to meet you."

"Toussaint, aren't you late for a meeting?" Guy joked as he pulled me into the elevator.

"I am, but trust me they can't start without me. It's been a pleasure meeting you Christian."

"Likewise," I said as the elevator door closed.

Guy was grinning like the Cheshire Cat as he pushed the button for the sixteenth floor.

"Toussaint is the playboy of the company if you couldn't already tell."

"What's his story?"

"He's head of our legal department and recently divorced," Guy continued to smile as if he was trying to start something.

"That's nice."

Guy looked at me out of the corner of his eyes, "Don't try to act like you're not interested."

"I'm not. He's handsome and all but I don't mix business with pleasure."

"Oh, live a little."

"Moving right along," I said trying to change the subject. "So who am I presenting to?"

"Mr. Theodore Carter himself."

"Stop lying."

"I'm dead serious."

"You mean to tell me I'm presenting to the president of the company."

"You got it sister."

As I sat in the break room for two hours following my meeting, I know I drank at least five cups of coffee nervously waiting for Guy to come back with an answer. I don't know how I was able to effectively deliver my presentation because the sheer knowledge and pressure of presenting to the president of a major company is enough to make anyone feel faint, but somehow I got through it. When Guy finally came back, he walked through the door with a huge smile on his face. Christian, don't get your hopes up and don't jump to any conclusions, I told myself as I prepared to hear what he had to say.

I got the account. Oh my goodness, I can't believe I got the account! I'm developing the total promotional campaign for Illum's new perfume, Luxe. From the launch party to the field marketing, my company was selected to manage it all. The ink on the contract was barely dry when I realized that this contract will take care of my rent and car payments for a full year, put a dent in my outstanding student loan and after that I'll still have more to spare. God is so good!

"I didn't see Faire in the office today. What's he been up to?" I asked Guy as we waited to be seated for dinner.

"He sold his interest in the company and left to go work for the competition. Good riddance."

"I thought you two were cool."

"Remember your whole business with pleasure rule? Well let's just say I should never have crossed the two."

"Enough said."

"Changing the subject, are you excited about winning the account?"

"Words cannot express."

"I know you're going to blow this campaign out of the box," he said smiling then began looking at me like he had something to ask. "I need you to do me a big favor when you come back next month."

"What's that?"

"I have a photographer friend who's shooting for an upcoming exhibition. He needs a brown-skinned, exotic model type to be his main subject."

"Okay…"

"And I need you to fill the part."

"Out of all of the women in New York City, you're asking me?"

"Why not? You've got the look and plus you owe me for hooking you up with the contract."

"I'm getting the sense that this will be an unpaid gig."

"You guessed it."

"I don't have to be naked do I?"

"Honey, this is not that type of shoot."

"Well okay then. I guess I don't see any reason why I shouldn't. I'm in."

"Great, I knew you'd do it."

After dinner, Guy said that he had a huge surprise for me, so after hailing a cab and speeding down the Westside Highway like a bat out of hell, we were on our way to an undisclosed location.

"You can turn on Warren, the building is between Greenwich and West Broadway," Guy said to the cabbie as he whipped around corners, ran a few red lights and dodged traffic before slowing down at our destination.

"Just wait until you see this!" he said, scooting out of the cab after paying the driver.

"What?" I asked, not noticing anything particularly special.

"This!" he said, pointing to a vacant looking warehouse. "You'll see in a minute."

The place was obviously still under construction because in order to get in, we had to walk up a long makeshift ramp while dodging tattered plastic swaying in the wind.

"You are going to shit when you see this!" he said, as he pulled out a large key ring and unlocked three deadbolts.

When we entered the space I couldn't believe what I was seeing. The place was fabulous! It was like we stepped back in time into an authentic ancient Egyptian palace. The floors were made of beautiful polished sandstone, the walls were enhanced by huge gold pillars inscribed with hieroglyphics and there were large palm trees that lined the main foyer and extended into the next floor up.

"This is where we're having the launch party!" Guy said to me. "Fierce isn't it."

"Unbelievable. What's the name of this place?"

"Third Dynasty or 3D Lounge as the insiders call it. It doesn't open until next year but they're making an exception for us."

"This is going to be fabulous."

"That's the only way we do it around here. I know you've been successful at doing your thing for a while, but trust me after this event you're going to be catapulted to another level. Be glad you have me in your corner."

SATURDAY, 9/2

I was so busy yesterday that I didn't even have the time to journal. I had to hit the ground running with vendor meetings back to back from nine o'clock until it was time for me to catch my flight at eight-fifteen. Throughout the hecticness of the day, I experienced a high like none other. Guy's words rang repeatedly in my head over and over, "You're going to be catapulted to another level." With this opportunity I truly believe that.

"Reese told me that she set you up with a hottie the other night," Carra said as she sat on the edge of the black cushioned pedicure chair grinning at me.

"Carra, haven't you learned to take Reese with a grain of salt. I wish you could've seen that brother. He had a mouth full of ice, a peanut head and no neck."

"That's not what Reese told me. She said his skin looked like smooth butterscotch and that he had...," she looked around then lowered her voice, "an ass out of this world."

"Trust me, it wasn't all that. Consider yourself lucky that you're already locked down because I don't know if you could handle the Reese Cambridge Settle-For-Less-As-Long-As-He's-Paid Dating Service."

"It's that bad?"

"You have no clue."

"I guess the after effects of the divorce have clouded her judgment."

"And taste. Trust me, it's not only with the men she tries to hook me up with, but with the men she messes around with."

"What happened to Martin?"

"Prime example. She uses him because he's a straight and narrow nice guy. She knows he's head over heels for her, yet she plays him like a fiddle."

"I don't get it. Martin's grade A," Carra said while choosing a polish color. "He's a handsome, intelligent Christian man."

"That's the problem. He's not the bad boy she's looking for. Although she'll never admit to it, I'm sure if one of the professional ballers she chases broke down and proposed to her, she would accept."

"I feel sorry for Martin."

"Oh, well. He'll learn. So how's your man?"

"Aaron's doing alright, just a little frustrated because he was passed over for yet another promotion. This is the second time since the beginning of the year."

"What's the deal with that?"

"I don't know. He's far more educated and intelligent than anybody at his company. They keep giving him the excuse that he's such an asset to his department, they can't bear to lose his expertise."

"Then they need to give him more money."

"Exactly. But when it's all said and done we're not worried about it. God has a blessing on the way."

"Amen to that."

"So do you have big plans this weekend?"

"A little something," I said, trying to look away to conceal my smile.

"What are you smiling about?" Carra asked as she leaned over to look at my face. "Why are you blushing? Who do you have a date with?"

"Why does it matter? Just know that I'm going out to see one of the last living jazz greats of our time. It should make you happy just knowing that."

"Okay, that's nice, but who are you going to see this jazz legend with?"

"No one."

"Chris, don't act like that. Tell me."

"Oh, alright. I'm going with Darius."

"*Darius who?*"

"Carra. You know exactly which Darius I'm talking about. Darius Paterson, president of the Jazz Renaissance Society."

"Don't you mean Darius Paterson, president of the Jazz Renaissance Society who also happens to be Mekhi's best friend?"

"You're forgetting that I knew Darius way before I met Mekhi."

"Wow, you don't feel weird about this?"

"Not at all."

"So you and Darius are an item now."

"An item? Carra come on it's just a date. We're just going out to enjoy a night of jazz, that's all."

After we left the spa, Carra and I met up with Celeste and Reese for a breast cancer awareness luncheon that Celeste's mom invited us to. It's a little depressing that between the four of us, we've all been affected by the disease in one way or another. Nanna is a fifteen year survivor who had a mastectomy, Celeste's mom was recently diagnosed, Reese's cousin died a couple years ago from the disease and Carra, who has a family history of breast cancer, has been keeping an eye on a small lump in her own breast.

"Christian, don't make me have to call you to see if you're doing your self-examinations," Reese scolded.

"Why'd you have to single me out?" I asked.

"Because I know how you forget those kinds of things," Reese said, looking at me like I should have already known. "You are the queen of going a year and a half before you realize that you should've scheduled your pap smear. I'm just trying to look out for you."

"I do my self-exams, I don't know what you're talking about. After seeing my Nanna suffer, you better believe that I'm on it every month."

"Speaking of which, how is she?" Celeste asked.

"She's fine, but can you believe that she has a boyfriend."

"What?" Celeste replied smiling with her mouth wide open.

"Nanna's getting her groove, bump and grind on!" Reese sang, dancing out the door towards the parking lot.

"Oooh, that's so out of line," Carra said, laughing. "She's probably just dating a friend, similar to her granddaughter."

When Carra said that, all of the girls stopped mid-trek and stared at me.

"Don't pay any attention to her, she's talking crazy," I said, trying not to look guilty as I rushed to my car. "Gotta go!" I said before slamming my door and speeding off.

Darius arrived at my door at a quarter after six looking wonderful with roses and card in hand.

"It's awkward going out with you on a 'first date' since I've known you for so long. I hope that this can lead to bigger and better things to come in the future. Love, Darius."

From the moment we left my place, Darius was the example of a perfect gentleman. He opened every door, held onto me as I walked up or down stairs in stilettos, during the performance he gave me his coat when it got chilly and to my surprise he gently stroked my wrist and fingers as we vibed to the sounds of Sonny Rollins.

"Do you still paint?" Darius asked afterwards at dinner.

"Wow, I can't believe you still remember that," I said, taking a sip of mineral water. "I just finished a piece a couple of weeks ago. Since then, I've been taking a breather because of my hectic schedule."

"What was the inspiration behind it?"

"I was home one evening during a thunderstorm. I had the windows open and just feeling that warm breeze and smelling the scent of rain somehow inspired me. The whole vibe put such a calm over me that I didn't think about what I was about to paint, I just let the brush do its thing."

"Sounds deep."

"It is. I actually surprised myself."

"I hope I get a chance to see this masterpiece."

"If you're up for dessert I can whip up some cookies and you can see it tonight."

"Hey Chris, is this the painting you were telling me about?" Darius asked as I grabbed a bottle of wine out of the fridge.

"Yeah, the one on the easel by the window!" I yelled out to him.

"This is nice. You should consider approaching an art dealer about your work."

"You know, I already like you. You don't have to try to butter me up."

"I'm not trying to butter you up. Someone just needs to master the art of accepting a compliment."

"Well in that case, thank you," I said as I handed him a glass of wine.

"Thank you," he said tapping his glass against mine.

Between the two of us, we ate an entire tray of cookies, a half a pint of ice cream and killed a bottle of wine. We ordered an Eddie Murphy double feature OnDemand but by the time the second movie came on, Darius was sprawled out across my couch knocked out.

"Darius," I whispered as I knelt down on the floor in front of him and tapped him on his shoulder. "Darius, wake up."

He slowly opened his eyes and gave me the sexiest bedroom stare.

"You are so beautiful," he whispered, unfolding his arms and wrapping them around my waist.

"Darius…" I said attempting to derail the direction of this scenario. "I think you should be going."

With his arms still around me, he pulled me even closer, "Are you sure about that?" Then kissed me slow and gently, leaving the sweet scent of Riesling on my lips. Before I could even think, Darius sat up with his fingers moving up my spine to my neck then gave me the most sensual, judgment clouding kiss I've experienced in a very long time. I admit I got a little caught up. Okay, extremely caught up because I allowed myself to be picked up and whisked off into my own bedroom—without a fight. Who knows how I'll feel in the morning, I just know at that very moment I didn't really care.

SUNDAY, 9/3

For the second Sunday in a row, I was awakened out of a deep sleep by the sun beaming through my window. I reached to grab the pillow next to me to cover my head, but as I felt around for the pillow all I got was a handful of dreads and an ear. Oh, how soon we forget, I thought before opening my eyes.

"Good morning gorgeous," Darius said in a groggy voice.

"Hey," I said, noticing the makeup smeared all over my pillowcase. I quickly turned my face in the other direction because I was certain I looked like Bozo the Clown.

"What's wrong," he said, rolling over to my side of the bed. "Let me see how beautiful you are."

"I'm not ready for my close up," I joked as I buried my head in my pillow. "Go back over to the other side."

"Let me be the judge of that," he said as he pulled the pillow from over my head.

"I need to run to the bathroom," I said jumping up from the bed headed towards the bathroom door, pulling the sheets along with me and exposing Darius full frontal.

"Wait a minute!" he said, grabbing back the end of the covers and jerking them away from me, leaving me standing there butt naked.

I could hear Darius in my bedroom cracking up laughing after I ran into the bathroom.

"Neither one of us will ever look at each other the same!" he yelled.

He's right. I never thought beyond last night. I never considered how awkward it's going to be at Jazz Society meetings, where he's the president and I'm the hired marketing consultant. Would he be obvious about our little escapade or would he play it cool and keep it professional? Looking in the mirror, I didn't know whether I liked what I saw and it wasn't because of the smeared makeup, bloodshot puffy eyes or the tangled hair. I lost control which isn't like me. I was okay with hanging out, but I had no intentions of sleeping with him.

"Hey Chris, I'm going across the street to the market. What kind of bagel do you want?" Darius yelled from outside the bathroom door.

"Cinnamon and raisin."

"Cream cheese?"

"Low-fat," I replied, while squeezing eye-drops into my eyes.

"Okay, I'll be right back."

I was all washed up and dressed by the time Darius came back. When I opened the door to let him in, he placed the bags down on the floor, picked me up and began spinning me around and kissing me like he hadn't seen me in three years.

"Okay. Good morning to you too."

"You know what? I can really get used to this," Darius said, as he held my hand.

"This is nice, but let's just take our time."

"I'm willing to do that—later," he said as he walked behind me and brushed his lips across my ear. "But right now I can go for round two," he put his arms around me and pulled me in to his obviously alert counterpart. "Maybe round three or four while we're at it."

"Darius, let's chill out for a minute."

"Uh oh, what's wrong?"

"Nothing's wrong, I just need some time to digest everything that's happened."

"This is about Mekhi isn't it?"

"This has nothing to do with Mekhi, I just think we moved way too fast last night."

"Funny, I don't. I've known you for a long time and even before Mekhi, there was an attraction between us, the timing was just always off. Do you know how pissed I was to have to introduce you to Mekhi? The more I hesitated, the more he pressed the issue. If I were single at the time I would have never hooked the two of you up. He didn't deserve you, but I think that I do. I know you think this is moving too fast and I'm sure what I'm about to say will scare you, but Christian this is our time."

MONDAY, 9/4

You saw her last month and now she's back for her encore performance! Starring in an abdomen near you, it's the Christian Cullen "Menstrual Show," I thought and chuckled to myself as I fumbled through my linen closet for a box of tampons and ibuprofen. After I popped the pills and ate a light breakfast, I hauled myself over to my work desk and began pulling out drawers. I really didn't feel like moving into my new office today, but I had no choice. My sunroom was beginning to look like a darkroom because I had file boxes practically stacked to the ceiling. The movers were supposed to arrive at eleven but they ended up coming over almost an hour early. I directed them towards the sunroom so they could start moving the boxes out while I rushed to finish packing. Every time they came in to get another box one guy was frowning and huffing and puffing like he was pissed about something.

"Man, I'm not trying to be here all day. If she ain't done by the time we get these last couple of boxes, I'm out. I gotta barbecue to hit up," I overheard him say in the living room.

"Excuse me?" I yelled from the sunroom, as I got up from the floor. "You're going to be here until the job gets done. You guys weren't even supposed to be here until eleven but I didn't say anything. Regardless, I'm paying you the holiday rate to move my stuff not to be standing around complaining and wasting time."

The other guy started snickering at his partner while the loud mouth one just rolled his eyes, picked up another box by the front door then walked out.

"He's got issues," the other guy said, picking up a box. "Just ignore him."

That dude caught me on the wrong day, I thought as I went back into my office to finish packing. I was done within fifteen minutes and the guys still had my office furniture and nine boxes left. I didn't say a thing to them when I walked back into the dining room, I just sat at my table and read the newspaper.

Once the guys were done loading the truck, I put on my shoes and followed them to my new office space. It didn't take long for them to get everything moved in and within an hour, I had a brand new loft office decorated in the finest cardboard money could buy. I honestly didn't feel like unpacking so I just arranged all of the file boxes in alphabetical order and pushed them towards the back of the room.

Even though I was dead tired after leaving my new office, I talked myself into going to the gym. While changing clothes I thought about everything Guy and I had talked about last week in New York, mainly about me modeling for his friend. A hundred and fifty-six pounds at five feet seven inches, isn't horrible, but it isn't exactly model material. I could stand to lose a few pounds here and there.

"Do you like what you see?" a muscular and heavily tanned woman asked as I was stepping off of the scale.

"I have a photo shoot coming up so I'd like to tone up and lose a couple of pounds. Are you a trainer?"

"Yeah, my name is Janet. I would give you my card but this is my last week here at the club. I'm about to move to Cali," she replied. "I can give you a few pointers though."

Janet suggested that I participate in a spinning class for my cardio, followed by a circuit-training program paired with a strict low carb, high protein diet.

"By doing this program you should begin to see results pretty quickly," she said, showing me a class schedule. "There's a spinning class that's just about to start. Why don't you go in and give it a try."

"This sheet says intermediate spinning. I don't know if I can…"

"You're in pretty good shape, you should be able to handle it," Janet said, cutting me off. "Remember your goal."

"Okay, if you say so."

After my workout, I went in for the first fitting of my bridesmaid dress. I love Celeste for selecting elegant, little black cocktail dresses for us. Finally, a bridesmaid dress that I can actually wear again. I would have preferred that the fitting be on a day other than the first day of my period, but even though I was bloated like the Michelin Man I felt good after my workout.

Later in the evening, I attended a few art festivals and picked up a great new sculpture for my office before heading back to my apartment. My family was in Michigan spending the holiday with my great uncle, each one of my girls had their own plans and since there's no boyfriend in the picture I decided to spend the rest of my Labor Day relaxing at home by myself.

TUESDAY, 9/5

"Oh, so you're screwing my best friend now?"

"Excuse me?"

"I can't believe you gave it up to my boy! What the hell's up with that?"

"I don't have to explain shit to you, Mekhi," I snapped, pissed off that he would call me talking crazy.

"Then you just confirmed it. Just another high class ho..."

I hung up on him fuming at his audacity to confront me, but even more pissed at Darius for running his mouth!

I was completely ineffective during my two meetings today, still reeling over the phone call from earlier. When I went to the gym this afternoon I exercised like a mad woman. Anger is an awesome stimulant because I went to the advanced spinning class today and didn't feel a thing. My adrenaline was pumping and even after my workout I couldn't calm down. I tried to work on a new painting, but I couldn't concentrate. I tried to catch up on a little reading and again, I couldn't concentrate. I tried calling Carra to hear a positive voice, but she wasn't around. I tried Celeste and Reese's home and cell phones, but they weren't answering. I tried calling my sister and parents. I even tried calling Guy, but no one was answering their phones. Just as I was about to dial Nanna, I got a call from guess who, Darius. His small talk was laughable as he began the first couple minutes of the conversation as if nothing was wrong. I couldn't take it any longer when he had the nerve to ask me if I'd thought about him today.

"Darius, where do you get off telling Mekhi about what happened between us?"

Dead silence.

"Darius I asked you a question."

"It's not what you think."

"What do you mean it's not what I think?"

"Mekhi came over Sunday night and your name came up."

"Why?"

"Somebody told him that they saw us together at the Walker event." Darius said, slowly and carefully.

"That still doesn't explain anything."

"Christian, look. Mekhi started trippin' about us going out and he got out of line saying that I was trying to pick up where he left off. Things got heated, stuff was said and he ended up putting two and two together. I told him straight up that he didn't know how to handle a situation with a good woman like you. That's when Mekhi asked, 'and you do?' Then I blurted out without thinking, I'm taking care of business as we speak."

After talking to Darius I was so happy to get a message from Carra inviting me to dinner tonight. I needed to take the long tranquil drive to her house to help me sort out my thoughts. Carra lives in one of the most affluent areas in the city, simply known by the name of the reservoir it surrounds, Geist. This is the type of neighborhood that status symbols are made of. You either feel good or depressed when driving in this part of town because it's such an image of the "perfect world." Custom homes, wooded lots, four cars garages housing four luxury cars, blacks and whites living harmoniously next to one another in wealth, professional women with advanced degrees that choose to stay at home to tend to their gorgeous children who have more money in their trust funds than I'll ever see in my lifetime—it's so storybook. Everyone isn't destined for that life but Carra has been prepping for it for as long as she could crawl. She's got the suburban black professional starter kit with the great job, the right organizational memberships, the successful husband who's fighting up the corporate ladder, the luxury SUV and sedans, the dog, the five bedroom, four and a half bath, three-car garage home with the library, family room, living room, rec room, formal dining room, good morning room and numerous other special rooms in this titanic home for just the two of them. There's only one thing left that would complete the package.

When Carra answered the door, she looked adorable sporting a sassy new hair cut, wearing the old sorority shirt we received when we were initiated.

"Girl, where did you dig up that shirt?"

"I wear this all of the time. I bet you don't even know where yours is."

"Unfortunately you're right. I see Celeste and Reese have already beat me to the punch."

"Yeah, they're in the family room eating. Go ahead and get yourself a plate," she said, ushering me into her luxurious kitchen.

Carra had ordered a massive sushi spread along with shrimp fried rice, vegetable tempura, spring rolls and edamame. I channeled my willpower to resist the tempura and fried rice and only put two salmon rolls and some edamame on my plate.

"Tonight will be the beginning of a new tradition within the sister circle. After we eat, we shall begin the ceremony," Carra said dramatically, as we all looked at her confused.

"Whatever you say," Celeste said as she smiled at Carra then looked at Reese shaking her head.

"Will you get me two more spring rolls," Reese asked just as I was about to sit down.

"And you're all of a sudden crippled because…"

"You were about to get back up anyway because you forgot to get something to drink," she said, noticing me look at her like she was crazy. "Please?" she said, smiling.

"That's more like it," I said as I got up and playfully snatched the plate out of her hand but didn't get away in enough time before she popped me on the thigh.

"Did anyone even hear me? I'm serious about this," Carra said in a whiny voice.

"Alright girls, Car has something special planned for us and I think we'd better give her our undivided attention," Celeste said like a school teacher with a sinus problem.

"Well what the hell is it?" Reese asked.

"Do you really want to know?" Carra said in a suspenseful tone.

"Yes!" the three of us said in unison.

"Come on, follow me," Carra said as she popped up from a big pillow on floor.

We followed Carra upstairs to her bedroom where soft violin music played and candles flickered all over the place. She told us to sit down on her bed as she went into the bathroom and brought out a small wooden box.

"In this box lays the key to my future," Carra said, as the three of us sat on the bed looking confused. "This box holds something more precious than money can buy. This box represents..."

"Carra just open the damn box," Reese snapped, interrupting Carra's soliloquy.

"Fine," she said, while taking a deep breath and handing the box to Reese.

"This better be good," Reese said while sliding the cover off of the box, then paused. "*Whaaat...*" she said, passing the box to Celeste.

Celeste took one look in the box and said, "Oh my goodness," then passed the box to me.

When I looked in, I couldn't believe what I saw. There was a pregnancy test wand turned upside down on a bed of cotton balls. I looked up at Carra and she nodded at me.

"Turn it over," she said, as everyone looked at me nodding.

"Why do I have to be the one to touch it?"

"Just give it here," Reese said reaching over for the box.

"Fine, I'll do it."

I reached in the box and used my fingernail to flip the wand over on its other side then couldn't believe what I saw. A pink plus sign was showing through the small window.

"Well, what does it say?" Celeste asked as Reese leaned on her shoulders to see.

"Carra, do you have any baby names picked out?"

Carra stood speechless in disbelief as Celeste jumped up off the bed to give her a hug.

"Are you okay?" I asked as I put the box down and walked over to her.

"Yeah," she said with a dazed look.

"You don't look okay," Reese said, getting up to get her a cold washcloth.

"I'm pregnant. Oh, my goodness, I'm pregnant," she said quietly, then began squealing. "I can't believe it, I'm pregnant!"

"Congratulations sweetie," Celeste said as she used the washcloth to wipe the tears from Carra's eyes.

"Are you happy?" I asked, giving her a hug.

"I'm so happy. This is exactly what Aaron and I need."

Reese looked at me with a furrowed brow as if to say, *what's that supposed to mean?* I replied by slightly shrugging my shoulders.

Reese got up from the bed and gave Carra a hug, "You know, you're always the first one to break the sister code. You were the first one to run off and get married, now you went and got yourself all knocked up," Reese said, laughing. "I just don't know about you girl."

"Thank you guys for being here. I love you all so much," Carra said, dabbing her Bambi eyes. "Now you know this has to be tradition from now on."

"What?" Celeste asked.

"Having a pregnancy test ceremony."

"Anything you say Car," I replied, knowing good and well that this would probably be our last and only one.

"Okay, I'm still hungry. I don't know about you all but I'm about to get back to my food," Reese said as she made her way to the door.

"Oh, damnit! I can't eat sushi anymore," Carra announced. "And oh, I shouldn't have said damnit because the baby will hear me."

"Oh my goodness," Celeste said walking down the stairs with her hand on her head before turning her attention on me. "So Christian, tell us about your New York trip?"

"Well you know I got the account but what I forgot to tell you is that I've also been offered to do some modeling."

"For who?" Reese asked sarcastically, following me into the kitchen.

"For one of Guy's friends," I said while washing my hands. "You remember me telling you about him. He's the one that basically hooked up the Illum opportunity for me."

"Do you have your first gig lined up?" Celeste asked.

"Yeah, it's for an art exhibit for some photographer. Nothing's set in stone just yet. I'm still finding out all of the details."

"Guy's the one you met last year when you got caught trying to sneak into the fashion shows, right?" Carra asked as she fixed herself a big plate of rice.

"Yeah. He's really cool."

"I bet he is. How many times are you going to have to sleep with him in order to get more business?" Reese joked as she popped the rest of her California roll in her mouth.

"I'm offended," I said playfully with my mouth wide open.

"I'm just saying. I remember when you came back from your Fashion Week trip. All you could talk about was Guy this and Guy that. I just figured that he'd already hit or that he was about to."

"That approach may work for you," I replied and jokingly rolled my eyes at her. "Anyway Guy's gay for your information. I think he's using this whole modeling thing to get closer to the photographer."

"It figures," Reese replied.

"Speaking of getting closer, what's up with you and Chocolate Thunder? What's his name, Tee? It didn't look like he had any intentions of leaving your house that night," I said to Reese as she avoided direct eye contact with me. She didn't say a word. All she could do was smirk and hide her face behind a nearby newspaper.

"Shameful," Carra said as she snatched the paper away from Reese. "Didn't you just go out with Martin the other night?"

"Since when has that meant anything?"

"Ugghhh, next subject," Carra said as she turned her nose up at Reese. "How's the wedding coming along Celeste?"

"Just what you'd expect from a rushed, last minute ceremony. If it weren't for you guys, I wouldn't know what I'd do. My mother is driving me crazy and John is being spastic about everything. Trust me if he and my mother changed their minds about this big production and opted to go downtown for a civil ceremony, I wouldn't object. It'd be a hell of a lot cheaper."

"Just take it all in and enjoy the happy times and the stressful times because before you know it, it will all be over," Carra said while rubbing her belly.

"It's getting late. Carra, you need to get some rest and I have leave. I'm driving to Chicago first thing tomorrow morning and I still need to pack," I said, while Celeste chimed in.

"Yeah, I need to be going too."

As we walked to the foyer to put our shoes on, Carra had to ask the question that would keep us there for another hour.

"Oh I almost forgot to ask, how was your date with Darius?"

Reese and Celeste stopped what they were doing and stared at me.

"Date with Darius?" Reese asked while widening her green eyes.

"Look, I just went to a concert with him. That's all," I said and gave Carra the evil eye.

"What? I thought you told them," she said, replying to my gesture.

"It really wasn't a big deal," I said as I fumbled through my purse for my keys.

"Isn't Darius one of Mekhi's best friends?" Celeste asked, picking up my keys from one of the end tables and dangling them in front of my face.

"You're not getting these until you cough up some information," Reese said, as she snatched the keys out of Celeste's hand.

"There isn't any information," I said as I walked over to her and reached out my hand. "Now quit playing and give me my keys."

"I'm not giving you shit until you tell us what's up with you two."

"Like I said before, he took me to a jazz concert on Saturday night."

"And?" Reese prodded.

"And we went out to dinner afterwards, now give me my keys so I can go home to get ready for tomorrow."

"Nah, I know there's more. What else?" Reese said as she jingled my keys and grinned. All the while, Carra and Celeste were cracking up laughing on the stairs.

"Nothing," I said, trying to keep a straight face.

"I knew it!" Reese yelled. "You know you can't keep shit from us!"

"I was wondering why you were glowing at the fitting yesterday," Celeste said, shaking her head.

"I never said anything went on," I said, trying to control my smile muscles.

"You don't have to, it's written all over your face," Carra laughed.

"Okay, it happened. But I guarantee that it won't happen again," I said, trying to be serious.

"And why is that?" Reese asked, making a face as if she didn't believe me.

"Because he told Mekhi."

"What? That doesn't seem like Darius's style," Carra said in disbelief.

"He claims that Mekhi put two and two together. Regardless, when it's all said and done it never should've happened in the first place."

WEDNESDAY, 9/6

It hurt to get up this morning. I didn't get home until after one and in order to make my eight o'clock meeting in Chicago, I had to be on the road by five. I was making good time for the first hour of my drive. I had my energy bar, a big bottle of water and my old school hip hop playlist. I was good to go until I tried to pass a slow minivan and ran over a piece of metal lying in the middle of the highway. After I heard a loud pop then a wobble sound, I knew I had a flat. Thankfully, I managed to pull over to the side of the highway just as the lanes were merging into one for an on-coming construction zone. I don't have roadside assistance, so I may have to change this flat myself, I thought. Magazines always have articles about women handling their own car care, showing pictures of ladies in business suits and heels checking their oil and changing their own tires. That thought was quickly overturned with every passing semi that shook my car as they passed, nearly missing me and running me off the road. I tried calling Jean to let her know what was going on and that I'd be late, but being out in the middle of nowhere I didn't have a cell signal. To make matters worse, when help finally arrived by way of a county sheriff, he spent more time checking my background than he did actually assisting.

When I arrived at the Jean Co. office it was ten twenty-seven, and although I called her as soon as I was in range of a signal I knew she wouldn't be a happy camper. As I walked down to the end of the hall, I noticed Jean through the glass door of her lobby pacing back and forth from one end of the room to the other. She looked up when I opened the door then ignored me and began pacing again while

111

mumbling something in Russian and shaking her head. I was trying to make out anything that sounded like Negro, noir or black because I knew exactly what she was probably thinking. Moments later she finally looked up at me and growled in her thick accent, "This is not what I expect from someone I just paid twenty-five thousand dollars advance to handle my promotion! Never again, late, late, late!"

I didn't even bother arguing with her. Whatever I said would've sounded like an excuse to her. I just apologized and went on with the meeting as if everything was fine.

I'm so glad this day is over, I thought as I sped down Lake Shore Drive and turned on Michigan Avenue for some retail therapy. I bought two bra and panty sets, a sexy black knit wrap-shirt, skinny red jeans, some bad-ass spiked ankle boots and a ton of toiletries.

I'm not driving home tonight, I said to myself as I pulled into one of my favorite hotels. I grabbed my work-bag, iPod, purse and shopping bags, then left my keys with valet to enjoy a much needed change of scenery tonight.

After a power nap, I walked across the street to a hole-in-the-wall jazz club for dinner. Even though the only thing I'd eaten all day was an energy bar, I was able to withstand the temptations of ordering the house favorite, barbecued chicken and garlic mashed potatoes and instead ordering only a small garden salad with a side of lime vinaigrette and a glass of Pinot Blanc.

"Will that be all for you?"

"Yes, I'm trying to keep it light tonight."

"Why? You look great," the waiter replied flirtatiously.

"I've been doing so good thus far, I can't let an order of succulent barbecue chicken and mashed potatoes get me off track."

"If you say so. I guess I should leave the breadbasket in the kitchen."

"Please do."

When I got back to my room, I felt more relaxed but I still felt hungry. I took an appetite suppressant that I'd picked up about a week ago and within a half hour I was fine. A little jittery but nonetheless, fine. Part of me feels guilty about my extremely restrictive diet but the other part of me feels empowered that I'm able to control my hunger and dedicate to my goal of losing a couple pounds. When I took my clothes off before getting in the tub, I stood in front of the full-length mirror and stared at my body. I couldn't believe that I was already beginning to lose weight. I haven't really eaten anything heavy or fattening over the past week or so and I'm pretty surprised that my energy level is as high as it is. My goal was to be at my target weight within the next couple of months, it's honestly looking like I'll be there in half the time.

THURSDAY, 9/7

"Hey Angela, give me a call. We need to chat about you helping with Celeste's wedding."

I can check that off my to-do list, I thought after leaving the message for my sister. On the road back home, I teleconferenced with two clients, solved three major issues dealing with a few of my current projects, secured a venue for an upcoming event, hired a DJ for my fashion show fundraiser, secured a sponsor for a volunteer charity ball and called at least seven client prospects before I crossed the Indianapolis city line.

"Hello Chris, this is mom. We're grilling today and since we haven't seen you in over two weeks I figured I'd call you to formally invite you over for dinner. If you need directions to the house, feel free to call us back. Just joking, but seriously we know you're busy so just drop by if only for a little while. Love ya."

"Hey mom, how are you?"

"I'm fine. Did you get my message?"

"Yeah, I'm actually on my way now, I just wanted you to know that I'm bringing over a couple loads of laundry."

"That's fine, just come on over. Dinner should be ready in about an hour."

"Do you need me to bring anything?"

"Just you."

My twin brother and sister were outside washing dad's new car in hopes of him letting them borrow it for their football jamboree tomorrow night. I couldn't believe that they were already juniors in high school, I thought as I greeted them both with hugs and kisses. They offered to wash my car for a hefty fee of twenty dollars. I felt so guilty about not seeing them in such a long time, I ended up giving them both twenty dollars each.

I opened the door that lead from the laundry room to the kitchen and yelled into the house to let my parents know I was there. After I started my first load of laundry, I went back outside to catch up on old times with the twins. When I asked them what they'd been up to, Eva began talking a mile a minute. From her debutante cotillion, his growing popularity as a DJ, their Jack and Jill activities, fall sports, cheerleading, SAT's, homecoming and a laundry list of other things, these two were getting the most of their teenage years.

"Oh, I haven't told you about James have I?" Eva said as she put her long arm around my shoulder.

"No, who's James?"

"He's her punk boyfriend," Everett said, moving away just in time to avoid the sponge that Eva threw at him.

"Your boyfriend?"

"Correction, my man," she giggled, as I cut a sharp look at her.

"How old is he?" I asked.

"Eighteen," she replied, dreamy eyed.

"Then he's still a boy."

"Who is this James character that Eva's so head over heels about?" I asked my mother as I leaned in to give her a kiss.

"He's the guy she's been going out with and the reason I need you to help me talk to her," my mother said, stirring a large pot of collard greens. "He's been keeping her out every weekend until the last few minutes of her curfew. She's been really cutting it close lately."

"I'll talk to her."

"Good," she said as she shook some spices into the pot then looked at me. "Are you losing weight?"

"A little."

"Why?"

"No particular reason."

"Well you looked great before."

"Thanks."

"Are you feeling alright?"

"Yeah mom, I'm fine," I said as I turned my attention back to the window where I could see the twins outside washing my car with a group of their friends. My baby brother and sister have grown up to be quite attractive, I thought. Eva now has curves and Everett has a cute, thin little mustache. "Have you seen Angela lately?" I asked my mother.

"She was over here last week. She'll be here tonight and she's supposed to be bringing her new boyfriend."

"Wow, everybody's got a new man."

"Yeah, I guess they've been dating for about a month now."

"No wonder I haven't heard from her," I said stirring a pitcher of lemonade.

"You know how she becomes missing in action when she starts a new relationship."

"Whatever happened to Dr. Elliot's son, Tyson?"

"When he got accepted into Meharry, they decided that a long distance relationship wasn't going to work. He moved to Nashville a few weeks ago and they've been broken up ever since."

"This new boyfriend must be pretty special if she wants us to meet him so soon."

"I guess."

"Hey baby!" dad belted as he walked in from the family room.

"Hey daddy," I replied, giving him a big hug.

"Andy, would you go outside and wipe the chairs down for me," mom asked while batting her eyes.

"Yes love," he replied then winked at me as he walked out the door.

As I helped my mom set the patio table for dinner we heard the sound of a car door slamming in the driveway. About five minutes later Everett walked through the sliding glass door with a weird look on his face.

"What's wrong with you?" mom asked.

"You'll see in a few minutes."

Just then Angela walked through the gate beaming and holding the hand of a guy who looked like he could've been in the band Nirvana. His messy beach blond hair was half loose and half dreadlocked, he had lip, eyebrow, chin and nose piercings, his clothing was dingy, saggy, baggy and torn in all the wrong places and he wreaked of patchouli oil mixed with a musty, slightly weeded, not so fresh scent.

"Hey everyone, this is Frankie," Angela proudly announced as we all stood there speechless.

"Hello Frankie, I'm Andy Cullen and this is my wife Mariam," dad said as he and my mom extended their hands to him with constructed smiles on their faces.

Angela began introducing Eva and I to her new boyfriend while the both of us stood there a little stunned.

"Christian, I've heard so much about you," Frankie said as he smiled, exposing a large tongue ring

"That's nice," I replied, looking at Angela as she glowed and held on to his arm.

In theory Frankie wasn't such a bad catch on paper. He had a degree in photography, spent three years in India with the Peace Corps and just took the LSAT with plans to go to law school. With all that said, I just didn't like him and it wasn't because he was white. Okay, not so much. I hate to say this but maybe if he were a different kind of white, like clean and groomed, I know I would've felt differently. Regardless of my feelings about him, my bigger issue is with Angela. One day she's practically the leader of the Black Panther party and then the next she's so grungy that she might as well move to Seattle and join a garage band herself. Angela just hasn't been the most consistent person in the world. It just seems as if she's dating Frankie for attention.

Before I left my parents' house, I got a moment to ask Angela about helping out with Celeste's wedding and the Illum account.

"I'm available as soon as tomorrow."

"Great, let's meet before the end of the week to go over exactly what needs to be done."

"Not a problem," Angela said as she put plastic wrap over two plates of leftovers then looked at me a smiled. "Hey, what do you think about Frankie?"

"We'll talk."

FRIDAY, 9/8

"Girl, do I have a surprise for you. Wake your lazy butt up and meet me for brunch at Mimosa."

"What is wrong with you? Do you know what time it is?" I asked, looking at my clock with one eye open.

"Yes, and you ought to be ashamed because it's almost nine and normal working people are usually up and out of bed by now. I'm giving you an hour and a half to get dressed and drag yourself five blocks to hang out with your girl."

"Reese, I don't have any appointments scheduled until four o'clock today and I didn't go to bed until a quarter after one…"

"Like I said, I'll see you there at ten thirty," she said, followed by the dial tone.

I can't stand Reese! What was so important that she couldn't just tell me over the phone, I thought as I stumbled into the bathroom. Why was it so urgent that I meet her for brunch and not for a late lunch or even dinner?

"She better not!" I yelled as I ran out of the bathroom and grabbed the phone from the counter.

"Reese, who's meeting us for brunch?"

"Some brothers from corporate. Don't worry they're both fine."

"I don't care if they look like Morris or Boris, I'm not in the mood to go on a blind date this time of morning."

"We're just meeting them for brunch, damn."

"Reese…"

"Oh, don't wear anything blue because I'm wearing my new navy suit."

"Who cares what you're wearing," I said, rubbing cleanser over my face. "I don't think I'm going."

"Why? You ought to be happy that I'm hooking you up."

"Reese, you haven't been the best judge of character lately when it comes to men, or looks and class while we're at it," I said, referring to the Tee and Romeo incident. "Besides, my eyes are all puffy and swollen."

"Put some Visine in your eye and come on! You'll look fine. Now hurry up because you're going to end up running late as usual."

On my way to the restaurant, I kept wondering if I was making a big mistake. Reese and I have never shared the same taste in men and I know that today's brunch probably wouldn't be any different than a couple of weeks ago. Nevertheless, I might as well try to have some fun. I was actually sort of glad that Reese woke me up to get out this morning. It would've been a shame to not enjoy such a gorgeous day.

When I arrived at the restaurant, I was relieved to see Reese's car already in the parking lot. It would've been really awkward to meet these guys without her being there since she hooked the whole thing up. After giving the host Reese's name he walked me to the table where she was sitting across from two of the finest brothers I'd ever seen in my life. As the host pulled out my chair, both men smiled and greeted me.

"Hello, I'm Erik Masters," the first handsome guy said while standing and extending his hand.

"Hi, nice meeting you," I replied, trying not to look obviously giddy.

"And I'm Alain Hughes," the other one said, extending his hand.

"And nice to meet you too," I managed to say as we shook.

Erik was fine, but Alain was absolutely stunning! Actually, he was far beyond stunning he was unbelievable! His skin, the same dark reddish-brown tone as a new copper penny, was even and smooth, his hair was shiny and jet-black and his face was chiseled like a statue.

Christian breathe, I kept telling myself as I tried to sit down gracefully.

"So, I hear you two have been friends ever since college," Erik said.

"Yeah, but we couldn't stand each other at first," Reese said and then elbowed me in my arm.

"We really didn't get a chance to know one another until we pledged," I said.

"I forgot, what sorority? No, no let me guess," Alain said, chuckling.

"Nah man, sisters get touchy about the sorority thing. Let them tell you because if you get it wrong you'll have serious hell to pay," Erik replied, laughing.

"Well, let me put it this way. I consider one of you a brother in more ways than one," I said, winking. "I noticed someone's Navigator in the parking lot with the Illinois plates and the Gamma license plate frame."

"Okay, alright!" Erik said loosening up a bit. "Now I feel like I'm amongst family. Alain and I are both Gammas."

"Hi, I'm Heidi and I'll be your server today," our waitress interrupted. "Are we ready to order or do you need a little more time to look over the menu?"

"We'll need just a few more minutes," Reese replied.

"That's fine. I'll be back in a few," Heidi said while smiling at Erik.

"Uh oh, I think someone wants a little chocolate in her life," Reese teased Erik.

"You just had to go there," Erik laughed as he studied his menu.

After a few minutes passed, Erik asked Reese a question about a sports radio station in Cleveland that their company was trying to acquire. While Reese and Erik discussed work, Alain and I sat there trying to look preoccupied by staring at our menus and periodically taking sneak peeks at one another. After about two minutes or so, Alain finally decided to break the silence.

"Since this is my first time here, I'm not quite sure of what to order. Everything just looks so good," Alain said smirking and emphasizing the words *looks so good*. "What do you recommend?"

"Well it depends. Are you in the mood for something sweet?" I replied flirtatiously, trying to conceal the emerging smile on my face.

"As a matter of fact I am," he said, flashing the most perfect set of teeth I'd ever seen.

"Well then, I'd recommend either the banana, pecan Belgian waffle or the strawberry & cream pancakes."

"I think that I'll try the strawberry pancakes. Now you know if the pancakes aren't on point you owe me," he said, trying to disguise his smile with a phony scolding look.

"Oh, they're on point," I replied seductively.

"Okay beautiful people are we ready to order here?" Heidi asked bringing us back to reality.

"I think I am," Reese replied looking at all of us as we nodded our heads. "I'll have the spinach & cheddar quiche and with a Bellini. Oh, and please make it with Prosecco if you have it."

"Not a problem, and for you ma'am?"

"I'll have the low-fat yogurt parfait, with blueberry yogurt please, and a bottle of La Croix," I said folding my menu and looking at Alain.

"And for you sir?"

"I'll have the strawberry & cream pancakes with a side of turkey sausage and a large orange juice," Alain told the waiter and then winked at me.

"How about you sir?" she asked smiling at Erik.

"I'll have the southwestern omelet with picante on the side, the five grain toast with mango jelly and I think I'll have a Bellini as well."

"I'll have this right out to you," she replied.

"Reese mentioned that you own your own business," Alain said. "What do you do?"

"I own a marketing and events company," I said before taking a quick sip of water.

"She shows companies how to look fabulous and throws parties for a living," Reese joked.

"Sounds cool," Erik said.

"Do you just do business locally?" Alain asked.

"No, as a matter of fact my biggest clients are in Chicago and New York."

"Look at you!" Alain replied smiling with a look of approval.

"What do you two do at UniLink?" I asked.

"I'm vice president of national sports programming," Erik replied.

"And what about you Alain?"

"I'm the director of print media for our sports division."

"They're here because corporate is moving the Sports Division to Indianapolis," Reese said with a Kool-Aid grin.

"So I'm assuming that both of you will be moving as well."

"You've assumed correct," Alain replied.

"Are you guys here for the whole weekend?" I asked, trying to figure out if I'd get another chance to see Alain.

"Yeah, we're actually here until next Friday," Erik replied. "Our meetings don't begin until Monday so we decided to come down and check out the scene a little early. I deal with Reese over the phone quite a bit and she convinced us to come down to hang out over the weekend."

"So, what's there to do in Indianapolis?" Alain asked, directing the question to me but Reese butted in before I could say anything.

"Well since you're here all weekend, you can start by checking out Christian's fashion event tomorrow night. It's a huge fashion show and wine tasting fundraiser she started two years ago," Reese said then pinched my thigh under the table.

"Is that so?" Alain asked.

"Yes. I hope you can make it," I said to him with a flirty smile.

"Fashion models plus unlimited alcohol, don't worry we'll be there," Erik said as our food was brought out on two large trays.

After we all said our silent grace, Reese and the guys began chowing down. I, on the other hand, couldn't even pick up my spoon. I don't know what came over me but all of a sudden I felt awkward about eating in front of Alain. What is wrong with me, I thought as I sat there feeling stupid watching Reese chomp away. I hesitated for a good minute or so before I finally built up the nerve to take the first bite of my yogurt parfait. Just as I was putting the yogurt and granola filled spoon up to my mouth, Alain asked, "So what should I wear tomorrow night?"

There I was with my mouth wide open and half the glob of yogurt on my top lip. I quickly licked it off while trying not to blush.

"I'm sorry," Alain said with a slight chuckle.

"Wear whatever makes you feel good," I said, regaining my composure.

"Good, in that case I'll just wear my dingy old Morehouse sweats."

"Alright, but I'm sure the alumni association won't be so proud when they see your picture in *Ebony*."

"Oh, so you're ballin' like that! You've got *Ebony Magazine* coming to your events?"

"I sent them an invite and they may or may not attend, but just in case leave the sweats in your room," I joked as he smiled, making me blush.

"How's your omelet?" Reese asked Erik.

"It's great, do you want to taste a piece?" Erik asked as Reese pinched my leg again.

"Uh huh," Reese replied as she poked her fork onto Erik's plate.

"How's your yogurt?" Alain asked me.

"It's fine."

"Christian's on a starvation diet right now," Reese blurted out. "She's trying to be the next Naomi Campbell."

"Are you modeling in your show tomorrow night?" Erik asked.

"No," I replied then responded to Reese's accusation with a swift thigh slap under the table.

"Then what's up?" Alain asked, gazing at me.

"Don't pay any attention to Reese. She's just talking crazy."

"Well you definitely don't need to change anything. You look beautiful," Alain said.

As we walked out to the parking lot, Alain and I exchanged business cards.

"Your name is spelled the same as Alain Locke's," I said, reading his card.

"You're right," he said, putting my card in the front of his wallet. "Not many people even know who Alain Locke is, let alone realize that our names are spelled the same."

"Well what can I say, I happen to be intrigued by black intelligentsia," I said as he walked me to my car.

"Well then, we need to meet for coffee sometime soon to have a vibe session," he said as he leaned up against my car. "What do you know about the Harlem Renaissance?"

"I'm an expert on the subject," I said as my heart raced from the thought of finally meeting someone who shares the same personal interests as me. "What do you know about classic black cinema?"

"Are you talking 1950's musicals or do you go as far back as Oscar Micheaux?"

"I'm talking Micheaux."

"Okay, we definitely need to hang out soon."

"Yes we do. Let me write my home number on the back of my card," I said as Erik pulled up behind my car and began honking at Alain like a mad man.

"Can I call you tonight?"

"You can, but I'll tell you right now I won't be able to talk. I'll be hectic getting ready for tomorrow."

"That's right. Well I'll definitely be there. Hopefully I'll be able to steal a few moments from you after the show."

"I think I can make that happen. Just look for me at the reception."

"Will do," he said as his eyes lit up. "I'll check you out later Ms. Cullen. Hey, you wouldn't be any relation to Countee Cullen would you?"

"Who knows?" I said as I winked at him.

SATURDAY, 9/9

"Girl, I think you've hit the jackpot!" Reese screamed through the receiver.

"I know but I can't talk right now. I'll see you tonight."

I was able to get all of my beauty appointments out of the way by eleven this morning so I could spend the afternoon running errands before heading to the event site. When I got there I couldn't believe my eyes because most of my family and friends were there to help set up before the event, including Erik and Alain, who by the way looked adorable in his faded Morehouse T-shirt and sweatpants.

The men started setting up the chairs while the women helped to unload my car. After watching him pass by several times, I stopped Alain to personally thank him for his help.

"I don't mind it at all," he said, winking.

"I saw that," my mother teased as we pulled mirrors out of my trunk. "He's cute, what's his name?"

"Alain Hughes," I said, blushing.

"Hughes? Is he any relation to Attorney John Hughes?"

"Probably not. He's not from here. He lives in Chicago, but he's moving to Indy in a couple of weeks."

"I see he went to Morehouse," she said, smiling at me. "What does he do?"

"He's the director of sports publications for UniLink."

"Oh nice. Did Reese introduce you to him?"

"Yeah. She did a good job this time."

"Have you gone out with him yet?"

"No, but I have a feeling we'll be making plans very soon."

"Well who knows? This one just may be my future son-in-law."

"Mom, it's way too early to be thinking about that. Just cross your fingers and hope that we have a good first date."

As we decorated the room, I couldn't help but watch Alain as he helped to set up the backdrop. I could see his muscles flexing through his form fitting T-shirt every time he lifted his arms. That man was absolutely beautiful. Periodically he would look up at me and flash that amazing smile that made my knees buckle and my cheeks hot. Every time he looked at me, both Reese and my mother would always have something to say about it.

At around seven-thirty a big rush of people began to arrive and just looking out into the crowd from backstage got my adrenaline flowing. As I was about to do a pre-show interview by with local lifestyle magazine, Darius walked back stage and rushed over to me.

"Hey Chris. How have you been?"

"I've been busy with the show," I said, walking away from him.

"Do you have at least five minutes?"

"Darius, look. There's nothing left to talk about. I've said all I needed to say to you and I've heard all that I needed to hear, so would you please excuse me, I have an event to put on."

The show was a success! Everything went smoothly, the fashion was fabulous, the press loved it, and most importantly we raised over forty-five thousand dollars for the Urban Arts Council. Alain congratulated me with a big bouquet of pink roses and a long, warm hug.

"You did a wonderful job!"

"Aww, how beautiful. I appreciate this," I said beaming, still wrapped up in his embrace. "Oh, and thanks again for all your help."

"No problem," he said. "So, is there a possibility that I can see you again sometime this week?"

"How about tomorrow?" I replied.

"Sounds good to me. What time?"

"I'm free all day."

"Then I'll pick you up around noon," he said as he reached for my hand and gently squeezed it.

"I'll be waiting."

SUNDAY, 9/10

"So what do you want to do today?"

"Well, I figured since I'm not from here I'd let you show me around."

"I'm thinking we can hit up a few museums, go for a relaxing walk then come back to my place for dinner."

"I'm cool with that," he said as I imagined him smiling on the other end. "Where do you live?"

"About ten blocks from your hotel. Call me when you leave and I'll give you directions."

"Great. I'll be there in an hour."

Alain looked like he just stepped out of a J. Crew ad wearing a nautical style striped shirt and slim fit khakis. Words cannot stress how handsome he is.

Our first date turned out to be absolutely wonderful. We checked out some art, grabbed some ice cream then took a casual stroll on the downtown canal, which gave us the perfect opportunity to get to know each other better.

"So where did you grow up?" I asked as we sat down on a bench near a large fountain.

"Savannah, Georgia."

"Do you have any sisters or brothers?"

"No, now it's just me," he said as his face slowly became somber. "I had a brother who was two years older but he passed away a couple of years ago."

"Oh, I'm sorry to hear that."

"You know, it's weird how some days I can go on with life and feel that I've come to terms with his death. Then there are those times when I wake up wanting to call or hang out with him. It just hits me all of a sudden and reality sets in that I'll never see him again, not in this lifetime."

"What was his name?"

"Aaron. He was named after Aaron Douglass. I'm sure you know who he is," he said, beginning to beam again.

"Yes. I have a few copies of his paintings."

"I figured you would," he said, pinching my cheeks. "Miss renaissance black woman."

"I wouldn't have it any other way," I replied.

"So how about you? What's your family like? I briefly met your mother and your sister but I really didn't get a chance to talk to them."

"Well, all of my immediate family lives here in Indy. My parents were born and raised here. You met just one of my sisters, Angela, at the show. She's twenty eight and is a graphic designer and artist. I also have another younger sister and brother who are twins, Eva and Everett. They're sixteen year old juniors in high school. My dad is retired and my mother is a guidance counselor."

"Are your grandparents still living?"

"Only one of them. My dad's mother is the only one still living—and boy is she living."

"What do you mean by that?"

"Well to start she has a hot red sports car, she's more active in our sorority than I am, she lives in a snazzy condo community near the art museum and here's the kicker, she has a new boyfriend."

"Ha, nothing wrong with that. She seems like a classy lady. I'm sure that's where you get your poise and sophistication from."

"Aw, thanks. I can only strive to get to her level," I said as I lifted the collar of my wrap sweater to shield off the cool breeze. "She's a well-known socialite in the city. She's pretty much on every influential board you can think of."

"I can't wait to meet her."

"I can't wait for *her* to meet you. She's going to absolutely love you."

"Your place is fly! I can use your help after I get settled into my new apartment."

"I'd be more than happy to. Decorating is therapeutic for me."

"Well, you definitely have the eye and taste for it. Your style is real cosmopolitan."

"I love minimalist modern design."

"Where do you get your furniture?"

"There are a handful of places here that have never let me down, but for the most part I'll just jet up to Chicago and shop. Sometimes I'll find and ship a few pieces when I'm in New York or Cali or I'll just buy online."

"Are your paintings originals?"

"Yeah, originally by me and some by my sister Angela."

"Wow, you never cease to amaze me."

As I was in the kitchen cooking, Alain was in the living room looking at some of my old photo albums.

"Now who's who in your circle of friends? I already know Reese but who were the other people helping you out?"

"Well, there's my other pledge sister Carra. The cute brown skinned girl with the curly hair. She's a veterinarian and she just found out that she's pregnant."

"Is she married?"

"Yeah."

"I'm glad you told me that because Erik was scoping her out at the show."

"I thought Erik was checking for Reese?"

"I don't know what's up with that," he said easing back into the couch. "Does she and her husband live around here?"

"No, they live in an area called Geist about forty-five minutes north of here."

"Who's your other friend, I think she's Italian or something?"

"You're talking about Celeste. She's Italian and Greek."

"She seems cool. How did you two become friends?"

"Celeste and I were roommates my first two years in college. We became really good friends right after her father died."

"What does she do?"

"She's a drug dealer," I said laughing.

"What?"

"She's a pharmaceutical sales rep," I joked.

"That's what I was hoping."

"Believe it or not her last name, Venditore, means sales person in Italian."

"You're lying."

"I'm telling the God honest truth."

"Is she married?"

"She's getting married in a couple of weeks."

"Is her fiancé cool?"

"Yeah. He's been a good friend of her family ever since she was a little girl."

"What part of town does she live in?"

"She lives in Broad Ripple, the neighborhood where we got ice cream."

"Okay, the village-like area."

"Right."

"And where does Reese live?"

"She lives about seven minutes from here. About a year and a half ago she bought a huge old house for next to nothing and renovated it. She had an appraiser come out a month ago and do you know that the value has almost quadrupled. All of the renovated houses in her neighborhood are selling for top dollar."

"I may look into doing that. I'd like to live downtown."

"Well, you better act now before prices skyrocket," I said as I took the fish out of the oven.

"Do you need any help?"

"No, I've got everything under control," I said as I made our plates. "You can turn on some music though. My iPod is connected to the stereo."

"Ah, let's see here," he said as he scanned my playlist. "John Coltrane, Miles Davis, Mint Condition, Maxwell, Jill Scott," Alain said then paused. "Mos Def, The Roots, Talib Kweli, A Tribe Called Quest? Now I know I like you."

"Did you like Common's last album?"

"Pure genius."

"I agree," I replied as I uncorked a bottle of Chablis.

"Okay, I have to test you on your hip-hop knowledge to see if you're really down. What does KRS-One stand for?"

"Knowledge reigns supreme over nearly everyone," I said, looking at him like he could have done better than that.

"Oh my goodness, I think I've found my soul mate," Alain said to himself out loud.

"You're too silly," I said as I shook my head. "I know what I want to hear. "Bumpin" by Wes Montgomery."

"Ooh yeah, Wes Montgomery, candlelight and wine. The makings of the quintessential chill out vibe."

After dinner Alain helped me clean the table and load the dishwasher. Just as we were finishing up, Alain noticed my list of goals for the year on my refrigerator.

"This is cool. They say writing down your goals and putting it in a place where you can always see it is a good way to stay motivated," he said as he began reading them out loud. "Exercise more, grow Image Brokers by sixty percent, spend more time with family, paint more, practice celibacy…"

Oh my goodness, I thought to myself as Alain said those words. I wrote it down, but celibacy was the one goal I haven't been able to achieve and I'm still torn whether I can or not, especially now that Alain's entered my life. Not that I planned on sleeping with him anytime soon, but I feel a connection and chemistry between us that if I were to become intimate with someone in the near future, I see him being the one.

MONDAY, 9/11

I invoiced clients and set appointments all morning, so by the time noon rolled around I was more than ready to call it a day. As I was packing up my laptop, Guy called and wanted to schedule a face to face meeting next Wednesday to discuss the details of the launch party and to meet Eden, his new boyfriend, the photographer.

"Whatever you're cooking, I can smell it all the way down the hall," Angela joked as she hung her graffiti-print jean jacket in my coat closet. "Smells good though."

"It's curry chicken."

"Indian or Jamaican style?"

"Jamaican."

"Did you make rice and peas too?"

"Yep."

"I'm going to have to make a plate to take back to Frankie. Rice and peas are his favorite."

Angela and I discussed all of my current projects over dinner. We reviewed the upcoming Illum campaign, specifics of Celeste's wedding and the proposals I'm working on for several potential clients.

"I'll get right on it," she said as she surveyed the project plans then looked at me and smiled. "I know what I wanted to ask you. Who was that fine brother that gave you the roses after the fashion show?"

"That was Alain. He's moving here from Chicago."

"When and where did you meet him?"

"Through Reese. She introduced me to him a couple days ago."

"And he's already giving you flowers? This man seems like husband material."

"So far that's what it's looking like. I'll definitely be spending a lot more time with him once he moves here."

"Nanna's going to love him."

"I know," I said, remembering a cute artist that I met a few weeks ago who I wanted to introduce to Angela. "While we're on the subject of husband material, I met the cutest guy a couple of weeks ago. He's a sculptor from the Ivory Coast and I think you two would hit it off."

"That's okay Chuck Woolery. I'm dating someone right now."

"But you guys have so much in common."

"I said that I was dating someone at the moment," she said with her lips pursed together. "I know what you're thinking. Go ahead and say it. Ask me why I'm with Frankie."

"You better believe I was going to ask you. Why *are* you with him? He seems like good friend material but you are way out of his league. You deserve someone who's going to complement everything about you. Frankie just isn't it."

"Why?"

"Look at you! You're gorgeous, intelligent, artistic and driven. You can have anyone you want. Why him?

"Why not? You don't even know him and you're judging him."

"Forget I said anything."

"Too late for that. Say what you have to say Christian."

144

"Angela look, I don't know what you see in him. I don't know if you're just experimenting or if you're doing this for attention, it just doesn't seem real."

Angela gave me the most bitter look I'd ever seen. She snatched her things and marched to the door. The overreacting has now begun.

"I don't know if anyone's ever told you but you can be a bougie bitch sometimes."

"Oh goodness gracious, here we go."

"You act like you're the most perfect person in the world and everyone has to measure up to your standards, well you know what, fu..," she paused and refrained herself from cursing me out. "Forget you and your shallow opinion. This is me, take it or leave it."

Whatever Angela, I thought as she slammed the door behind her. Throwing a tantrum and storming out of a room is so typical. That'll be the last time I ever try to look out for her with her oversensitive self.

TUESDAY, 9/12

Darius called me three times this morning and left two pitiful messages about wanting us to start over again. *Delete*, I said to myself as I pushed number seven on my phone keypad. This guy just can't seem to get a clue.

"Hey baby, how are you?"

"Hey Nanna. What are you doing up so early?"

"Just cooking breakfast. I thought you might want to join me."

"I've already eaten," I said disguising the fact that I hadn't really eaten anything. I just knew that it'd be too tempting to pig out over her house since she makes the best pancakes and omelets in the world. I've been doing so good with my weight thus far, I couldn't backslide today. "I can come over to chat."

"Nonsense, you've always had room for my pancakes."

"Maybe I'll just take some home with me, how does that sound?"

"You know they don't taste as good when you warm'um up in the microwave. It'd be best to eat them over here."

"We'll see," I said, wondering why she was being so persistent. "I'll be over in about forty-five minutes."

"Good."

When I got to my grandmother's house, not only did she make pancakes and omelets but she also had oatmeal, turkey sausage and bacon, hash browns and fruit salad.

"Nan, whose army is coming over to eat?"

"What are you talking about child, get yourself a plate and quit all of that babbling."

"I'm really not all that hungry Nan," I said as I slowly picked up a plate then went straight for the fruit salad. "I'll just have a little bit of this."

"Girl what is wrong with you? Are you sick or something?" she asked, frowning at me.

"No ma'am. I've already eaten this morning and I'm stuffed," I said patting my stomach.

"Why are you losing so much weight?"

"I'm not losing any weight."

"I'm not stupid nor am I as blind as you think. What's going on?"

"Nothing," I said, surprised by her interrogation.

"Nothing my foot. Are you worried about something?"

"No, Nan. I've just been busy moving into my new office and planning the big show last weekend. I was a little stressed out but now I'm back to normal."

"No more losing weight?"

"No more losing weight."

"Fine, then wrap up a plate to-go and come out to the patio so we can chat."

"Yes ma'am."

"Now who is this new gentleman your mother was telling me about on Sunday?" she asked, pouring a cup of peppermint tea.

"His name is Alain," I replied, stunned that my mother had already told her about him.

"Alain who?"

"Nan, he's not from here so I doubt if you'd know his family."

"Then where is he from?"

"Chicago by way of Savannah."

"What does he do?"

"He's an executive for a national sports magazine."

"Impressive. What fraternity is he in?"

"He's a Gamma."

"That's good."

"Nanna, I've only been on one date with him. It's a little too early to be sizing him up for his tuxedo don't you think."

"It's never too early," she said while smoothing out the wrinkles on her tan linen pants then looked at me smiling. "I haven't even met him but I have a good feeling about this one."

Alain was sitting in the hotel lobby when I arrived, wearing a loose white oxford shirt, navy chino shorts and a pair of navy, leather Sperry's. Mmm, mmm, mmm was all I could think as I approached him.

"So where are we headed?" he asked, walking towards me with his arms out for a hug.

"To one of my favorite places."

"Will I like it?" he asked, still holding on to me.

"I hope so," I replied, gazing into his beautiful chestnut eyes. "Have you ever had Ethiopian?"

"No but I hear it's pretty good."

"It is. I'm sure you'll like it."

I noticed that Alain had his phone in his hand as we walked into the restaurant. After we were shown to our table and I took a seat, he walked behind me kneeled down.

"Would you mind taking a picture of us?" he asked our server, handing her the phone.

"Not at all," she replied. "You two make a beautiful couple."

Neither one of us responded to the comment, although what she said was true, we looked wonderful together.

"Say cheese!" she said as Alain wrapped his right arm tightly around my waist.

"It looks good," Alain said as we all crowded around to view the picture. "Really good," he said, smiling at me.

"How long have you two been together?" the waitress asked.

"Oh, we're not a couple…" Alain said then paused. "Yet."

I know I had a goofy looking smile on my face but I was completely speechless. Thank you God!

After my lunch date with Alain, I met up with Celeste to help her pick out flowers and décor for the wedding.

"How was your date the other night?"

"It was great," I said as a warm feeling rushed throughout my body. "I just left him a half hour ago."

"Wow. This guy may be the one."

"He just might be," I said as I inhaled a large bouquet of red roses.

"Is he the guy Reese set you up with?"

"Yeah, and for the first time in history, I'm actually thankful for that. How's John doing?"

"He's fine. He should be all moved in by the end of the week," she said as she flipped through a fabric catalogue then pointed to a sheer, pale yellow fabric with a rhinestone starlight effect. "Do you like this?"

"It's nice."

"It is, isn't it," she said as she flipped through a few more pages. "You know, I can't believe that I'm actually about to get married. In a few weeks, I'll be spending the rest of my life with John."

"I'm so happy for you."

"I only wish my dad could be here to experience this."

"I'm sure he's smiling down on you from heaven," I said as I tickled her nose with a feather pen.

"You're right," she said then paused. "You know, I haven't really told anybody this but I'm nervous."

"This is a big step for you. I'm sure everyone feels nervous before the big day."

"I guess you're right."

"Just shake it off, everything's going to be okay."

As we stood at the cashiers' counter, Celeste's phone began to ring.

"Hello...Hey sweetie, what's wrong...It's too early to be getting all worked up about it...Have you made a doctor's appointment...Well go see what she has to say, I'll go with you if you need me too...Yeah, I can come over tonight...No need, she's standing right here...Yeah, I'll ask her...Alright, you just calm down and I'll see you tonight...Bye."

"Who was that?" I asked.

"Carra. That lump in her breast is sore and swollen."

"I hope it's just hormones."

"I hope so too. She's going to the doctor tomorrow to get it checked out."

"Good."

"She wants to know if you could come by tonight?"

"Aaron must be out of town again."

"Yeah he left this morning."

"I'll be there," I said, trying not to get myself too worked up and worried about Carra. "Is Reese in town?"

"She's in Cleveland now but she'll be back tonight. Carra left a message for her."

"What time are you going out there?"

"Probably around seven or so."

"I can get there around the same time," I said, fumbling through my purse to find my keys. "Has she ever told you what's up with her and Aaron?"

"She won't talk about it," Celeste said, popping the trunk of her car. "The only thing she's alluded to is that the baby will help their relationship."

"I didn't realize they were having problems like that."

"Neither did I until she made that comment."

I brought my old photo albums over to Carra's house to help take her mind off her worries. It was fun reminiscing and laughing over good times and bad fashion. It took a while, but we were able to cheer her up by the time Reese arrived.

"Hey ladies," Reese said as she walked into the family room.

"Hey girl," I said while trying to find the picture of Reese wearing an incriminating orange and blue FUBU outfit.

"How was Cleveland?" Celeste asked.

"Cleveland was great, but Tank Reynolds was better."

"Tank who?" Celeste asked.

"Tank Reynolds from the Cleveland Browns. He's their new tight end," she said, fanning herself. "And boy is it tight."

"You have no shame," Carra said laughing and shaking her head.

"None at all," Reese proudly proclaimed. "So what's up? Did you go to the doctor?"

"No, my appointment isn't until tomorrow afternoon. I'm trying not to think about it."

"Don't, because there's nothing to worry about. You're fine, a little on the bloated side but other than that you look healthy," Reese joked.

"I'm going to ignore that last comment," Carra replied giggling. "You're right though, no worrying for me tonight. We're here to have a good time."

"Here, here," I said as I lifted my flute of sparkling water.

"Here, here!" the girls replied as they each grabbed a glass, lifting them to the ceiling.

"Oh, I found it!" I screamed, pulling out the embarrassing picture of Reese.

"Well would you look at that," Carra said as she grabbed the picture. "Don't we look like Homey the Clown!"

Reese laughed as she snatched the picture out of her hand, "Oh, I remember that night. We were on our way to the Gamma talent show. I only wore that outfit because I was being pledged. They told me to come out looking like that."

"You are a bold faced liar because I was there that night and we were not being pledged!" I said to Reese as she ran to the other side of the room and stuffed the picture up her shirt.

"Right! No one even knew we were interested in pledging at the time," Carra said.

"You wore that outfit because you thought it was fly and you thought you looked good," I said cracking up laughing. "You swore you were the finest thing on campus. Oooh, I couldn't stand you back then!"

"I second that!" Celeste chimed in.

"Reese if it weren't for you being my line sister, I don't think we would've ever gotten along," I joked as I pulled out a picture of Carra, Reese and I right after we crossed. "Look at this," I said, giving the picture to Carra.

"Look at my hair! I forgot I had those finger waves!" Carra said in embarrassment.

"And those huge glasses," Celeste said.

"And Chris, what was wrong with your eyeliner? Looking like a broke Cleopatra," Reese said, laughing at my poor make-up techniques.

"That was the style back then," I said, in tears laughing.

"Christian was going through an experimental time in her life," Celeste said. "I remember when she would spend hours in front of the mirror, putting on fake lashes and bright red lipstick to go to class. Remember when she would wear heels and suits around campus to make it seem like she was so sophisticated?"

"She'd be looking so crazy trying to walk all the way from the business building back to the dorm in those high heels," Reese said, cracking up laughing.

"I forgot all about that," Carra said.

"Oh, let's not start on you Celeste," I said, pulling out a picture of all four of us right after Carra and Reese moved into a house off campus. "At the time Reese and Carra didn't realize your hair had just gotten itself back together. She basically had a mullet right before then."

"Why did you have to bring that up?" Celeste said while covering up her face with a throw pillow.

"I don't know what possessed you to cut your own hair with kitchen shears?" I said as I scratched my head.

"I was trying to go for a Demi Moore look," Celeste said, shaking her head at the picture. "It just didn't quite work out that way."

"Look at this," Carra said as she handed me her old sorority scroll that had our initiation date, time and listed each of our names. "Do you still have yours?"

"Yeah, I think mine is in my parent's attic," I said, trying to remember the last time I'd seen it.

"Hey you guys, remember this?" Carra said as she held up a picture of all four of us in bathing suits.

"I wish I didn't," Reese said, turning up her nose.

"That night wasn't *that* bad," Carra replied.

"Yeah, it was," I said while Celeste nodded her head with me.

"That was the first time Seth ever saw you guys. It was love at first sight," Celeste said chuckling.

"You mean lust at first sight," I said, thinking back to when we first met John's brother, Seth. He'd invited Celeste to come to his fraternity's annual pool party and demanded that she bring some of her friends. I don't think he was prepared to see three shapely black women following her into the back gate of their frat house that night. The moment we walked in their jaws dropped.

"Seth and his frat brothers hadn't seen that much tail in their lives," Reese said.

"But they were cool. I remember them treating us like queens, waiting on us hand and foot," Carra said.

"That's because they thought that they were going to get some," I replied. "And Reese's flirty little fuchsia bikini didn't help any."

We spent the rest of the evening in tears laughing and reminiscing, but more importantly helping Carra by just being there for her and keeping her mind positive.

WEDNESDAY, 9/13

"How was your day?" Alain asked after taking a sip of a Riesling, unconsciously licking his sexy lips.

"Let's just say I'm glad it's over. I was in meetings from eight this morning until six. Thankfully I was able to get away for a few moments to meet my friend Carra for her doctor's appointment."

"Is she okay?"

"She's got a lump in her breast that's bothering her."

"I hope it's not serious. Isn't she pregnant?"

"Yeah, that's what's making this situation so scary. Just keep her in your prayers."

"Most definitely."

Alain and I tried to rush back to my apartment after dinner because it looked like it was about to be the storm of the century. We initially decided to walk to dinner because it was so gorgeous earlier, but as we walked back with only four blocks left to go, the rain began pouring down so hard that we had to run for cover. I grabbed Alain's hand and ran across the street after spotting a small awning above the entrance to an architectural firm. Even though my clothes were soaked and the humidity had taken its toll on my hair, it was kind of fun cuddling up to him to keep dry. The rain lasted for over ten minutes but I certainly didn't mind because Alain took that time to give me a much needed head rub, neck massage and I can't neglect to mention, our first real kiss. I couldn't have planned it better, almost like it was straight out of a movie. There we were, passionately kissing in the rain like Audrey Hepburn and George Peppard in *Breakfast at Tiffany's*. Wow, if my life is playing itself out like a movie, then let's hope the happy new couple to-be will live happily ever after. I can totally see it happening and I can definitely see the possibility of getting a little more serious with him. As early as it seems, he's really beginning to take up residence in my heart.

THURSDAY, 9/14

For the first time in a while I had a very relaxing morning. I slept in with no interrupting phone calls from Reese, no bright sunlight through my windows and no emergency emails from Guy. I didn't have any meetings scheduled and no projects pending, so I spent the day catching up on a little housework, going to the grocery store, exercising and painting before meeting the girls for our second dress fitting.

When I arrived at the seamstress's boutique, Carra was standing on a wooden platform in front of a three-sided mirror with a stressed out look on her face. The seamstress was having trouble zipping up the back of her dress and she kept telling Carra to hold her arms up and to quit sucking in her stomach so that she could take accurate measurements.

"How is she?" I whispered to Reese as she scooted over on the ruffled stool to let me sit down.

"The doctors said it was the same cyst but this time they're going to drain it."

"Ouch," I said at the thought of the procedure. "She's not going to take that very well. Carra's not the biggest fan of needles."

"Yeah. She told me at her first prenatal check up it took the doctors almost a half hour to calm her down so that they could take her blood."

"That's pitiful," I replied, focusing my attention back to Carra. When she noticed me, she waved and gave me a half smile before her attention reverted back to her new growing figure. "Look at her little belly—and those boobs. I think she looks cute."

"She does. Carra's just not used to wearing any clothes larger than a size four," Reese said, smiling a little. "She had to buy a pair of elastic waist pants in a size eight the other day because she's been so bloated."

"I'm sure she enjoyed that."

"Yeah, so much that she had to go home and lay down after she bought them."

"Oh my goodness," I said not able to hold back my snicker.

"You guys, this isn't funny," Carra sulked and frowned at us through the mirror.

"Carra, no one's even talking about you. Quit being so self-conscious all the time," Reese said, trying to disguise her laughter by rubbing her face with both of her hands.

I got off the stool and walked over to Carra, "What's the problem, huh?"

"Nothing," she huffed. "I'm just exhausted, plus I'm sick of everything being too tight."

"You look beautiful Car," I said as I rubbed her back.

"I told her that but she doesn't believe me," Sarah, the seamstress said. "All I have to do is take out a couple of inches around the waist and allot for about four more inches of growth between now and the wedding day."

When Sarah said that, Carra let out a long sigh and held out her arms.

"That's a good girl," Sarah said to Carra, then winked at me.

I walked back over to the stool and sat down next to Reese again, "So where's Celeste?"

"She's in the back picking out a veil," Reese said as she checked her watch. "You should have seen the way she acted when she put on her dress."

"What happened?"

"She was damn near as bad as Carra."

"What?"

"She's been stressing out and getting all moody about this wedding that she's picked up a few of pounds."

"I can't tell."

"No one can."

"Maybe I should have fasted today. That tape measure seems brutal," I said, hoping that my measurements would be the same as they were during the first fitting.

"Why am I the only one around here that doesn't mind having a little meat on her bones? I'm a size ten and damn it, I know I look good! Why you and Celeste are so obsessive about being skinny is beyond me. Especially you Chris. You know brothers don't like skin and bones."

"First of all, you know what I'm losing weight for. Secondly, contrary to belief, I'm not obsessed with it so chill," I said as Reese slowly looked me up and down.

"So you mean to tell me losing almost two dress sizes in less than a month is not obsessive?" she said with a slight attitude.

"Reese, I don't feel like talking about this."

"Fine," she replied then got up as Sarah motioned that she was ready for her.

"What's she frowning about?" Carra asked as I made room for her on the stool.

"Nothing. Just being Reese."

When Sarah finally called me over to the platform to try on my dress, I began to regret sneaking a few bites of Alain's cheesecake yesterday during dinner. When I took off my clothes and waited for Sarah to make the final adjustments to Reese's dress, Reese let out a big gasp and rushed over to me.

"Not obsessed my ass! What are you trying to do, starve yourself?" she asked as she lifted up my arm to view my waist.

"Do you mind?" I said as I snatched my arm back.

"How much weight have you lost?" Carra asked as she walked over to me then circled the platform.

"Hurry, hurry step right up and view the lady in the blue bra and panties," I said sarcastically. "Would everyone please calm down?"

"No, we won't. What are you doing to yourself? You were never overweight. You looked fine before but now you're trying to whittle down to nothing," Reese snapped.

"Chris, we just care about you," Carra said as she held my hand. "I've noticed that you barely eat when we have dinner together and I wasn't going to say anything about it, but I can't keep silent anymore. This isn't healthy."

"Which one do you like?" Celeste asked as she held up two veils from the back room then focused her attention on me. "Oh my goodness I can see your hip bones," she said as she marched over to me in her corset and petticoat.

"She's anorexic," Reese said to Celeste matter-of-factly.

"I am not anorexic. Would you please?" I said as I tried to shew them away.

"Alright girls, let me get finished with her," Sarah said to my onlookers. "Lift up your arms."

As she draped the dress over me and smoothed it out over my frame, it was noticeably big and gaping at the waistline.

"Okay, let's get this off so I can take your measurements," she said as she helped me get the dress over my head. "I didn't want to say anything while they were over here but are you okay? They're right, you've lost a lot of weight."

"I've just been under a lot of stress, that's all."

"Are you sure? Reese said that you were trying to do some modeling."

"I am but that has nothing to do with it."

"Okay, just don't lose anything else before the wedding. If you do your dress is going to look crazy on you."

After I put my clothes back on and walked to the front of the boutique, the three of them abruptly stopped talking and looked at me.

"What?" I asked.

"You know what," Reese said. "The question is, what are you going to do about it?"

"Look, like I told you before, I'm fine. Now just let it go."

165

"Either you're in denial or you're just embarrassed because you know we're right."

"Reese, I'm not going to tell you again, let it go."

"No I'm not gonna let it go. Someone needs to check you on this. You're not stupid, you know what you're doing isn't healthy. Carra was right, we've noticed that you barely eat anything when we're together. Who knows what you're eating or if you're even eating at all when you're by yourself."

"Enough already! You guys are blowing this out of proportion. I'm fine. End of discussion."

"I see the truth hurts doesn't it? At least I can say I attempted to help," Reese said as she turned around and walked out the door while Celeste and Carra stood there with their mouths wide open.

"I hate to admit it but Reese is right," Celeste said then followed her out the door.

Before Carra left she gave me saddest, most puppy dog face I'd ever seen before opening the door and leaving. I walked over to a full length mirror and stared at myself. Aside from my clothes being looser I honestly didn't see what they were talking about. To me, I basically looked the same. I still had a puffy stomach, my legs still seemed thick and my boobs were still big and round. To me it looked like I still had work to do. As I smoothed my hair back I heard the door opening and saw Carra's reflection through the mirror. Now what, I thought as I continued to fiddle with my hair.

"Chris."

"What?" I said with an attitude, not turning around.

"I just thought you could use these," she said as I turned around to see her holding a white envelope.

"What is it?"

"Tickets to see the Alvin Ailey Dance Theater. Since Aaron will be out of town I figured it would be fun for you and Alain to go."

"Carra," I said feeling awful. "Why don't we go together instead, it'll be fun."

"No, I want you and Alain to enjoy them."

"Thanks Car. I appreciate this."

"No problem," she said walking out the door.

"Hey Carra. I didn't mean to get upset with you."

"It's alright," she said standing in the doorway. "We just love you and care about you Chris."

FRIDAY, 9/15

Last October, I was elected to chair one of my favorite events of the year aside from my fashion fundraiser, the Flatlands Jazz Festival. Today the committee held its last meeting before the big event on Sunday and I actually feel like this is going to be the best one ever. We spent all morning ironing out the final details and by eleven o' clock we were all amped up for the event. When I got home, I fell out on the couch for about fifteen minutes and was just about to drift off to sleep when Carra called.

"What are you and Alain doing tonight?"

"I'm not sure. I haven't spoken to him all day."

"Well if you'd like, you're free to join Aaron and I for dinner at the Ocean Room."

"Sounds good, what time?"

"I'll make reservations for seven, so let's plan on meeting there around six forty-five."

"I'll let Alain know. Are Celeste and Reese coming?"

"Yeah, Reese already knows and I'm calling Celeste after I hang up with you."

"Alright, I'll see you there."

After I hung up with Carra, I called Alain, both on his cell and at his hotel, but ended up having to leave messages about tonight's plans. I didn't want to appear like a stalker or anything so I didn't leave any more messages, though I called him a few more times throughout the day. By the time six o'clock rolled around, I still hadn't heard from him so I started to get ready for dinner hoping that he will get my messages and show up at the restaurant to meet me.

When I arrived Carra, Aaron, Celeste and John were already there. I tried calling Alain one last time as Reese walked in the door arm in arm with a very handsome, older looking man. It was not only rare to see Reese with a man who actually matched her caliber, it was rare to see a man who was truly smiling in her eyes and not at her chest. They were in such deep conversation that she didn't even notice I was alone until we sat down at the table. When she started to put two and two together, she flashed me a slightly confused look but decided to remain silent. I felt like the big, rickety seventh wheel as the only one without a date.

All eyes were on me when we placed our orders. I got a half order of the grilled swordfish salad with Balsamic Vinaigrette and Reese instantly gave me the evil eye after I placed my order. While waiting on our food we were engaged in a discussion about everyone's hectic work week. Just as I was mid-sentence telling Aaron about the jazz fest I heard Reese say, "Where's Alain?"

I turned and looked at her with the same evil eye she gave me after I placed my order and replied, "I haven't talked to him all day. I don't know."

"I said *there's* Alain, not where's Alain," she said with an attitude pointing to the bar area. There he was, looking for us in the crowd and without even thinking I popped up out of my seat nearly knocking over a waiter with a tray full of food and rushed over to meet up with him. As soon as he saw me, he immediately held out his arms, pulled me close and kissed me.

"Sorry I wasn't able to return any of your calls earlier. I've been tied up in meetings all day," he said as we walked hand in hand towards the table. "You have no clue how happy I was to hear your voice when I listened to my messages."

"I'm so happy to see you," I whispered as he pulled out my chair. "Let me introduce you to everybody."

Alain came by after dinner for a little wine and sorbet. As I walked into the living room with drinks in hand I heard the sax intro to John Coltrane's, "A Love Supreme." Alain walked over to me, removed the wine glasses out of my hand and pressed his body against mine as we slowly began to sway side to side. It felt like heaven as we danced in each other's arms.

"I'm beginning to get used to this," he said as he traced the small of my back with his fingertips.

"I feel the same way," I said as I locked my fingers together around his waist and floated into heaven.

SATURDAY, 9/16

Alain and I stayed up talking until six this morning. We completely lost track of time and before we knew it Alain had to leave to go check out and meet up with Erik to get back on the road to Chicago. I was able to fall asleep after he left and got up just in time for dinner over my parents' house. When I arrived, I surprised them with ten jazz fest tickets and a low-fat cheesecake for dessert.

"Low-fat cheesecake is the biggest oxymoron I've ever heard in my life. Cheesecake wasn't meant to be low-fat," dad grumbled as he put it in the refrigerator.

"Oh hush up Andy. Why don't you make yourself useful and run to the store to get some laundry detergent," mom playfully scolded then blew a kiss at him.

"Only under one condition," dad said then let out a growl and nibbled on the side of her neck.

"Get out of here!" she giggled as she swatted him with a dishtowel. "He just doesn't know when to quit."

"I think it's cute!" I said, smiling.

"You're right. It is," she said as she smiled big and wide. "So how are things with you and Alain? Did you guys go out this week?"

"Yeah, we had a great time. We spent almost every day together. He came over last night and didn't leave until early this morning," I said as my mother gave me a shocked look. "Oh, no, no! We were just talking and hanging out."

"I was about to say," she said, dramatically placing her hand over her chest. "So tell me, what's he like?"

"Wonderful. We have so much in common. He...."

"Could he be the one?" my mother asked, cutting me off.

"Mom," I said then paused. "He might be."

After dinner, Everett left to go play video games with some friends while Eva lounged out in the family room watching videos. This is the perfect opportunity to have *the talk* with her, I thought as I finished helping my mother clean the kitchen.

"Hey Eva, wanna hang out with me tonight?"

"Might as well. I don't have anything else to do since James is out of town," she said as my mother looked at me and frowned.

"You shouldn't be planning your weekend around him. He's not *that* important," my mother scolded as Eva turned and rolled her eyes then looked at me as if to say *here we go again.*

"I know, I know. Next subject," Eva said as she joined us in the kitchen. "So Chris, who's this new guy you're seeing? Angela said he was fine!"

"His name is Alain."

"Do you have a picture of him?"

"Actually I do," I said, heading over to my mother's laptop in the breakfast nook. "Mom, what's your password?"

"Hotmama."

"Hotmama?" Eva and I said at the same time.

"Is there a problem?" mom said with her hands on her hips. "Your father always calls me hot mama and I figured..."

"You don't have to justify yourself," I joked while nudging Eva in the arm. "Everyone has a secret life."

"Oh hush!" she said laughing and removing her apron. After I signed on to her computer then logged into my email account, I pulled up the pictures Alain emailed me from the Ethiopian restaurant.

"Oooh he *is* cute," Eva squealed as she grabbed the mouse and zoomed in on Alain's face.

"Would you calm down," my mother said, smacking her behind. "It's not right to be so boy-crazy. Isn't that right Chris?"

"That's right."

"Oh please Christian. I remember when you were in high school and all you could talk about was Bobby Thompson."

"Yeah, but the difference was that I admired Bobby from a distance, he wasn't my boyfriend. You, on the other hand, seem to be consumed with this James boy."

"I can't get a break from anybody. No one understands me," she said in a dramatic voice then slouched over to the staircase. "Just yell when you're ready," she said then threw a balled up napkin at me and ran up the stairs.

"Goofy girl," I said to my mother as we listened to Eva dance down the hall while singing a mash up of Rihanna songs. "What are we going to do with that child?"

"I'd do anything to keep that way, a child."

At Eva's request, we saw a movie then afterwards went for ice cream. As she ate her double chocolate chip, brownie ice cream and I ate my fat-free strawberry and kiwi sorbet, I thought it would be a good time to have *the talk* with her but I couldn't figure out how to bring it up. I figured if I made small talk about school and friends, it could lead into her so-called relationship with this James boy. As soon as I was about to ask her what her favorite class was she beat me to the punch and asked, "How old were you when you first had sex?"

"What?" was all I could say after being stunned and caught off guard.

"How old were you when you first..."

"I heard you the first time," I said cutting her off as I pulled my cell phone out my purse.

"Who are you calling?" she asked as I dialed my parent's number.

"Hey mom, how are you?"

"No different than when you left a couple of hours ago. Are you on your way back to bring Eva home?"

"No, I'm going to have her spend the night with me tonight."

"Don't you need to come by so she can pack an overnight bag?"

"We'll just stop by Target and pick up some stuff. She should be fine," I said, looking over at Eva's beautiful, young face.

"Thanks for letting me spend the night!"

"Eva, why did you ask me that? Are you and James intimate right now?"

"Intimate? You sound like mom when you say that," she said laughing.

"I'm serious Eva," I said, feeling a queasiness developing in my stomach.

"No, not yet," she said as I let out a deep sigh. "I was just wondering what age you were when you realized you were ready."

"I had already started college before that ever happened," I said, glad that I was telling the truth but refrained from telling her that it happened within the first month of my freshman year.

"Really? I know for a fact that Angela didn't wait that long."

"Don't even worry yourself about what age Angela and I were when we made that decision, you just need to realize I'm not being crazy or old fashioned when I tell you it's okay to wait. There's no big rush."

"I know, I'm just confused. Sometimes I feel like I should and then there are other times when I feel that I shouldn't."

"Why do you feel like you should?"

"Because he's cute, smart and sometimes I feel like if I don't, he'll find someone who will."

"Oh, Eva. If he did that then he doesn't care about you as much as you think," I said as I rubbed her arm and tried to keep from tearing up. "What are some of the reasons you feel you shouldn't?"

"Well first of all, I don't want to end up like Alicia."

"Cute little Alicia from down the street?" I asked as she nodded her head. "Don't tell me she's pregnant."

"Yeah, she is."

"Oh my goodness."

"I know. She just found out two weeks ago," she said as her eyes began turning red. "Since freshman year we've always talked about rooming together at Spelman. That's not going to happen now."

177

"Eva, please don't let yourself end up that way. You deserve to go away to Spelman and have the best time of your life. Don't let this James boy talk you into doing something you're not ready for. Believe me, there are better guys out there than him."

"What if there aren't?"

"Trust me there are. Don't let him make you feel bad for not having sex with him."

She couldn't hold back the tears as she leaned over and rested her head on my shoulder.

"Come on sweetie, let's go back to my place," I said as I stood up with my arm around her.

"He keeps pressuring me every time I go out with him. I like him, I just don't know what to do."

"You should stand your ground and do what you know is best," I said, but also felt compelled to deal with the realism of what young woman go through. "Please wait, but if the time comes when you feel that you're ready, Eva talk to me first so you don't end up like your friend."

"Thank you Chris. I love you."

"I love you too."

When we got back to my apartment, we stayed up talking and listening to music all night. Once Eva finally wore herself out I made a vow to myself to spend as much time as possible with her until she goes away to school. I want to make sure she knows that no matter what, I'm always here for her.

SUNDAY, 9/17

I had to be at the park no later than eight o'clock in the morning and since I had to stay and oversee the set-up, Eva dropped me off and I let her use the Rover for a few hours until the festival began and boy was she happy about that. I couldn't have asked for more perfect weather, we even had two news stations air their weather reports live from the festival site. One of my volunteers was so excited that he ran across the entire event site to tell me that there were cars lined up for twelve blocks waiting to get into the parking lot.

My whole family arrived raving about the number of people lined up to get tickets and how there wasn't a parking space for miles around. Eva felt extra special because she and her friends were able to park in the special parking lot behind the stage since she had my VIP entrance pass. My parents, grandmother, brother, sisters, their friends and even Frankie seemed to be proud of my first Flatlands Jazz Fest. The line-up was awesome and the record crowd grooved in the park from noon until midnight. I received major kudos from my committee members, the festival founders and the press, but the praise that really touched my heart was from my family. Well at least most of my family. After saying my goodbyes to Nanna and my parents, Angela gave me a strange look but finally came over to talk to me.

"I'll call you about Celeste's wedding," she said with a stern face then looked over towards Frankie as he packed up their stuff. "Let's just try to squash this, okay."

"Fine with me," I replied as Eva and her girlfriends bopped over.

"Good job girl!" Eva squealed.

"Thanks sweetie. You didn't wreck my car did you?" I joked as I watched Angela and Frankie walk away hand in hand.

"I wish James could've been here," she mumbled to one of her giggling friends.

"Eva, remember what I told you," I said sternly as she handed me my keys.

"Don't worry, I will," she replied as I gave her a big hug and kiss.

When I arrived home, there were two-dozen red roses on the mat outside my door.

"Dear Christian, I don't like not seeing or talking to you. I want to start over from scratch. Can we please talk? I want to make everything right again. Love, Darius."

I realized that I couldn't avoid him any longer so I called and left a message to finally settle the score.

"Darius, I got the roses. Thanks, but you didn't have to do that. I guess I need to be open and tell you that I think we're better off just being friends. I'm also going to be honest by telling you that I'm seeing someone else. He makes me happy and I've never felt this way in my life so I know it's real. I'm not saying this because of what happened with Mekhi the other week. I'm telling you this so we can both move on. Take care and I'll talk to you soon."

MONDAY, 9/18

Although the jazz fest wasn't nearly as stressful as I thought it would be, I kept my eleven o'clock spa appointment for a half day of relaxation after I finished my Monday morning invoicing. Afterwards I met up with Reese and Carra to shop for some naughty and nice items for Celeste's bridal shower and bachelorette party. Our first destination, Victoria's Secret to partake in a huge clearance sale. When I walked in the store, Reese was already there hovering over a bin full of bras and fiercely stuffing lacy, silky items into her wire mesh shopping basket.

"Slow down, you're going to get a stomach ache," I joked as I began sorting through a pile of bras.

"Oh, please. You're the last to talk," she replied as she held up a sexy orange see-through bra. "Last time we were here you acted like you were a contestant on *Supermarket Sweep*. Running around the tables, grabbing thongs like a mad woman."

"Hey girls!" Carra said as she walked in the store.

"Hey," I said, giving her a hug. "How are you?"

"Oh, I'm alright, just a little hungry," she said, sounding almost scripted as she tried to inconspicuously nod at Reese like she was giving her a cue.

"I am too. Let's grab something to eat after we leave here," Reese said, sounding like she was reciting rehearsed lines as she and Carra simultaneously looked at me as if I would oppose.

"You two are horrible actors," I said, playfully rolling my eyes and shaking my head. "I'm not as anorexic as you think."

"Let me be the judge of that," Reese said as she held one of her bras up to my chest. "Skinny ass thing."

"I bet if you put that up to me, it'd look like a washcloth," Carra said as she lightly pressed down on her swollen breasts. "I'm not used to this just yet."

"I'm pretty sure Aaron isn't complaining," I said.

"I'm hip! Aaron finally has something to grab on to!" Reese joked.

"Exactly!" I laughed then turned to Reese. "But what I'm trying to figure out is why you just felt the need to reach back into a time warp, circa nineteen eighty-six, to pull out the phrase *I'm hip*. I haven't heard anyone say that in years!"

"Right M.C. Resse's Pieces," Carra laughed as she held on to my arm.

"Oh, both of you know where you can go," she said as she tried to hold back her laugh.

After about a half hour, we realized that we were actually there to shop for Celeste so we all got to work to try to find the sexiest lingerie in the store. I decided on a steamy black, long, sheer nightgown and a short, white, laced nightie. I also gave in to my temptation to buy a little something for myself. A sexy gold nightgown marked sixty percent off. I deserved it.

TUESDAY, 9/19

I try not to jump to conclusions when people act rude. I try to sum it up as a bad day and not jump to racial or sexist conclusions, but sometimes that's exactly what it is. I came to that realization before a client meeting early this morning with the Midwest Cancer Foundation to manage their first annual 5K walk/run. I was all geared up and excited to meet with Richard, the executive director, whom I met through mutual board involvement with another foundation. We had a great first meeting earlier in the year and he made sure to mention how big of an impression I made on him.

Our meeting was at nine this morning and the plan was for me to meet Richard in their lobby five minutes til' since their receptionist recently quit and nobody would be there to page him. That didn't seem too hard. As I pulled in the parking lot, a young white woman pulled up next to me. When I entered the building it turned out that we were going to the same place because she followed me upstairs to the office, no big deal. In the lobby there was a middle-aged gentleman standing at the door that only employees can open with a code. When I walked over to him, the gentleman half-heartedly looked up at me, pointed over to the row of chairs against the wall and mumbled, "Just take a seat over there." When the white woman behind me walked in, his entire tone changed. He fully acknowledged her and smiled, offered her a magazine, a cup of coffee, asked her about the weather then directed her to a plush cushioned chair by the window. At first I thought she was there to see him then I realized she was there waiting to see someone else just like me. When the guy came back into the lobby with a cup of coffee on top of a clipboard, he smiled as he served her the coffee then walked over and handed me the clipboard.

"Just fill this out and leave it at the receptionist's desk when you're done. Someone will call you when they have a chance to review it," he said arrogantly. When I looked at the coffee stained paper attached to the clipboard it read: *Application for Employment- Receptionist.*

"Excuse me sir," I said, fuming as I walked to face him. "I'm not here to apply for a job, I'm coordinating the walk/run and I'm here to meet with Richard," I said slowly, trying my best not to go off, though giving him a serious side eye and shaking my head.

"I'm here to apply for the job," the woman said timidly as she set her coffee on the side table. "Sorry about that," she said to me as I handed her the clipboard.

"You don't need to apologize for anything," I responded while waiting for the guy to say something.

"Can I have another application? This one has a coffee ring on it," she asked handing the clipboard back to the guy who was standing there beet red.

"Christian!" Richard belted as he walked through the doors. "It's so good to see you!"

"Good morning. Good to see you too."

"Uh, Richard I was just about to call you to let you know your guest was here," the guy said nervously as I gave him the eye.

"Thanks Bill. Oh by the way, can you run downstairs to the copy center and pick up the packets for today's meeting, thanks. So Christian, how's your day been so far?" Richard asked sensing that something was a little off.

"Great until I ran into an extremely rude person this morning," I said to Richard but within earshot of the man. As soon as Richard took me back to his office he asked if Bill had done something out of line. After I told him what happened, Richard began fumbling through his Rolodex.

"I am so sorry Christian. That was completely unacceptable and I'll make sure he's reprimanded for not being professional," he huffed as he picked up his phone and began dialing. "Hello Phyllis…Yeah this is Rich…No everything's not fine…It's Bill, I don't think that he's working out…No, we've given him plenty of chances and it's just not going to work…Phyllis, I'm really sorry but I tried, I really did…Yeah you too…Bye."

It was a little awkward overhearing Richard order for Bill to be fired, but I really didn't care. Some people only learn the hard way.

"Pardon my language but that prick was only a temp. We brought him on as an office assistant and he's actually been the acting receptionist while we're in the process of finding a new one. It's amazing what assholes with low self-esteem will do to feel powerful," Richard said then smiled. "So other than the events from this morning, how have you been?"

I had two missed calls while I was in my meeting with Richard, one from Alain making sure I was having a good day and an urgent one from Celeste asking if I had time to come by later for something she described as an unforeseen circumstance.

"When did you find out?"

"This morning when I went in for my annual. My doctor only confirmed what I've feared all week," Celeste said with her eyes closed.

"How far along are you?"

"Six weeks."

"Are you okay?" I asked as Celeste opened her eyes letting out a big sigh.

"I guess. I'm just a little worried. For the past couple of weeks I've been downing Cosmos like water," she said with both her hands on her belly.

"Did you tell your doctor?"

"Yeah, she said that I shouldn't have anything to worry about. She's going to keep an eye on me though. She assured me that this happens to women more often than you'd think."

"You should be fine. Try not to worry."

"Christian to be quite honest, I'm just not ready. It's hard enough dealing with my mother being sick so adding a baby to the equation will make things even more difficult."

"I thought your mom was doing better."

"So did I until I spoke with her doctor yesterday and found out she had a relapse. She knew but she'd been keeping it a secret for weeks," Celeste said as she nervously ran her hands through her hair.

"Please don't worry yourself sick," I said as I grabbed one of her jittery hands. "Let me get you a glass of water."

On my way to the kitchen, I heard a light tapping sound then noticed a figure peering through the front storm door.

"Hey!" Carra yelled from outside. "What's going on in there?" she asked as I unlocked the solid glass door.

"How come you didn't ring the bell?"

"I did," she said as she took off her jacket and locked the door behind her. "I've been out there for over five minutes."

"Her doorbell must not be working, sorry."

"Is everything okay?"

"Yeah, Celeste just has a lot on her plate right now," I said, opening the kitchen cabinets. "I'll bring you something to drink. Why don't you go on back and talk to her."

As I walked back to the den all I could hear was Carra complaining about Celeste breaking the pregnancy ceremony code.

"Not now Car. A pregnancy ceremony is the furthest thing from my mind," Celeste said frowning.

"Does John know?" I asked.

"Not yet. I'll tell him when he gets home."

"Your mother is going to be so happy," Carra said as Celeste let out a deep breath and rubbed her temples.

"Look, I don't know why I'm stressing. Everything's going to be just fine," she said trying to look pleasant. "This is about to be the happiest time of my life," she said turning pale.

WEDNESDAY, 9/20

I got good rest last night after arriving in New York. My Illum meetings went well today and I was able to secure catering, entertainment and staffing for the perfume launch party, as well as iron out the details for the investor's reception at the home of Illum's president in the Hamptons.

I had a six o'clock appointment for my test shoot with Guy's photographer boyfriend, Eden. The heavy, steel entry door was propped open when I arrived at the studio and after I got off a slow freight elevator, Guy and a man who I assumed to be Eden were in the middle of the room arguing. Because their backs were facing me, I was in the room for at least two minutes before they even knew I was there. I didn't want to interrupt, but I didn't want it to seem as if I was eavesdropping either, so I slowly walked backwards toward the elevator and purposely dropped my purse. They immediately turned around and stopped arguing. Guy began walking towards me with an apologetic smile on his face while the other man looked at me as if I was interrupting something important.

"Eden's really hungry, would you be crushed if we postponed this until tomorrow?"

"Not at all. It'll give me time to wash my hair tonight. It's looking a little frazzled right now," I said lightheartedly.

"You're right, it does," Eden said in a snide tone as I stood there in shock. Before I could say anything else, Eden walked over to us with a sour look on his face. "I've got a million and one things to do tonight. We need to get going—NOW!" Eden growled at Guy then stormed out the door.

"What's his deal?" I asked Guy who tried to downplay the situation by laughing and waving him off.

"He's just being bitchy right now," he said then paused. "It's just bad timing. Tonight's not a good night. A lot of things have come up unexpectedly and he's just stressed. Why don't we just meet here tomorrow around noon."

"That's fine, I needed the rest anyway."

THURSDAY, 9/21

Alain called me first thing this morning to pump me up before my photoshoot. Although this was just a test shoot he acted like I was about to be on the cover of Vogue.

"I can't believe that I'm dating an international supermodel," Alain joked.

"Sweetie, I doubt if more than five people will ever see these pictures."

"Whatever, you're about to give Tyra a run for her money!"

"See, that's why I like you."

Before entering Eden's building, I could see Guy frowning through the small, glass window on the door. After I rang the buzzer, he walked over with a stressed out look on his face. He opened the door and gave me a half smile as he turned and walked towards the elevator without saying anything.

"Is everything okay?" I asked as Guy pushed the up button.

"Eden's still being temperamental so consider yourself forewarned."

"We can always do this another time," I said holding on to brace myself from the jerk of the elevator.

Guy grabbed onto the rail next to me then pushed the stop button and let out a deep sigh.

"I don't think that's a good idea. We need to get it done and out of the way while you're here."

When we got off the elevator and walked into the large studio space, Eden mumbled something that sounded like *late*.

"I've been downstairs talking to her, she's not late," Guy barked back.

"Whatever, let's just get this over with," Eden said as I began freshening up my makeup. "Hello! I said let's get started!"

I turned to face him and he was fiery red and scowling, "Are you talking to me?" I asked, irritated by his funky attitude.

"Who the hell else would I be talking to?" Eden said annoyed. "I have other things to do so let's get started."

"First of all, you need to take it down a couple notches. I'm doing *you* a favor..."

"Everyone just calm down! We're all here so let's just make the best of the situation," Guy said, looking at me with an apologetic expression.

"Fine," I said brashly as I unbuttoned my long cardigan. "I'm about to walk over to my bag to get a hairbrush, is that okay with you?"

Eden didn't respond and Guy tried to stay preoccupied by flipping through a big photography magazine.

"Just do what he says," Guy whispered to me as I touched up my blush. "I know he's difficult but just suck it up and it will be over in a few."

"Guy, I didn't ask for this. I'm volunteering my time to help him out. By the way he's acting you would've thought he was paying me thousands of dollars to be here," I said, blatantly ignoring Guy's gestures for me to whisper. "I'm not going to kiss his ass and I'll tell you one thing, he has one more time to talk crazy and I swear I'm putting him in his place."

The shoot took a little over a two hours and although Eden steered clear of any smart aleck remarks, he consistently gave me a look like I wasn't really impressing him. Needless to say by the end of the day, I made up my mind that I couldn't care less.

FRIDAY 9/22

I took an early flight back home and if I thought my time with Eden was stressful nothing could prepare me for the bomb my mother dropped. My cousin Josie was coming to town.

"How about letting Josie stay with you?" mom asked in a casual tone.

"What's wrong with her staying at your house?"

"Well nothing's wrong with it, I just thought that you two would like to spend a little time together since it's been so long and..."

"You just don't want her to stay with you," I said, cutting her off.

"Uh, no."

"So you're putting her off on me?"

"Don't think of it as us putting her off on you, think of it as you spending quality time with the only female cousin your age."

"When will she be here?"

"Tomorrow night around seven."

"Why will she be here?"

"She said that she needed to get away somewhere where there was peace and quiet."

"In other words, away from Jejuan."

"Exactly."

"Well we most certainly won't have any peace and quiet. We'll have to listen to her complain about how all men are dogs and how black men aren't worth two cents or how she's gonna' go out and find a white man to take care of her. Can't we put her up at a hotel?"

"I tried to subtly hint around to your father but he wouldn't hear of it. I didn't want to press the issue and start an argument."

"If I let her stay with me how long is my sentence?"

"Just for a couple of nights."

"And my reward for doing this?"

"Your reward is thicker skin and a lesson in patience."

"Dad doesn't know it but he owes me big time," I said as I chuckled along with my mother.

Great, I thought sarcastically after hanging up the phone. Tomorrow is going to be a night of pure hell. My cousin isn't a happy person to begin with and now that she's going through a divorce, I'm sure she'll really be a delight to be around.

"Hey girl, what's up?"

"Nothing much, just sitting here with John trying to figure out which flowers I'm going to use for my bouquet. How have you been?"

"Good, just trying to get back into the swing of things after being in New York."

"Have you heard from Car? I spoke to her briefly this morning and I got a weird vibe from her," Celeste said. "She's been acting really odd lately."

"Odd like how?"

"Well, take this for instance. We all know most pregnant women have cravings, even I'm starting to feel it, but Carra's taking the cravings thing to another level. Yesterday she told me that she went to the grocery store at one-thirty in the morning, by herself, because she had a craving for tuna fish and corn starch," Celeste said while John snickered in the background, then abruptly stopped after a loud slapping sound.

"Oww," John moaned while laughing.

"Anyway," Celeste giggled, getting back to the subject. "Then she told me that she had a taste for real snow and it was killing her that winter isn't here yet. Too weird."

"You're next."

"I hope not."

"I'll try calling her. So what are you and John doing tonight?"

"I have to play Martha Stewart for some of his friends in from Ohio," she said then whispered. "A bunch of boring white people."

"Hey, I heard that," John laughed in the background.

"They're bringing stroganoff and a deck of cards to play euchre, enough said," she said joking. "Oh, by the way, I was wondering. Have you heard from Alain lately?"

"Yes, as a matter of fact I plan on seeing him next week while I'm in Chicago."

"Oh really?"

"Uh huh."

"*Uuh huuuuh?*"

"What?" I said laughing, knowing exactly what Celeste was thinking.

"Where are you staying?"

"In a hotel, smartass! This isn't Reese you're talking to."

"Oh, I know who I'm talking to, miss Darius and I are *just friends*," Celeste teased.

"Shouldn't you be warming up a pot of fondue right now?"

"Funny," she said. "But seriously, I guess I should start cleaning up before our guests get here. Call me later tonight if you hear from Car *and* to finish this conversation about your Chicago accommodations."

As I was catching up on a week's worth of personal emails, Carra dropped by unannounced armed with nachos, tacos, refried beans and ice cream.

"Put this in the freezer before it melts," she said, handing me the cold, wet grocery bag.

"What is all of this?"

"Goodies," she said, opening my kitchen cabinets then stopping dead in her tracks and began looking around my apartment like it was the first time she'd been over. "Oh my gosh, I'm sorry. Am I intruding?"

"Carra, what are you talking about?"

"You have the lights all dim, with incense burning and Maxwell playing. I'm sorry, I can leave," she said as she opened the freezer, removing the bag of ice cream.

"Now who in the world do you think would be coming over here tonight? Alain's still in Chicago."

"Whew, that's a relief because I don't feel like driving all the way back home tonight. You don't mind if I stay do you?" she said kicking off her shoes and curling up on my couch.

"Not at all," I laughed thinking about my conversation with Celeste earlier. "But what I do mind is you bringing all this greasy, fattening food in the house," I said, jokingly giving her the evil eye.

"*Chris*," she said in a sing-songy tone. "I don't want to confirm what is now popular opinion amongst the girls when I report back to them."

"*Carra*," I replied in the same tone. "I don't care about popular opinion. Like I've told you guys a million and one times, I'm fine."

"A little ice cream has never hurt anyone," she said with a sly grin as she swayed over to the freezer and pulled out the bag.

"Fine, Carra. I'll eat some ice cream. What flavor did you bring?"

"Crunchy peanut butter chocolate swirl."

"Well now I have an excuse. I despise peanut butter. After all the years we've been friends I assumed you knew that."

"I thought it was Celeste that hated peanut butter."

"No, it's me."

"Fine then. You're off the hook this time."

"I know I'm off the hook. Peanut butter ice cream? Ugh, sounds disgusting."

"It may be to you but I've been craving it all week. You wouldn't believe the trouble I went through to find that flavor. I went to eight different grocery stores and only one had it in stock. Who knew it'd be such a rare find?"

"We'll I'm happy that after all those days of searching, you finally found it."

"All what days?" Carra said as she crunched on a nacho overflowing with cheese and chili. "I started looking this afternoon when I got off work."

"You mean to tell me that you've been to eight different grocery stores in the last four hours?"

"Yep."

To appease Carra, I ate a small bowl of beans and grazed on a few nachos as we spent the rest of the night enjoying throw back cinema, watching the original *Sabrina* with Audrey Hepburn and *The Wiz*. Even though I'd seen both movies a million times, I enjoyed the nostalgia. Carra's hormones were truly getting the best of her and I couldn't keep from laughing as she cried on every ballad sung in *The Wiz*. She was especially moved when Diana Ross sang "Be a Lion" to the cowardly lion with tears running down her face as she mouthed the words and clutched a pillow. Wow, pregnancy has definitely done a number on her.

SATURDAY, 9/23

"Where do you keep your facial cleanser?"

I opened one eye to see Carra sitting at the foot of the bed smiling and swinging her legs, before glancing at the clock which read seven forty-seven.

"Why are you up?" I asked trying not to sound pissed off.

"I want to go down to the market before it gets crowded."

"It doesn't get crowded on Saturday mornings, now go back to bed."

"No, look," she said as she bounced off of the bed and walked over to the window. Before I could say anything, she flung open the curtains. "It's going to be a gorgeous day!"

"Carra!"

"It's so sunny and pretty already."

"Look, we'll go to the market together at ten. Just give me a few more hours to rest."

"Suit yourself, but I bet it'll be crowded."

"Close the curtains on your way out," I grumbled, rolling over and putting the covers over my face. As she closed my bedroom door, I tried falling asleep again but that damned sun beam that made my whole room orange stuck in my mind. I laid there for another twenty-five minutes before I realized it was a lost cause.

"Here," I said, walking into the living room, handing a tube of facial cleanser to Carra.

"Oooh. You look awful," she said smiling as she looked over at me. As much as I wanted to say something snarky, I didn't. I just gave her the cleanser and plopped down on the couch.

"I know you're not watching this," I said to Carra as I looked for the remote control.

"As a matter of fact I am."

"Sesame Street? Where's the remote?"

"This is actually very interesting. You see Elmo's trying to..." Carra said then looked at me with her mouth wide open as I changed the channel.

"Are you staying over here until it's time to go to Celeste's shower?"

"Yeah. I have some extra clothes in the car. I just need to throw my leggings in the washer."

"Well if there's any place that gets crowded on a Saturday morning it would be the laundry room. Did you remember to bring Celeste's gift?"

"It's in my trunk. Speaking of which, I'm pretty sure you'll be showing off all the naughty little items you bought at Victoria's Secret on your trip to Chicago trip next week."

"My goodness," I laughed. "I only bought one thing, one measly little nightgown that isn't really all that sexy. Alain and I aren't even at that stage in our relationship yet. Hell, we're not even in a relationship yet."

"That never seemed to matter before," she said smirking as she folded up her sheet.

"What is with you and Celeste? You would've thought that I was superhoe, flying around the city seeking out helpless men to screw," I said as I hit her with a pillow. "A sister messes up one time in her life and from that point on I have a permanent scarlet H branded on my chest."

We arrived at Celeste's house the same time as her mother, so we didn't feel quite as bad about being twenty minutes late. I hadn't seen Ms. V for weeks and quite a bit had changed. As she pulled up behind us the first thing I noticed was the bright orange scarf she wore wrapped around her head and the considerable weight she'd lost.

"How are my girls?" Ms. V belted as she held out her arms.

"Just fine," I replied.

"It's so good to see you again. Did Celeste tell you I was expecting…" Carra went on as she and Ms. V walked up to the door arm in arm.

Celeste opened the door wearing a sexy, little black dress with a plunging neckline and Reese, you gotta' love Reese, she was wearing the same dress that she'd tried on at my house several weeks ago. She gave me the smuggest grin as I sat down next to her on the loveseat.

"I see you stuffed yourself into a size eight," I joked.

"No sweetie, I found a size ten and as you can see, it fits like a glove."

"You just had to go out and buy my dress didn't you?"

"Uh, the last time I checked the tag it said Nina Ricci, not Christian Cullen," she said smiling before biting into a finger sandwich.

"Look on the bright side, now you get to see how you're really supposed to rock the dress. I'd take notes if I were you."

Before I could reply, John's sister, Heather walked over to us and started drooling over Reese's outfit.

"Your dress is absolutely gorgeous. I'm dying to know where you got it."

"As much as I like giving away helpful hints and trade secrets, I'm not able to divulge that information," she said, winking her green eyes.

"Nordstrom's," I blurted as Reese looked at me as if I'd just stolen her purse. "I'd go now if I were you, I think they're having their big semi-annual sale."

"I'm there tomorrow!" Heather replied then yelled over to a group of women talking next to the punch bowl. "Nordstrom's!"

They all nodded and gave Reese the thumbs up as I laughed and threw my arm around her.

"I have one word for you. Karma," I said as she thumped me on my arm.

After about two hours of playing games, eating and watching Celeste open countless boxes of lingerie and bath products, Ms. V did something that changed the whole mood of the party, she took off her scarf. I wasn't prepared to see Ms. V without her long, thick black hair. She was completely bald and despite everyone else's shock, she seemed to be unnaturally calm and unfazed.

"Maybe I'll have enough to tie back in a French twist for the wedding," Ms. V joked as the room filled with delayed, hollow and confused chuckles. I didn't know whether to laugh or cry. "And to think, they only gave me one year to live. You guys are already dead! It's okay to laugh, it's just hair," Ms. V announced as Celeste excused herself and rushed into the kitchen. "Come on everybody. Don't let a little lady with cancer dampen the mood, this is supposed to be a party!"

"Who made these delicious meatballs?" a young lady asked trying to change the subject. "The sauce is amazing!"

"Can you believe they're store bought?" another lady answered.

As the women continued to sit around the living room intrigued by a five-dollar bag of meatballs, I excused myself and followed Celeste into the kitchen.

"Are you okay?" I asked as Celeste rummaged through a drawer, not looking for anything in particular.

"Why does she always have to do this?"

"What?"

"Cause a scene!" Celeste said in an elevated whisper as she threw a serving spoon into the sink, making a loud echo noise against the stainless steel basin. "Did she really have to go there?"

Just as I was about to say something, Ms. V walked in.

"What are you two doing in here when the party's going on out there?"

"Just getting some aluminum foil," I said, looking at Celeste. Just as she looked like she was about to say something, she squinted her eyes and walked back into the living room.

"What's the deal with her?" Ms. V asked as I grabbed the box of foil.

"Probably just pre-wedding jitters," I said trying to make my way back to the living room.

"Chris, let me ask you something."

"Yes ma'am," I said, turning around to face her.

"Are you sick? You look like you've lost weight."

"No. I'm not sick."

"Are you sure, because your eyes look really sunken in."

"I'm just a little tired from working hard all week. Believe me, I'm fine."

"That's what I thought was wrong with me, fatigue. But as you can see I was mistaken."

"Believe me, I'm alright."

On the way back to my apartment, Carra and Aaron argued over the phone for most of the twenty minute drive. She, voicing her frustration with him being gone all of the time and he, on the other end, trying to plead his case.

"When I get home are you going to be there or not...Well we'll just finish this conversation when I get there...I disagree, I don't think we should just squash this...I'm sorry you feel that way...Whether you like it or not, we're going to finish this conversation when I get home goodbye," she said before ending her call as we pulled into my parking lot.

"Am I being unreasonable by asking my husband to spend a little time with me since I haven't seen him in over a week?"

"Not at all."

"I'm glad you agree because he makes it seem like I'm crazy for bringing it up," she said, unbuckling her seatbelt. "I think he's having an affair."

"Carra, he may be gone a lot but do you really think he would cheat on you?"

"I don't know for sure, but I have my suspicions."

"Then you need to talk to him about it."

"That would seem like the logical thing to do but I'm debating whether I should or not. Once the baby arrives, he'll snap out of whatever is distracting him and things will get back to normal."

"Or they'll get worse. Car, if you have suspicions you should get it all out in the open now, before the baby's born."

"Chris, just let me handle things my way. Aaron can only deal with so much at a time. He already feels like I'm nagging him about the time we spend together and I know he's stressed out over the pregnancy, I just don't want to overwhelm him and really drive him away."

"And who suffers in the long run?"

"Chris," she said then paused. "I need to go."

"Carra, I'm not trying to upset you, I just want you to put yourself first for a change."

"I know," she said as she turned to walk to her car with tears in her eyes. "It'll all work itself out. That's all I can hope for."

At seven o'clock I got a call from my mom informing me that my cousin Josie was at Union Station and needed to be picked up.

As I approached the train station I saw Josie standing at the curb laughing on the phone. Maybe she's changed, I told myself though still trying to mentally prepare for what could possibly be two days of sheer misery. As I pulled into the entrance, I honked the horn to get her attention. She gave a half-hearted wave as she ended her call and gathered all of her bags.

"What took you so long?"

"I got here as fast as I could."

"I'd been standing out there for the past half hour," she said as she pulled down the visor mirror to refresh her lipstick. "Anyway, how have you been?"

"I can't complain," I said almost running a red light. As I slammed on the brakes Josie lost control of her lipstick, smearing it above her lip line. I couldn't help but laugh at the red streak extending from the corner of her lip to the bottom of her nose. Thankfully, she still had an ounce of humor left because she managed to crack a slight smile, then rolled her eyes as she wiped the lipstick off of her face.

"Nice car," she said, more sarcastically than approving. "I thought you were an entrepreneur."

"What does that have to do with my car?"

"Isn't this a little too expensive for someone trying to grow a small business?"

"Trust me, I'm doing alright."

"No need to get touchy. Anyway, how are things with you and the party promoter guy?"

"I broke up with Mekhi about a month ago."

"That's too bad. What happened?"

"I don't feel like getting into it. I'll just say this, I feel like God took him out of my life so the right one could enter."

"It's obvious that he must've cheated."

"Josie."

"What? I'm not trying to make fun of the situation, I'm just thinking out loud. If he did I wouldn't be surprised, it's in a man's nature to cheat."

"Not all men cheat."

"Not all men get caught."

"That's your opinion."

"It's fact. Take my dad for instance. Everyone thought he was the perfect husband and father until he got caught in an affair with a woman half his age after thirty years of marriage to my mother. Your friend Reese's husband did her the same way, all of my married friends husbands cheated and don't get me started on Jejuan's trifling ass," she hissed.

Josie met Jejuan during her junior year in college, married him the summer before her senior year, dropped out of school to play step-mommy to his three kids and never held down a job because he wouldn't let her.

"I quit school to be with that punk."

"It's not too late, you can always go back."

"I know that," she said with an attitude. "It's just the fact that I gave up my life to be with him."

When we arrived at my house, Josie immediately plopped down on my chaise lounge and began studying the look of my living room while I grabbed some clean linens for her.

"Isn't your place a little small?"

"No. It's the perfect size."

"I'm just saying, since you work from home."

"I have an office now."

"I can see why," she said, walking into my sunroom with her nose turned up. "I don't think I could live in a place so old. I bet this building was built over a hundred years ago."

"As a matter of fact it was. It used to be a hotel," I said, trying to remain patient. "Actually I wouldn't live anywhere else. I love this place."

"If you say so," she said, looking at me like she didn't believe me. "So tell me more about this little business of yours. What exactly do you do?"

"I create and manage promotional campaigns, plan events, develop marketing materials…"

"Anybody can do that, hell I can do that."

"Trust me, it's not as easy as it seems."

"Yeah, but it can't be that hard either."

"If what I do is that easy then I'd be out of business due to massive competition. I'm good at what I do and right now I'm growing with more clients than I can even keep track of."

"Tell me anything," she said with a smug look. "How much do you make?"

"None of your business."

"You don't have to get an attitude, I'm just curious."

"Just put it this way, in the past year alone I've been able to double my old salary from when I was a marketing manager in corporate America barely scratching six figures."

"So you're trying to tell me that you make six figures doing this?"

"Yes."

"Well since you claim to have more clients than you can count, let me be your partner."

"I don't think that's a good idea."

"Why not?"

"Because you don't know anything about my business. You can work on special projects for me if I ever need help in the D.C. area, but to make you a partner isn't going to happen."

"You're too bougie for your own good. Here I am going through a divorce without two nickels to rub together, making pennies working at my dad's restaurant and you don't want to help a family member get ahead. Stingy!"

"Stingy? I worked hard as hell to get where I am today. I went a year and a half barely making it, but I never gave up. This is what I went to school for, this is what I earned two degrees for, this is why I dedicated seven years of my life working and paying dues at a major PR firm, this is what I devoted my life savings to! I'll be damned if I stand here and let you call me stingy in my own house just because I won't make you partner of my company!" I said walking over to her. "Now if you want to take the time and learn the business, I'll let you intern for me."

"Whatever," she said under her breath as she headed to my bathroom, slamming the door.

"Mom, I don't think this is going to work out."

"Why, what's wrong?"

"She's on a rampage. In the course of an hour, she's insulted me, my intelligence, my business, my apartment. I can't take anymore."

"I'm so sorry. Look, why don't you two come by for dinner. Nanna's over here and I'm sure Josie would like to see her while she's here. That'll help the time go by faster, don't you think."

"I'm out the door now."

When we arrived at my parents' house, Josie did a total one-eighty and put on a complete show for Nanna and my dad. She was so sweet and nice that my mother pulled me aside to tell me that it appeared Josie had changed her ways.

"Well, she must have changed from the driveway to the front door. Trust me, before we got here she was the same old Josie."

"Well, try to get through dinner because after that you won't have to deal with her anymore today."

"Hallelujah! Angels must be looking out for me!"

"Your angel is Angela. She offered to let Josie stay at her place since she has an extra bedroom with a full size futon."

"Thank the Lord!" I shouted, as my mother playfully motioned for me to lower my voice.

"Speaking of thanking the Lord, I think tomorrow at church would be a great place to do it," mom said then changed to a serious tone. "You've been too blessed to not devote just two hours a week to God."

"Mom, I'm not an atheist, we've been through this before."

"Christian, you're missing out. Nothing can compare to being in a place filled with a spirit and energy so great that it moves you to tears."

"Or being in a place where people talk about you and treat you worse than the people on the street. No thanks, I prefer my spirit-filled living room."

SUNDAY, 9/24

At three o'clock, I did what I told my mother I was going to do. I watched worship service and felt as much spirit as I would if I were actually there. After service I started on a new painting entitled, *Alain*. In the middle of a brushstroke, I started to get excited about seeing him later in the week. My heart raced at the thought of kissing him again and my body shivered as I remembered the scent of his cologne.

"I can't wait to see you this week."

"Hopefully you'll have time to pencil me into your busy schedule."

"I'm sure that I can spare five minutes," I joked.

"How about ten," he laughed then paused. "Hey, I wanted to ask you something."

"Yeah."

"What hotel are you staying at?"

"Actually, I haven't made my reservations yet."

"Good."

"Why is that?"

"Because you shouldn't have to spend extra money when you don't have to."

"Meaning?"

"Meaning, I would love it if you stayed with me."

MONDAY, 9/25

"How are the new pills working out?" Dr. Brown asked as she flipped through my medical charts.

"I stopped taking them."

"Any particular reason?"

"A couple. The weight gain and nausea were the main reasons but I was also thinking about celibacy at the time."

"Sounds like you've changed your mind," she said smiling. "Celibacy's a big commitment."

"I just started seeing someone new and I'm not sure what's going to happen between us."

"Would you like to learn about other birth control options?"

"Yes."

When I got back to my office I got an email from the Jazz Preservation Society of San Diego inviting me to present my proposal for their major music festival next year. I was one of three other planning companies in the running. Nothing could explain the excitement I felt after reading the message. This was by far the biggest opportunity of my career. From a monetary standpoint, this account would be over three times bigger than Illum! I replied immediately to confirm my availability and express mailed a thank-you note to the president. I blew off working for the rest of the day and called everyone to share the good news.

"Okay, let's say that I get this project, I'd have the option to do nothing else but focus on it for the entire year. Could you imagine?"

"Girl, you could sit around in your thong all day long and do absolutely nothing for a whole month and still be getting paid more than you ever had in your whole entire life," Reese joked.

"I know!"

"I'll keep my fingers crossed for you," she said then paused. "So, are you going to see Alain on Thursday?"

"Yes, and don't say what I think you're going to say."

"Alright, I'll say it in a different way. Do you think you'll still be celibate by the end of the week?"

TUESDAY, 9/26

I had a lunch meeting with Angela to go over Celeste's wedding and the Illum project. I contracted her to do all of the graphics for the big perfume campaign and she had the first drafts ready for me to see today.

Angela ended up being twenty-five minutes late to the meeting and when she finally arrived she was wearing an odd looking print headband with her hair braided erratically, a few of the braids interwoven with some type of yarn. She had on a long hippie looking floral skirt, a white tank top and an orange gingham shirt tied around her waist. Not to be outdone by her outfit and hair, she had on mismatched gold earrings and bright orange lipstick. She couldn't possibly think that ensemble was working. She looked like a drugged up gypsy from hell.

"Sorry I'm late, I overslept."

"You were obviously out partying last night."

"How'd you guess?"

"Oh, probably by the fact that you look like you rolled out of bed to meet me here the same way you rolled into bed last night."

"I resent that."

"Angela, please do me one favor. When you help with Celeste's wedding please wear the suit that I gave you, and please do something to your hair."

"I'm not dumb, I know how to dress for a wedding."

"Do you know how to dress for a meeting?"

"Damn Chris, I thought this was just lunch. I didn't expect you to be so formal," she said as she looked both surprised and hurt. "I figured I was here to spend time with my sister. Yeah, I planned on showing you these proofs and discussing the wedding for a few minutes, but really, I was looking forward to hanging out and filling you in on my time with Josie. Sorry."

Terrible is not a strong enough word to describe how I felt. I didn't realize Angela just wanted to spend time with me. My life is so scheduled during the day that I'd forgotten that meeting up with my sister for lunch shouldn't just be a check off of my to-do list.

WEDNESDAY, 9/27

As I sat, burning up underneath the dryer, I did some serious soul searching about spending the night with Alain tomorrow. The reality is, although I really like him and could see myself being with him, I've known him for less than a month and I've only spent one week with him in person. Would I be able to take it easy and know when to stop or would I get caught up in the moment and give into temptation like the Darius incident? One thing's for sure, let the girls predict it and I'm as good as gone.

I decided to stop by Nanna's house after I left the salon. When I arrived, she was outside watering her flowers and as soon as she saw me pull up she started spraying my car.

"How are you going to have such a nice car and drive it around town with poop all over your windshield?" she said as I got out and walked over to hug her.

"I've been so busy that I've been neglecting a lot of things lately."

"Well at least you look good. There's nothing prettier than a brown skinned girl with long shiny hair."

"I got it from you."

"I know," she said laughing as we went into the house. "I'm even getting used to all of this weight you've lost. You don't look sick anymore."

"I never looked sick."

"Oh yes you did."

"No I..."

"Don't you argue with me child," she said, playfully. "Did you just get your hair done? It's cute."

"Yeah, I just got back from the salon."

"Are you still dating that guy?"

"Alain?"

"Ah yes, Alain. I can't wait to meet him. Your mother told me how handsome he is."

"Handsome is an understatement."

"Oh really. So how would you describe him?"

"He's indescribable."

"I bet that he doesn't look better than your grandfather did in his younger years."

"They're running about neck and neck."

"Well then, I can't wait to meet him. I should probably warn you, don't get upset if he ends up falling in love with me instead."

"Nanna, I just may have to fight you for this one."

As I packed my bags, I stared into my lingerie drawer and thought, should I or shouldn't I? After I figured out the answer to that dilemma, the next question was, the red one or the black one? Although I decided on the black one, it didn't mean that I planned on being bad in Chicago, I just wanted to be prepared.

THURSDAY, 9/28

I went straight to Jean Co. as soon as I arrived in Chicago this morning—on time by the way. The investors meeting went well from my standpoint, everything ran smoothly and the board loved the attention to detail in the activities I planned. Unfortunately for Jean, the meeting was such a disaster that even my impressive planning couldn't overshadow it. The company's earnings were a quarter of a million dollars under projection and her investors were not thrilled. She was in such a pissy mood after the meeting that she stormed out of the office without even discussing the investors reception tomorrow evening.

"She probably figures there isn't anything worth celebrating," Alain said after meeting up with me in the Jean Co. parking lot.

"Well she can cancel it if she wants to, my checks have already been cashed."

"Must be nice," he said, smiling and looking at me like he wanted to tell me something. "Let's get out of here. Are you hungry?"

"Not really. I'm just tired."

"Well let's head over to my place and relax for a few. We can go out for dinner later on."

Alain lives in a beautiful residential neighborhood that has the best of both worlds. It's a quiet and tranquil park-like setting that's only two blocks from Lake Shore Drive and ten minutes from the heart of downtown.

"I know you're going to miss this neighborhood," I said as I opened my trunk.

"A little. The apartment I found in Indianapolis is in a neighborhood similar to this."

"Oh, so you finally decided on a building. Where's it at?"

"Lockerbie? I think that's the name of the area. Does that ring a bell?"

"Yeah, you'll love it there," I said as I laid my bags in the grass and closed my trunk.

"Is this all you have?" Alain asked as he picked up my tote and dress bag.

"You seem surprised."

"I am! You look like the type who would have one of those huge Louis Vuitton trunks that takes five men to carry."

"I thought I've already proven to you that looks can be deceiving."

"You're right. You just never cease to amaze me."

Alain's apartment building was really nice. It appeared to be an old Victorian-style home that had been converted into several apartment units. There was a large stained glass window at the end of the long common hallway with beautiful mahogany hardwood floors all throughout the building. When we arrived in front of Alain's door, I could hear the sound of jazz from the other side. When we walked in, I was inundated by a total sensory experience. There was the relaxing smell of frankincense, the soothing sounds of Grant Green, the marvelous image of Alain's breathtaking home and the feeling of his hand on the small of my back as he guided me into his place. About seventy-five percent of Alain's house was all boxed up and bare but from the way his apartment was constructed and the items that were still unboxed, I was very impressed.

"I wish I could say make yourself comfortable, but as you can see…" he said as he began removing boxes from his couch. "Can I offer you something to drink?"

"Yeah, just water," I said as I managed to catch a glimpse of his chiseled physique as he walked into the kitchen.

"So aside from the fact that Jean Co.'s earnings were low, were there any positive aspects to the meeting?" Alain yelled into the living room.

"I received major recognition from Jean's assistant as being the person responsible for the great meeting," I said as I walked into his sunny kitchen. "I also exchanged business cards with a few investors looking for me to assist with some of their other ventures."

"That's great."

"Yeah, considering some of the other companies they finance are multi-million dollar businesses."

"Well then, I'd like to propose a toast to you and to Image Brokers. May you be blessed with continued success so that maybe one day, we can get married and I can retire early—here, here!" he said as he raised his glass of water in the air and smiled in the sexiest way. I slowly walked toward him and wrapped my arm around his waist.

"We can negotiate your early retirement but I think I could agree to the rest," I said as I tapped my glass against his.

"Can I be truthful here?" Alain said softly then took a quick sip of water. "The moment you told me you were coming to Chicago, I've been on a high that I can't even begin to explain. For the past couple of days, all I've been able to think about was kissing and holding you. I'm a little hurt since that hasn't happened yet," he said as I ran my fingers along the back of his ear then down across his jaw line. He took a deep breath, reached up to grab my hand and interlaced his fingers into mine. I could literally hear my heart beating as he bent down to kiss me.

We ended up ordering dinner from a Thai restaurant up the street then stayed at his house all evening laughing and talking.

"Uh oh Chris," Alain yelled from the living room while I was in the bathroom brushing my teeth. "The new Jean Co. commercial is on!"

I ran into the living room with the toothbrush hanging out of my mouth.

"I haven't seen this one yet," I said with a mouth full of bubbles, watching the skinny model with her arms crossed over her topless body roll around on a bed covered with jeans. This scene goes on in silence for about twenty seconds before Jean's voice comes in and says, *"Jean Co. is not about the jeans, it's about the genes behind the jeans."*

"Puh-lease," I said as I ran back into the bathroom to rinse out my mouth. "Jean is too arrogant for words!"

"Where is she from?" Alain asked as he walked into the bathroom, watching me wipe my mouth from the mirror on the medicine cabinet.

"Russia."

"Is she at least friendly when she's not stressed out?"

226

"It depends on your definition of friendly," I said as I walked back into the hall with a pouty face and stood in front of a closed door that I presumed to be his bedroom. "I'm offended that you haven't given me an official tour of your place."

"I'm almost embarrassed to since it's so junky," he said as he grabbed my hand and led me into his bedroom. "Okay, this is the king's domain."

"I like it," I said as I took in the strong African décor. "Where did you get this?" I asked, pointing to the mudcloth throw at the foot of his bed.

"My mother bought that from a Malian woman at an African festival in Atlanta last year. It's actually a wall hanging, but I thought that it would look better on my bed."

You lying naked with the cloth draped across your body would look better on your bed, I thought to myself.

"Let me show you the den," he said as he guided me into the hallway. "This is where the creative juices flow. I do all of my writing here."

"And what is it that you write?"

Alain walked over to his bookshelf and picked up a thin book bound in brown leather. He handed me the book that was entitled *Queen* then smiled.

"I guess I never told you."

I looked at the bottom of the book and to my surprise it read Alain Hughes.

"You told me that you dabbled in writing but you didn't say anything about being published."

"No one really knows except for my family and a few people here and there."

"I'm so proud of you," I said, flipping through page after page of poems and short stories. "Would you read some of it to me?"

"I suppose I could," he said as I handed the book back to him. "I don't need that. It's all up here," he said, pointing to his temples. "What type of vibe are you in right now?"

"Mellow."

"Okay, then I'll give you my favorite one. This is part one of the title poem entitled, "Queen":

She knows no challenge to stand in her way

A confident presence, standing toe to toe with the elements of the world

She makes deals with the mountains and the stars in the skies

Tells the moon when to beam and the sun when to rise

The earth stops rotating when she enters the room

Thaws the winter's rigid earth and commands roses to bloom

Wraps herself in midnight like a blanket of fleece

Emboldens the sparrows and tames the wildest of beasts

She enters my world as a force yet unseen

My heart, my soul, my love, my queen

I was awestruck as I stood there and listened to this beautiful man recite his words.

"I love that!"

"Thank you," he said beaming as he walked over to the futon, picked up a stack of books and placed them on his desk. "I guess I could go ahead and bring your bags in here."

"Huh?" I said, trying to act as if I didn't really hear him.

"I'm going to bring your bags in here so you can get settled in."

"Okay," I said in a neutral tone as I looked down at the futon, which appeared fluffy and comfortable but not as cozy as the large king-sized bed in his bedroom.

"Don't worry, it's actually pretty soft," he said, noticing me as I stared down at the futon.

"Oh, I'm not worried about that," I said and smiled up at him. "It's just that—you know what, I'm fine."

After he went into the living room to get my things, I couldn't help but think about how unexpected the sleeping arrangements turned out to be. There will be approximately fifteen feet separating us as we slept tonight.

"Here you go," Alain said as he placed my bags down next to the bookshelf then walked over to the futon and bent down. "Let me pull this out for you."

After he set up my bed, he walked over and kissed me on the forehead.

"I'm so happy you're here with me," he said then walked over to the door. "I'll let you get situated. I'll be in the living room for a while. If you want, I can read you some more poetry before you go to bed."

"That'll be nice."

"Good," he said then walked out of the room, closing the door behind him.

I opened my tote bag and pulled out the black nightgown, "So much for this," I said out loud as I stuffed it back in the bag and pulled out my old T-shirt and shorts. As I put on my nightclothes something dawned on me. Alain was only doing what he thought I wanted. That damned celibacy goal on my fridge. And to think three days ago I was fitted for a diaphragm specifically for this trip when all the while Alain had set up a guest room for me because he was trying to be respectful. Christian, you played yourself this time.

FRIDAY, 9/29

While in the bathroom this morning washing my face and brushing my teeth, I accidentally knocked my case of hair pins off the sink. As I was picking them up, I noticed an empty medicine bottle in the trashcan. I used a piece of toilet paper to turn the bottle around so I could see the label. It was a prescription for Xanax that was initially prescribed to Alain two years ago. He didn't appear to be sick but unfortunately since I didn't know what illness Xanax was used for, I didn't know what to think.

Alain was on the couch reading the newspaper when I walked into the living room.

"My goodness, you are so beautiful," he said as he got up and walked towards me. "Did you sleep alright?"

"I did, how about you?"

"I was thinking about you all night," he said, kissing my forehead. "Are you hungry?"

"A little."

"You should be, you barely ate anything last night," he said as he put on his tennis shoes. "I'm gonna run down the street and pick up some fruit and donuts. How's that sound?"

"Sounds good."

"Just make yourself at home. I'll be right back."

I waited for about five minutes before going to the window to make sure that Alain was gone. When the coast was clear I called Celeste.

"Please say that you know the answer to the question I'm about to ask you."

"Huh?"

"Why would a person need to use Xanax?"

"Okay," she said in a confused tone. "Depression, panic attacks, anxiety, things like that. You sound as if you need a hefty dose. What's wrong with you?"

"Oh, nothing."

"Then why'd you ask? And aren't you supposed to be in Chicago right now?"

"I am in Chicago."

"And?"

"And I found an empty bottle of Xanax in Alain's trashcan."

"Well if you were worried that Xanax is for AIDS or something like that you can relax. No need to worry."

I bet he was prescribed those pills after his brother died, I thought as I plopped down on his couch and picked up the newspaper. Underneath the stack of papers was Alain's wallet on the coffee table. I couldn't resist the urge to be nosey so I picked it up to see what was inside. Nothing out of the ordinary, just his driver's license, some credit cards, his library card, a couple of frequent flyer cards, business cards, an old picture of a little boy and a picture of an older couple who could possibly be his parents. As I studied the picture, I heard the sound of a car door slamming. Sure enough, it was Alain walking up the sidewalk to the main entryway. I stuffed the picture back into the wallet and put it back on the table just as I found it.

"Hey gorgeous!" Alain announced as he opened the door. "I have some strawberries for you."

"What'd you do, rob the store?" I said, laughing as I held up his wallet.

"Funny girl," he said, bending down to kiss me. "I always keep money in my ashtray, so I was fine. I didn't realize it until I was in line though."

"Do you have to go into the office today?" I asked, wrapping my arms around his neck.

"Yeah, I'm gonna go in for about an hour or so. I won't be there long because I have to finish packing."

"I can help. I don't have to be at the party site until four o'clock."

"No, you just sit back and relax."

"I insist," I said, looking around the living room. "You have a lot to do before Monday."

"I know."

"So let me help you."

"Okay, but only worry about the easy stuff," he said, walking into the bathroom.

As I sat down at the dining room table and reached into the grocery bag, Alain said something from inside the bathroom.

"I didn't hear you babe, what did you say?" I yelled back.

He opened the door and walked back into the living room.

"I was saying, I hope that empty Xanax bottle didn't scare you. I was cleaning out my medicine cabinet yesterday and threw away a bunch of things."

"Are you okay?" I asked, hoping to find out why he was taking them.

"I'm fine. I was on Xanax right after my brother died. I haven't been on it for over a year. It was just real tough for me after the funeral—I was literally haunted with the sight of my brother lying dead in a casket. For weeks I would wake up in the middle of the night and have hallucinations of his casket in my bedroom. I was off work for a month from fatigue," he said then looked away. "I know you probably think I'm crazy."

"No sweetie, you're not crazy," I said walking over to him. "You're human."

After breakfast, we sat in the middle of his living room floor and wrapped up his dishes while joking around and flirting with each other. When Alain left, I finished wrapping and packing the dishes then went into the den to begin boxing up some of the items in his desk drawers. At the very top of his main drawer, I found two pictures in elegant silver frames that really bothered me. One of a tall, pretty light skinned girl and the second of the same girl and Alain kissing. I knew I shouldn't be upset or even concerned, but the sight of him with that girl made me feel queasy.

"So how was it?" Reese asked with excitement.

"What are you talking about?"

"How big? How long? You know, the details!"

"I don't know."

"*What?*"

"There's nothing to tell. Nothing happened last night."

"Okay then, I'll just call you back tomorrow morning."

"I still won't have anything to tell."

"Why? Is Alain gay too?"

"No fool, he's not gay."

"Then what's the problem? How can you predict that nothing's going to go down tonight?"

"Because he thinks I'm celibate."

"Why in the hell would he think that?"

"He read it on my refrigerator."

"I told you a long time ago to take that shit down. You know good and well you never had any intentions of going celibate."

"Actually I was really serious about it after Mekhi."

"Yeah, serious for about three weeks before letting his best friend hit," she laughed.

"It was the wine, my judgment was impaired," I joked.

I left Alain's invitation to the Jean Co. event on the small table where he keeps his mail. He still had a great deal of packing to do but hopefully he could spare a couple of hours to come to the event.

About two hours into the party, after the majority of my work had been done, I felt someone tap me on the shoulder.

"Is the marketing and events guru allowed to dance?" Alain asked, smiling and looking extremely sexy in a white slim fit dress shirt, light gray British-cut suit, navy tie, white pocket square and modern framed glasses that were a cross between serious intellectual and fashion forward.

"Why yes," I replied, beaming as he bent down to kiss my jaw.

"Busy day?"

"In the afternoon, but not so much after you left this morning. I was able to finish packing up all of your dishes and desk stuff by noon."

"You have no clue of how much that helped. Thanks queen."

Wow, did he just call me queen?

Alain stuck around and waited for me to wrap things up after the party ended, which only took an hour. Afterwards we ended up at a nice jazz club off Lake Michigan and stayed until two in the morning. Luckily we were able to find a wonderful balcony seat overlooking the water before the crowd started filing in. We sat and talked the night away, and the later it got, the more I found myself staring at him in amazement. How can a man be so handsome? I honestly didn't hear half of what he was saying because I was watching his lips more than listening to them. Before we left, he took my hand as we walked over to a quiet secluded corner of the balcony. He stood behind me and wrapped me in his arms as we watched the hypnotic waves of the water, then after a few minutes he turned me around to face him and gave me a different kind of kiss. This time, the way his tongue caressed my lips so lightly, yet intensely, I could tell that he was on the same sensual vibe I was. When he pulled me closer, my instincts were validated in a different way, one I could feel throbbing against my lower abdomen.

Back at his apartment, we could barely get in the door before we were ripping away at each other clothes. My heart was racing a hundred miles per hour as his fingertips traced the form of my bra as we engaged in the most passionate kiss I'd ever experienced in my life. Just as I was about to undo my bra strap, he stopped me.

"Not yet," he said smiling. "I want to savor this."

We fell asleep on his living room couch in each other's arms, still in our underwear, wrapped up in a fuzzy blanket.

I felt Alain get up a couple of hours later then heard the sound of the shower in his hall bathroom. Although my inner voice was telling me to open the door, get in the shower and strike up a hot, passionate lust session with him, I didn't. I was actually enjoying this game of sexual charades. The only way I can explain it is, not having him is only making me want him that much more.

SATURDAY, 9/30

We woke up early this morning, packed a few more boxes then caravanned back down to Indianapolis. Alain took a nap at my apartment before he had to go pick up the keys to his new place while I went to work out. After I left the gym I went to check on Celeste to see how she was holding up before the big day. She had a house full of hectic people, mainly John's family, fussing over things like the wedding program and napkin rings, yet surprisingly she was relatively calm.

"Celeste, let me know what you need me to do to help."

"Chris, everything's fine. As you can see I have an army of people helping, actually too many people because they're starting to get on my nerves. Besides, your sister just left an hour ago to set up the church for tonight. She's actually been the biggest help. Can you believe she got here at six this morning and ran errands for me all day? I've got to give her a little something extra for all she's done above and beyond what I originally asked. That girl is a God-send."

"I'm proud of her."

"You should be. You taught her well," she said as she remembered something. "Oh, I forgot to ask, is Alain in town?"

"Yeah, he's pretty much here for good."

"Well let him know that John wants him to come to his bachelor party tonight."

"I'll do that."

"Maybe he can be a mole and fill us in on what happened."

"You know, that's not such a bad idea!"

"Is John having strippers at his bachelor party?" Alain asked as he laid his clothes out for tonight.

"His brother is planning it, so knowing him, yes."

"Well, you don't have to worry about me getting buck wild," he said laughing.

"I'm not worried, I trust you," I said, pinching his cheek.

"I'm glad to hear that because as your man, you can trust that I won't disrespect this beautiful thing we have. Oh, did I just say that? What I meant was, as your friend," he said smiling as he put on his shoes.

"Are you really ready to be my man," I asked as I straddled him and sat on his lap.

"Girl, you've had my undivided attention since the fashion show. I've been your man longer than you've realized."

I had to get my nails done, pick up an outfit for tonight and get a wedding gift for Celeste before getting ready for the rehearsal. When I got home I instantly smelled Alain's cologne lightly floating in the air, I could also hear the water running from the bathroom and the sounds of Alain humming "Drop It Like It's Hot."

"Honey, I'm home," I yelled, laughing from the living room. "I see that you're already singing strip club carols."

He started laughing with embarrassment from inside the bathroom as he shut off the water then walked into the living room.

As good as he looked, he could have been singing a medley of country hits and I wouldn't have cared.

"Aren't you running late for your photo shoot?"

"You are too funny," he said then kissed me on the side of my neck.

"I love this look," I said as I began to circle him. "You've got this whole neo-soul, preppy, sophisticate thing going on."

"Now if it doesn't work then tell me. I don't want to walk around looking crazy."

"Oh, believe me, it works."

Alain and I drove to the rehearsal together and when we arrived, Angela was already there hard at work setting up decorations. She looked gorgeous in the black tailored suit I bought for her and a white Image Brokers tank top underneath. She'd gotten her long, thick hair ironed out and probably visited the M.A.C. counter before she arrived because her make-up was flawless. As I stood there admiring my sister on how good of a job she was doing representing Image Brokers, I was startled out of my thoughts.

"Christian, what's up?" Frankie said in a drugged out voice.

"Oh, hi Frankie," I said, trying to look pleasant while wondering what Angela saw in this man.

"And you are?" Frankie said as he extended his hand towards Alain.

"Alain Hughes."

"Dude, nice meeting you."

"Nice to meet you too," Alain said. "So are you related to the bride or groom?"

"Neither," I reluctantly interjected. "He's one of Angela's friends."

"Ah, a little more than that," he said laughing. "So Alain, am I saying it right?" he asked as Alain nodded yes. "That's a pretty unique name. Does it have an origin?"

"Well it's French but I was named after Alain Locke."

"I'm not familiar with him. Is he famous?"

As I listened to Alain give Frankie a crash course in black history, I looked over at Angela again, then back at Frankie. I couldn't figure it out and the confusion gave me a headache.

"Okay everyone, please gather around so we can get started," Angela said assertively through the microphone then looked at me and smiled.

"I'm going to go have a seat. I'll be watching you," Alain said as he squeezed my hand.

"I'll sit over here with you," Frankie said to Alain, patting his back as if they were old chums from back in the day.

"We're going to need to get this right, fairly quickly, because dinner reservations are at nine and we have to be out of here by eight thirty. Bridesmaids and groomsmen, Celeste doesn't want anything fancy, just a basic walk down the aisle with your arms linked. Mom and uncle, walk slowly and don't forget to smile. Alright, I need all of the girls and guys to go to the back of the sanctuary and line up by height. Mom and uncle just stand-by until I give you your cue. Okay, let's get this show on the road," Angela said while clapping her hands for us to get a move on it.

"Angela better work it out!" Reese said to me as we walked down the aisle to take our places.

"She's doing pretty good."

"She's doing very good," Carra said.

"You're right, she is."

"And she looks so much different than she did the last time I saw her. She's always been cute, but Angela's really stepped her game up," Reese said.

"She's absolutely gorgeous," Carra added. "I see someone else over there looking good too," she said tapping me as she directed her attention towards Alain.

"I probably already know that answer to this, but did you guy's ever…"

"Girl, we are in church," I said as Resse laughed and shook her head.

"Where's Celeste?" Carra asked looking around the massive sanctuary.

"Good question. I don't know," I replied, realizing that we hadn't seen the bride all evening.

"Ms. V, where's Celeste?" Reese asked Celeste's mother.

"She's back in the dressing room getting her dress altered."

"Could someone go and get the bride?" Angela asked through the mic.

"I'll get her!" I yelled up to Angela.

As I rushed down the dim, long and borderline scary halls of the cathedral, the eyes of the statues and pictures of Christ were following me.

"I know what you're thinking, I haven't forgotten about you. I still believe," I whispered to a large painting of Jesus.

When I got to the dressing room Sarah, the seamstress, was standing beside a hunched over Celeste, patting her back and trying to calm her down.

"What's wrong?" I mouthed to Sarah trying not to startle Celeste.

Sarah rolled her eyes up, shook her then sighed, "Enough already, we're already running late and there's nothing you can do about your face and boobs. You're pregnant, that can't be reversed. The dress looks wonderful on you so sit up and get out there because they can't begin the rehearsal without you," Sarah snapped as Celeste slowly sat up and frowned at her.

"Give me a moment, please," Celeste said to Sarah.

"I'll be in the sanctuary," Sarah said, walking out the door shaking her head.

"What's wrong?"

"Would you look at this?" Celeste hissed. "I look like Jabba the Hutt in this dress."

I tried to hold back my laugh but I couldn't.

"See, I knew it."

"Celeste, you look the same as you did at the last fitting. You've only gained nine pounds."

"It looks like fifty."

"You look fine. We need to get you out of this dress before Angela comes back here. We're running behind schedule and everyone's irritable and hungry."

"What's going on back here?" Reese yelled as she, Carra and Angela busted through the doors.

"Celeste's upset because she thinks she looks fat."

"Give me a break," Reese snapped. "No one can even tell that you're pregnant."

"I don't mean to rush you Celeste but we only have forty-five minutes left to rehearse. Now, we can go ahead and practice so that things will run smoothly or we can just wing it tomorrow and hope for the best." Angela said patiently.

"My goodness, can't I get an ounce of sympathy over here?" Celeste asked as she looked around at all of us.

"No!" we all said in unison.

"Okay, okay I'll be right out."

When we walked back into to the sanctuary the whole room fell silent. Everyone was trying to figure out what was going on, especially John who looked the most puzzled.

Rehearsal went on as planned for about forty-five minutes then immediately after we all left on two plush charter buses for dinner. All throughout the evening the guys kept mumbling and laughing to one another and although they thought that they were being slick, it was blatant and obvious they were talking about their post dinner activities. John's brother Seth kept excusing himself from the table to make suspicious phone calls on his cell and every time he would return Chad, the best man, would give a gesture as if to say, *is everything still okay?*

"I guess they're trying to make sure the stripper's still on for tonight," Reese whispered to me, noticing the same suspicious activity. "Don't worry, I've got the ladies taken care of this evening. I hired four men."

"Four men? Do we really need that many?" I asked as the waiter interrupted to take our drink orders.

"I'll have a Bailey's Shaken but served Straight with a shot of Frangelico," I said then turned to smile at Alain as he joked and laughed with the other guys.

"I'm just going to have a virgin daiquiri," Reese told the waiter.

"A virgin daiquiri? Since when have you ever been associated with anything virgin?"

"I'm on this new medication and I'm not supposed to be drinking. Believe me, I'm not thrilled about it at all."

"Are you feeling okay?"

"Yeah, just peachy," Reese said sarcastically.

After dinner, the elders said their goodbyes and the sexes parted ways because it was time to get the parties started.

"I'll have Carra bring me home tonight," I said to Alain as we walked down the street towards the parking lot.

"Have fun," he said, winking at me.

"You too, but not that much," I said, winking back.

As we turned the corner and walked toward the buses, there was a sleazy looking late-model Bonneville parked behind the bus that the guys were staking claim.

"Uh, uh ladies the first bus is ours!" Seth yelled out to the girls as we walked toward their sacred bus.

"What's the difference?" Reese snarled at Seth.

"Reese, you really need to get laid more often. You know, to release all of that pent up sexual frustration," Seth yelled out in his frat boy tone as the guys ran towards the bus.

Reese replied with a nice, long, manicured middle finger in his face, and Seth caught her off guard by grabbing and kissing it.

"Call me, I can help you with that. I'm an equal opportunity lender," he said as she snatched her hand away.

Once we got settled on our bus and before we were about to pull off, two skanky looking blonds hopped out of the Bonneville onto the guys' bus. As soon as the girls boarded, their driver took off with fury.

"What in the…" Celeste said as she squinted to catch the last glimpse of their bus speeding away.

"Never fear ladies, the mistress of sin has everything taken care of! Forget them!" Reese said as she opened one of three big bags she had in her hand. Just then, she began distributing large, life-like, cherry flavored candy penises, equipped with veins and testicles, to everyone on the bus.

"You are too nasty," I said, examining the package while Carra nodded in agreement.

"I would've thought you'd be happy to get this since you've been missing out on the real thing lately," she whispered to me before continuing down the aisle to pass out the edible, anatomical party favor.

After it was all said and done, I would have had a better time hanging out on the couch with Alain for the rest of the night. We ended up going to a male review where there were hundreds of desperate women screaming and shoving to get a glance at The Dark Hurricane, Bullet Proof, The Ebony Knight and Atomic. After the show, Reese arranged for our group to get a private showing in a smaller banquet room within the building. These men were obviously confident about their endowment because each one of them stripped down to nothing to dance, bump and grind for us for the next two hours. Maybe if they weren't so greasy or didn't look like long lost members of the group Full Force, I would've had a better time. As a matter of fact, the only person who seemed to really enjoy the show was Reese, who rubbed, hugged and stroked each one of the men personally.

"You two are a bunch of sorry, sexless, old-maids who don't know how to have a good time," Reese barked after Carra and I got back on the bus.

"Reese please," I said, just wanting to go home and end the night.

"I'm serious. I'm embarrassed about what happened in there," she said, frowning and rolling her eyes. "I went out of my way to get that private room for you tricks. You don't know the hoops that I had to jump through to get the guys to do a private performance for us. The promoter was dead set against it until I assured him that the guys would make good money in tips. I bet they didn't even make twenty dollars between the four of them."

None of us had the will or energy to argue with Reese, we just let her rant and rave until she wore herself out.

When I got home I found Alain sleeping on my living room couch under my fuzzy flannel blanket, barely covering his naked chest. Although I tried my best to shut the door quietly, it clicked so loud that he woke up when he heard it.

"Hey gorgeous," he said, rubbing his eyes. "Did you have fun tonight?"

"It was okay. We went to a sorry excuse for a male review, then had to suffer through two additional hours of watching the same broke down men gyrate in our faces. You should have seen the way those Italian girls were looking at those brothers."

"I bet they didn't know how to react."

"To say the least."

"I'm sure Reese had a good time."

"Yes, and she couldn't understand why she was the only one turned on by a big greasy dude with an S-Curl!"

"Oh it was like that?" Alain laughed.

"You have no clue. So enough about the girls what did the guys do?"

"I can't tell you that."

"What?" I said, hitting him with a pillow.

"Okay, okay. First off, I know you saw the two girls who got on our bus. Well they ended up looking like trashy trailer park chicks, so needless to say the guys weren't too happy about that. Then to top it off, they were only hired to dance for us on the bus on our way to play laser tag."

"Laser tag?"

"I know. What made matters worse was in the middle of the bus performance one of the dancers tripped and twisted her ankle so bad that she wasn't able to finish, and since she was hurt the other girl refused to dance by herself."

"Ha ha. After all the hard work Seth put in."

"Yeah, he was pissed."

"So did you have fun playing laser tag?"

"It was too crowded so I didn't play. I basically sat in the arcade area and talked to Frankie the whole time."

"Umm," I said as I turned my head.

"I take it you don't like him?"

"I don't dislike him, I just dislike the relationship he's in with my sister."

"I could tell."

"Alain, believe me when I tell you, this is just another one of Angela's stunts," I said as Alain looked at me confused. "I'll explain it later, let's just get some sleep."

SUNDAY, 10/1

Thank goodness our bridesmaid gowns are black because it's *menstrual show* time again. I should've known this would happen to me today.

Alain and I woke up late at nine fifty-three and scrambled to get ready for the ceremony, which began at twelve thirty. I rolled my hair, jumped in the shower and shaved my legs in record time. Alain jumped in after me and although he didn't want to, he ended up using my lavender body wash because he forgot to bring his. It was fun teasing him about the benefits of smelling feminine fresh all day.

Since Celeste wanted this ceremony to be low maintenance, she asked for us to arrive at the cathedral dressed and ready no later than 11am. Luckily my apartment is only a few blocks away.

At ten twenty-five I called Angela who was thankfully already at the church.

"Is everything okay?"

"Sort of."

"What do you mean sort of?"

"Well, the florist hasn't arrived and they're not answering the emergency number, also the violinist got sick and won't be showing up so we're scrambling to hire one last minute and to top it all off, we're going to have to reorder the back-up tent we cancelled a few days ago for the reception since it's now a seventy-five percent chance of rain," she said as I looked out the window to a sky full of gray clouds.

The moment I got off the phone with Angela, I called every florist and violinist in my network to see if they could help save the day. Last minute flip-ups don't typically get me frazzled, but since this is my girl's big day, I started to get nervous. I tried to regain calm by fixing a cup of chamomile tea, but my tranquility turned into chaos after dropping a gallon jug of spring water all over my kitchen floor.

"Damn it!" I yelled as I jumped to grab a roll of paper towels and slipped.

All the while, Alain was standing in the doorway watching me look like a deranged lunatic in a half open bath robe, underwear, stockings with a head full of rollers and a clay mask on my face. Now he, on the other hand, stood there looking delicious with a towel wrapped around his waist, flashing that million-dollar smile. I quickly forgot about my problems when my eyes focused on a special muscular area right below the waistline, the one that my girls commonly referred to as *the V*, made famous by D'Angelo in his "How Does it Feel" video.

"Are you going to make it?" he asked, smirking at me.

"I guess," I said, trying to look away from his towel and regain my composure. "I just can't believe everything that's happening this morning."

"What do you mean? Everything was just fine before I got into the shower."

"Yeah, but now all hell has broken loose. I just spoke to Angela and things are starting to fall apart."

"Let me give you a hand," he said, grabbing a large wad of paper towels. "Why don't you check in with Angela while I finish up in here."

"Hey Angela, is everything okay?" I asked, obviously sounding hectic.

"Yeah, we're getting everything under control."

"Do you still need my help?"

"No disrespect but I didn't need your help to begin with. You called me wanting to know how everything was going and I told you. Everything's fine now. Chill out," she replied, sounding a little annoyed.

"Is everything alright?" Alain asked handing me a cup of tea.

"Angela says everything's fine."

"I knew it was going to turn out to be okay," Alain said matter-of-factly.

"I guess I just need to concentrate on getting ready," I said as I got up and walked into the bathroom.

As I washed the mask off of my face, I began to wonder how anal I must come off to Angela. She probably won't ever want to work for me again, I thought as I unrolled my hair. Unfortunately with every roller I removed, my morning got worse. To my horror, my hair looked like George Washington's wig.

"Aaaugghh!" I cringed as I tried to comb it back into an up-do, but it just turned into a frizzy, bushy mess.

"Are you alright in there?" Alain asked as he knocked on the door.

"Now my hair isn't cooperating."

"Can I come in?"

"I guess, but be prepared. I don't look like the same woman from last night."

"As far as I'm concerned, Christian is Christian," he said opening the door.

As he stood there looking at my hair he couldn't hold back his laugh.

"I don't believe this. You're supposed to be consoling me in my time of need."

"I'm sorry queen. I like the look. It's Ronald McDonald chic."

"You're really not helping any."

"I know, I know. I apologize," he said cracking up as my phone started ringing, only making me more nervous.

"Why are you still at home?" Reese asked.

"Because my hair is a big swollen mess. I kept my hot rollers in for too long."

"Girl, spray some oil sheen on your hair, wrap it up tight and come on here!" she said then hung up on me.

When we got to the church at a quarter after eleven, I had Alain drop me off at the back entrance so I could sneak in without anyone seeing me in my elegant gown and greasy head rag.

254

"I'll see you inside," Alain said, leaning over to kiss me then teasingly tugged at my scarf.

I tried to be inconspicuous as I darted to the back staircase but sure enough guess who I saw, Darius and his date, who looked at me like I had the plague.

"Christian, aren't you in the wedding?"

"Yes, and I don't really have much time to talk. I'll see you at the reception," I said running up the stairs, smack dab into a crowded hallway.

"Looks like somebody had a rough one last night," Seth said as I rushed past all of the groomsmen who were already lining up to go downstairs.

"Not now Seth."

Once I entered the dressing room, Reese attacked me with a wide tooth comb and bobby pins.

"Sit down. You're going to be the reason this wedding runs on C.P. time."

"Am I the last person to arrive?"

"Yes."

"Where's Car?"

"Over there about to commit suicide," Reese said, unintentionally jabbing me in the scalp with a bobby pin.

I looked over to find Carra sitting on a pillow in the window-seat staring out into the heavens while dabbing her eyes.

"Now what's wrong with her?"

"Who knows, probably hormones or something. Whatever it is, I can't take much more of it."

"Just leave her alone," I said while trying to adjust my bustier. "Are you and Martin still going to Negril this week?"

"Yeah, we're leaving on Wednesday," she said nonchalantly.

"You don't sound too thrilled."

"Girl, this trip is going to be dry as hell. Just thinking about spending more than three days straight with him is like overdosing on Nytol."

"Then don't go."

"Are you crazy? This is Jamaica we're talking about."

"Reese, you need to quit playing with that brother's head. Martin is a good guy. Yeah, he can be a little stiff at times but I know a lot of women who would give anything to be with him."

"Well if they want him they can have him. Until then, I'm going to continue to enjoy these free trips and pretend that I have a headache every night."

"All of this is going to come back to you, just wait and see."

Once Reese finished styling my hair, I looked like a new woman.

"See there, just leave it up to me and I can transform frog into a princess."

"That's right, you did a great job getting yourself ready this morning."

"Whatever," she laughed as she went over my hair with a little oil sheen and hair spray.

"Let me go over and see what's wrong with Car."

"You'll be wasting your time," Reese said, looking towards Carra and shaking her head.

When I walked up behind Carra, I placed my hand on her back and smiled, "What's wrong, sweetie?"

She just shook her head and dabbed her eyes.

"Something has to be wrong or you wouldn't be over here all teary eyed."

She was about to say something until she looked up and saw Reese walking over, after that she turned back to face the window.

"Are you going to tell us what's bothering you or what?" Reese asked as she tried to pull Carra's hands away from her eyes.

"I'm reflecting on…" Carra said solemnly then took a deep breath. "Love."

Reese let out a half laugh and began clapping, "Academy award winner for the best dramatic performance."

"Reese, cut it out. Carra, is everything okay with you and Aaron?"

"No."

"Come on, let's talk in the hall."

"Where are you two going? We're about to line up!" Angela barked.

"We're just going out in the hall, we'll be right back!" I replied as she rolled her eyes at me. She was taking this power thing way too seriously.

"Now what's up with you and Aaron?"

"Christian my marriage is falling apart," she said, crying.

"What's going on?"

"We're just not close anymore. He barely touches me anymore and last night…"

"Everyone needs to start lining up. Now!" Angela interrupted with an attitude as she stormed passed me and ran down the stairs.

"I'll talk to you about it later," Carra said then let out a big sigh.

As we walked down the hall to line up, Ms. V rushed up behind us with her hands waving in the air.

"You girls just have to see Celeste, she looks so beautiful!" she said, grabbing our hands and pulling us down the hall to the dressing room where we found Celeste standing in front of the mirror smiling at herself, trying to hold back the tears. I knew exactly what she was thinking. She deserved this. Celeste had been so patient and loving to John. I really hope he realizes what a treasure he has.

"Doesn't my princess look…," Ms. V said as she began to get choked up.

"Celeste, you look absolutely gorgeous," I said to her and gave her a big hug.

"This is the last call to line up!" Angela instructed to everyone with a stern look on her face.

"Congrats, girl. You've waited so long to go on lock-down and here it is. Today's the day!" Reese joked.

"Thanks," Celeste said then gave her a hug.

"Celeste, always be there for John no matter what. He can't always be the strong one when times get rough. Never forget to remind him of how much he means to you," Carra said and kissed Celeste on the cheek as Reese gave me a look.

"Did she tell you what's going on?" Reese whispered in my ear.

"I don't know just yet, but you need to be more sensitive to her."

"Alright ladies, it's show time," Angela said, trying to bring some excitement back into the room. "Everybody wipe the running make-up off of your faces and get happy! This is a celebration, not a funeral!"

"Amen to that," Reese said under her breath.

As we began to walk down the stairs to the main foyer, all you could see was a sea of people through the stained glass window leading into the sanctuary. It was the largest wedding attendance I'd ever seen. Despite the big crowd, I was able to spot Alain from a mile away. My goodness he's handsome. Every time I see him my heart flutters. He is definitely my soul mate, I thought as I took my place in between John's sister Heather and Reese.

As the orchestra began to play, a bright ray of sunshine beamed in through the windows. It was almost as if the heaven's opened up on cue with the music.

"Do you Celeste Alonna Venditore take John Alfred Marinucci to be your lawfully wedded husband?"

"I do with all my heart."

"Do you John Alfred Marinucci take Celeste Alonna Venditore to be your lawfully wedded wife?"

"You bet!" he belted as the crowd began to laugh.

As the ceremony went on, Alain stared at me the whole time we stood at the altar. I couldn't help but wonder if he was thinking the same thing I'd been thinking all afternoon. As Celeste and John were making this big commitment to take their relationship to a higher level, Alain and I were at the very early stages of something extremely beautiful.

The sun finally came out when we arrived at the art museum for the reception. It was a wise choice to reorder the tent because every time the wind blew, rain droplets fell from the leaves on the trees. The setting was absolutely beautiful and best of all, Celeste seemed to be so pleased with how everything turned out. After dinner was served and everyone began to relax, Angela came over to me and whispered that she needed to talk later on. I could tell that she was pissed so I tried to save face by complimenting her on the great job she was doing. All she did was look at me like I was patronizing her and walked away. I was being truthful, the whole day went flawless and she did it by herself.

Everyone sniffed and dabbed tears from their eyes as the new couple danced to the first song. Celeste looked oblivious to the world as she gazed into John's eyes while they danced the night away.

MONDAY, 10/2

Alain left for Chicago early this morning to get more stuff still at his old apartment. Since he was planning to make two trips today, I cleared my schedule to go back with him later on tonight. UniLink provided him with a moving company but Alain took it upon himself to rent an extra truck to tote his books, files of his poems and writings, his rare jazz albums, his family pictures and original artwork, "the priceless things" as he calls it.

"You should sleep in this morning," Alain whispered as he lightly kissed my cheek. "I'll be back no later than four o'clock."

"I'll be ready when you get here," I said, groggy and half-asleep.

For the most part I worked on invoices all day, scheduled a couple of appointments for the week then went for a quick workout. By the time four o'clock rolled around I was all set and ready to meet up with Alain. By a quarter til' seven, I still hadn't heard anything from him. Once eight o'clock rolled around with no word from him, I started to worry. When he finally called a little after nine I was almost on the verge of contacting highway patrol.

"Christian, please don't be upset with me."

"Upset? I'm not upset I'm worried. Are you alright?"

"Yeah, I'm okay."

"I should have gone with you this morning. I didn't realize you had that much left to do."

"It wasn't that much."

"So what took you so long?"

261

"I had a few things come up on my way out."

"I don't mean to pry, but is everything okay?"

"Just some unfinished business. It's nothing."

I didn't want my mind to go there but I've seen *Love Jones*. I know what unfinished business usually means, I thought as I tried not to get upset.

"So where are you now?"

"I'm still in Chicago."

"Alain, what's going on?"

"Christian, it's really hard to explain."

I hesitated for a second then decided to go ahead and say what I was really feeling.

"Does this have to do with some woman?"

"Christian it's not what you think. She…"

"Just do what you gotta' do," I snapped then abruptly hung up the phone.

I didn't mean to pull a Reese on him but damn it, I'm not stupid. Unfinished business, does he think I was born yesterday? The phone rang minutes after I hung up on him but I was too pissed to answer it.

After being asleep for several hours I was startled awake by the sound of something falling in my living room. I laid there petrified for about five minutes and listened for the sound again. After a few minutes I heard my living room window open and the sound of footsteps on my fire escape. Shit, I thought as I mustered up the courage to slide out of bed and dash into the bathroom. Standing there in fight or flight mode, I was so nervous that I had to pee like crazy. The more I thought about it the more urgent I had to go but common sense was telling me that this wasn't the time to take a restroom break. I couldn't hold it anymore and could barely get my pants down all the way before I heard more noises, this time coming from the hallway. I quickly wiped then looked around for the sharpest item I could use as some sort of weapon. I have a butcher knife under my mattress for this very reason and of course I didn't think to bring it or my cell phone, I thought as my heart raced a mile a minute. I put my ear against the door and soon as I did someone on the other side pushed the door open.

"*Aaaahhh!*" I screamed at the top of my lungs as I hit the person on the hand with my big barrel curling iron.

"*Owww!* A voice yelled after I whacked them on the knuckles. "Calm down, it's just me," Alain said, coming in and shaking his hand in pain.

"What's wrong with you? Why didn't you call me to let me know you were coming?" I said, trying to catch my breath. "If I'd remembered to bring my knife to the bathroom you'd be bleeding right now!"

"I tried calling back after you hung up but you wouldn't pick up the phone," he said clutching his hand. "Christian, how could I not come back after what happened earlier?"

"Who is she?"

"A woman I dated off and on."

"So what's the status? Are you still seeing her or what?" I said with my arms folded.

"No, I'm not still seeing her. But I think I should let you know that I plan on remaining friends with her."

"Do what you gotta do," I said as I walked back into my bedroom.

"Queen, she was recently diagnosed with lupus," he said then gently held my face. "The relationship I had with her is over but I still love her as a friend. *You're* the only woman in my life."

I felt bad about over reacting. I had my guard up because I didn't want to set myself up for heartbreak and disappointment if they ever decided to rekindle what they had.

"Do you have to go back to Chicago tomorrow?"

"I have to make one more trip," he said giving me a sincere look. "If you're free will you come with me?"

"Yes," I replied as I reached for his hand. "I'm sorry for blowing up earlier. Let's get some rest, tomorrow's a new day."

He stood there and gazed at me.

"You are a true queen," he said, stroking my cheeks then closed his eyes and rested his forehead against mine. "I only wish you knew how I feel about you."

TUESDAY, 10/3

On the road to Chicago, we kept the conversation light and free of any mention of what happened yesterday. Shortly after paying our first toll outside of Gary, Indiana, Alain got a call on his cell.

"Hello…This is he…How serious is it…Which hospital…What's her room number…Thanks," Alain said, distraught.

"Is everything alright?"

"No," he said then paused. "My friend Paula, the one with lupus, well she was admitted to the hospital this morning."

"How's she doing?"

"I'm not sure."

"Do you need to go and see her today?" I said feeling embarrassed by how I acted yesterday.

"Yeah."

"Go ahead and drop me off at your place. I can finish boxing up your records while you're at the hospital."

"No, I actually want you to come with me."

"I don't know…"

"I need you to come with me so you'll feel more comfortable about this."

"Does she even know about me? I mean, how is she going to feel laying in her sick bed and you come strolling in with your new woman?"

"Everything will be fine."

We headed straight to the hospital as soon as we arrived in Chicago. When we got to Paula's room she was asleep and unaware that we were there. She was definitely the girl from the pictures I found while packing Alain's stuff the other day. There were two other people in the room who at first seemed very pleased to see Alain then changed their tune once they saw me.

"Christian, this is Paula's sister Lynette."

"Nice meeting you," I whispered as I extended my hand, only to find Lynette hesitant to shake it. After a tight and damn near painful handshake, Lynette looked back at Alain, squinted then rolled her eyes.

"I think it'll be best for me to sit out in the lobby and wait for you," I whispered as Alain began walking towards a small sofa in the room.

"You don't have to. You can stay right here," he said as he pulled me alongside him while Lynette stared with the most evil look anyone has ever given me.

"Alain, I think it'd be best if I sat outside," I said then lightly snatched my arm away and walked out the door to the nearest bathroom.

I felt like I was I thrown in the middle of some obvious static between Alain and Paula's family. I didn't plan on being here today and I don't want to be here now, I thought as my blood boiled. Alain tried to make it seem as if everything was cool but that obviously wasn't the case.

I found a quiet table in the lobby next to a window and as I sat there pondering the situation at hand I looked up towards the elevator and saw Alain wandering around looking for me. I didn't say anything and I didn't move, I just turned back towards the window and acted like I didn't see him. About a minute later I got a call on my cell.

"Babe, where are you?"

"In the lobby."

"I've been looking all over for you."

"I'm right here," I replied, lifting my hand as he walked towards me.

I turned back around to face the window while he pulled up a chair.

"I'm so sorry about what happened up there."

"What's going on?"

"I didn't realize Lynette was going to act like that."

"This is too weird for me. I'm just going to wait down here until you finish doing what you need to do."

After being at his house for several hours, we sat on the floor in silence as we finished packing his albums and pictures. I didn't have any idle conversation or small talk to strike up and when Alain did ask me a question I rarely had a full sentenced response.

"I can't take this anymore. Christian, will you please talk to me. What's on your mind?"

"It shouldn't be a big mystery."

"What do you mean by that?"

"What do you think?"

"Haven't I already apologized?"

"Alain, it didn't appear that her family had any clue that you've moved on," I said with a hint of attitude.

"Like I said before Paula and I are no longer together. I was only trying to be a friend by visiting her today and I guess I made a mistake by bringing you to the hospital."

"Her sister made that very clear."

"I've apologized to her, I've apologized to you, what more do you want?"

"You need to use better judgment next time."

"Christian, you're overreacting."

"I'm overreacting?" I said fuming before getting up and going into the den. Alain immediately followed me.

"I'm sorry, I shouldn't have said that. I don't want us to start off like this," he said then kneeled down in front of me and laid his head in my lap. "Queen, I just want for this to work," he said then wrapped his arms tightly around my waist.

WEDNESDAY, 10/4

"Hey girl, I just called to let you know we're about to leave for Negril."

"I don't know whether to be happy or not," I replied laughing.

"Don't start. Anyway, has the bedroom status changed between you and Alain?"

"No, and I won't say anything else about it," I said, looking at Alain who never took his eyes off of the road.

"I don't know. Like I said before he might have a little sugar in his tank."

"Shut up Reese."

"I'm just saying, I don't know of any man who would restrain himself from trying to get down with a beautiful woman prancing around his house in lingerie."

"You are truly one of a kind. I'll talk to you later."

"And?"

"And I shouldn't say it, but have fun."

"That's more like it. I'll tell you all about my trip when I get back on Monday."

We ran into a lot of traffic on our way back and after Alain dropped me off at my house, I had a ton of work to catch up on then had to rush to attend two meetings across town. On my way to the last meeting I made a pit stop back home to wash my face and grab my gym bag. As I was brushing my hair back, my door buzzer rang.

"Here's your stuff," Angela said as she walked in and laid the Image Brokers reference books on my coffee table.

"Thanks. How's it going?"

"Fine," she said in a dry tone.

"I've been meaning to congratulate you on doing such a good job at Celeste's wedding."

"Don't mention it," she said sarcastically, glaring at me.

"Look Angela, I know you're mad at me but I was only trying to help you."

"Is that what you call help?"

"Why can't we ever be civil? Why is it there's always something that prevents us from being cool?"

"Because you always create static between us. I can never do anything right in your eyes. You don't like the way I dress, where I live, who I date, how I live my life. If it doesn't adhere to your siddity ass standards then it's trash."

"Where in the hell is this coming from?"

"If you didn't think I was competent enough to handle the wedding by myself then why did you ask me to do it?"

"Obviously I thought you could manage it or else I wouldn't have asked you."

"Then why the hell were you following up behind me the whole time? Better yet, why were you purposely trying to not follow my directions when I needed things done? Instead of cooperating with me, you not only ignored my orders you yelled at me in front of everybody."

"I did not yell at you."

"Yes you did."

"*You* yelled at me."

"That's because I was trying to get you to line up."

"Fine, I'm sorry for yelling. Can we get over this?"

"No, because there are a few things I think little miss Christian needs to hear, things that everyone else is afraid to tell you because they don't want to ruffle miss high and mighty's feathers."

"Now you're trippin'."

"Look who's talking, someone who's going through an early mid-life crisis trying to be a supermodel. Don't think we don't know that you've basically been starving yourself. Reese told me all about your little escapades in New York and how you don't eat anything but Slim Fast bars, diet pills and water. You want to be skinny so bad that you'd rather kill yourself to do it quickly than to do it right. Secondly, you are the most superficial and judgmental person I know, that's why none of my friends want to be near you."

"I'm crushed," I said sarcastically.

"See what I mean. You think you're too good for everybody and since my friends don't mean anything to you, it doesn't make any difference whether they like you or not. Now, if they were members of high society and affiliated in all your little bourgeois sororities and fraternities then you'd be bending over backwards to get them to like you. I really hope Alain knows what he's getting himself into," she said, shaking her head.

"It's a shame that you feel this way after all these years. You obviously don't know me."

"Actually, I know you all too well."

271

THURSDAY, 10/5

Today was just one of those days where all I wanted to do was stay in bed. I didn't want to talk anyone. I didn't want to see anyone. All I wanted was to keep my blinds closed and to listen to Sade. The first lively move I made was to call all of the day's appointments to reschedule. After that, I turned off all the lights and got back in bed. As I was drifting off, Alain called wanting to come over for breakfast.

"Babe, I'm going to have to take a rain check. I just don't feel up to breakfast this morning."

"Well how about a candlelight dinner over my house? I've got some comfortable cardboard boxes we can sit on," he joked.

"That's cool. I'll come by around six."

"Don't try to back out of it either."

"Huh?"

"You are the only person I know who can function off of two lettuce leaves and a gallon of water a day," he said then chuckled.

"I eat, I just haven't had an appetite lately."

"Well you need to stop stressing out so much. You're too pretty to stress."

"That's why I like you," I said, beginning to feel a little better. "What are you getting into today?"

"I have to go to the office and try to get some things organized for my trip."

"What trip?"

"I thought I told you. I have to be in San Francisco all next week for a conference."

"When do you leave?"

"Sunday."

"When do you get back?"

"Next Sunday."

"That's the Sunday I leave for San Diego. We won't see each other for two whole weeks."

"Maybe I can do something to change that."

At noon, I finally dragged myself out of bed to check email. Guy had the nerve to send me a message saying that I was picking up heavy on film, especially in the arm and bust areas and that I needed to lose a few more pounds. How much more weight was I supposed to lose and ultimately for what? This was just for a measly art shoot that will nine times out of ten turn into nothing. My goodness, I thought as I headed out to the gym.

I ignored the loud and painful growling of my stomach as I ramped up the speed on the treadmill. For the first couple of minutes at a steady jogging pace I felt fine, then all of a sudden I got really dizzy and nauseous. All I can remember after that was reaching up for my water bottle and never actually grabbing it. The next thing I knew I was laying on a table in a small room with several people standing over me doing random things, including one who was holding an ice pack pressed against my right eye.

"What's going on?" I asked, trying to sit up.

"Just calm down ma'am. Everything's going to be okay," a tall, bald white guy with a red beard said as he lightly pressed against my shoulder to get me to lay back down.

Just then, my dad rushed through the door in a panic.

"Is she alright?"

"She's just fine, her blood sugar's low and she's a little bruised up but other than that, she'll be okay," the guy said to my father. "If I've seen it once I've seen it a million times, people under eating and overexerting themselves."

I felt awful as the bald guy and another gentleman helped me out to my dad's car. My head was pounding and my stomach felt queasy.

I vaguely remember getting to my parent's house and them helping me into my old room. Shortly after, my mother opened the door and demanded that I eat the grilled chicken sandwich, popcorn and sherbet she had on a tray for me. Shortly after, I dozed off.

FRIDAY, 10/6

This morning I was awakened by the loud but heartwarming sounds of family life. I could hear the twins scrambling to get ready for school, my mother's aerosol hairspray can and the sound of my father's coffee cup clinking to the backdrop of Matt Lauer's voice. These were the very sounds that made me count down to the day when I could move out on my own. It's funny how now these same sounds are as safe and comforting as my favorite warm blanket.

"Are you awake?" Eva asked, lightly knocking on the door before peeking in.

"Yeah, I'm awake," I said, feeling a little lightheaded as I tried to sit up in the bed.

"Can I come in?"

"Yeah, come on in."

"How ya feelin'?"

"A little better. I'm still kind of dizzy but I should be fine."

"The scratch over your eye looks better."

"It still stings."

"You lucked out cause' it's pretty much in your eyebrow. I can barely see it," she said as she put some alcohol on a gauze pad and handed it to me. "I'm about to head off to school. I just wanted to check in with you before I left."

"Thanks, that's sweet of you," I said as she walked towards the door. "I want you to remember what we talked about, okay."

"I will. I'll never forget it," she said as she opened the door then paused. "There's something I want you to remember."

"What's that?"

"I think you're the most beautiful person in the world and you don't need to change a thing," she said, walking back to give me a hug. "Take care of yourself, Chris. I love you."

"I love you too."

When I finally got out of bed, I went downstairs to the den to find my dad in his favorite chair laughing at something Al Roker said. When he noticed me standing there his smile turned into a look of disappointment.

"How are you feeling this morning?" he asked in a dry tone.

"I feel better. Well, at least better than yesterday."

"You know, Angela came by here the other night and told us about you trying to do some type of modeling. Is that what this is all about?"

"What do you mean?" I said, playing dumb.

"I'm talking about you going on this crash diet," he said looking at me like I should have known what he was talking about. "You losing a considerable amount of weight in a little over of a month."

"Dad, you're jumping to conclusions. I'm just under a lot of stress with my company," I said as my dad looked at me as if he didn't believe me.

"Whatever you say. Just let me know when you want to go and pick up your car."

On our way back to the gym, my dad lectured me on the importance of living a healthy lifestyle. I felt like I was fifteen years old by the way he was carrying on. All of the things he said may have been more relevant a couple of weeks ago, hell even yesterday, but little did he know I'd already made it up in my mind that yesterday was the last day I would do anything like that ever again. No more being anal about calorie counting or exercising until I'm faint. Forget Guy and screw Eden, I'd had enough.

When I got home, I had three voice mail messages. Two from Alain, wondering why I didn't show up for dinner and the other from Nanna, scolding me for passing out at the gym.

"You ought to be ashamed of yourself, walking around here passin' out like some crazy person. Any other time I would've jumped to your rescue, but in this instance I thought, no, let her learn this lesson. I want you to remember how bad it feels to starve yourself. All this time you walked around here lying to everybody, but Angie told me the truth, uhh huh, she told me just what I'd been thinking all along. I can't figure out why someone who is already so beautiful would want to go out and change themselves so drastically—and at your age? What message do you think you're sending to Eva, huh? She looks up to you more than anybody. Eva is your clone. Not only does she look just like you, she's shaped like you too. You're sending her the message that it's not okay to be curvy and she should strive to be what society thinks we ought to look like. With the exception of Angela, and Lord only knows where she got her beanpole genes from, black women are meant to be voluptuous and curvy. Not obese but curvy. Black men don't want a little toothpick, they want an all true woman, complete with all the curves that come with it. If you don't believe me, ask your new boyfriend.

279

Now, I've pretty much said what I had to say and I hope that you think about what you're doing. You're not only hurting yourself, but also everyone around who loves you."

I'll just let her cool off for a couple of hours before I return her call, I thought as I deleted the message. Anytime my grandmother gets upset like that she goes on a rampage and won't let the other person get a word in edgewise. I did call Alain back to apologize for standing him up yesterday.

"Queen, are you okay?" Alain asked with a sense of urgency.

"I'm fine."

"Angela called this morning and told me everything."

I suppose Angela sent out a press release to the *Indianapolis Recorder* as well, I thought, annoyed that she felt the need to tell the whole world about what happened.

"Oh she did."

"That's beside the point," he barked. "Something told me that I should have been more vocal about your eating habits."

"Alain, I really don't feel like getting into this right now. Just trust me, you don't have to worry about that ever again."

"You promise?"

"I promise."

"Do you have dinner plans for this evening?"

"No."

"Well, I want to cook dinner for you tonight."

"Cardboard and candlelight?" I joked, attempting to lighten the mood.

"You know how we do," he laughed.

"After dinner do you want to come with me to the twin's homecoming? Eva's the co-captain of her cheerleading squad and Everett's deejaying for the party. I want to go and show a little support."

"I'd love to."

Alain and my dad really hit it off. During the game they talked politics, finance, sports and plethora of typical guy topics all while periodically jumping up and hollering at a touchdown. Everyone cheered for Eva as she led her squad in the tumbling stunts during halftime. She looked so cute as she waved back at us and gave me a cue that she knew Alain was sitting next to me. After the game was over, I introduced Alain to Eva who smiled from ear to ear as she talked to him. I looked around for Everett but he was nowhere to be found.

"He's probably setting up his equipment right now. We shouldn't bother him and make him nervous," mom said after my dad suggested that we all go into the gym full of kids to look for him.

After we left the game, my parents, Alain and I walked to an ice cream shop a couple of blocks from the twin's school. Everyone clapped and cheered when I ordered and finished a brownie fudge sundae. Alain even proposed a toast for me when we got back to his house.

"To the most beautiful woman in the world. May she realize her worth and accept that she is more stunning than any supermodel in the world. Here, here," he said, raising his glass.

"Here, here," I replied as I gladly welcomed back the old Christian.

SATURDAY, 10/7

Alain and I met up with Carra and Aaron this morning for brunch before the Circle City Classic game and it turned out to be a living hell. Alain discretely pinched my leg under the table as we sat and watched those two go at each other's throat about everything from which fork was the correct fork to use for salads, to what year Grambling's former coach, Eddie Robinson, retired. Whenever it would start to get bad, I would interject and try to change the subject to a more neutral topic. After brunch we walked around the pre-game outdoor marketplace before it was time for the game to start. After about an hour of browsing, Alain and Aaron sat down to listen to a local jazz musician which gave me a chance to talk to Carra alone.

"What's going on with you two?"

"Point blank, at the beginning of the year Aaron had this hair-brained idea that he wanted to quit his job and invest all of our savings into a startup technology firm with two of his colleagues. I flat out told him no, but he kept trying to convince me that we'd be better off in the long run. Well, he begged and begged for a couple weeks until I got fed up and couldn't take it anymore. I told him that either he go forth with the deal and find another wife or give it up and maintain a happy home. From the moment he told the guys that he wasn't going to go through with the partnership, he's been a complete asshole. Especially when he found out that..." she said then paused.

"That what?"

"That his two would-be partners just landed a multi-million dollar contract."

"If you don't mind me asking, how much was everyone supposed to invest?"

"A hundred and fifty grand."

"Whoa."

"Christian can you blame me? What was I supposed to do, let him gamble on our future and possibly blow all of our money? How was I supposed to know this business was going to succeed?"

"Carra, you don't have to explain anything to me. I understand," I said. But as an entrepreneur, I also understood Aaron's perspective as well, I thought as we stood in front of a booth full of African sculptures. "This would really look good in Alain's living room," I said as I picked up a small mahogany tribal mask mounted on a stand. "I think I'm going to get this for him. Are you getting anything for Aaron?" I said jokingly to lighten up the mood.

"I'd rather get something for myself," Carra said while browsing through the art pieces. "How about this?" she said, holding up a long, sharp spear.

"Are you sure it's big enough?" I asked sarcastically as I pointed to a longer spear with a sharper arrowhead displayed behind the merchant's table.

"You're right. Sir, I'll take that long spear behind you," Carra said to the vender as he smiled and pointed to the tallest one behind him.

"This one?" he asked as Carra nodded her head. "Good, good choice. That'll be one hundred and thirty-five dollars," he said, smiling from ear to ear.

"Do you take Visa?"

"Yes we do," he said then looked at me. "And is that all for you ma'am?"

"Yes."

"That will be twenty-five dollars."

As I handed over my cash, I looked at Carra who was gloating as she watched the vender's assistant wrap paper around her new spear.

"Carra, we're at least ten blocks away from the car, not to mention the game starts in a half hour. Where are you going to put that thing?"

"I'm sure these fine people will hold my spear while we're at the game," she said as she batted her eyes at the two men.

"Oh yes, yes, yes. We'll be happy to hold it for you. How about you ma'am? Would you like for us to hold your mask?"

"No, it's small enough for me to carry."

The merchant smiled then looked back at Carra, "You have to come back before midnight or else we're all packed up and gone."

Aaron and Carra had game seats on the other side of the stadium, so after Alain and I said our goodbyes we headed up to the Unilink suite, got a couple of drinks and sunk into our plush box seats overlooking the field.

"I have to admit, you were right about Carra and Aaron. What's up with them?"

"It'll take until halftime to tell you," I said, taking a long sip of my pomegranate martini. "I can just sum it up as drama at its finest."

SUNDAY, 10/8

"Can you believe that we were pulling into the driveway last night before I realized that I'd forgotten my spear?" Carra said, smacking on something.

"Did you go back and get it?"

"No. By the time I realized it, it was already after midnight."

"So you basically just threw away a hundred and thirty dollars."

"Yeah, but believe me, it doesn't even compare to the amount of money Aaron blows on a daily basis."

It is way too early to get into all of this extra drama, I thought, almost missing my turn.

"Hey Carra, let me call you back because I'm about to drop Alain off at the airport."

As Alain and I sat at Starbucks before he went through security, he said something that surprised me.

"Paula and I were a lot like Carra and Aaron towards the end of our relationship. When it was good, it was good but when it was bad, it was a living hell. The bad days started to out weight the good and that's why we broke up."

"Well, breaking up is not an option for Carra. She'd rather live like that for the next forty years than get a divorce."

"I'm sure they'll work it out."

"Hopefully so."

Reality hit me as Alain prepared to go through security, it will be an entire two weeks before I see him again. Before he got in line, I pulled him close and simply held him.

"I know everyone probably thinks that you're about go away for a year by the way I'm acting, but who cares, I'm going to miss you," I said as onlookers smiled as they passed us.

"I'm going to miss you too."

"I better let you get in line before you miss your flight."

"Two weeks is too long Queen," he said before closing his eyes and leaning in to kiss me.

As I pulled into the parking lot of my apartment building, I saw Angela walking out the front door. She gave me a half smile and waved when she noticed my car.

"I was in the neighborhood and I thought I'd come by to check on you."

"Well isn't that sweet," I said smiling with a hint of sarcasm.

"I'm just fulfilling my sisterly duties," she said smiling.

"So you're not mad at me anymore?"

"Not at this moment, no."

"Do you still think I'm a bougie bitch?"

"Yeah, but I can learn to deal with it," she joked. "Christian, I'm sorry about the other day. Can we start over?"

"What do you think?" I said as I walked over to embrace my sister. "I'm sorry too. I didn't mean to disrespect you."

"No problem. Now that we've gotten that out of the way, do you have a little time to hang out?"

"Yeah. You know what, I'm actually a little hungry, what about you?" I asked as Angela gave me a shocked and surprised look.

"*You're* hungry?"

"That's what I said."

"It's a miracle! She's saved!" Angela shouted in the middle of the parking lot.

"Would you shut up?" I said, laughing at her.

"No, I just can't contain my joy!" she joked as she threw her arm around me. "Seriously, I'm happy that you've come to your senses."

"Trust me, you don't ever have to worry about me starving myself again."

"Good, now where do you want to go eat? I'm buyin' today."

"*You're* buying? You're right, it is a miracle! I better enjoy this now because I'm sure it'll never happen again," I laughed as she playfully squinted her eyes at me. "I'm in the mood for a good deli sandwich, let's walk over to City Market and chill out for a while."

"Sounds good to me."

During our walk, I was reintroduced to my sister. There's always so much tension between us that I'd honestly forgotten just how great a friend she is.

"Guess what?" Angela asked after taking a big swig of her lemonade.

"What?"

"Frankie and I broke up."

"You're kidding me?" I said, trying not to sound overjoyed.

"Go ahead and cheer. You know you want to."

"Yes!" I said, pumping my fist in the air. "Sorry, I couldn't contain myself."

"That's alright," she said, shaking her head. "You know what, I saw it coming."

"Really? I couldn't tell."

"That's because I didn't want to prove you right, miss-know-it-all."

"I tried to tell you, but you wouldn't listen."

"I should have but you know what, Frankie wasn't a bad guy. I still really dig him as a friend."

"So what happened?"

"Let's just say that his recreational habit was starting to become full time."

"I knew he was on something."

"You could tell?"

All I could do was look at her and laugh. She had to laugh herself because anyone with sight could sense that Frankie was high at any given time from a mile away.

"I have some other news for you."

"What?" I asked on the edge of my seat.

"Tyson and I are back together."

"You're talking about the future Dr. Tyson Elliott?" I said, smiling with my mouth wide open.

"Yeah."

"This is indeed a glorious day," I said. "So when did this happen?"

"Well, technically it never really ended. Tyson and I have kept in touch ever since he left for Meharry. I hung out with him yesterday in his parents' Circle City Classic suite, then afterwards I went to dinner with his whole family. Christian, even as bougie as they are, I had a ball."

"I bet you did. I can't believe you're back with Tyson. He is so sexy!" I said as I held up my hand.

"You don't know the half of it!" she said, giving me high five. "He handles his business in *every way* imaginable."

"Freaky thing!"

"Girl, he's got that super stroke."

"My ears are bleeding! Control, alt, delete!" I said, cracking up. "I don't want to know about you and Tyson doing it."

As Angela laughed, she gave an endearing look and shook her head. "Chris, let's just squash everything that we've gone through this year and stay like this."

"I'd be more than happy to," I said leaning in to hug her.

"I love you."

MONDAY, 10/9

While I was tied up in a client meeting, Alain left a message asking for me to call him as soon as possible. I called him back and left a message and he, in return, did the same. By the time I'd finished all of my meetings, invoicing, appointment scheduling and follow-ups, I'd managed to miss two more of Alain's calls. We were now in double overtime of a very long and serious game of phone tag. On his last message, Alain said it was very important for me to call him before six o'clock Pacific time because he had something urgent to tell me. Once I finished up at the office and ran home to change clothes for a gallery opening, I took a chance calling Alain back.

"Is everything okay?"

"Yeah, everything's fine. I just need you come out here to be with me."

"Boy, quit playing. You know I can't do that."

"Why not?"

"Because."

"That's not going to work, I need a real answer."

"Okay, how about the fact that I already have a flight booked for San Diego on Sunday."

"That's not a good enough reason. Try again."

"Alright then, how about the fact that I have a ton of work to finish before I leave."

"Better, but still not good enough," he said as I envisioned the smug smile on his face. "Girl just pack up your work and come on. Your ticket's refundable so call the airline to cancel."

"Can you imagine what it's probably going to cost for me to buy a spur of the moment ticket to see you?"

"You don't need to concern yourself wit all dat," he said in his best pimp impression. "You just need to carry yo fine ass out here to see big daddy."

"Alain, baby I wish I could. I've got a lot of past due invoices that I'm still waiting for payment. I can't afford to be spontaneous right now."

"Queen, I'm paying for you to come."

"I can't let you do that."

"Too bad."

"What about my San Diego meeting?"

"If you wouldn't mind, I'd like to join you."

"So let me get this straight, you're paying for a three-legged flight to take me from Indy to San Francisco, San Francisco to San Diego and then from San Diego back to Indy?"

"Yep."

"You're serious?"

"Very."

"I don't believe what I'm about to say, but okay I'll go."

"Can you come tomorrow?"

"Can I come tomorrow?" I said then hesitated. "I guess I could, but I'd have to take the last flight out."

"It doesn't matter, as long as I have you here," he said as I beamed from ear to ear. "I'll email you your itinerary tonight."

"You're crazy you know that. I can't believe you're doing this."

"Baby, this is just the beginning."

As promised, he sent my itinerary a couple of hours later. For him to do something like this means so much to me. San Francisco is actually one of my favorite cities and being there with Alain is going to mean that much more. As I finished printing my itinerary, I got a text from Celeste, *"What's married, pregnant and tan all over? It's me and I'm back! Call me after you read this message, I have so much to tell you!"*

"Welcome back girlie!" I squealed when Celeste answered the phone.

"Chris, you have to come over tonight to see the pictures from our trip."

"I don't know if can. I have two weeks' worth of packing to do and I have to reschedule the rest of my appointments for the week."

"Where are you going for two weeks?"

"I'm meeting Alain in San Francisco. We'll be there for a week then down to San Diego the next for a big presentation I have to give."

"Can't you break away for a couple of hours? Car and Reese will be here and it wouldn't be the same without you."

"Is Reese back already?"

"Yeah, their flight got in around the same time as ours. We saw them at the airport earlier."

"Sorry I can't. Hold on, let's compromise. I can hang out with you guys tonight but only under one circumstance."

"What's that?"

"You all come over here instead to help me pack."

"You know what, that actually works out better. Seth is supposed to come over tonight and I know Reese and Car don't want to be bothered with him."

"You got that right."

"We were going to hook up around seven. Is that okay with you?"

"That's fine."

"I'll call Carra and Reese to let them know."

For a Monday night, the girls were in full party mode. Reese arrived with sparkling cider, cheese and crackers, Carra brought over a ton of DVDs and Celeste couldn't wait to share all of her pictures and movies from the honeymoon.

"Carra tells us that you actually ate a whole slice of quiche, a full Caesar salad and two rolls when you guys went to brunch the other day," Reese announced as she walked in the door.

"It's true," I proudly replied.

"Well what's gotten into you?" Celeste asked as she grabbed a blanket off my couch and wrapped it around her shoulders.

"Definitely not Alain! He hasn't gotten into anything lately!" Reese screamed. "I know that brother's dick is midnight blue!"

I patiently waited for them to settle down and stop laughing before I announced my new outlook on life.

"No, Alain and I haven't done anything, but a lot has happened over the course of the past few days," I said in a very long, formal and drawn out tone. "With several of you out of my hair, I've been able to reevaluate my life and make changes accordingly."

"Like what?" Celeste asked.

"Finally kicking that dieting shit to the curb!" I hollered as the girls began cheering.

"Well, in honor of Christian's new diet ban, I move that we order a big ass pizza overflowing with cheese!" Reese said picking up the phone. "What else do you guys want on it?"

"Pepperoni and mushrooms sound good to me," Celeste said.

"Um, also add spinach and onions," I added.

"Don't forget anchovies and pineapples," Carra said as we all looked at her like she was crazy. "What? I thought it sounded good!"

After we placed our order, the girls chipped in and helped me pack my bags while Celeste gave us the details of her honeymoon. As I listened to Celeste, something made me look over at Reese who was trying to be slick by stuffing four sexy nightgowns into my suitcase.

"Celeste, I don't mean to cut you off but I have to go and slap Reese for a second. What are you doing?" I asked as Reese quickly zipped my bag.

"Nothing."

"Then what's this?" I asked, pulling out a sheer black nightgown.

"I'm just trying to help a sister out," she said as she put the nightgown back in the bag.

"I don't need your help," I said, playfully pinching her hand to let me unzip the suitcase.

"It's beyond me that you two still haven't done it. What the hell are you waiting for?"

"We're not rushing it. It'll happen soon enough."

"Well soon may be this weekend so you need to be prepared."

"Oooh, you definitely need to take this with you," Celeste said holding up a sexy bra and panty set. "I have to agree with Reese."

"This is a first, so do I!" Carra chimed in. "Have you guys even slept in the same bed together?"

"Yeah, several times."

"Show us what you wore," Celeste said.

I hesitated for a second but then walked over to my dresser and pulled out my favorite cotton pajama set.

"What the…" Reese said as she snatched the pajamas out of my hand. "No wonder nothing's gone down."

"What?" I said laughing.

"Girls, from now on let's refer to those as the birth control pajamas!" Celeste yelled laughing.

"No shit! How the hell do expect a brother to get it up when you're walking around in this?" Reese said while nearly hyperventilating from laughing so hard.

By this point, Carra had tears rolling down her face in laughter.

"Christian, listen to me carefully. Alain just dropped at least a grand for you two to spend time together in Cali, the least you can do is give the man something to look at," Reese said as she stuffed my old pajamas in the trash.

"Okay, okay, okay!"

TUESDAY, 10/10

Hectic is not a strong enough word to describe the first half of my day. I had to squeeze in the seven appointments previously scheduled throughout this week into one day then finalize a laundry list of items for Illum.

When I arrived in San Francisco, Alain was waiting for me at the airport with a single red rose.

"Thank you sweetie," I whispered as I walked up to him and slowly kissed his beautiful, soft lips. "It's so good to see you."

It took about a half hour to get to our downtown hotel and when we arrived I was taken aback by how elegant it was. When the uniformed doormen greeted us, I felt like royalty.

"Great place isn't it?" Alain said as he led me to the elevator.

"Absolutely gorgeous. Did you happen to notice the two blue paintings in the lobby?"

"Yeah, they were nice," he said as the elevator door opened.

"Nice? Boy, those are original Matisse paintings."

"Who?"

"You mean to tell me you don't know who Henri Matisse is."

"No."

"And all this time I thought you were cultured," I joked.

"Well excuse me," he said with a high brow. "I guess I need to do some research."

"Don't worry, I'll teach you," I said, hugging him from behind as we exited the elevator to go to our room or shall I say our five room deluxe suite.

"I'd like to teach *you* a thing or two as well," Alain said, taking off his coat and tossing it on the arm of the couch.

"Oh really," I replied as Alain held my hand, opened the balcony door and led me out into the chilly bay air.

"Wait right here while I take care of a few things."

Alain walked back into the room and made a quick phone call. After he hung up he went to his suitcase and pulled out several large pillar candles and began placing them all around the room. After they were all lit, he turned off the lights and walked back to the balcony.

"I want you to relax and enjoy this little escape," he said, standing behind me massaging my shoulders. "I know you have a lot to do before your big presentation next week but for the next couple of days, take it easy."

"I'm not going to argue with that," I said as I closed my eyes and melted into my massage.

"Our room service should be here shortly, until then I'm here to cater to you. So which would you prefer, a scalp or foot massage?"

I have died and gone to heaven!

When our room service arrived and Alain was busy at the door signing for the bill, I went into the bathroom to wash up and figure out what to wear to bed tonight. Since it was the first night, I decided to go with a long cotton nightgown that was more nice than naughty. Reese would kill me for this, I thought as I slipped it over my head.

When I walked back into the bedroom, Alain had the duvet on the floor, picnic style, with a gorgeous array of fruits, cheeses and meats in one corner and piles of soft, feathery pillows in another. Off to the side was a large silver wine bucket holding two bottles of chilled Moscato and two wine glasses.

Now that I think about it, the silk nightgown wouldn't have been such a bad choice. I felt like a fool wearing conservative cotton pajamas after Alain spent all that time to create a romantic scene.

"I see you have on my favorite pajamas," he said, smiling and walking over to pull me into his arms.

"Let me go change, I'll be right back."

"No, I think you look comfortably cute."

I could practically hear his erection deflating when he said that. He was trying to be nice. Comfortable has never been associated with sexy, I thought as I sat down.

"Do you want to order a movie?" Alain said as he got up and walked to the bathroom.

"Yeah, what do you want to see?" I asked, sorting through the movie categories on the screen.

"Something funny," Alain said from inside the bathroom.

This selection is pretty lame, I thought to myself as I scrolled through the comedy options. Most of the titles available were low brow, frat boy movies like *Jackass* that have been out for several years.

"Even though I've seen it a million times, the only thing worth watching is *The Devil Wears Prada*. Is that cool with you?"

"I'll watch whatever you want," Alain said as he opened the bathroom door and walked out in his Morehouse sweats.

"*The Devil Wears Prada* it is," I replied, tickled that he put on his old sweats to match my look.

After eating and downing two glasses of wine, Alain fell asleep in the middle of the movie. Once the movie ended, I blew out all of the candles and snuggled up behind him. As I laid there I wondered, how early was too early to know if you're in love with someone? I'd like to believe that it's the quality not quantity of time that determines the strength of your feelings. So if that is indeed true, my heart is saying I love you Alain.

WEDNESDAY, 10/11

I felt Alain gently kiss my lips before he left for his meeting this morning. To his surprise, I grabbed him by the neck and pulled him back down to give him a big, long embrace.

"I'll be back for lunch around one, in the meantime I want you to order anything you want for breakfast and please make use of the spa downstairs. Everything's on the company and I definitely wouldn't want any of those spa services to go to waste. If you want to go shopping or sightseeing, just give the valet captain the room number and use my rental car. What else is there?" he asked himself. "Oh, if you feel up to it I'd like to introduce you to some of my clients during dinner tonight. Is that alright?"

"How could I say no?" I said as he lifted me out of bed and carried me into the living room of the suite.

"Call me if you need anything."

"Okay," I replied, kissing the back of his neck as he was leaving out the door. "What time should I be ready for dinner?"

"Let's aim for around seven-thirty."

"I can't wait. Have a good day."

"You too queen," he said then gave me a slow, passionate kiss on the lips.

I'm in heaven, I thought walking into the bedroom and falling back in bed, which had a heavenly feather mattress top and was covered in one thousand and twenty count Egyptian cotton sheets. I only know this because I checked the tags. Just as I felt myself drifting away into a state of laziness, I immediately sat up and realized I could be falling asleep downstairs on the masseur's table. I'd been working hard all week and will be working even harder next week trying to land the jazz fest account. I deserve a little R&R, I proclaimed out loud as I got out of bed to take a quick shower.

Within the next five hours I'd received a manicure, pedicure, spa facial, body wrap and the best massage I'd ever had. I felt like I was walking on a cloud when I left the spa, so much that I didn't even notice it was after one o'clock. When I got to the room, there was a note from Alain saying that he saw me getting my nails done and he didn't want to bother me because I looked so calm.

I drove over to Union Square for a light lunch and to indulge in a little retail therapy. A new outfit is exactly what I deserved after a year of hustling and paying dues. By the time I'd left the mall, I was juggling six bags full of shoes, make-up, clothes and scarves. When I got back to the hotel, I leisurely got ready for dinner. It felt good to not have to rush for once.

Alain arrived at a quarter 'til six and when he saw me he did a double take.

"Now that's what I'm talking about," he said as he smiled, giving me those sexy eyes.

"Do you like it?" I asked as I whirled around for him to see my new ensemble.

"Love it."

"Then prove it by kissing me here," I said, pointing to my cheek.

"I'd rather kiss you here," he said as he began sucking on my neck. That sensation sent a chill through me like none other. He ran his hands up my neck into my hair then kissed me in the most sensual and passionate way, making me want to tear off his clothes. It had gotten so hot and heavy that I started undoing the buttons on my dress while his hand gently made its way up my thigh, then it all ended when we were interrupted by the hourly beep from his watch, which meant that it was six o'clock.

"I guess I need to start getting ready," he whispered as he gently ran his fingers down my cleavage.

Okay, tonight I'm breaking out the sexy lingerie.

Dinner was at a bustling and trendy Nob Hill steakhouse. Even though we had reservations we still waited for almost forty-five minutes to be seated and another twenty to get our first course. I ordered grilled swordfish and Alain ordered blackened shark, which was surprisingly delicious. About halfway through my meal, jet lag began to set in. I tried my best to keep my eyes open but Alain's middle-aged clients weren't helping the situation any with their bland discussions and bad jokes.

When we finally got back to the suite, Alain cracked the balcony door, turned off all the lights then led me to the bed.

"The view is breathtaking," I said as I gazed out into the skyline.

"My view is even better," he said, staring at me. "I love you Christian," he said then paused. "I admire your intelligence, success, spirit—everything about you. When I call you queen, I call you that for a reason. I feel connected to you in ways that I can't even explain."

"Alain, I feel the same about you," I said, leaning over to kiss him. "I love you too."

Alain gently rolled on top of me and held me so tight, I could feel his heart beating. As we kissed, the spark we had before dinner was back stronger than ever. My body shivered from head to toe when he slowly loosened the buttons on my dress, grazing his lips lightly over my neck and collarbone.

"I love you so much," he whispered in my ear. "I can stay like this forever," he said as he nestled his head into my chest. Shortly after, we both drifted off to sleep, wrapped in each other's arms.

Several hours later, I felt Alain get up and turn on the shower. I thought back to when I was at his apartment in Chicago and how tempted I was to join him but chickened out. That was then and this is now, I whispered to myself as I got out of bed, lit a few candles and poured two glasses of wine. I was definitely ready to take this to next level. I quietly opened the bathroom door and grew more excited when I saw Alain's naked silhouette through the glass of the steamy shower wall. I slowly dimmed the bathroom lights to a warm glow, took off my robe and stepped into the shower with him. I could feel his heart beating as I held his wet, muscular body from behind. He slowly rolled his head back, let out a deep breath then turned around to look at me. When he faced me, my heart raced because I'd never seen such a handsome man in my life. He stood there and gazed at me with the most loving eyes then pulled me close to him as his lips and fingers explored my body for the first time. We stepped out of the shower, consumed with one another, bodies dripping wet and the shower water still running.

"I've never seen anything more beautiful," he whispered as he laid me down on the bed and revealed a sensual side of him that absolutely blew my mind.

Tonight was the most passionate experience I've ever had in my life. No one has ever taken me to that level of climax not once, but four times in a row. I knew Alain was my soul mate but being this close to him completely sealed the deal.

THURSDAY, 10/12

"Good morning queen," Alain whispered before getting out of bed to join his morning conference call. After washing up I ordered breakfast, poured two cups of tea and joined Alain in the living room of our suite. He put his finger over his lips and held his arms out for me to sit on his lap. With the phone on speaker, I could hear several men arguing back and forth about how the competition was catching up with them and how they needed to be more innovative in their business approach. As I sat there watching him on his conference call, in nothing but his boxers, I was intrigued to see him in work mode. He was in control, confident and most of all he was a leader amongst his peers because everyone seemed to defer to him when they needed a resolution. That scene added about one hundred more points to his sexy score.

Alain's final meetings wrapped up around six o'clock and when he returned to the hotel he was hyped to go out on the town. Our first stop was to Sausalito for dinner at one of my favorite restaurants, Scoma's. I love it partially because of the food, but mainly because of the romantic atmosphere. The last time I was there I vowed I would never go back unless I had someone special to experience it with me. As I drove, Alain tried his best to figure out where I was taking him but by the time we crossed the Golden Gate Bridge, he had no clue.

After our delicious meal, we hit a few bars for drinks and dancing but the highlight of the evening was later on in our suite for a very sweet repeat of last night.

FRIDAY, 10/13

At the crack of dawn I felt Alain get out of bed, not to get up and start the day but to close the huge balcony blinds so we'd be able to sleep in. It wasn't until ten thirty that we finally woke up to begin our lazy day. We went downstairs to the spa and while he got a massage, I sat in the hot tub and savored the new feelings of love I was experiencing. I thought back to all of the people I'd dealt with in the past and thanked God that He allowed the timing to be right for Alain to enter my life.

"Is there any room in there for me?" Alain asked, standing at the edge of the hot tub.

"Plenty," I replied. "Have I told you that I love you today?"

"No."

"Well then," I said as I waded close to him. "I love you and I can't imagine life without you."

"Queen, love is not a strong enough word," he said, holding me with his lips on my forehead. "This is indescribable."

SATURDAY, 10/14

Alain and I woke up early to drive up to Napa for the day. Our first stop was the town of Yountville where we enjoyed a picnic lunch by the countryside, a visit to the Napa Valley Museum then later rented bikes for a leisurely ride around town. We ended the night by visiting Domaine Chandon. While listening to the guide discuss the history of the winery, Alain gave me a quick nudge when she mentioned that Chandon is the product of world renowned Moet-Hennessey.

"No wonder this was the only winery you suggested. You were hoping they were giving out free Hen," Alain joked while doing a little two step.

"Quit before you get us put out," I whispered back to him as I smacked his leg.

"Alright, I'll stop," he said and began doing the dance again.

"I can't take you anywhere."

"For real, I'm serious now. I'll stop," he said, pinching my behind.

Alain and I joked and had a blast throughout the entire tour.

We ended our evening at the winery's amazing restaurant and luckily we were able to be seated without a reservation.

"This is the life—a beautiful woman, exquisite wine and a five star meal. Who could ask for more?" Alain said then raised his eyebrow at the sound of John Coltrane's "A Love Supreme".

"Ah, to add to your list of great things," I said as I closed my eyes and let the genius of Coltrane take over me.

"I'll always think about us dancing in your living room whenever I hear this song," he said in a smooth tone. "This will forever be our song."

I opened my eyes and stared at Alain's handsome face. Yeah, he's definitely the one.

SUNDAY, 10/15

After a busy morning and a quick flight we arrived in San Diego at three-thirty. When we got to the hotel I was presented with a large fruit and cheese basket along with a bottle of Prosecco from Karen, a banquet manager who I worked with while coordinating a sales meeting last year.

"Well look who's here! How's it going?" Karen said with her thick Dominican accent as she ran from behind the front desk.

"Ask me on Wednesday after I get this presentation over with," I said, giving her a big hug. "You didn't have to do this Karen."

"Nonsense, I need to be doing more after what happened with your meeting last year," she said gazing at Alain, then sharply at me. "I'm Karen and who might you be?"

"Alain Hughes," he said with a cute smirk. "It's a pleasure meeting you."

"Likewise," she said then cut her eyes back at me. "Ms. Cullen never once mentioned that she had such a handsome man."

"Yeah and I better not catch you flirting with him," I joked as she swatted me lightly on the back.

"Don't worry honey, I won't steal him," she said then looked at Alain. "Just call me if she ever messes up."

"Then let me get one of your business cards," Alain said, playfully.

"You two are a mess."

"All in fun my love. Hey, if you two aren't doing anything tonight, I'd be delighted to treat you to dinner at The Wharf on the boardwalk."

"Sounds good to me," Alain said, looking over at me.

"Yeah, does six o'clock work for you?" I asked.

"Perfect."

"There's no shame in her game," Alain said as we got on the elevator.

"None whatsoever. She's a sweetie though."

"You better not leave me in the same room with that woman. I'm afraid I might get raped," he joked.

"I know," I said, laughing at Alain's facial expression. "I can't begin to tell you how much she helped me at an event I had here last year. Everything that could've gone wrong did."

"Well, it looks like she hooked you up again," Alain said as he fumbled through the gift basket. "Fruit and cheese, nothing out of the ordinary…but chocolate body paint? I'm surprised there isn't a whip and handcuffs somewhere in here."

"I'm gonna' let you in on a little secret, a little birdie may have told her I was bringing you," I said winking at him. "I think she knew what she was doing."

After dinner, Alain and I took the trolley a couple of blocks to the Gaslamp District and settled into a chic little lounge to relax over a few drinks. As calming as the scene was, feelings of anxiety began to overwhelm me. What happens if I bomb during my presentation, I thought as I looked over at Alain who was oblivious to my worries, completely enthralled in the live neo-soul performance. I didn't come all the way out here to not get this account. I'd worked so hard at perfecting my career that I couldn't let this opportunity slide through the cracks. My heart began to beat so hard that I could not only feel it with the slightest touch to my chest, I could hear it.

"Baby, are you okay? You look a little green," Alain whispered.

"I'm fine," I said, trying to disguise the panic I was feeling.

"No, you don't look so good. I think we better go," he said as he flagged down the waiter and asked for our check. "Besides, we need to get you back to the room so you can go over your presentation."

"I think you're right."

"I'm here if you need to practice it on me."

"I'll definitely take you up on that."

Alain and I worked on my presentation for five hours straight before turning in.

"Baby, I don't want you worrying about anything. You're going to walk in that meeting on Tuesday morning and claim what's yours. Believe me sweetie, this account belongs to you."

MONDAY, 10/16

I picked up right where I'd left off when I woke up this morning, finalizing the budget, revising the promotions strategy and outlining my vision for the artist tribute ceremony. Alain left to give me a little peace and quiet while he went for a morning jog on the pier then made plans to visit one of his old childhood friends. I was so consumed with perfecting my presentation that the next time I glanced at the clock it was already one thirty-five in the afternoon.

"I'm so sick of looking at my presentation. Every time I review it, I hate it and I feel like I should just delete it and start over. I'm making myself crazy," I said to Alain from inside the shower.

"You need a break. I'm meeting my friend Jeff for lunch, why don't you join me."

"Maybe I should," I said before looking at my frizzy hair in the reflection of the steamy mirror. "Oooh, I look horrible. I can't go down there looking like this."

"Trust me you look delicious. Besides, he's already downstairs waiting."

"If you say so," I said, smiling as I quickly grabbed my towel and wrapped it around my body.

"Here, let me do that," he said as he pulled the towel from my hand and began gently patting my body dry.

"You better get back downstairs before you start something you can't finish," I said kissing the top of his head as he lightly brushed his lips against my legs while drying them. "Just give me a few minutes to pull my hair back and I'll be right down."

I was actually happy that Alain asked me to join him for lunch. I seriously needed a change of pace. I scrambled and rushed to get ready and when I made it down to the lobby and saw Alain sitting in the bar, I nearly choked. I couldn't believe what I was seeing. It was like a sick, twisted episode of *The Twilight Zone*. Alain's friend was the spitting image of Mekhi.

"So this is the gorgeous woman I've heard so much about! You better be glad you came down here with A.J. cause if I would've seen you here all alone, you'd be snatched up," Jeff said as he greeted me with a big, uncomfortable hug. As I leaned my head back away from the side of his face, I noticed that he even wore Curve cologne, just like Mekhi.

"Nah bruh, I'd have to fight you for this one," Alain responded as he playfully tagged Jeff in the arm. "Plus, I'm sure Cynthia wouldn't be having that."

"Cynthia who?" Jeff joked, unconvincingly trying to look confused while still holding on to my arms. "Oh, that Cynthia. You mean, my wife Cynthia. Aw, she wouldn't mind. She realizes that variety is the spice of life."

"Nice meeting you," I said as I politely wiggled away from his grasp.

"Yeah, she knows that if she wants me to stay happy, I need to be out doing my thing."

"Some things never change," Alain said, shaking his head.

"Once a player, always a player," Jeff said then looked over at me like a horny, prepubescent schoolboy.

When Alain walked over to the hostess desk to check on our table, Jeff showed his true colors, "So how serious are you two?" he asked, scooting his barstool way too close to mine.

"Very serious."

"Oh really? Well I'm happy for A.J. It's good to know that he's tagging some grade-A tail."

"Excuse me?" I said with a disgusted frown on my face.

"I'm just playing. Take it as a compliment."

"Compliment?"

"Hey our tables are ready," Alain said walking over to us. "You weren't over here messing with my lady were you?"

"Of course not," he said smiling like the Cheshire cat.

Jeff had officially grossed me out. Not only did he look like Mekhi, he was just as crude and uncouth as he was.

On the elevator Alain could read all over my face that I wasn't impressed with Jeff in the least bit.

"I have to apologize for Jeff," Alain said while kissing me on the forehead. "I'm pretty sure he wasn't the most tactful guy you've ever met."

"That's putting it mildly. Babe, Jeff's an asshole."

"I know, I know."

"I can't believe he's married."

"None of us can. You'll meet her tonight at dinner."

"Babe, I'm not just saying this because I never want to see Jeff again, but I have too much work to do. Why don't you go without me."

I worked on my presentation for the rest of the day and by the time dinner rolled around, Alain was so insistent upon helping me that he canceled his dinner plans with Jeff and stayed up with me as I practiced my presentation until two in the morning. After that he had a special presentation that he wanted to practice on me. Needless to say his performance was stellar.

TUESDAY, 10/17

I arrived for my eight o'clock meeting at seven thirty-five, but waited in the lobby until the receptionist finally called me back at a quarter til' nine. As I waited for my big moment, I looked around the room at the other prospective companies bidding for this account. One of the groups consisted of an older, wealthy looking white woman and two middle aged white men. They smiled pleasantly at me while we all sat and waited to be called in. The other group consisted of two *"Real Housewives of Beverly Hills"* types with dark tans, dark suits and even darker demeanors. When I looked at them and smiled, they looked at each other and snickered. Christian, don't stoop to their level, I thought as I refrained from rolling my eyes at them. As the time passed the two rude women who were once smug began looking nervous. One was frantically looking at her watch while the other lady nervously tapped her toes in anticipation. I opened my portfolio to review my notes one last time and as soon as I finished, the receptionist called me in. As I stood up and walked over to the door I started shaking uncontrollably. I paused for a minute to take a deep breath and regroup. Once inside I was greeted by Molly, the director of the organization, then stood in front of the jam-packed room of seventeen board members, who were all peering at me like they were ready to open fire. Why should these people dish out premium money for my company to plan their festival? I know I can do it, but how am I going to convince them of that. Now that I think about it, what if I can't handle it? What have I gotten myself into? I thought as my heart pounded and I could barely swallow. I had never felt so nervous about anything in my life. Christian, now is the time to put all of your yoga breathing and relaxation techniques to use, I thought as the board members reverted their attention back to each other while I set up my displays.

"Ms. Cullen, we're ready when you are," Molly whispered over my shoulder and patted my back.

Just as I was about to turn around, I heard Alain's voice in my head, *"You have to claim this account. Queen, you have to believe this project is yours. Once you do that, you have nothing to worry about."* I couldn't help but smile at the thought of Alain's support and belief in me. When I turned around and approached the large mahogany conference table, Molly began my introductions and before I uttered one word to the crowd, I channeled the first thirteen words to God.

"Lord, thank you for this opportunity. Please help me to do my best."

He did just that.

WEDNESDAY, 10/18

Molly called me at nine o'clock this morning and asked if I could come back to answer some additional questions. I immediately got up and raced across town for the meeting. Once there I restated my budget figures in detail, explained my vision for the festival and reassured them that Image Brokers was the best firm for the job. After the meeting, Molly pulled me aside and guaranteed that I would hear from them by the end of the business day. She also mentioned that I shouldn't have anything to worry about because my presentation was the most impressive. Regardless of what she said, I left the meeting a nervous wreck. Alain tried his hardest to calm me down, but to no avail. He lit aromatherapy candles, ran a hot lavender oil bath, gave me a massage and even tried his hardest to sing to me but none of it worked. By the time four o'clock rolled around, I couldn't think straight.

"I knew this would happen. There's a reason the other companies laughed when I walked in the lobby. What was I thinking?"

"Christian, what time do their offices close?" he asked as I laid on his chest while he massaged my head.

"At five o'clock."

"Is it five yet?"

"No, but it's damn near."

"But it's not quite, so relax."

At a quarter til' five my phone rang. I frantically looked at Alain and he looked back at me pointing to the phone, "Don't look at me, answer it!"

"Hello Christian, this is Molly. How are you?"

"I'm fine, how are you?"

"Just fine. I bet you thought I'd never call."

"I was beginning to think just that," I said as I tried to laugh.

"Well, I'm sure you'd like for me to just cut to the chase and tell you what we've decided."

"Yes," I said as Alain stared at me wide eyed.

"Are you sitting down?"

When I hung up the phone, I screamed at the top of my lungs.

"Yes! Thank you Lord! Yes, yes, yes!"

"You got the account?" Alain asked with excitement as I frantically nodded my head. "Yes! Baby, I knew you would!" he said as I pulled him on the bed, jumping up and down on the mattress like a kid. "You never cease to amaze me!"

THURSDAY, 10/19

Alain and I drove up to L.A. and spent the day sightseeing. We decided to take the coastal highway instead of taking interstate five which turned a two hour trip into nearly five, but who cares. I was with my man and still on a high from my good news. We visited Hollywood Boulevard, strolled up and down the street taking pictures of the stars on the Walk of Fame and toured Mann's Chinese Theater. Afterwards, we drove around Beverly Hills then ate dinner. At the end of the day in the midst of trying to find our way back to the highway, we rode past the Hustler Store. To my surprise Alain made a swift u-turn and the next thing I knew we were pulling into the parking lot. I've always had a thing about not wanting to be seen in a sex store but we were thousands of miles from home, what the hell. The Hustler Store was huge, who knew there were that many sex toys, racy lingerie, books and videos in the world? They even had the nerve to have a café! I'm not sure why anyone would want to eat there, but oh well. Two hours and three bags later we headed back to the car eager to get back to the hotel. With all the toys we bought and every piece of lingerie worn, my girls would definitely be proud!

FRIDAY, 10/20

We spent our morning packing and resting until we checked out at one. Since our flight wasn't until ten o'clock this evening, we killed time by visiting the San Diego Zoo and Sea World.

As soon as we boarded the plane, Alain snuggled up to me like a baby and fell asleep before we even took off. I couldn't help but smile when I looked down at him. Just the sight of this man makes my heart melt. All I could do was gently kiss him and hold his hand as I marveled at this awesome life of mine.

SATURDAY, 10/21

I hate red-eye flights. I was so disoriented by the time we arrived in Indianapolis this morning that we barely made it home. Today was one of the rare occasions that I was able to fall into a deep sleep despite seeing the light of day. We woke up around one o'clock but stayed in bed until two-thirty eating, talking, joking and doing what lovers do.

After finally getting out of bed and as soon as I stepped in the shower, my phone began ringing off the hook. I jumped out to get it but didn't answer in time.

"Hey sis. I thought you were supposed to be back in town today. I wanted to see if you could hang out with me while I get my debutante pictures taken. Hopefully it's not too late when you get this message because I really want you to come. Plus I have something I need to tell you about James. Anyway, call me when you get a chance. I get my pictures taken at four-thirty. See ya!"

I caught Eva just in time before they left to take her to the photographers'. Mom drove and Nanna sat in the front while Eva and I were in the back trying to keep her ten pound debutante gown from wrinkling. When we arrived at the photo studio, mom and Eva went back to the dressing room while Nanna and I sat on stools behind the camera waiting for Eva to get ready.

"So, Mariam told me all about your business trip. How did it go?"

"I landed the deal."

"Congratulations! I knew you would," she said with a mischievous look on her face. "What else happened?"

"What do you mean?" I said in a cautious tone, hoping that she wasn't about to go there.

"Did you enjoy your getaway with Alain?"

She went there.

"It was okay," I said, embarrassed.

"Child, I wasn't born yesterday. If a woman spends two whole weeks alone in a hotel room with a man, it needs to be more than just okay."

"Nanna, *please.*"

"Don't *please* me. Is he the one?"

"I'm pretty sure he is."

"Girl, you better know for certain. You can't go around giving men all of your goods without a clue if he's the one you can picture yourself marrying."

"You know what Nanna, he is the one," I said smiling at my grandmother. "And for your information, what happened during my trip is not what you think."

"Whatever you say my love," she said laughing then turned her attention to the dressing room door as my mother walked into the studio with tears in her eyes. When Eva walked out behind her, I barely recognized my baby sister.

Nanna gasped and rushed over to give Eva a hug.

"Look at her!" Nanna gushed. "Would you just look at how beautiful she is!"

"Thanks," Eva said then bashfully lowered her head.

"Oh no you don't. You need to hold your head up high and proud," Nanna said while raising Eva's delicate chin. "Let your confidence radiate when you walk into a room."

"She's right, baby. You need to show the world who you are and why you're going to become the phenomenal woman you're destined to be," my mother added.

"Okay," Eva said as she stood up straight and lifted her cute little head into the air. "I think I'm ready for my big debut."

"That's my girl!" Nanna belted as we watched Eva prance in front of the backdrop for her pictures to be taken.

"This is freaking me out," I said silently as we watched the photographer get Eva situated for the shoot.

"What is?" Mom asked.

"It seems like it was just yesterday that I was her age. Sitting here looking at Eva makes me feel old."

"That's because you are old," Nanna said, jokingly.

"Oh stop it, you're not even in your mid-thirties yet," mom said.

"It doesn't matter if you're thirty or eighty, old is what you make it. It's all in the mind. If you want to become old, sit around and do nothing. If you don't want to be old, be like me," Nanna said winking at me. "I bet I go out on more dates than you do."

"That I wouldn't doubt," I said, putting my arms around her.

After the shoot, I treated them to an elegant dinner at a new seafood restaurant downtown. There was an hour wait when we arrived and since the restaurant was directly across the street from the mall, I used it as an opportunity to spend some more one on one time with Eva.

"Oh, I've been meaning to ask you," Eva said as she tossed her long black hair to one side and kept her chin up just as Nanna had instructed. "Will you be in town on November seventh?"

"I'll be getting back from New York that week. What day is that?"

"Tuesday."

"Whatever I have planned, I'll make time for you. What's going on?"

"I want you to come and speak at our debutante meeting."

"No problem, what's the topic?"

"Health, beauty, careers, that kind of stuff."

"I'll put something together. Have you all learned your dance routines yet?"

"Yeah and they're so cute. Our dance instructor brought her new boyfriend to our practice last weekend and whew he is fine!"

"Look at you. You ought to be ashamed," I said laughing.

"He was there hanging out with our escorts, showing them how to twirl a cane. I tell ya, there's just something about those Kappa men that make me weak."

"What in the world are you talking about?"

"You know what I mean. The Kappa's got it going on."

"Alright, it's that very mentality that'll get you in trouble as a freshman."

"Hold on, if I'm not mistaken those were your exact words when you came home for Thanksgiving your freshman year."

"My goodness, you don't forget anything."

"You're right. Now what was his name again, I think it was Bill."

"Okay, you got me. But what made me fall for him was his personality not his affiliations."

"You have to take the fun out of everything don't you," she said with a pouty face.

"There's nothing fun about being labeled a Kappa groupie, or worse."

"Oooh, I guess you're right," she said, shrugging her shoulders and tightening her mouth.

"I know I'm right," I said then paused to look at her. "So what's going on with this James dude?"

Eva looked at me briefly then looked away.

"You didn't, did you?"

"No I didn't and guess what? He broke up with me."

"Babysis, you did the right thing. Believe me he's just one amongst a million other guys."

"I know Chris, I couldn't care less about that loser."

"Well look at you," I said, giving her a big hug. "I'm proud that you got over him and moved on with your life."

"Exactly, that's why I'm dating David Hudson now. He's tall, cute, has dimples and hazel eyes. He's also the captain of the varsity basketball team and he's only a junior! Can you believe that?"

"Lord have mercy, here we go again," I said as I shook my head at my goofy baby sister.

"Don't worry, I still remember what you told me," she said as she bounced along in front of me. "Anyway, he's got curly hair and he looks just like Kobe Bryant. Just wait until you see him!"

Mom and Nanna were being seated just as Eva and I returned. The restaurant was very nice and the service was impeccable. Eva and I both ordered the penne puttanesca and shared steamed mussels as an appetizer, mom ordered the Chilean sea bass and Nanna ordered tilapia. All in all each one of us gave the restaurant a ten, that was until we were half way back to my parents' house.

"So what do you have planned for the rest of the day?" mom asked.

"I think I'm going to go home and lay down, I'm feeling a little light headed."

"You're still functioning on west-coast time that's why," Nanna said.

"Maybe that's it," I replied. "What about you all?"

"I've got laundry to do," mom said.

"So, do I," Nanna replied.

"And Miss Eva back there has to help her brother rake leaves tonight," mom said, looking back at Eva through the rear view mirror with a stern eye.

"Mom, I don't know if I can do it today. I need to lay down too."

"Well you won't be going over to Lisa's house tonight."

"That's fine," she said in a moan.

"What's wrong with you?" Nanna asked

"My stomach feels queasy," Eva said.

"I thought it was just me," I said to Eva.

"Do you think it was something you ate?" mom asked.

"It was probably the mussels," I replied while breathing deeply and cracking the back window to get some fresh air.

"Did they taste fresh?" Nanna asked.

"Yes, they tasted fine to me."

"Sometimes you can't tell by taste," mom said as we pulled into their driveway. "Are you going to be able to make it home?"

"Yeah, I think I can make it."

I barely made it before sickness hit me full throttle.

SUNDAY, 10/22

Even though water was the only drink I had yesterday, it felt like I was suffering from a severe hangover when I woke up this morning. My head was pounding, I was burning up and could barely stand from the pain in my stomach. Miraculously, I was able to disconnect the phone, turn on the air conditioner and close the blinds because every sound and ray of light made me feel worse. I did all of this by crawling around the house because I was too nauseous to walk. Alain came by later in the day to see if I was still alive. When he saw my condition, he went to the store and came back with some club soda, crackers, chicken broth and Milk of Magnesia. Within a couple of hours of consuming the contents of Alain's care package, I was able to get up and join him in the living room.

"Hey Queen. You feeling better?"

"A little. Thanks for taking care of me."

"No problem, I was worried about you last night when I didn't hear from you."

"I thought I was going to die when I got home yesterday."

"What's happened?"

"We went to The Blue Oyster and I think I got a hold of some bad seafood."

"Did anyone else get sick?"

"Eva did. We both ordered the same thing."

"That's not good."

"Tell me about it. I probably need to call and inform them that they gave me food poisoning."

"I would if I were you."

"What did you end up doing last night?"

"Just hung out with Erik," he said then paused for a couple seconds. "Do you know that he and Reese have slept together nearly ten times since the first time we met for lunch?"

"I think Erik may be exaggerating a little."

"I don't know Chris. Erik usually doesn't lie about that kind of stuff."

"Well in this case, let's hope that he is."

MONDAY, 10/23

After I finished invoicing, I updated my company website, called Angela to invite her over for dinner tonight and ran errands outside of the office for the rest of the day. Later on when Angela arrived, we went over the plans and travel arrangements for next week's big Illum event. It warmed my heart to once again be able to talk to my sister like long-lost best friends. We ended up having a really good time becoming close again. I couldn't wait to fill her in on my Cali trip and she could barely contain herself as she told me all about her road trips back and forth to Nashville. The small amount of time that we did spend on discussing the Illum event was very productive. I was extremely impressed with her designs for the investor kits and program books. Angela completely outdid herself. When I told her that I wanted her to be my partner for the big jazz fest project and how much she'd be making, she gave me the biggest and sloppiest kiss on the cheek. She hadn't done that since we were little. After dinner, we ran a few more errands then went to The Canal Room for cocktails. We sat in a cozy corner booth for hours singing, clowning and people watching—just like old times.

Spending time with family, free of drama, really allows you to appreciate the moments you have together. Alain would kill to be able to hang out with his brother again. It hurts him so much that they took each other's lives for granted and didn't spend enough quality time together. I don't ever want to feel that way, that's why I savored every minute I spent with Angela today.

TUESDAY, 10/24

As I was leaving a client meeting, Carra called to tell me that Ms. V was back in the hospital and that this time it didn't look good. I went home for a brief moment to change clothes then headed straight to the hospital and saw Reese in the waiting area outside of the oncology ward. Carra arrived shortly after and we all quietly walked to Ms. V's room together.

"Celeste's not doing well," John said, standing by the door with bloodshot eyes and a distraught look on his face. "Ms. V's cancer has spread and the doctors aren't offering much hope."

Celeste was sitting at the edge of her mother's bed when we entered the room. She looked up slowly then hung her head down again. The three of us walked over to console Celeste and to pray over Ms. V. We sat in the room silently for an hour before a nurse came in and asked us all to leave. We went down to the cafeteria for coffee and as we sat there, Celeste finally broke her silence.

"I wish we could've had a better relationship," she said with tears running down her face. "Ever since my parent's divorce and dad's passing, I've subconsciously resented her."

"Everything will be okay sweetie," Carra said as she pulled Celeste close to her.

"I've already lost one parent, I'm not ready to lose another," she said then paused before glaring at John with a disgusted look. "I just feel like my life is falling apart."

WEDNESDAY, 10/25

I spent the night over Alain's house and I woke up just as he was in the bathroom getting ready for work. I rolled out of bed, slipped on one of his oxford shirts and quietly walked down the stairs to fix him a quick breakfast. When he came downstairs, I surprised him with a big bowl of oatmeal, turkey sausage, fried eggs, toast and orange juice. He smiled at me as he sat down at the kitchen table and I seductively I tied a cloth napkin around his neck then handed him the morning paper. Alain immediately laid the paper on the floor and pulled me down on his lap.

"That can wait, this can't," he said as he cradled me into his chest, leaned me back and kissed me.

"I want you to have a good day today sweetie," I whispered in his ear.

"How can my day be bad with you in my life?"

When I got to the office my main goal was to get everything prepared for the big events next week. I called Guy to go over some final details and after we got everything squared away he asked me the question that I hoped he wouldn't.

"How's the weight loss coming along? Eden said that he could re-shoot you while you're here."

"Actually Guy to be quite honest, I don't think this modeling thing is for me."

"Uh uh, you can't quit," he said in a sharp tone.

"I'm afraid I have to."

"After all of the persuading I had to go through to get Eden to even look at you."

"With all due respect, I didn't ask you to do that. I'm sure he'll be able to find someone else with no problem."

"That's not the point. You committed to this and now you're trying to back out."

"Eden never liked me in the first place."

"But he used you."

"And you know what, that's exactly how I felt when I left his studio, used."

"I can't believe you're being so hypersensitive," Guy said in a huff. "Shame on me for trying to give a small town girl a big city opportunity. From this point on, don't expect me to ever do anymore favors for you."

I can't believe Guy had the nerve to argue with me about something so irrelevant. And to think, he was really mad.

My mom invited Alain and I over for dinner tonight and when we arrived he gave my mother a big hug and kiss. I tried my best to not look at Nanna because I could feel her smiling at me and I didn't want to blush in front of Alain.

"Chris, could you help Nanna with something in the kitchen?" she asked as she smiled walking out the room.

I followed her into the kitchen and before I got through the door she was already hollering.

"Child, I was only hoping that he looked half as good as you said! He's so handsome!" she said, pinching my cheeks and sashaying back into the den but abruptly stopped and turned back around to face me. "You better not let this one go."

I walked up to her and threw my arms around her shoulder, "Don't worry, this one will be in my life for a very long time."

After dinner, Alain sat in the den and talked to my dad for over an hour then went outside to shoot hoops with Everett. Meanwhile mom, Nanna, Eva and I looked through hair magazines to help Eva decide on a hairstyle for her cotillion. Angela even came by and hung out for a while. All in all this was one of those picture perfect days that I'll always remember. Not because anything significant happened, but the fact that my whole family was together, hanging out and loving one another on an ordinary autumn day.

THURSDAY, 10/26

Alain and I woke up sniffling because the temperature had suddenly turned chilly. This first day of blustery weather was a harsh reminder that winter was well on its way. We could literally see our breath as we walked out to the parking lot, shivering and fumbling with our keys before we kissed each other goodbye. I had a busy day today, with a nine o'clock Urban Arts Council meeting, where I was nominated chairman of the board, an eleven o'clock luncheon that lasted until three, a client strategy meeting at four and a last minute meeting with a prospect at six. Just as I was trying to decide whether to go home and rest or partake in a big sale at Macy's, Reese called wanting to go out.

"Do you have plans tonight?"

"No, actually I don't."

"Good, then you can go to the Circle City Professionals networking mixer tonight."

"The last time I went, I vowed that I'd never go to another one of those tired mixers again. Plus the last time I went, I begged for you to come and you refused."

"It's different this time."

"Why?"

"They moved to a better location, plus William Devereaux's going to be there."

"And who is that?"

"My next victim," she said, letting out a sinister chuckle.

"You are so pitiful. Oh but guess what? I'm not going."

"You're just scared that you're going to see Mekhi, that's all that is," she laughed.

"I'm not even thinking about him."

"Then what's holding you back? You haven't come up for air to hang with your girls since you've been back from California. Which brings me to another point, what happened? Did you and sexual chocolate finally slip and slide?"

"I'm not telling you."

"You're either telling me now over the phone or tonight at the mixer. Take your choice because I'm not getting off of the phone otherwise."

"Look, if I go to this wack mixer will you leave me alone?"

We ended up having a halfway decent time at the event. I got a chance to meet Reese's new prey, William who wasn't half bad. Once he left to get back to mingling, Resse began prying again.

"Please tell me that you and Alain finally hooked up."

"Reese, you won't believe me when I tell you that we made love but we didn't actually have sex."

"Either you did or didn't."

"We've had plenty of passionate sessions but we've never actually had intercourse. I have to tell you, as strange as it sounds it's extremely satisfying."

"And you guys are doing this why?"

"It just is what it is."

"So, Alain still thinks you're celibate?"

"We've never officially talked about it, so I'm assuming yes."

"Are you ever going to talk about it?"

"Eventually. Things just feel so good and pure right now."

"You're a good one."

"It'll happen sooner or later but trust me I'm not missing out. This non-sex is the best sex I've ever had. Alain is the first man to ever make me reach my peak not once, not twice, but multiple times in a row."

"It's wonderful isn't it?"

"Words cannot describe."

As Reese and I continued to discuss our love lives, her original prediction came true. Mekhi walked into the room.

"Well would you look at who just slithered in," Reese said. "Oh shit, here he comes."

"What's up ladies?" Mekhi said as he squeezed in between Reese and I, then gave her a look. "Reese, do you mind?"

"I'm not going anywhere."

"Mekhi's there's nothing that we have to talk about in private, what do you want?"

"You're right, I'm not ashamed to have witnesses for what I'm about to say. First off, I wanted to tell you how good you look."

"Is that all?"

"No. I want to say I'm sorry about how I acted the last time we talked," he said as Reese started laughing out loud.

"I really don't have time for this," I said as I stood up.

"Hold up Christian. I've been thinking about some things over the past couple of months and I think there's a chance for us to start over. How 'bout we finish this discussion over dinner this weekend?"

"No he didn't," Reese said as I turned around to face Mekhi.

"I sure hope you don't think I'm sitting around lonely, waiting to get back with you. Understand this, I'm more happy now than I've ever been," I said as I slowly walked towards him. "I have a man, a real man that treats me like a queen. So believe me when I say, no, I don't want to get together this weekend, next year or anytime."

"Get that?" Reese co-signed as we left him sitting there stunned.

Men can really be a trip sometimes.

FRIDAY, 10/27

This morning, Guy made it a point to make my life as chaotic as humanly possible. He and his staff called me every five minutes wanting to change things or bothering me about things that had already been done. I'm guessing that he and Eden had a lover's quarrel last night and he decided to take it out on me today. After dealing with all this morning's drama, I found time to go to the mall and shop for Alain's birthday tomorrow.

Sitting on my living room floor wrapping all of Alain's gifts, I still wasn't one hundred percent satisfied with the book on the history of jazz, the bottle of Acqua Di Gio cologne or the sexy robe I bought for him. Everything I got was nice, but none of it stood out as extra special. That was until I got a bright idea and made a detour to the nearest AAA.

SATURDAY, 10/28

I called Alain at six this morning and made him get up and get dressed because I was coming over to pick him up at eight. The day was sunny and mild in the mid-fifties, a perfect day in my book because I was now able to sport some of my new fall gear.

"What's on the agenda?"

"I'm not telling you. Just wait right here and I'll be back in few minutes," I said then walked up to his bedroom and closed the door. I quickly packed a couple of his outfits and essential toiletries into an overnight bag. When I walked back into the living room, he was lying across his couch with his eyes closed. I stood behind him and gave him a quick neck massage. When I did this, he cracked a cute smile.

"Happy Birthday baby," I whispered in his ear.

"I thought you forgot," he said sitting up.

"You know I'd never forget your birthday. After we eat breakfast, I'll give you the first part of your gift."

Alain got really suspicious when we got on I-74 East towards Cincinnati.

"Where are we going?"

"You'll find out when we get there so just sit back and be quiet!" I joked as Alain made a face like a spoiled little boy who had just gotten in trouble. In an hour and a half we exited the highway and Alain immediately spotted the image of a huge roller coaster in the distance behind a line of trees. As we pulled into the entrance of the amusement park, Alain began smiling from ear to ear.

"Aw, thank you baby!" he said getting out of the car.

"There's more to come later," I said as he turned around and kissed me in the parking lot.

A few kids behind us, decked out in Halloween costumes, got a kick out of our public display of affection and began ooh'ing and aah'ing. Alain turned around and made a funny face at them as we laughed and rushed up to the park entrance hand in hand. Once we were inside, Alain acted like a kid in a candy store. When we got to the start of the line of the first roller coaster, I pinched his cheek and told him to have fun as I began walking toward the nearest park bench.

"Oh no. You can't bring me all the way out here and not ride anything."

"Baby, I haven't ridden a coaster in years. I don't think I can handle it."

"Are you scared love? I won't let anything happen to you."

"Nah, babe. I don't think I can."

"Pleassssse, it's my birthday," he said pouting. "You can't let me ride all by myself on my birthday."

I stood there for a couple of seconds staring at the tallest hill of the ride, watching people scream at the top of their lungs, "No, I'll wait."

"Look, that little girl just got off of the ride and she's probably only eight years old. Don't let her outdo you," Alain joked as the giggly little girl exited the ride with her father.

"You'll be fine by yourself," I said as Alain turned to look at me with basset hound eyes. "Okay, okay I'll get on the stupid ride."

When I sat down in the car I immediately wanted to stand up and get off but before I could, one of the park attendants pushed the brace bar down over our waists and we could no longer move. Alain held my hand as I leaned over and laid my head on his shoulder while the coaster began to move. We slowly rolled around a corner then approached a steep hill. As the ride crept up the incline, I closed my eyes as Alain put his arm tightly around me. When it was all over I can honestly say that I had fun. After that ride, Alain was able to talk me into getting on almost every ride in the park, with a few exceptions. There were some rides that were just clearly out of my league, and to my surprise, out of Alain's as well.

After we left, we checked into our hotel where he later unwrapped the rest of his gifts. He tore into the wrapping on his book, destroyed the paper on his cologne, demolished the box containing his robe and delicately peeled the wrapping off of me.

SUNDAY, 10/29

On the road back to Indianapolis, Erik called Alain inviting us over to watch the Pacer game tonight.

"I told Erik that we'd come by, is that okay with you?"

"Yeah that's fine. Who else is coming over?"

"He didn't say," Alain said as he turned on the radio and scanned through all of the Cincinnati stations.

"My iPod is in my bag in the back seat. I don't think I can reach it."

"Don't worry about it. I'm trying to find some gospel music," he said stopping on a station playing Yolanda Adams. "Man I feel bad. I haven't been to church in over a month. I can't believe you haven't gotten on me about that."

"It's not your fault, you've been busy."

"I know but that shouldn't be an excuse. Let's go to church together when you get back from New York."

"I guess I should be honest with you, I really don't go to church. I watch it on T.V. but I'm not into actually going."

"You're kidding me."

"No, I'm serious."

"Why?"

"Alain, it's a long story."

"We've got over an hour before we get home, fire away."

After I explained all about my past experiences in the church and how it's changed my perspective, Alain's reaction sounded just like my mother's.

"You can't let people keep you from getting your spiritual house in order. Queen, I hate to tell you this but that's not a good enough excuse."

"You just don't understand," I said, ending the conversation.

As we rode for the next thirty miles in silence and I could see Alain peering over at me out of the corner of my eye. Finally, he broke the silence.

"It would mean a lot if you'd go to church with me when you get back. Will you go?" he asked, stroking the side of my cheek while I kept my eyes on the road. "Christian, I asked you a question."

"Yes, I'll go."

When we got back to the city we headed straight to Erik's house. He lives in a very attractive warehouse loft not far from Alain. For the most part, we had a good time watching the game, although the Bulls were defeating the Pacers, but that all changed at the beginning of the fourth quarter.

"So when was the last time you spoke to your girl?" Erik asked while I was in the kitchen pouring myself a glass of club soda.

"Who, Reese?"

"Yeah."

"I talked to her two days ago."

"Did she say anything about me?"

"No, why?"

"Your girl is buck wild."

"Reese is a person who likes to have fun, what's wrong with that?"

"She likes a little more than fun. Reese puts herself out there."

"Be careful now, that's one of my best friends."

"I'm not trying to talk greasy about her, I'm just telling it like it is. Now that I know you, it's hard to believe you'd associate yourself with someone like her, sorority sister or not."

"Erik, I guarantee that I know her a lot better than you do. Reese is a wonderful person."

"Well since you know her like that, you may want to inform her that people are talking and it ain't good. Your girl gets around. Trust me, I know firsthand."

"If you know firsthand then apparently you're just as guilty as she is."

"You don't have to get defensive."

"Trust me, I'm not defensive I'm just sick of the double standard."

"Christian, calm down."

When I went back into the den, I grabbed my jacket and whispered to Alain that I was heading out. When he asked why, I just simply explained to him that the Pacers weren't the only losers in downtown Indianapolis tonight.

"Girl whatever you do, please don't mess around with Erik anymore," I said to Reese, juggling the phone to my ear as I stood in the closet, picking out my outfit for tomorrow.

"What are you talking about?"

"I'm talking about him putting all of your business in the street. Not to mention, you work with him. You don't want that kind of information swarming around the office."

"Believe me I'm not worried about that fool. He can say whatever he wants, people don't take him seriously."

"Well just in case they do, you should leave him alone."

"Chris, it's not that big of an issue. I have my boy toys and Erik just happens to be one of them," she said.

"Wow," I said in disbelief. "I guess I'll just let you handle this however you see fit."

"You know I love you but I think your time would be better spent concentrating on your own relationship, no offense."

"Classic," I said, stunned at Reese's reaction. "I'll let you get back to whatever you were doing and I'll talk to you later."

Reese didn't reply, she just immediately hung up.

So much for looking out for a sister. I guess some people simply have to learn the hard way.

MONDAY, 10/30

I spent the majority of today with Angela, trying to finalize and strategize any last minute situations that may arise in the next couple of days. Most of our planning was done underneath the dryers and the pedicure chairs at the salon. We both walked out looking like a million dollars. I got subtle honey highlights to my newly layered hair and Angela totally flipped the script by braving the big chop.

"This morning your hair was down your back. You're more courageous than I am," I said, running my hands through her gorgeous mountain of shiny natural curls.

"It's just hair. It'll be back by next fall. Besides, I'm about to go to NYC so I gotta represent!" Angela said as she unlocked her car door.

"I heard that!"

"Wow, she looks good," she joked, checking herself out in the rear view mirror with a smug smile. "You know, I just thought about something. I moved out of my old place a week after Josie left. It's almost been a whole month and you still haven't seen my new apartment. Do you have time for a quick tour?"

Angela's new apartment building was the epitome of a bohemian paradise. The artwork that adorned the halls and elevators were original paintings by the tenants who lived there, including Angela. When you stepped off the elevator there were large velvet pillows and incense burning in an alcove with a big picture window overlooking an urban playground. All of the apartment doors were painted in various jewel tones, deep purples, golds and reds and

Angela's was a deep burgundy shade with a huge gold knob that reminded me of Alice in Wonderland. Inside Angela's apartment she had original artwork displayed all over, some on easels, some on the walls and some in her windowsills. Her bedroom was just an elevated area on one side of the apartment that held her bed, two nightstands and a floor lamp. Her bathroom had original subway tile with a claw foot tub and her kitchen was cute and retro in design contrasted with modern stainless steel appliances.

"Although it's a studio, it has way more square footage than my old two bedroom apartment," she said, beaming as she showed me around her place. Angela had every right to be proud. Her apartment looked like a chic art gallery that just happened to have a bed.

"You should bring me some of your pieces, Chris. I'll be more than happy to put them up. You know I have to give my sister a little showcase," she said to my surprise.

"You really want one of my paintings?" I asked as she nodded her head.

"I already have one in mind. It's the blue and yellow one in your sunroom."

"You like that?"

"Yeah. That painting is just another example of how creative and talented you are," she said then paused for a few seconds. "You not only have a business and analytical mind, but a creative one as well. I admire you. Not many people are blessed like that."

"Thank you," I said, honored that Angela felt that way about me, especially since I'd gone throughout life with the impression that she despised me.

"So can I have the painting?"

"It's all yours."

TUESDAY, 10/31

Before going home after a day full of meetings and client calls, I went to the drugstore to pick up some Halloween candy for the adults who annually come to my door trick or treating, particularly the guys directly above me who really get into the masquerade thing. The few kids who do come by are usually from a youth group or something, but my average trick or treaters are gay men in their thirties out having fun.

I was in the kitchen making tortilla soup for Alain when Carra called to catch up. After about fifteen minutes, in mid-conversation about work, Carra moaned, "hold on". The next thing I know, I hear Carra in the background coughing and gagging. A few minutes later she got back on the phone and picked up the conversation right where we left off, "So, as I was saying…"

"Are you okay?"

"Morning sickness. Well I guess you can say evening sickness."

"Yuck! How are you going to be in mid-conversation with me, excuse yourself to go puke then come back to the conversation like nothing happened. You need to go lay down somewhere."

"Oh, I'm used to it now. I'm fine."

"Where's Aaron?"

"Do you even need to ask that question?"

"So I take it he's out of town."

"Correctomondo."

"How have you two been since the last time we spoke?"

"A little better. Remember when I told you about the business deal he was supposed to get into?"

"Yeah."

"Well, my instincts were right because that million dollar deal fell through."

"Really?"

"Yeah. One of the guys is threatening to dissolve the business if they can't get a new client by the end of the year."

"Carra, I know what you're thinking but try to resist saying I told you so."

"That's the same thing our marriage counselor told me."

"I didn't know you guys were in counseling."

"Yeah, for about three weeks now. I'm actually going to refer Celeste and John to our counselor. It may be a far cry but she may be able help their situation."

"What situation?"

"Oh, she didn't tell you."

"Tell me what?"

"Well John…" she said then got quiet. "Oh I'll let her tell you when she's ready."

"What's going on?"

"I don't know if I should say."

"Carra just tell me."

"Chris, John has a one year old son in Cleveland."

"What!"

"She found out the night before her mom got sick. Don't tell her that I told you. When she tells you, act like you don't know."

"Maybe this is all just hearsay. Maybe it's a huge misunderstanding."

"No, it's true."

"How did she find out?"

"The child's mother called their house while John was at work. She was crying, saying that she hopes John doesn't forget about them now that he's married."

"Did Celeste confront John about this?"

"Yes."

"Did he deny it?"

"No," she said softly.

Alain and I ate dinner as we watched *The Shining*, though I couldn't concentrate on anything but Celeste's situation.

Alain pushed pause for the tenth time while I got up to answer the door for the trick or treaters and when I sat back down, I turned the movie off.

"Uh oh, I think somebody's getting scared," he said then noticed the serious expression on my face. "What's wrong queen?"

"Carra told me that John has a one year old son that no one knew about."

"What?"

"Yes."

"Have you talked to Celeste?"

"Not yet. I really wouldn't know what to say."

"Man, I knew that John was wild but I didn't think he was that bad."

"Why do you say that?"

"Well, put it this way. He had a very good time at his bachelor party."

"I thought you said you guys went to play laser tag."

"We did but afterwards we went to his brother's house. That's when things got out of control."

"I don't believe you're just now telling me this. What happened?"

"I don't know the details, all I know is that John and one of the dancers were in Seth's bedroom for over an hour."

"Alain I thought you were better than that. How come you didn't tell me?"

"Babe, I didn't want to make a big deal out of it."

"Well you should've. This is one of my best friends we're talking about. I think I need to know if her man was screwing some trailer chick within twenty-four hours of them getting married."

"Hold on here, we don't know what went on so let's not jump to conclusions," he said calmly. "Look, I didn't say anything because I didn't want to cause any static."

"No, you didn't want to break the male code of silence, I get it. So tell me Alain, how much fun did you have that night?"

He looked at me like I was crazy, "Christian stop it."

"How am I supposed to know you didn't join in on the reindeer games?"

"Because you know me better than that."

"I thought I did. I also would've thought you'd tell me that my best friend's fiancé was cheating. You being silent all this time makes you just as guilty as he is."

"I don't believe this."

"Since men think it's alright to do things behind closed doors as long as they don't get caught, let's forget about the bachelor party for a moment and talk about Chicago. How am I supposed to know that you aren't juggling me and who knows how many other chicks you were messing with when you lived there?"

"This is getting out of hand. Christian, all men are not out to dog women. John f'ed up, that doesn't mean I did or ever will because that's not my style. I care about you too much. Even early on, I was doing everything possible to win you over. I would never compromise this."

"If John could do it after five years then what would make me think…"

"You know what," Alain said, cutting me off. "I came over here with the intent to hang out and spend some quality time with my woman. I'm not used to this kind of drama."

"Then leave."

"Oh, it's like that?" he said standing up, staring at me. Once he saw that I wasn't responding, he grabbed his jacket and left.

What the hell have I done? Damn it Christian, Alain has been nothing but a true king and here I am acting crazy, going off on him about something John did. I'm so used to the men I've dealt with in the past that I didn't want to accept that this one was different. I can't believe that I just sat there and let my fear of being hurt again rear its ugly head and ruin a great evening. After a few minutes of pacing back and forth, I couldn't take the feelings of guilt anymore. I had to go get my man.

Once I got to the security door of his apartment, I tried to remember his code. 346019 didn't work. 364109 didn't work either. I tried several sequences of those numbers but none of them worked. Just when I was about to try one last time, my cell phone rang,

"It's 361094. I saw you pull up five minutes ago."

"Thanks," I said shamefully. "I'm on my way up."

When he opened the door, he looked a little unsure of how to react. He looked so confused that I couldn't help but to walk up to him and give him a long, deep kiss.

"I'm so sorry Alain."

"It's okay. I know you're upset," he said holding me tight. "You're right, I should have told you about the bachelor party. I'm sorry about that. Just remember this, you got me. I'm all yours and I'm not going anywhere."

"Thank you."

"I know what we can do to make this night go a little better."

"What's that?"

"You need some ITT time."

"ITT?"

"In the tub time," he said, running his fingers through my hair. "You need to relieve some stress."

"I think you're right," I replied as he took my hand and lead me to the bathroom.

As Alain drew the bathwater, I walked behind him and held him for what seemed like forever.

"I promise I won't ever act like that again."

"And I promise to be open and honest with you about everything," he said, pouring bath oil into the tub. "Queen, I'm in this for the long haul. I'm not interested in getting back on the dating scene, especially now that I've found you. Christian, you're my soul mate."

"I feel the same way. I can't picture myself being with anyone else."

"I hope not," he said, flicking water at me.

While in the tub, I sat feeling melancholy as Alain rubbed my shoulders and temples. When the water started to get cold, we quietly wrapped each other up in large towels then got underneath the covers.

As we lay in bed holding each other, tears began streaming down my face. I can't imagine how Celeste must feel knowing that she's carrying John's second child.

"I know you feel awful about Celeste's situation, but everything will work out the way it's supposed to. In the meantime there's something the both of us can do to help," Alain said, grabbing my hand and kneeling down at the edge of the bed. "We need to pray for them."

"Christian, are you awake?" Alain whispered in my ear.

"Yes."

"I want you to know something. We were put together for a reason. There isn't anyone out there more perfect for me than you. And I'm the only person God has equipped to love you the way you need to be loved. Don't ever forget that."

WEDNESDAY, 11/1

I called and left a message for Celeste first thing this morning. I didn't get specific, I just let her know that I'm here for her no matter what she's going through.

Angela met me at four o'clock and at four forty-five we took a taxi to the airport and barely made our six thirty flight. On the plane we discussed every little detail concerning the event. With every topic I uttered the more excited she became.

"I can't believe I'm going to New York!" Angela said, fidgeting in her seat.

"I can't believe that I'm producing this event," I said as I held on to the armrest of my chair during a moment of turbulence.

"After this event you'll have every clothing designer and cosmetics company beating down your door."

"With you as my partner?"

"You bet," she said as she searched for a file on her laptop. "Here are some preliminary ideas I have for the jazz fest."

"Wow Angela," I said marveling over her design that incorporated influential jazz artists from past and present.

"I have some other concepts that I came up with. I'll show you when we get back home."

"I can't wait to see them. You are so talented."

"I get it from my big sis," she said then paused after noticing my hands tapping nervously. "We need to get you a stiff martini after we check in."

"Why do you say that?"

"Look at you. Your hands are shaking like an old woman."

"I don't know why I've become so anxious lately. This happened to me in San Diego. I'm usually not like this."

"Well calm down and breathe. Everything's going to be okay."

"I know," I said, closing my eyes. "Everything's going to be just fine."

After we checked in, we went to Angela's room to map out our game plan for tomorrow. When I got back to my room, I cracked the windows and took a couple of deep Yoga breaths to calm down. When I tried to fall asleep I tossed and turned for what seemed like eternity then it dawned on me, just like yesterday I needed to pray. After that, I felt calm.

THURSDAY, 11/2

I woke up at five thirty this morning and got right to work. I called Angela's room to give her a wake up call and she moaned, groaned and grumbled until I threatened to come over and beat down her door. Come to find out, the reason she was so tired was because she met up with a friend from Queens and decided to hang out all night.

"Girl, don't you go leaving your room in the middle of the night without telling me. What if something happened to you?" I said as we sat down for breakfast.

"Mariam, are you finished?"

"Yeah, I may sound like mom right now but you know what, I can send your little tail home," I joked as she playfully rolled her eyes.

When we arrived at the Illum headquarters, I gave Angela the lay of the land before the board members and investors arrived. Guy tried his best to give me the cold shoulder until I introduced him to Angela. He barely said two words to me but he was all in her face trying to get buddy-buddy. I swear some people are so transparent.

The investors meeting began at eight thirty and from that point on, I was in total manager mode. Forget anxiety, forget nervousness and forget Guy, Christian was on a mission. Perfection is what I aimed for and the results were as close to perfect as I've ever seen. I was so happy that everyone, with the exception of Guy, chipped in to make the day run as smooth as possible.

After the morning meetings, I scheduled four limousines to pick up the investors and board members for a power lunch at Aquavit. After the last group of people left, Angela and I raced down Fifth Ave. to prepare for the evening events at The Rainbow Room in Rockefeller Center. As the day progressed I felt less stressed. By the time dinner had ended and we were making our way back to the hotel for cocktails, I was on top of the world. Never would I have imagined things would run so smoothly.

While Angela and I were sitting at the bar chatting, Guy came over and rudely interrupted our conversation by standing in front of me and began talking to Angela.

"So Angela," Guy said then paused with a puzzled look on his face. "Do you go by Angela or Angie?"

"Both," she said smiling at him. "Call me whichever one you want."

"Well, Angie," he said, never once looking at me. "Is this your first time in New York?"

"Yeah, it is."

"How do you like it so far?"

"I love it," she said oblivious to the fact that Guy was being a complete asshole towards me. "Hopefully I'll have time to hit up some museums and galleries while I'm here."

"You sound like an artist."

"I am," she said then leaned around Guy towards me with a confused look. "Didn't Christian tell you that I designed all of the graphics for this project?"

"No, she told us that you were her personal assistant," he said in a snide tone.

"That's cold Christian," Angela said, looking disappointed.

"Excuse me," I said sharply at Guy and lightly pushed him over to the side. "Angela you know me better than that. I told *everyone* that you were the brains behind the designs. I just don't think *some people* were listening."

"Anyway," he said smirking, obviously satisfied that he caused some minor tension between my sister and I. "So Angie, what type of art do you do?"

"Well as you now know graphic design, but I'm also a painter, illustrator and sculptor."

"I've gotta get you over to the Studio Museum in Harlem."

"It's on my list of places to go while I'm here."

"I'll arrange something for you in the next couple of days," he said then dramatically scratched his head. "Do you have any free time tomorrow?"

"I'll have to check. Why?"

"We're having an open call for our spring make-up line. Have you ever modeled?"

"Only in art class."

"Well, you've got the perfect look for Illum."

"What time is the open call?"

"Noon."

Angela looked at me for some feedback, "Do you think we'll be done by then?"

"Oh you'll be done," Guy answered, indifferent to whatever I had to say.

"Actually, we won't be done," I said giving him a pissed-off look then noticed Angela looking disappointed. "But I guess by that time I'll be able to handle it on my own. Go ahead and do it."

FRIDAY, 11/3

As I was putting on my makeup this morning, Angela called to tell me that she and Guy were meeting for breakfast. I tried not to be irritated by the fact that they didn't invite me, but deep down I was. After hanging up with her, it dawned on me that I hadn't spoken to Alain since Wednesday morning. I tried calling him but he didn't answer.

"Hey baby, I can't wait to tell you how great things are going so far. I've got the big party in the Hamptons tonight so I won't be available to talk until after midnight. I hope you're having a good day. I'll talk to you later. Love ya."

After I grabbed a quick bite for breakfast I hailed a cab and sat lonely through the heavy Manhattan traffic. When I arrived at Illum, Angela was already in the conference room setting up for me.

"Hey girl," she said light-heartedly.

"Hey. How was breakfast?"

"Good. I got a chance to show Guy some of my artwork."

"That's cool. Are you excited about this afternoon?"

"Yeah. Now are you sure that you can handle everything on your own?"

"It shouldn't be a problem. What time are you leaving?"

"Eleven."

"That's fine. The group breaks for lunch at eleven forty-five and the meeting adjourns at two. I'll be able to handle it from there."

About an hour before the meeting broke for lunch, Angela whispered that she had to go get ready for the audition and asked one last time if it was still okay for her to go. After I reassured her that it was, Guy came to the door and discretely motioned for her to come out into the hall. She got up and slid out of the conference room with confidence and as soon as she stepped out, I could see the two of them through the frosted window skipping down the hall like happy little elves.

After the meeting, which ended an hour late, I scrambled to politely shew people out, oversee the return of the audio-visual equipment and get myself ready to go to the investor's reception. I looked out the window to the atrium below and I saw waves of Illum staff filing into the limos that were transporting everyone to the Carter Mansion in Bridgehampton. That nervous feeling began rushing all throughout my body again as I darted to the restroom, applied make-up, put on my gown and fixed my hair in under ten minutes. Just as I was zipping up my bag to head downstairs, one of the interns peaked in to tell me that the last limo was about to leave. I rushed downstairs and jumped in the limo, panting and out of breath. As we were about to pull off someone tapped on the window.

"I barely made it," Toussaint smiled as he slid in the seat in front of me.

"I haven't seen you in a long time."

"Not since I mistook you for one of our models. You know, you made me late for my meeting that day."

"I did not make you late," I replied, remembering the day I gave my final presentation for this project and I met Toussaint flirting with me in the hall. "So, how's the job treating you?"

"Aside from the continuous contract discrepancies and a potential trademark infringement with one of our slogans, the job's fine."

"Ah, the life of an attorney."

"Ain't that the truth."

"Is that an accent I detect?"

"Yeah," he chuckled. "Comes out every now and then."

"Where are you from?"

"New Orleans. I left about ten years ago."

"Was moving here a big adjustment for you?"

"Not really. I came to New York because my ex-wife landed her dream job as an art specialist for Sotheby's. My then father in-law purchased an apartment for us on the Upper East Side and secured a job for me as a corporate attorney for a real estate developer."

"That's cool."

"Not really. Her family controlled every aspect of our lives. Everything we did was because they set it up," he said slicking back his thick, wavy hair. "I swear, my dad will deny it until he's blue in the face but I was part of an arranged marriage."

"Stop lying."

"One hand on the bible, I swear I'm not."

"So you don't feel like you had a choice in marrying your ex?"

"In so many words, no."

"Wow, so how does an arranged marriage happen in this day and age?"

"Trust me, prominent families in Louisiana have long rooted systems in place to ensure their children will only associate with who they want them to. I knew her all of my life, courted her throughout prep school and college and eventually grew to love her."

"Did you really love her?"

"I still love her 'til this day, but we weren't ever in love."

"Why'd you end up divorcing, if you don't mind me asking?"

"Just like I said, we realized that we weren't in love. We came to that conclusion together and although we were fine with it, our families lost their minds."

Toussaint and I talked for most of the two-hour trip then managed to steal a quick nap for the last half hour or so. Once we arrived at the mansion, Toussaint met with the rest of the Illum staff for dinner while I put my game face back on. To my dismay, none of the grounds contractors had begun any of the work they were scheduled to do. They were all sitting around smoking, laughing and listening to loud music. As I walked up the courtyard they all looked at me, looked around at each other then began talking and smoking again. I didn't want to do it, but at that point I switched on total bitch mode because we only had two hours before guests would begin to arrive.

"Why are you guys just sittin' out here chillin' when you're supposed to be working? Has anyone started any anything?"

No one said a word.

"Hello? Am I speaking a foreign language here? Has anything been done yet?"

"Look around, does anything look like it's been done?" A guy said in a thick Long Island accent while his buddies laughed.

"Oh I'll give you something to laugh about. Your pay doesn't start until you start working and your overtime doesn't start until two hours after that! By a show of hands, how many people out here are brand new on the job?"

No one raised a hand.

"That's what I thought, now get to work!" I said as I approached an older electrician. "Is Mr. Carter here?"

"He's out back on the lawn," the gentleman replied.

"Shit!" I said under my breath, knowing that he wouldn't be happy with the lack of progress at the main entrance.

As I hustled up the stairs, I could feel the unseasonably warm wind blowing on my calves and thighs through the split in the back of my evening gown. A few of the guys got a kick out of it and started whistling, until I turned around and gave them the sixth grade math teacher stare. From that point on they all shut up at once and began scrambling to start working.

Luckily the people inside weren't as shiftless as the groundsmen. I was pleased to see they had all of the rooms set up and decorated just like I'd requested. When I walked through the house out to the terrace, I saw Mr. Carter and two older European men with croquet sticks in their hands.

"My, my, my. The wind blows beautiful this time of year. How are you my dear?" Mr. Carter said, giving me a double kiss.

"I'm good."

"Glad to hear that," he said, noticing the other two gentlemen looking at him. "Christian, let me introduce you to my new partners, Jean-Claude and Laurent."

"Nice to meet you both," I said, extending my hand.

They both nodded and instead of shaking my hand, they kissed it. After the formal greetings, Mr. Carter mumbled something to the two men in French and they nodded at me once more before walking off.

"Is everything coming along okay?" Mr. Carter asked as he laid down his croquet stick.

"Yes, everything's running smoothly so far."

"Good, so there's no need for me to worry about the slow progress on the front lawn," he said smiling.

"I've taken care of it."

"I'm just teasing with you. I know you're on top of things. So have you given any thought to how you want to make things better for next year?"

"I have a few ideas," I said, completely taken aback by his statement. I had only hoped to be reconsidered for next year, but after Guy's attitude I figured it was a lost cause.

"I'm anxious to hear what you propose," he said as he noticed his wife on the terrace. "Carmen! I have someone I want you to meet."

"It's a pleasure meeting you," I said as I shook her hand.

"So this is the woman responsible for this event? I've invited a few members of my art guild tonight and I'm sure they'll be taking notice. We're in the early stages of planning our major fundraiser for next year and we're looking for someone with a fresh approach. You never know," she said winking.

"I'll make it a point to introduce myself to them tonight," I said as my walkie-talkie began beeping.

"I'll let you get that," Mr. Carter said as he took a sip of Carmen's champagne.

"Yes?" I said into the receiver.

"Hey, I've got a guy up front saying that he's from *The Times* but he doesn't have a press pass and he's not on the list. Can you come up here and see if you can straighten this out?"

"I'll be there in a minute," I said as the Carter's stood there smiling. "Excuse me, I need to go handle this."

"We understand," they said in unison as I rushed across the lawn back into the house.

About two hours later, guests began arriving and the limousines were lined up at least a quarter of a mile outside of the estate. As I stood at the door helping with the guest list, I began to wonder where Angela was. I knew that she had her audition, but afterwards she was supposed to meet me to help with the set-up. The answer to my question came a half-hour later. There she was, getting out of a limo all glammed up with Guy and two other model type girls. As they glided up the stairs, camera's flashed from every angle. The interesting thing about the whole scenario was that Angela was a natural in the spotlight. She walked the walk and definitely looked the part. This was her element. As she and her entourage made their way up the last flight of stairs, we made eye contact. Her look of confidence quickly became a look of fear as she stared at me as if to say, *Uh oh, I'm in trouble now*. All I could do was nudge my head towards the door and motion for her to just go on inside. She winked at me, put her game face back on then sashayed up the stairs into the party.

For the majority of the evening Guy acted like a complete and utter ass. Every five minutes there seemed to be an issue with him.

"Is Jeffrey Rubenstein here?" he said looking over my shoulder at the guest list.

"He's not on the list."

"He doesn't need to be, he's the new fashion editor for *The Times*," he said with an attitude.

"Is he a short Jewish guy with square glasses and curly hair?"

"Yeah, is he here?"

"No because we had to turn him away earlier."

"Why in the hell would you do that?" Guy yelled.

"Because he didn't have a business card, he didn't have a press pass, he wasn't on the list and you weren't answering your phone, plus you made it painfully clear that no one and I quote 'not even Donald Trump himself' gets past the door without being on the list."

When I said that, he turned around and stormed off. As if that weren't enough, while I was outside informing one of the electricians of a blown string of bulbs on the rear lawn, one of those 1980's chicken cars pulled into the driveway. Please don't let Guy see this, I thought as I ran up to security to tell them to redirect the car. Luckily someone else had beaten me to the punch because I saw them hustle over to talk to the driver. Seconds later, Guy rushed out and stomped down the stairs pointing. When he stood in front of me he closed his eyes, dramatically held up his hand and started speaking in slow, low tone, "There's a car, with a four foot chicken on the roof, wearing a cowboy hat, in front of the Carter Mansion," then started spazzing out and began yelling, "What the hell is wrong with this picture! Do you not realize there are millionaires in this house? Are you that incompetent?"

"Would you calm the hell down," I accidentally blurted out.

"What did you just say?"

"Guy, they're about to leave."

"That's not the point. Why are they here in the first place?"

Just then, a security guard walked up behind me and addressed Guy's question. I'm glad he did because I was honestly about to go off on him.

"It's all taken care of. They were here to pick up someone from the kitchen staff. We told him to go to the parking lot at the gate entrance but he made a wrong turn and wound up in front of the house. It's fine."

After security backed me up, Guy pretty much stayed out of my hair for the remainder of the night, though he made it a point to be catty and roll his eyes every time I passed him. Instead of getting mad, I just thought about that big number on my check and mentally told him where he could go.

"Who's that?" Angela asked, drooling over Toussaint as he helped Mr. Carter bid farewell to the last remaining guests.

"He's Illum's general counsel."

"Whew. He's beautiful."

"I know."

"You know? Ooooh, I'm telling Alain."

"And I'm telling Tyson."

"Tell him. I may be on lock down but I'm not blind," she said fanning.

"You need to go douse yourself with some cold water."

"You know I'm just playing," she said noticing me looking at my watch, hoping those were the final guests. "I'm sorry about not helping tonight. You don't have to pay me for anything after this morning's meeting."

"I wasn't going to," I said with a phony attitude. "But I will anyway."

"Thanks Chris."

"No problem. What are you about to do now?"

"I think Guy's going to take us clubbin'," she said then began doing a little shimmy dance.

"Well have fun."

"You're not going to be stuck here all night are you? If so I can stay."

"Go," I said, waving my arms like an old woman. "Have fun and just meet me at my room tomorrow afternoon."

"Not a problem," she said then walked off to join her newfound friends.

Although I knew I'd be stuck at the mansion all night, I didn't want to ruin her fun.

After the final guest left, I oversaw the first portion of the cleanup process then at midnight, I jumped into the last limo headed back to Manhattan. As irony would have it, guess who I saw running down the stairs flagging down the driver as we were about to pull off.

"Driver, stop the car for a minute," I said opening the door.

"Thanks," Toussaint said slamming it behind him.

"I'm leaving you next time," I joked.

"You wouldn't do that," he said smiling. "You know what? The Carters are really impressed with you."

"Is that so?"

"I'll let you in on a little secret. I overheard Carmen Carter raving about you to one of her friends."

"You're kidding me," I said trying to control my grin.

"No lie."

"I was talking to Mr. Carter earlier about the potential for me to plan next year's investor meeting."

"You've got it in the bag."

"And how do you know that?"

"Trust me, I know," he said then started cracking up laughing. "I have to admit, seeing that chicken car pull up in the front of the mansion was funny as hell."

"Don't tell me you saw that."

"Yeah, I saw it. So did Mr. Carter."

"Oh, no."

"Yeah, he laughed it off though."

"Thank God he has a sense of humor."

"So when you're not working with us what other companies do you work with?"

"My major clients are Jean Co. Jeans and one I just landed a few weeks ago, the San Diego Jazz Preservation Society. I'm producing a week long jazz festival for them next year."

"That's really good. I guess your man has to get used to you being out of town a lot."

"He's fine with it. He travels just as much as I do."

"Are you two serious?"

"Yes," I said giving him a look.

"I'm just asking. I gotta' scope out the competition."

"I don't know where this conversation is going."

"I'm just playing with you," he said then paused, "beautiful."

"I didn't hear you, what was that?" I joked.

"You heard me. I called you beautiful."

"Thank you."

"Like you don't already know that."

"You're right. I know it," I said laughing.

"What about me?" he asked, leaning across the seat smiling.

"What about you?"

"Girl, I'm from the south. Anytime someone pays you a compliment you're supposed to return the favor."

"You're alright, but not all that," I said with a straight face then busted out laughing. "You know I'm just playing."

"I know you are," he laughed, running his hands over his wavy hair.

"Can I ask you a question?"

"Shoot it at me."

"I hope this isn't offensive, but what are you? Are you Creole, are you Moroccan?"

"You got it right the first time. My family's Creole. Although I never got a chance to meet him, everyone in my family says I'm the spitting image of my grandfather. Same eyes, same hair, same complexion, same everything. What about you? You've got a different, exotic look. I'd guess your family's from East Africa because you remind me a lot of Iman."

"Wow, that's a huge compliment. To tell you the truth, I couldn't tell you where my family's from."

"I'd do some research if I were you. I can trace my family history back nine generations."

"Uh, probably because a particular side of your family kept proper records of your lineage. Not everybody has it like that."

"Yeah, but keep in mind the majority of my family were descendants of slaves and there are plenty of good records about them too. Just do some digging around, you'll find something."

"I'll have to look into it."

"I'll see you tomorrow at the launch party," I said after getting out of the limo and extending my hand.

"I'm not shaking your hand, you better come here," he said pulling me back in the limo for a hug.

"Are you about to call it a night?"

"I haven't decided. If you want to hang out I'm down."

"No, I'm beat. I'll have to catch you tomorrow night."

"Well get some good sleep tonight," he said with the most hypnotizing smile.

"I will."

"Dream about me tonight," he said laughing before I slammed the door shut. Immediately he rolled down the window and said, "You know I'm just playing with you. Beautiful."

SATURDAY, 11/4

"Hello?"

"Who is this?"

"Paula. Who is this?"

"This is Christian. Why are you answering Alain's phone?"

"Christian who?" she replied.

"Christian who? What do you mean Christian who? His girlfriend Christian, that's who! Why in the hell are you answering his phone this early in the morning and where the hell is Alain?" I asked before she hung up.

What the…I thought as I called back repeatedly and every time going straight to voicemail. I took long deep breaths as I replayed that short conversation over and over in my mind. I don't hear from Alain for days and when I finally get through, his ex answers the phone then hangs up on me. It was six in the morning, why in the hell would they be together this early? I don't believe this shit. This is Mekhi version 2.0, I thought as I paced the room fuming. After all the time we spent together and all the lines he fed me, it boiled down to this?

I tried calming my nerves by starting a pot of water to make some tea but the coffee maker in my room refused to heat beyond lukewarm. Without thinking, I grabbed a bottle of rum from the mini bar and took a shot. Within an hour I'd killed three of the miniature bottles and as I contemplated a fourth, I decided to call and leave a message this time.

"What the hell is Paula doing answering your phone? And why is she answering your phone at six in the morning then hanging up on me? I should have

known better. All that my queen this, my baby that, you definitely had me going. Not anymore. You and Paula have a wonderful life. Screw you Alain! I thought you were different. I thought you were the one!"

"I got the gig!" Angela yelled then immediately noticed my red face and puffy eyes when I opened the door. "Christian, what's wrong?" I tried not to but I broke down and started crying again. Angela walked me over to the bed and wrapped her arms around me. "What is it sis? Talk to me."

I couldn't. I couldn't say anything. As Angela held me and rubbed my back, we sat there in silence until I was all cried out.

"Don't worry about helping out this evening. I can handle it."

"Chris, I'm worried about you."

"I don't really want to talk about it, trust me I'm fine. You just go and enjoy yourself today."

"No, I'm going to stay and help you."

"Really Angela, I can manage on my own," I said perking up my tone. "So, you got the modeling job. Congratulations."

"Christian, I'm still worried about you."

"I'm fine, really. I want to hear about your new opportunity. Trust me, I'm fine."

"If you say so," she said with concern in her eyes. "Well, I found out that I got the Illum gig this morning."

"I'm so proud of you."

"Thanks. I'm excited," she said, reaching over the nightstand and grabbing a handful of tissue for my runny nose. "But that's just the beginning. Guy got me a meeting with a modeling agency. Keep your fingers crossed."

"Definitely. Good luck."

"Thanks. Hey, do you have any more invitations for the party tonight? I have a couple friends I want to invite."

"Go ahead and take the rest of them. There should be about five on the desk."

"Thanks. Now are you sure that you'll be okay tonight? I feel bad for not helping."

"Don't because I'm going to need for you to work extra hard on the jazz fest."

"Not a problem. You know I'm still worried about you though. Whatever you're going through, it'll work itself out, okay."

Christian, you have a job to do so forget Alain and move forward with your life, I thought on my way to the event site. Thankfully when I arrived at 3D everything was set up and looked perfect. Today the workers did exactly what they were supposed to do at the scheduled time they were supposed to do it. By ten o'clock, a sea of people formed outside, anxiously waiting to get in. From the balcony, I could see several husky bouncers making a fortress between the entrance and the eager people waving their invitations, which Angela so beautifully designed, in the air. There were news reporters and press from all over, including Jeffrey Rubenstein from *The Times*, who I made sure to add to the guest list after last night's fiasco. As the night grew, the crowd inside became more influential and affluent.

There was an abundance of models, up and coming designers, the who's who of indie music and film, not to mention a ton of industry big wigs and execs. The thing that most surprised me was that Guy kept his cool and didn't come to me with one complaint. The whole night was a success and I'd finally accomplished producing the largest project of my entire career.

"Hey Christian! I wanted to come by and congratulate you on such a great event."

"Faire! It's so good to see you," I said reaching in to hug him. I hadn't seen him since my initial presentation to Illum this past spring. "Guy told me you're working for another cosmetics company."

"I'm sure he did. He's telling everyone that I went to work for the competition, which isn't true."

"What do you mean?"

"I'm working to launch a new hair color line through Illum's sister company in Paris. He wanted the job but didn't get it."

"Is that so?"

Faire chuckled and directed his attention towards Guy, who was fake laughing with a group of people, "I'm sure he's been an absolute joy to work with."

"You couldn't imagine," I said sarcastically, smiling at Faire.

"The biggest mistake I ever made was going out with him. Not just because we worked together, but he's got the most venomous personality of anyone I've ever met."

"Don't I know," I said without thinking. I shouldn't have said that. Although Guy wasn't my favorite person, I still needed to keep the conversation professional.

"With over three months of dealing with him, I'm sure you do," he said laughing. "I bet he also told you that I sold my interest in the company."

"As a matter of fact he did."

"Well to set the record straight, I did, but so did Mr. Carter and the other initial investors. We were bought out and we all took active employee roles throughout the different divisions of the company."

"Well, I'm happy to know that you're still around."

"Thanks. I shouldn't be telling you this but Guy's on his way out. He's ruffled one too many feathers in this organization and has burned his fair share of bridges. Next year you can breathe a sigh of relief because you won't have to deal with him."

I held back any comments in an attempt to regain some sort of professionalism, however I'm certain my smile said it all.

"I'm having a get together tonight at the Gansevoort. You should come by when you wrap up."

"Thanks, I'll definitely be there."

I was on top of the world after the event ended. I'd survived this weekend and pulled off the most successful project of my career. Standing in the middle of 3D and watching all of the people hustling around me, I couldn't help but smile because for the first time in my professional career I felt validated.

When my taxi pulled in front of the Gansevoort, there was a long line of anxious party-goers snaked around the corner.

After ten minutes of waiting with no movement I was about to give up until I heard, "If you're here for the Faire Mattheson event, please step to the front."

Once escorted to the rooftop lounge, I was ushered past the velvet rope towards Faire and his colleagues.

"Everyone, this is the mastermind behind the Luxe launch party, Christian Cullen."

"Hello," they all said in unison.

"It's a pleasure to meet you all."

"What a wonderful event," a stylish Asian woman said while extending her hand. "I'm Helen Nakamura, president of the Westchester Japanese Cultural Institute. I'd like for you to call me sometime next week. We're premiering a major exhibition next year and I'd like to discuss the possibility of working together on the opening gala."

"Most definitely," I said with confidence. "Do you have a business card?"

As Helen handed me her card another woman in the group inquired, "Was it your idea to collaborate with NYU's department of Egyptian studies to set up that pop up exhibit?"

"Yes. I felt like it was a great opportunity to provide a little insight on how ancient Egyptians used fragrance throughout various aspects of life. More importantly, it served as a great bridge to marry the theme and venue to the brand."

"Very well executed."

"Thank you."

"You have to be hungry," Faire said smiling while rubbing my back.

"Famished."

"Well there's plenty of food over there so dig in."

"I think I'm going to take you up on that offer. It was a pleasure meeting everyone." I said before making my way to the lavish buffet.

The food wasn't the only thing that was plentiful, the host bar was fully stocked with top shelf liquor and throughout the night Faire kept the bubbly flowing with toasts to every and anything he could think of, including a special toast to Image Brokers.

Two hours into the party, I acquired three major business prospects and one solid account for Image Brokers. It's amazing where good first impressions mixed with perfect timing and a little liquor can take you. Faire went out of his way to introduce me to all of the power players at the party not to mention, verbally committing to hire Image Brokers for an international hair show his division is sponsoring. After all I had to deal with earlier in the day this was the high that I needed to get me going full throttle when I return home. More than enough work to keep my mind occupied so I'm not sitting around thinking about Alain.

"You're leaving already!"

I turned to see Mr. and Mrs. Carter, Toussaint and a few other Illum executives crossing the street as I was about to hail a cab.

"I've been here for a few hours. I was just on my way back to the hotel."

"It's only two thirty, the night is still young," Mr. Carter joked as he helped his wife carefully walk across the cobblestone streets of the Meatpacking District. "This is your last evening in the city! You can't call it a night just yet. We're only going to pop our heads in to say hi then we're heading to Soho for tapas. You're more than welcome to join us," he said as Toussaint stood next to him smiling.

I took one look at Toussaint and replied, "Okay, you talked me into it." Without any additional convincing, I walked back into the party with the group.

"I haven't seen you all night," Toussaint said as we stood on the east end of the balcony, taking in the gorgeous views of the skyline.

"I know, there were so many people at the party."

"You outdid yourself. Mission accomplished, the event was hot. You should be proud."

"Thank you," I said turning around to face the city. "New York is so mesmerizing. The energy is magnetic."

"That's why I'm here to stay."

"Just look at how the city sparkles. What a perfect night, not a cloud in the sky."

"It is a gorgeous night, especially for November."

"I know."

"Mild, with a slight hint of chill in the air. This is the perfect weather for…" he paused then snickered a little.

"For what?" I asked as he smiled and walked away. I followed him to the other side of the balcony and stood next to him. "This is the perfect weather for what?"

"For making love," he said as I gave him a shocked look. "Yeah, I said it."

"Oh is it?"

"Indeed it is."

"Sounds like someone has a freaky side," I joked as we walked over to the bar.

"You have no clue."

"Is that so?" I said, feeling the hairs on my neck stand on end as I was starting to go down a forbidden path with this man.

"Yeah," he said slowly, southern drawl and all, then turned towards me gazing with his sensual grayish-blue eyes.

"You've piqued my curiosity," replied the liquor because I know in my right mind I would never have said that sober—well at least to a client.

"Are you two ready to go?" Mr. Carter interrupted.

"I am, how 'bout you Christian?"

"Oh, yeah," I said trying to regain composure. "Ready when you are."

We arrived at the tapas bar at three forty-five in the morning and unbelievably the place still had a wait time. Thankfully Mr. Carter's clout allowed us to be seated immediately, even better, we were at the best table in the house across from the stage where a middle-aged Spanish guitarist played some of the most heart throbbing and romantic music I'd ever heard. I felt like a girl in junior high all throughout our meal because anytime Toussaint's arm brushed against mine, I got all tingly inside. The sexual tension between us was obvious and undeniable. If Alain can have his fun so can I, I thought as I raised my glass of sangria to Mr. Carter's toast request. I've told myself before but now I really mean it, it's time to put Christian first. It's time for me to live a little and have fun. Free of rules, free of commitment and most of all free of restraint. Salud!

SUNDAY, 11/5

I did it.

I know I shouldn't have, but I did.

As I stared at Toussaint sleeping next to me, I replayed our encounter by following the trail of clothing from my hotel door to the bed. *Ummmm*, I thought as I tingled and shivered at the recollection. I know I should've felt shame, guilt even, but I didn't. I felt powerful.

I got up to shut the drapes and when I got back in bed, Toussaint pulled me close to him for round four, or was it five? I'd completely lost count.

"So when are you moving to New York?"

"Who said anything about moving?"

"You should," Toussaint said looking up at me with his head resting on my naked breasts.

"It'd be nice, but if I were to move anywhere it would be Chicago. It's in the middle of the country between all of my clients."

"Chicago's nice but it ain't New York," he said, slowly lifting up to suck on my neck while tracing his fingers around my nipples, trying to ignite another lust session.

"Toussaint...*whew*..." I said, nearly losing my breath as I gently pushed him away before allowing myself to get too excited. "I need to get ready to go. I have to check out in an hour."

"When are you coming back?"

"Sometime in January."

"Let me know because I want to take you out."

"Most definitely," I said, leaning in to kiss him. "Now I hate to do this to you but you have to go my love."

"I'm getting kicked out?"

"Yep."

"Can I at least hit the shower before I leave?" he said with the sexiest look, causing me to get all hot and bothered again.

"Only under one circumstance...I have to join you," I said as he pulled me out the bed and sensually led me to the bathroom.

I think Angela calls it the super stroke. Whatever it's called Toussaint was the epitome of it—goodness gracious.

I met Angela in the lobby after checking out and we rode to LaGuardia together, catching up on all the events of the past several days. As much as I wanted to tell her about Toussaint, I didn't. I'll just keep that naughty little secret to myself.

MONDAY, 11/6

Although I was physically in my office today, mentally I was out of it. I tried so hard to work but I just couldn't buckle down and focus. I had so many things on my mind. As I sat at my desk and stared out the window, I thought about my wild romp with Toussaint yesterday. As empowering as it felt when I was with him, today I was feeling an overwhelming sense of guilt. Just a few days ago I lectured Reese on mixing business with pleasure and I ultimately succumbed to it. I barely know Toussaint and I shouldn't have taken it there. I felt like I'd given up a piece of me that I'd been trying to hold onto for someone special. As good as I felt yesterday, today I was empty inside. I feel like I should take a step back and *honestly* revisit celibacy.

Another reason I felt guilty was because I hadn't watched church service in the past several weeks, I've barely skimmed over any word of scripture and my prayers have been few and far in between. The one good thing Alain inspired me to do was to go back to church. A few years ago I was in the house of the Lord almost every Sunday and this year I can count the number of times I've gone on one hand. Because of my immense blessings, I feel that this is my opportunity to reacquaint myself with a church family, be strong and start over again. Everyone's right, I can't let a few people serve as barriers between God and myself. I'd be fighting 'til the end if someone stood in the way of my business. I think back to how I didn't once let Guy get to me last week. I should have that same strength when it comes to my spirituality. The world is full of wrong doers, but regardless of if they reside in businesses, families or even churches, I have to be strong enough to fight whatever or whoever comes my way. At that moment I felt compelled to pray. I turned off my computer and put my cell phone on silent so I could meditate in peace. The emotions poured out as I reflected on all God has done for me. His favor and blessings towards me deserve way more thanks than I'd been giving.

After running some much needed errands, I decided to check on Celeste.

"How have you been holding up?"

"I've literally been taking it day by day. Chris, some nights I wake up and think that I could possibly find it in my heart to forgive John, but it isn't long after that I come to my senses."

"Is he back in Cleveland?"

"No, he's staying with Seth."

"Have you talked to him?"

"Not since the night you all came to the hospital. I honestly don't know when I'll be able to hold a civil conversation with him. I mean what in the hell do we have to talk about?" she said as tears began to well up in her eyes. "Christian, do you realize that he has a child other than the one I'm carrying! An f'ing one year old child with his name! While we were together, he decided to screw some other woman and didn't have the common sense to wrap it up to prevent her from getting pregnant."

I cradled Celeste in my arms and allowed her to go through this process, "You have every right to be mad. As much as it hurts me I can't imagine how you're feeling."

"Why would he marry me knowing that he had this horrible secret? How could he do this to me? And what about our baby? How in the hell am I supposed to explain this to them?"

"I know."

"And then I have to think about mom. She's been so sick that the doctors have given her life a deadline. Who am I going to have once she's gone?"

"Celeste, she's not gone. She's still here and she loves you."

"Do you know when I went out to visit her two days ago, the first thing she asked when she woke up was how John was doing? Can you believe that? That cheating bastard has everybody thinking he's perfect. I didn't have the heart to tell her what happened. I just told her that he was fine then excused myself to the bathroom and broke down. Then there's Carra. You gotta love her for being such an optimist, but for some strange reason she seems to think that the marriage counselor she and Aaron are going to could possibly help our situation. I had to tell her to save the referral for someone else because John and I are way beyond counseling. Right now I'm looking for a lawyer and a court date."

TUESDAY, 11/7

This morning I went to go vote, attended a breakfast meeting, gave two presentations, then spoke to a room full of Eva's chatty friends. After she introduced me to the group, it was time for me to remember how it felt to be a teenager and reflect on some of the things that may be affecting them.

From boys to politics, I felt as if I'd covered a solid range of topics with the girls. When I opened the floor for questions, every hand went flying up. There were questions asking my advice on how to choose the right college, how to select one prom date from six different boys and if Beyonce's hair was real, but the one that really stood out and caught me off guard was from my own baby sister.

"I'd like to ask a question," she said after everyone else's hands were down. "I've been hearing about eating disorders a lot lately. What are they and why do people have them?"

"Well Eva," I said slowly. "Eating disorders begin when people are obsessive about losing weight to the point that they either starve themselves or force themselves to throw up after eating. When people engage in this type of behavior, they generally don't realize that it's an illness, but it is. In many cases, these people have a negative and obscured perception about their appearance for one reason or another. People with eating disorders typically lose a noticeable amount of weight in a short amount of time that others will notice, but these individuals will still look in the mirror and see themselves as fat. The best thing to do if you know someone who is suffering from this is try to get them some help."

"Thanks," Eva said and smiled.

Before heading to bed, I called my mom to let her know how Eva's debutante event went and to tell her the good news that I planned to go to church on Sunday.

"Chris, I'm proud that you were able to speak on the challenges in your life and put them into perspective for those young ladies. You've gone through successes and difficult situations for a reason and it has enabled you to be a mentor for others. I just want you to know it meant a great deal to Eva. When I went to pick her up from the program she had tears running down her face because she was so happy that you're better. You really mean a lot to her and to the rest of us. We all love you and we're so proud of you."

"I love you too. Guess what?"

"What?"

"I'm going to church on Sunday."

"Praise the Lord!"

"Hello?" I said wearily as I picked up my cordless phone.

"Girl, I've been calling your cell all day," Reese said with stress in her voice.

"Sorry, I forgot it at home while I was out all day and when I got back the battery was dead. What's up?" I said trying to regain coherence.

"Christian, Alain was in an accident on Thursday."

"What?" I said sitting up in bed as my heart began racing uncontrollably.

"Human resources sent out an email today. He didn't come in to work Friday, yesterday or this morning and no one had heard from him. Erik went by his apartment to check on him this morning and he wasn't there, neither was his car. He contacted his parents in Georgia and they gave him the news."

"Is he okay?" I asked, fearing the worst.

"I'm guessing it's pretty serious because he's still in the hospital."

"Oh my God," I said beginning to feel faint. "What hospital is he in?"

"IU. When was the last time you talked to him?"

"Oh no!" I screamed as my heart sunk, retooling the timeline of the past couple of days. If he was in an accident on Thursday, when I called him on Saturday morning he was already in the hospital. "Damn!"

"Chris, I'm sure he'll pull through."

"Reese, I need to go. I gotta go see him."

"Chris, from what I hear I don't think it's life threatening."

"Oh no!"

"Chris, try to calm down and get some rest because it's too late for you to visit him tonight."

That was easier said than done.

I threw on whatever clothes were in reach and raced to the hospital.

"Ma'am, I'm sorry to tell you, visiting hours are over."

"Please, I need to see my boyfriend," I pleaded with tears streaming down my face.

"Sorry, you'll have to come back later. Visiting hours begin at eight."

WEDNESDAY, 11/8

From the time I got back home I stayed up crying and by seven o'clock my eyes were bloodshot and swollen as I got dressed to go back to the hospital.

I could see Alain resting and breathing deeply through a window from the hall as I approached his room. I let out a long exhale as I slowly walked in, trying not to startle him.

I couldn't suppress my emotions as I stood over him and looked at the I.V. needle going through his hand. I gently rubbed his arm causing him to jump a little at my touch before he slowly opened his eyes.

"Queen. Oh, queen," he sighed in a whispered tone as he brought my hand to his lips. "I'm so happy to see you."

"How do you feel sweetie?"

"A little better. My left elbow is fractured and I'm bruised all over my arms and back."

"What happened?"

"I was in the wrong place at the wrong time. I was driving through the intersection at Meridian and Thirty-Eighth Street and the next thing I know, crash! I blanked out after that. Supposedly I got hit by a guy who was being chased by the police."

"Oh my God," I leaned in to gently hug and kiss him. "I don't even want to think about what could've happened."

"I know. I think about that constantly. If I were just a few seconds off I probably wouldn't be here."

"Oh my goodness."

"Yeah, but all I can say is thank God. I'm lucky to be alive. I know you were probably wondering what happened to me."

"I didn't know what was up. I'd been calling you for the past few days."

"My cell phone's dead and my charger's at the apartment. This is really my first day being alert and for the most part pain free. They had me sedated all day Friday, Saturday, Sunday and most of the day yesterday."

My heart sunk even deeper when he told me that.

"I called on Saturday morning and I think Paula answered the phone."

"Yeah, I'm told she was here. The nurse said she left yesterday, probably because she had to go back to work. I'm guessing my parents called her after they were notified of my accident. My mother left a message with the nurse this morning and they're on their way."

"Alain, give me a second," I said, feeling nauseous as I rushed to the bathroom. I almost threw up before splashing my face with cold water to calm my nerves. I don't believe what's happening, I thought to myself as I overheard the nurse coming in to check on Alain.

"Is your guest still here?"

"Yeah, she's in the bathroom."

"Oh alright. This will only take a second, I just have to get quick temperature and blood pressure readings," she said then paused as I heard the sound of Velcro and Alain moving around on the bed. "You're looking good. Everything's where it should be."

"How much longer do you think I'll be here?"

"You should be able to go home in a few days."

"That's good to hear," I said, walking back into the room.

"He's looking good," she said beaming as she took note of how Alain was looking at me. "It doesn't take much to figure out that *she* must be the girlfriend."

"The love of my life," he responded.

"Hi, I'm Christian."

"I'm Stephanie, Mr. Hughes's day nurse. He's our favorite patient," she said chuckling then turned to Alain. "I don't want to get you in trouble, but I assumed the other young lady here was your girlfriend until she corrected me. She made it very clear that you two are just friends."

"Oh, yeah," Alain said seriously with wide eyes. "Just friends."

"Well, now that I see Christian I know why," she said while replacing Alain's charts. "I hate to do this because I know you two haven't seen each other in a while, but we're going to need to cut the visit short, you need your rest," she said then turned to me. "He had a rough one last night, a bad reaction to his pain killers. Poor thing barely slept a wink."

"Is everything okay?"

"Oh yeah, don't worry. He's fine now."

"I don't remember a thing," Alain said, still smiling at me.

"Probably for the best. Oh, just so you know, Dr. Stewart will be here in a few hours to check in on you so I'd suggest you get some sleep before he gets here. He wants to run some additional tests to check your internal organs."

"I'm really not that tired."

"You will be after you take these," she said, handing Alain a small cup of pills.

Within fifteen minutes, Alain grew groggy and quickly drifted off. I was teary-eyed again when I leaned in to kiss and hug him before heading out to the nurse's station.

"Thank you for taking such good care of him."

"Oh sweetie," she said handing me a tissue. "That's my job."

"I appreciate it."

"I'm assuming you'll be the one taking care of him once he's released."

"Yes."

"Just make sure he takes his medication and doesn't overexert himself."

"I will."

"He'll be out of it for the next several hours so you've got some time to kill. He should be up and alert if you come back tonight around eight."

"Have you recuperated from New York?" Angela asked as we perused the aisles of a party supply store, picking up items for Eva and Ev's birthday party.

"Yeah, how about you?"

"Yes, and I'm itching to go back."

"With all of the opportunities you have I'm sure you'll be back sooner than you think," I said as I picked up a donkey-shaped piñata and put it in the cart.

"What are you doing?" Angela asked, looking at me like I was crazy.

"What?" I said while trying to hold back my laugh.

"You might as well buy a couple of tails to pin on the donkey's ass while you're at it."

"I think they'd like it."

"If they were six."

"Well how about these?" I asked as I held up a bag of cone shaped party hats.

"You're pitiful. I hope you realize that," she laughed as she took the piñata out of the cart then snatched the hats away from me.

"I can't believe they're about to be seventeen. Time is going by so fast."

"I know," Angela said then started to say something else before pausing.

"What were you about to say?"

"Christian, what's going on with you?"

"Nothing."

"Come on now, this is me you're talking to. Are you and Alain okay?"

"Yeah."

"I don't believe you. Usually I can't get you stop talking about Alain, but lately I haven't heard you utter one word about him."

"Everything's fine," I replied as I sped up with the cart to prevent Angela from seeing my eyes well up.

"Christian wait," she said, catching up to me and stopping the cart. "What's wrong? See that's what I mean. What's up with all these tears?"

I took a deep breath and decided to come clean

"My life is spiraling out of control."

"Talk to me," she said, leaving the full cart in the middle of the aisle and walked me out of the store. Without judgment or opinion, Angela listened as I spilled my guts and told her everything—including the Toussaint situation.

As I approached Alain's room, I could hear several people talking in a low tone. When I entered, an attractive older couple greeted me with warm smiles.

"Hello," they said in unison.

"Hello, you must be Alain's parents."

"Yes, and you must be Christian. We've heard so much about you," Alain's father replied as he and Mrs. Hughes reached in to hug me.

"Yes sir. Did you two just get into town?"

"We arrived about an hour ago."

"From Savannah right?"

"That's right," Mrs. Hughes replied. "I'm so glad to see that Alain looks like he's going to be okay."

"How's he feeling?" I asked, gazing at Alain as he slept.

"He's fine, just a little groggy from the medication. The nurse said he should be waking up soon," Mr. Hughes said. "It's a parent's worst nightmare to get a call that your child has been in a car crash. Our hearts dropped when we got the news. As I'm sure you already know by now, we've already lost one child to someone else's reckless behavior."

"Alain told me."

"We're sorry that we didn't call you when we got the news. We didn't have your number."

"I understand. I was in New York when it happened. I just found out about the accident late last night. I was so relieved to see that he was alert and talking earlier this morning."

"That's a good sign. He's been asleep the entire time we've been here," Mrs. Hughes said as she walked over to Alain and held his hand.

A new nurse came in a few minutes later to check on him. The room was silent as she checked his blood pressure and changed his I.V. bag.

"Well, I thought he'd be up by now. He had such a rough one last night that his body is probably just trying to recuperate," the nurse said. "Hopefully he'll wake up before visiting hours are over."

When visiting hours ended at ten o'clock, Alain was in an even deeper sleep. On the elevator to the parking garage, Alain's parents invited me to grab a bite to eat with them. During dinner I got a chance to see exactly where Alain gets his most admirable traits. His humor and wit come from his mom and his caring and attentiveness come from his dad. I enjoyed getting to know them and by the time dinner was over, his dad was proclaiming me a member of their family.

THURSDAY, 11/9

Reese called first thing this morning inviting me to breakfast at her house.

"It's early Reese, why?"

"Can you come or not?"

"No."

"I knew you'd be the only one to trip. Celeste and Carra are already on their way."

"Reese, I'm tired. What is it?"

"I need your help with something."

"Fine, but I can't stay longer than ten thirty. I have to visit Alain before my meetings."

"Then jump in the shower and come on."

"This better be important."

"It's important as hell so quit wasting time!" she said, then as usual hung up.

"Never again," I thought as rolled out of bed.

When I got to Reese's house at a quarter after nine, Celeste was already there.

"So, what's the big issue?" I asked Reese as she handed me a blueberry muffin.

"You'll find out soon enough," she said as Celeste let out a sigh.

Carra finally arrived twenty minutes later and as soon as she did, Reese had us all go out to her car to help bring in a ton of shopping bags.

The three of us sat on the couch as we watched Reese lay out countless Saks, Burberry and Tiffany bags. She plopped down on a large pillow in the middle of the floor, smiling like a hyena, "Needless to say, I went shopping yesterday…"

"Okay…" Celeste said, trying to get Reese to elaborate.

"And I found some *really* cute things."

"And?" I said, becoming annoyed because I was going to end up running late for my meetings dealing with Reese this morning.

"And I need your help in deciding which ones you like best."

"Reese…" I said standing up.

"It's not time for you to go so sit down."

"We're wasting time doing all this talking, go ahead and show us what you got," Carra said growing increasingly annoyed herself.

"Okay, I'll start with Burberry," Reese said, pulling out a gorgeous tote bag. "How do you like it?"

"Reese, you can't be serious," I said, looking at Celeste and Carra. "You called us over this early in the morning to flaunt a new purse."

"Obviously you're not looking good enough, this isn't a purse," she said reaching in the bag and pulling out a piece of folded vinyl, laying it down on the floor.

"Okay, it comes with a laptop sleeve. Reese honey, I have to go," I said.

Carra walked over to inspect the situation closer and replied, "Uh, this isn't a laptop sleeve, it's a changing pad. Reese, what's going on?" she said as Resse begin pulling other items out of the bags. Little Ralph Lauren baby jumpers on satin hangers, a Juicy Couture pacifier set, Gucci baby slippers.

"Those are awfully expensive gifts. You two are getting hooked up," I said pointing to Carra and Celeste.

"I have a strange feeling these aren't for us," Celeste said giving Reese a perplexed look.

"Right about that," Reese said then belted, "Surprise!" As we all stood frozen in shock. "Don't ask me how it happened, but I'm pregnant."

It took the three of us a couple of minutes to digest the information.

"Pregnant?" Celeste asked.

"Can you believe it? Reese Cambridge is about to have a little crumb snatcher!" Reese said laughing.

"When did you find out?" I asked.

"A week before Celeste's wedding, hence why I was drinking a virgin daiquiri."

The three of us stood with our mouths wide open not knowing whether to jump for joy or be in a serious prayer session for this child.

"Okay, why am I the only one happy here?" Reese said, noticing our stunned looks.

"Oh, we're very happy for you, just a little shocked," I said slowly.

"Reese, who's the father?" Carra asked with concern.

"I'm about eighty percent sure it's Martin."

"Well, what about the other twenty percent?" Carra asked intensely.

"Oh calm the hell down Carra, I'm almost positive that it's Martin's. We had a condom accident right before Christian's fashion show."

"Does he know?" I asked.

"Not yet. He'll find out eventually," she said nonchalantly.

"What do you mean eventually?" I asked.

"I really don't feel like getting into this. Just put it this way, me being pregnant is guaranteed get Martin's hopes up. I just don't feel like dealing with that right now."

"You can't hide this from him," Celeste said sharply.

"Who said anything about hiding it from him? I'll just tell him when I feel like telling him."

"When, in your third trimester?" I asked sarcastically.

"If it comes to that."

"I can't believe you're saying this," Celeste said. "At least tell me that you're going to allow him to be a part of the child's life."

"It's debatable."

"That's about as stupid and backwards as anything I've ever heard in my life!" Carra snapped.

"Carra, that's your holier than thou opinion. I know what I'm doing. I'm very capable of taking care of this child by myself. He ought to be happy I feel this way instead of trying to milk him for every red cent he has."

"Reese, that's really twisted. You can't deprive your child of their father just because you don't want to have anything to do with him. Martin would be crushed to hear you talking like this," I said.

"Martin would be such a good father. That's so unfair to him!" Carra said.

"Why are we still talking about Martin? This isn't about him."

"Look, I'm running late for my meeting. I'll talk to you guys later," I said as I stood up and gathered all of my things.

"I need to be going too," Carra said as she and Celeste followed me to the door.

"So it's like that. No support, no lovey-dovey hugs like Carra and Celeste got when they announced their pregnancies," Reese blurted out.

"I have no problem supporting you," I replied. "I just wish you could see how selfish you're acting right now."

"She's right Reese. It's time to abandon your center of the universe attitude. You've got someone else to start thinking about," Celeste said walking out the door.

Reese marched outside as we got into our cars and started hollering on the sidewalk, "I can do this without Martin, you tricks or anybody else out there who doubts me. I'm strong enough to handle this by myself and I don't need any more input from any of you!"

"Fine, superwoman. Try to do this shit all by yourself. Let's see how many booty calls, uh I'm sorry, business trips to Cleveland you're able to make once this baby gets here. Let's see how fly you are when the baby's crying all night and you can't get an ounce of sleep but you still have to be up and ready to lead an eight o'clock meeting the next morning. Oh, and that sickening display of materialism in there, if you really want my opinion, I think you should take all that shit back and start a savings plan!" Carra yelled from behind her car door as if it were holding her back from jumping on Reese.

"No wait, even better than that. I can't wait to hear that good ass lie you're gonna to have to make up when the baby is old enough to talk and ask, 'how come I can't see my daddy?' What are you going to do then?" Celeste asked.

"Um, I'll probably look to you for advice. What do you plan on telling your child again?" Reese replied with a sarcastic smile.

"You did not have to go there," Celeste said with a crushed look on her face.

"Reese, that was low. You need to apologize," I said as she looked at me like I was crazy.

"Whatever," she huffed. "You know what, I really don't have to take this shit right now," she said rolling her eyes and walking back to her front door. "Don't call me, don't come by here, don't talk to me. I'm through with you arrogant, know it all bitches."

"You don't mean that," I said as she turned towards us, frowning one last time before giving us the finger and slamming the door.

I was running so late to my morning appointments that I wasn't able to see Alain until this evening. When I got there he was awake, alert and almost back to his old self. He appeared to be regaining strength because he was walking up and down the halls with little assistance when I arrived. I stayed with him for several hours before he took his medication and began getting drowsy again. His parents were grateful that I agreed to take care of Alain until he was able to move about on his own. I invited them out to dinner but they had to get back on the road first thing in the morning and they wanted to get some good rest. Before I left, I met with the nurses so they could prepare me for his release tomorrow. They gave me a long list of things to do and to have on hand when he gets to my house. I was looking forward to taking care of Alain and putting the past weekend behind me.

Later in the evening, I met up with my family at my parents' house to celebrate the twin's birthday. After cake and ice cream, my dad helped Everett set up his new turntables while the women gathered in the kitchen to help Eva go over her debutante recitation. Once Eva seemed to have it down pat, Nanna motioned for me to meet her in the family room.

"Guess who's in town?" Nanna said with a smirk on her face.

"Who?"

"Nathan."

"Nanna, you know Nathan and I broke up a long time ago. Why are you bringing him up? I thought you liked Alain."

"Child, do you think I was born yesterday? I know that."

"Then why are you telling me this?"

"Well, turns out that Nathan's got a little sugar in his tank."

"Nanna!" I said, shocked at my grandmother's revelation.

"Oh, don't go acting like you didn't know."

"Nanna, who told you this?"

"Delilah."

"His mother?"

"Yes. She's been suspecting it for years."

"How'd she find out?"

"Some guy from Atlanta called her and outed him."

"Andre," I said under my breath without thinking.

"That's him, that's who she said called. A man named Andre. I knew you'd know about this. Is that why you two broke up?"

"No, it was the distance. I never suspected anything when he lived here."

"Well believe it or not, he's going around telling everyone that he's still in love with you, emphatically denying that he's gay."

"Wow. I can't help him with that," I replied. "How is his mother handling it?"

"She's dealing with it. When it's all said and done, that's her only child and she loves him to death. Her only concern is that he's honest with himself and that he's safe."

"I should probably call him since he's in town."

"I'm sure that will make him happy," she said pausing. "And a little more confused I'm certain."

About an hour later as we were saying our goodbyes, my dad suggested that we say a quick prayer before everyone departed for the evening. He prayed a prayer of thanks and gratitude for allowing his family to begin spending more time together. He sent up a special prayer for Alain's speedy recovery. He revealed in his prayer that he'd asked God a couple of months ago to keep his family close-knit and he cried when he thanked God for answering his prayers.

FRIDAY, 11/10

"Chris, look…this baby is my responsibility and I don't need anyone telling me how to do this, I can handle it. You're right, maybe I should let Martin in for the child's sake but that doesn't mean I have to be involved with him. Point blank, I don't want a relationship with him. I don't like him like that. I know what you're thinking and I don't need to hear the safe sex sermon from you, I just need your help and support. Yeah, it's not right to deprive my baby of their father, so I'll give in on that. But while Martin's spending time with the baby, I'll be out doing my own thing. Look, I didn't mean what I said about not needing you. I do need you…a lot. I just don't like to be judged and preached to, okay. I'll talk to you later. Don't worry, I still love you."

What are we going to do with Reese, I asked myself as I saved the message. That was her attempt at an apology and for what it's worth, I'll accept it.

As I cleaned my apartment in anticipation of Alain staying with me for a few days, it dawned on me that he hadn't listened to his messages in over a week. I hated to do it but I had to hack into his voicemail to erase the drunken message that I'd left for him last Saturday morning. It took me a while, but I finally figured out his PIN number and was able to delete it. It felt like a huge weight had been lifted off my shoulders because not only did I erase that drama from his voicemail, I mentally erased it from my mind.

Later in the afternoon I caught up with Nathan over his mother's house. We spent nearly an hour clearing the air. His biggest concern was making sure that I wasn't mad at him any longer. I reassured him that I was never really mad at him, I was just taken aback by the situation. After we got that out of the way, everything was cool again.

Just as I suspected, he attempted to put his feelers out to see if I was involved with anyone. After I told him about Alain, he chilled out.

It felt good to smooth things out with Nathan. Even though we were good as a couple, we're even better as friends.

Angela and I met at the mall food court for a late lunch then decided to hang out until it was time to go to the twins' big birthday bash tonight.

"Guess what?" she said as we threw away our trash and headed back towards Nordstrom's. "I have a meeting with a modeling agent in two weeks."

"That's wonderful!"

"Even better, I spoke with a few people in Illum's marketing department and they said that everyone absolutely loved my pictures and they definitely want me to do their Urban Couture Campaign. I also spoke to a friend in Harlem who guaranteed that in between modeling jobs, he could get me a part-time gig at the Guggenheim as well as freelance work for several other people he knows in the industry."

"It sounds like you're going to be spending a lot more time in New York."

"Yeah, so much that I'll need to find some potential roommates," she said laughing.

She was still giggling as she began looking through a rack of clothes and pointed out a pair of leather pants.

"Mom would like these, wouldn't she?"

"You're serious aren't you?"

"Nah, you're right. Mom would never be caught dead in red leather."

"I'm not talking about the pants, I'm talking about New York. You're thinking about moving aren't you?"

"Chris, I can't pass this up. I have to do it now or else this opportunity may never come back around."

"So you're moving to New York," I said smiling but disguising the fact that I was actually really sad. Was it selfish of me to not want my sister to go away? I felt that we were just beginning to get close again and now she's about to move hundreds of miles out of my life.

"I know it seems like bad timing, but I promise that I'll still help you with whatever you need for the big jazz fest next year."

"And I promise to come visit you every chance I get."

"You better," she said as she leaned in to kiss me on the cheek. All the while an older lady standing across from us frowned and walked away. "She must think we're lovers," Angela said, cracking up.

"Forget her," I said as I threw my arm around my sister. "I love you girl."

"I love you too. So enough about me, have you thought about how you're going to handle the Toussaint situation?"

"I'm still trying to figure it out. I guess I just need to be straight forward with him and admit that it was a mistake and that we need to maintain a professional relationship from now on."

"He should understand that. Now as for Alain, I'm not advocating that you lie to him, I just suggest that you don't tell him."

"Girl are you crazy? I wasn't planning on telling him anything. This situation is just between you and me. From this point on, as far as I'm concerned, Toussaint never happened."

After we were done shopping, we headed over to my parents' house. Eva and Everett had what seemed like the entire school in the basement.

"I remember when we used to have parties like this," I said to Angela.

"Yeah. Eva and Ev used to sneak down here in their PJ's, quietly sit on the stairs and just watch us all night. They couldn't wait for their turn and now here it is," Angela replied.

"I wonder how it feels to be mom and dad right now. Their babies are all grown up. Eva and Ev will be out of the house in two years and they'll be here all by themselves. Time goes by way too fast," I said, watching the twins clowning with their friends.

When the first slow jam came on I noticed a tall, handsome, muscular boy grab Eva's hand then pulled her out to the middle of the floor to dance. All the while, Everett was in the corner finessing some young lady from the neighborhood. With everything he said, she let out a giggle and at one point he must have told her something really good because she took us both by surprise and gave him a long kiss on the lips.

"Did you see that?" Angela asked.

"Yes, and believe me I didn't want to."

"You can't get mad at him, he's seventeen now. It's about that time when boys start…"

"Please don't go there," I said as she cracked up laughing. Soon after, I turned my attention back to Eva who was all wrapped up in the muscular guy's arms with her eyes closed and a calm smile on her face. I'm so glad that we had our little talk not so long ago, I thought as I watched her.

About half way into the night, Eva bopped over to me while holding the hand of the young man she was dancing with.

"Chris, this is David. David this is my oldest sister, Christian."

"Nice to meet you," I said as I shook his hand.

"Nice to meet you too," he said as he gave me the Kobe Bryant smile Eva described to me a few weeks ago.

"David is our all-star basketball MVP," Eva squealed.

"That's wonderful," I replied trying to sound as excited as she did.

After they walked back to the dance floor and began laughing with their friends, I got a sudden flashback of when I was in her shoes. It seems so long ago, then again it feels like it was just yesterday. It's amazing how your life can drastically change in only a matter of years, months, even days. Take this year for instance. Back in January, Carra was celebrating her fourth year of marriage while Celeste, Reese and I were single, independent women enjoying life. Then in a blink of an eye, all three of them are now pregnant, one more is married though soon to be divorced, and I've finally found the love of my life. Earlier this year, Angela was a fly by night type who had little clue of what her true purpose and identity was and now she's New York bound with a whole new sense of who she is and what she wants to accomplish. As I sat there and thought, I couldn't help but wonder what was in store for all of us this time next year. How will life be? What major changes were headed our way? It really makes you wonder but it also makes you sit back and appreciate today and the fact that you'll never get it back. Once it's gone, it's gone.

I was startled out of my flashback when Everett kissed me on the cheek.

"My math teacher wants to dance with you," he laughed, pointing to a goofy looking guy wearing a plaid oxford shirt and thick glasses.

"Let's do it!" I said as I walked across the room and pulled his teacher out on the dance floor, taking him by surprise.

"It doesn't get any better than this!" my dad yelled to me, pointing to my mother as they slow danced cheek to cheek.

I looked around the room and saw Angela dancing with Nanna while the twins laughed with their friends, having the time of their lives. To make things even better, I was about to go pick up my soul mate to shower him with all the love and affection I can give.

At that point, I said a little prayer thanking God for my life then directed my attention back to my father who was holding my mother so lovingly and tight, almost as if his life depended on it.

That's when it became crystal clear, dad was definitely right. It doesn't get any better than this.

SATURDAY, 11/11

"Are you comfortable sweetie?" I asked as I positioned a stack of pillows under Alain's immobile arm.

"I'm fine baby. Now sit down and rest. You've been fussing over me all night."

"I just want to take care of you."

"I know and I appreciate it," he said, leaning in for a kiss.

"I stopped by your house this morning and got your laptop, cell phone charger, some more clothes and your toiletries just like you asked. I'm curious to see how you plan to type with one arm."

"I'll make it work."

"Speaking of work, do you need me to stop by your office on Monday?"

"No, Erik said he'd bring my work stuff over sometime tomorrow afternoon.

"Okay then, are you hungry?"

"Chris, sit down. I'm fine. I just want to relax here with you," he said as he patted on the seat cushion next to him.

"You sure I can't bring you anything?" I asked as he gave me an annoyed look. "Alright," I said sitting down, snuggling next to him.

"This is what I'm talking about," he said then wrapped his good arm around me and pulled me closer. "Ummm, I missed this."

"I know. Alain, I'm so happy that you're alright. Every time I replay what could have happened to you, I get light headed."

"Don't think about it. God is real and He's beyond excellent. He obviously saw fit to keep me around a little longer."

"I'm thankful that He did. Oh, guess what? You're going to be proud of me."

"Why is that?"

"I'm going to church tomorrow."

"You don't know how happy I am to hear that. I wish I could go with you."

"I'll bring home a CD of the sermon."

"Thanks love," he said then gave me serious look. "You know what I think? I believe this accident was a blessing in disguise."

"Why do you say that?"

"Because it revealed just how special you really are to me. I spent the first few days in the hospital completely unaware of my surroundings but the day you came to visit me was the first day I was coherent. I felt warmth and light when you touched me that morning. It was almost as if God gave me those first days to rest but made sure that He woke me up to see my angel. That's what you are to me, my angel. Love is not a strong enough word to describe how I feel about you. Christian, you're perfect in my eyes."

"Babe, I'm far from perfect."

"Not to me. You're my gift sent from heaven. I couldn't die last week. I couldn't leave this earth before I had the opportunity to make you my wife. God doesn't make mistakes and I'll thank Him every day of my life for delivering me from what could have been final," he said as tears streamed down his face. "I love you Christian."

"I love you too," I said as we held each other, allowing our emotions to flow out through our tears.

"I see us spending the rest of our lives together."

"I do too," I replied while trying to suppress the overwhelming feelings of guilt and shame that I'll likely carry every day of my life. I'm going to go above and beyond to make it up to him. I want him to feel like he's the most important and loved man on the face of the earth and I pray to God that He allows us to grow closer than ever while helping me to forgive myself in the process.

SUNDAY, 11/12

In an unusual turn of events, I actually woke up chipper at eight this morning. Undeniably it was God coaxing me out of my sleep by flooding my bedroom with blinding sunlight shining directly in my eyes.

"Early morning sunshine to give way to a severe snow storm this afternoon," the weatherman announced as I watched the morning news in my bedroom while getting dressed. I'll take my chances, I thought as I remained unfazed by the forecast and continued to get ready for church.

Alain was still asleep when I walked into the living room. Instead of waking him, I sat on the side of the sofa bed and stared at him for several minutes. Just looking at him, so handsome and peaceful made me smile.

"I'm going to treat you like a king for the rest of your life," I whispered before leaning in to kiss his lips. "I love you sweetie."

Two things happened to me on the way to church this morning. I almost ran out of gas on the highway then got into a minor fender bender when I pulled into the gas station. Luckily there was no major external damage to either one of our cars and since the guy that bumped into me was so forthcoming and apologetic, plus he was a member of my church, we just exchanged insurance information and I decided not to file a police report. He parked next to me in the church parking lot and when I got out of the car his little girl ran over and gave me a hug as they both continued to apologize.

"Everything's okay. The devil's just trying to prevent us from getting to church on time." Did I just say that, I thought smiling as I walked in with the man and his daughter.

It felt so good to be in the house of the Lord. I never fully realized the intensity of positive energy and spirit that moved through the building. Being there was a reunion of sorts. I saw friends and acquaintances I hadn't seen in years, I even saw the mean old lady who called me a hussy. I put all of that behind me and made it a point to walk over and greet her.

"Good morning ma'am," I said as she scowled and frowned. "You have a blessed day, alright." That felt good, I thought as I took my seat and opened my mind to receive the word.

I left church feeling completely fulfilled. The topic for today's sermon was Waking Up from a Dream Deferred. This was part one of a six part series on learning from and moving on after discouraging and difficult situations. Something I could definitely relate to.

Traffic was backed up for miles as snowflakes fell heavy and thick on the highway. My commute to church and back was usually fifteen minutes each way, this afternoon it was an hour. As I sat in park on I-70, I was mesmerized and hypnotized by the angular movement of the snowfall. Even though it caused mass chaos and the gray clouds that hovered over the city relentlessly continued to dump wet snow over everything in sight, the scene was eerily calming. When I finally got back downtown I made a quick pit stop to the grocery store to pick up a few items for a romantic candle light dinner with

Alain. Chicken scallopini, homemade mashed potatoes, macaroni and cheese with smoked Gouda and Piave, and my famous collard greens, all things I know Alain loves.

The house was completely quiet when I returned home and after I brought in all of the groceries, I went back to the bathroom to check on Alain.

"Sweetie!" I said from outside the closed door before opening it to find that he wasn't there. Oh my God, I thought as I scrambled around my apartment. I shouldn't have left him here by himself in his condition. What if he's back in the hospital, what if he started feeling bad again? I panicked as I called his cell phone only to get voicemail. As I was leaving a message, someone knocked on my door. Thank goodness I said aloud, putting two and two together that Alain must have gone downstairs to the laundry room. I'm going to kill him for leaving the apartment. The doctor specifically told him to stay put and take it easy.

"Forgot your key didn't you," I said opening the door, only to find my neighbor from two doors down. "Oh, I'm sorry Stan. I thought you were my boyfriend," I said, beginning to feel worried again. "What's up?"

"I'm so sorry Christian."

"Stan, what is it?"

"I hope I didn't get you in trouble."

"I don't know what you're talking about."

"The flowers."

"Stanley, what flowers?"

447

"The flowers I brought over this morning."

"I haven't seen any flowers," I said growing nervous and alarmed.

"Christian, I accepted a bouquet of flowers on your behalf two days ago while you were away and I brought them over here this morning. I didn't expect your boyfriend to answer the door. I'm so sorry."

I couldn't even think straight as I turned away from him in a trance walking back to my bedroom, my bathroom again, the sunroom then the kitchen looking for the alleged flowers only to find a bouquet of twenty four long stem red roses upside down in my kitchen trash can.

"Christian, he left an hour ago. I saw him and his friend leave with his bags, I'm so sorry," Stan said as I kneeled in front of the trash, digging through the discarded flowers to find the card. Even though I knew what to expect before I opened the envelope, I nearly collapsed as I read the words that have likely caused the love of my life to leave me for good.

"Christian, this is kind of hard for me to say, so I'll just put it out there. You're an amazing woman and the time we spent together last week, though short, was enough to leave a lasting impression on me. When I think about you, three songs come to mind, 'Simply Beautiful' by Al Green because that's what you are, 'Drowndeep' by Maxwell because it's your favorite song and I remember how pretty you looked singing it in the limo and lastly, 'Your Body Is a Wonderland' by John Mayer because, well it is and I want to kiss, touch, stroke and "drown deep" again, and again, and again...very soon. Looking forward to your next trip to the big apple, Toussaint."

FRIDAY, 12/15

I saw him today. I haven't seen or spoken to Alain in the past several weeks, but I saw him today. His reaction to seeing me was everything I expected, awkward, hostile and brief. Since I haven't written in my journal in over a month, I guess I should recap everything that's happened over the last six weeks. Angela is moving to Brooklyn right after the New Year to start modeling and build her artistic career. Celeste filed for divorce a few days before Thanksgiving and despite the obvious pain that caused, she's so excited to bring her new baby boy into the world. She plans to name him Christos after her grandfather. Her mother's still hanging in there which is such a blessing and Celeste has made it a point to spend as much time with her as possible so she'll never have any regrets. Carra and Aaron are doing much better. They swear by their marriage counselor and they should because she's taken their relationship to a whole new level. Aaron just landed a great new job as the Chief Information Officer for a start-up biotech company and Carra has decided to hang up her veterinary hat, temporarily, to pursue entrepreneurship. She plans to start an online pet accessories store and with the help of Aaron, it looks like it should be very successful. Carra doesn't want to know the sex of her baby, though we all have a feeling it'll be a girl, so she's picked out two names. If it's a girl, she plans to name her Sophie and if it's a boy she wants to name him after Aaron. And Reese, wow, Reese doesn't know what to do with herself after she found out she's having twin girls. Her due date's about a week or so later than Celeste's, however she's the biggest of them all. She looks absolutely adorable, all three of them do. I have to say, pregnancy has mellowed Reese out over the past few weeks. She's been more receptive towards the advice people give her, she's more patient and less abrasive, and she's even been acting nice towards Martin. How about that. As for me, I've been keeping myself busy with work as usual but I've also been extremely active with volunteering and serving on ministries in church. The most fulfilling ministry I'm currently involved with is the Christmas for a Child program. I volunteered to chair the program and since mid-November we've raised over sixty-five thousand dollars to purchase clothing, toys and food for needy children. We met the families this afternoon and it took everything for me to not tear up at the graciousness and thanks they showed. Out of everything I've done this year, this has to be the most rewarding.

I woke up this morning around seven to get a head start on wrapping gifts before I headed to the church. The snow had melted to practically nothing and the weather was a sunny and mild forty-nine degrees, balmy for December. I recruited a few of my neighbors to help transport some additional donated gifts and when I arrived at church, there were several hundred volunteers ready and waiting to help make the day a success. People joyfully worked at their designated stations, either wrapping gifts, filling out greeting cards, folding clothes, packing food into coolers or decorating miniature Christmas trees. As I was going from table to table to help where needed, I saw him. He was laughing with Erik as they packed and secured frozen turkey and dressing into an assembly line of coolers. I dealt with a moment of conflict as I debated on whether to approach him or not. We're in church and it would be the Christian thing to do, I thought making the decision to walk over and be cordial.

"How's everything going over here?" I asked smiling as Alain continued tape and secure the coolers, ignoring me.

"We're doing fine," Erik said half-heartedly.

"Alain, how's your arm feeling?"

"Erik, I'll be right back," he said walking away.

"Is he doing better?"

"What do you think?" Erik snapped.

"You don't have to have an attitude."

"Whatever," he replied with his attention squarely on loading turkeys and not on me.

"Erik, quit being judgmental. You don't even know what happened."

"All I know is birds of a feather flock together. You and Reese, definitely one in the same."

"You are the last to talk," I said, lowering my voice as I could tell bystanders were starting to tune into our conversation.

"Hey, I never claimed to be celibate. You on the other hand..." Erik snickered as I turned around and stormed off, all the while hearing people commenting in the background.

On my way to the restroom, I saw Alain walking down the hall. I ran up to catch him and as soon as he noticed me he kept walking.

"Alain, please stop and talk to me," I said as he continued to walk. I followed him into the kitchen and as he rinsed his hands off, I cornered him. "Alain, I'm sorry."

He continued to scrub his hands and ignored me as I stood next to him.

"Babe, please," I pleaded in a whisper as he turned to look at me as if he couldn't believe I had the nerve to call him babe.

"Christian, I don't have anything to say to you so I'm not sure what you want from me."

"I want you to hear me out."

"There's nothing to hear. I know what happened."

"No, that's just it, you don't.

"What else do I need to know? You screwed another dude while we were together. Do you want to give me the details?"

"Alain, please don't be this way."

"Christian move," he said, forcefully pushing his way in between me and the sink.

"I thought you'd at least listen to me. Babe, with all due respect, you're not living up to the Alain I remember."

Alain stopped dead in his tracks before turning around and walking up so close to me that I could feel his breath, "And with all due respect, after all your little extracurricular activities, you're not living up to your name."

"That wasn't fair."

"Fair? I'll tell you what isn't fair? I thought you were celibate," Alain said raising his voice, getting the attention of everyone in and around the kitchen. "I respected that. I was the perfect gentleman to you then you go off and sleep with somebody else? So excuse me if I don't get what it is that you still feel the need to tell me."

"I knew it," a voice came from over in the food prep area. I looked over to see the mean old church lady with her arms folded tightly, shaking her head. "I knew it all along."

"Why are you always in my business? You don't know anything about me," I said as Alain walked out in a huff.

"Umm," she sneered and rolled her eyes.

"Ms. Cullen," one of the associate pastors said from across the kitchen. "Can we talk for a few minutes?"

Nothing can describe the embarrassment I felt as everyone watched me follow the pastor to his office. What just happened, I thought as I felt my neck and face get hot and flushed. When he closed the door behind me, he gave me a warm yet concerned look.

"What's going on out there?"

"I'm sorry. I'm so sorry," I said with my head in my hand.

"Are you okay?"

"Yes," I replied, though as I was saying yes, my head was shaking no.

"Do you want to talk about it?"

"I hurt someone who means everything to me."

"No need to say anymore. Here's what I want you to do. Stay in my office for as long as you'd like. Feel free to lie down and rest, eat a little something, but more than anything I want for you to read this," he said handing me a small bible turned to the first chapter of Proverbs. "You've been here for the Dream Deferred series, right?"

"Yes."

"I want you to go back through those sermons because I think it'll help you," he said handing me a stack of CDs.

"Thanks."

"But I also want you to read through the book of Proverbs. After the holidays we're going to focus on the teachings in Proverbs to help kick off the New Year. There are a few chapters that I feel pertain to you," he said before walking towards the door.

"Which chapters?"

"You'll see," he said smiling. "I'll be back in about an hour."

Pastor was right.

When I got back home I felt a little better, however there was something I felt that I still had to do. This should have been done a long time ago, I thought as tears streamed down my face while I sat in front of my computer and emailed Alain. Not that I expected to change his mind, I just needed to write him to get things off my chest for my own sanity.

"I'm not asking for you to forgive me, I just want you to hear me out. Alain, I never meant to hurt you. Words cannot describe how much I love you and how horrible I feel knowing that I betrayed your trust. All I can do from this point on is be honest with you. I know you don't want to hear it, but I have to clear the air. When I got to New York and I didn't hear from you for several days, I didn't know what was going on. All I wanted was to fill you in on the wonderful and crazy things happening during my big Illum weekend, but I couldn't get through to you. I knew you weren't ignoring me, but it just didn't

make sense why you weren't reaching out to me. The day I finally got through to you, Paula answers your phone early in the morning then hangs up. I don't know why, but I snapped after that. The only thing I could think about was you two getting back together. It never would have occurred to me that Paula could be answering your phone in the hospital or that the battery died while we were talking, no, instead I assumed you were out cheating. I'm so sorry. In my anger I started drinking and my mind began going places it shouldn't have. I started thinking about the way I've been treated by some of my ex's and how John betrayed Celeste. I allowed things to get out of hand. I was celibate with you and I wasn't lying about that. I feel the shame and guilt every day for allowing liquor-induced, vengeful thoughts to take control of my actions and ultimately causing my world to fall apart. I was wrong and I miss you. Alain, words can't describe how much I miss you. Remember when you told me that you were the only one God has equipped to love me, well I believe it. I love you so much and even if you'll never feel that way about me again, please know that I'll always feel that way about you."

SATURDAY, 12/16

Right before the girls came by my house for a much needed sisterly brunch, I received a reply email from Alain. It took me almost an hour to open it because I was so afraid to read what he had to say.

"Do you want me to read it?" Carra asked.

"No, I'll read it," I said as I walked over to my desk and opened the message.

"I don't know what you wanted to accomplish by sending me this message. I read it, but I can't say that it really makes any difference. I will say that I apologize for causing a scene yesterday. I was caught off guard, so I'm sorry for that. There's no need for me to go into detail about my feelings because it doesn't matter. I'm moving on and one day this will totally be behind us both. It was good while it lasted and I wish you all the best."

My girls stood behind me with their hands on my shoulder as I tried to process Alain's response.

"It's okay Chris, go ahead and let it out," Reese said as I laid my head down and let the tears flow.

"I f'ed up big time," I cried as my girls led me over to the couch.

"Chris, everyone makes mistakes. This will pass sooner than you think," Carra assured me.

"I'm not a big religious person, but I do believe in miracles," Celeste said. "The doctors were convinced that my mother would be dead by now, but all of the cancer they thought had spread throughout her body is now gone."

"Well, I am a religious person and I know that God never fails. Just be patient, He'll deliver you from this pain. I guarantee it," Carra said.

"She's right," Reese chimed in as she put her arms out to collectively embrace all of us at once. "He's in control, all we can do is let go and let God."

SUNDAY, 12/17

"Are you getting ready for church this morning?" Reese asked after waking me up with her typical early morning phone calls.

"After the scene on Friday, I don't think so."

"I don't believe you."

"Reese you don't understand."

"Try me."

"Look, it's hard to explain. Just put it this way, I can't go back for a while. Half the church saw what went on."

"I know, I got two calls and five emails about it."

"Please tell me you're joking."

"It doesn't matter. What matters is that you're not going to let that derail you from continuing your walk. You've been doing so good, you can't give up now."

"Reese, I can't."

"You can and you will because I'm on my way."

"Reese, at least give me a few weeks to…" I said before she hung up on me mid-sentence.

Within a half hour, she, Carra and Aaron were at my house forcing me to get ready for church. If it weren't for them coming over, I would have still been in bed with the blinds closed, bawling my eyes out.

I didn't look anyone directly in the face as I walked in the sanctuary. Even though I didn't look at anybody, I could feel judgmental eyes searing the back of my neck. Being there was the most awkward and embarrassing moment of my life. Despite my shame, I did feel happy to be there because I was looking forward to hearing the final segment of the Dream Deferred series. Today's topic was about learning to move on and let go. How apropos, I thought as Carra looked at me and rubbed my hand. I closed my eyes and felt the spirit of song as the choir sang "How Excellent Is Thy Name". As my heart stirred with the spirit, I looked down at my program and my eyes fell on one particular sentence, *God's plan is beyond our comprehension, rely on faith to trust in it and let go of all your troubles.*

Before Pastor began his sermon, he invited the congregation to the altar for prayer.

"If there's something weighing heavy on your heart, lay your burdens down and join us in prayer. If God's blessings have been so immense that you can't contain them, walk down and give God the glory," Pastor said as Carra and Aaron made their way out of the pew hand in hand and started down the aisle. "If God has revealed something to you that has changed your life, come and give praise for your deliverance!" Pastor belted as Reese stood up with tears streaming down her face and started down the pew. "And if you know someone facing a dream deferred who is in need of loving prayer, grab them by the hand and lead them to the altar," Pastor requested as Reese stopped dead in her tracks and walked back from the middle of the aisle to extend her hand to me.

"Come on Chris," she said as she placed her arm around me and led me to the altar.

Everything around me was a blur and I felt dizzy and faint as I stood with the crowd at the front of the church. My face and neck were wet with tears as I slowly felt the spirit of God all around me. With my eyes closed and my tears flowing, I felt the pain and sorrow I was holding onto leave my body.

"What is ultimately meant to be has nothing to do with us. It's all in God's plan. We have people standing here at the altar in various stages of their faith. Some can bear witness at this very moment about the greatness of God and His promise. Others are wondering what God has in store for them. Some are trying to overcome their doubt that God will take care of them. Regardless of where you are, I have some good news to tell you, God is blessing you right now! Right at this very moment as I speak to you. It may be revealed next year, it may be revealed next week and it may even be revealed today, but trust me when I say God is blessing you right now. Can I get an Amen?"

"Amen!" The congregation said in unison as my heart began to race. I believe it, I feel it and I trust it.

"Before you return to your seats, I want you to turn to your neighbor and say, God delivers on His promise," I turned to Reese and she smiled at me as we said to one another, "God delivers on His promise."

"I want you to turn to your other neighbor and say, whatever it is that's troubling you, just let it go." Time stood still when I turned around to my other side. Alain and I faced each other with tears in our eyes, sorrow on our minds but faith in our hearts. Alain stood silent as I reached for his hand and repeated, "Whatever it is that's troubling you, just let it go."

"Now give that neighbor a hug and tell them God loves you and so do I."

"God loves you and so do I," I said crying as I wrapped my arms around him. At first, he stood there stiff and rigid, then something inside him clicked because he lifted his arms, pulled me close and wouldn't let go.

"I'm so sorry Alain..." I said as he slowly placed his fingers up to my lips and nodded.

The associate pastor that helped me yesterday looked over at the two of us, waved his hand and smiled. I smiled back and mouthed the words *"thank you"* to him.

On the way back to our seats, Alain held my hand and guided me into the pew where he'd been sitting. Reese and Carra couldn't contain themselves as they smiled and looked over at us throughout service.

"Before I close this message today, I want to remind you of something. We've talked about letting go and moving on from the disappointment of things not happening the way you want it, *when you want it*, but I need to remind you of something, don't lose sight of your dream. When something's deferred, it only means that it's been put on hold. If what you hope and dream for fall within God's will for you, He'll provide, but only when He sees fit. And trust me, when He does, it'll be more than you ever imagined."

Alain squeezed my hand and looked over at me with the most loving and forgiving eyes. He smiled at me before saying, "I love you too."

It was at that very moment, I knew that not only my dreams, but my prayers had been answered.

Thank you God.

45856116R00259

Made in the USA
San Bernardino, CA
01 August 2019